Dedication

For Avra, Sunny, Lisa and Carroll
And for my father Stanley

Prologue

In The Middle

The aroma of the ocean and the sound of lapping water against his raft were all he knew. Floating alone.

There were moments when time became obscured and ceased to exist. Even the memory of why he was there got lost. But he did know he was sickened by his circumstance compounded by the constant vibrating pain in his temples.

His reality was a canvas of disorientation. Almost forgotten was his escape and his reason for it. Neither night nor day provided solace or salvation from the soreness of the oozing welts that covered his body.

Hypnotic confusion caused him to believe he was floating, looking down on himself. Imagining it was midday due to the relentlessness of the sun's rays directly overhead. But what difference did it make? Regardless, he tried rolling over and covering his eyes with his only possession, a soiled t-shirt. It didn't stop the devilish rays reflecting off the ocean's surface from blinding him.

Every excruciating movement reminded him of the hopelessness of his circumstances.

It's simple, Amaury, just slide off the raft into the warm inviting water, so silky and smooth. It'll be so easy. The pain will finally be over forever.

Again, he shook his head to erase the terrible thoughts. He knew his mind was playing tricks on him. He tried to stimulate his mind by recalling the names of his family members, their faces, moments of his youth, and other familiar things to distract himself from the fear that gripped him.

His mind wandered to his brother Ernesto. *I can't believe he's gone. Why would he leave? How could he leave me?* Ernesto slipped away in the eerie darkness of night. Occasionally, Amaury would yell out his name hoping for a response, but he only heard deafening silence. Sadly, he murmured, "I wish he was still here."

Amaury forced himself to take control of his mind. If he was going to make it, he needed to sharply focus on why he was here. He vowed to himself to never allow anything to distract him from survival. He realized being free was why he was in the middle of the ocean. *I loved my brother,* he thought, *but I know he'd want me to make it through and reach our goal—America. Freedom is what must sustain me now.*

The battle he faced to maintain control of his mind and future was his greatest challenge. It required a strenuous effort floating from illusion to reality. He was a lonely soldier desperately searching for an oasis in a barren desert. He tried to recall his prior Army Ranger training, coaxing himself to review steps of survival. Consciously, he forced himself to maintain even breathing, staying cool and remaining calm. At this moment, the only way to stay alive was to rely solely on himself; his memory was the only aspect in his young life he truly still owned.

Time passed very slowly and then...

Chapter 1

It All Begins

A young five-year-old Amaury Torres held his mother's hand as they walked home. His family lived together in a small apartment building in Old Havana, a smaller part of the city originally known as *Bélen*.

Much of Old Havana's rundown residences were groups of neighborhoods known as Solars. As Amaury and his mother walked through the tall arched entryway, it opened to a well-packed dirt courtyard. The large open space was divided into sections with several large buildings on the perimeter and sparse weeds all around. In the back of the courtyard was a walled-off area that separated the hygiene facilities including toilets, showers, and a few sinks for food preparation, all unfortunately without basic running water.

The multi-layered residential buildings were essentially ghettos, built from cement with stairwells in the corners. It was the communists' idea of economically efficient housing for their citizens.

Amaury, an inquisitive child with a great penchant for learning, was happily walking alongside his mother Rosa Aleida, who was not often home in the evenings. She worked many hours with three jobs. He looked up at her and thought about how happy he was to have her home that night.

"When we get upstairs Amaury, I want you to be a good boy and help begin the preparation for dinner," his mother said. "Clean the vegetables and cut the onions to start."

"Okay, Mama, I will. What are we making for dinner?"

As they turned to approach the stairwell, Amaury heard a threatening voice from a hidden corner. Amaury immediately looked up and saw his mom's eyes grow wide from fear. He felt her hand grab his even tighter.

"Hey, you bitch. Give me your money!"

Rosa grabbed Amaury's hand as hard as she could and rushed toward the stairwell. Amaury suddenly felt a tingle in his neck that he couldn't understand.

"Hey, you with the kid! Damn it, I'm fucking talking to you!"

Rosa carried packages in her arms while securely holding her son's hand. She knew they were in a serious situation, their safety threatened. Chunks of wind-battered cement had fallen into crumbled piles strewn about the ground near the footing of the walls. Other broken pieces previously kicked about created hazardous pathways. She swiftly navigated their path so as not to trip over the crumbled debris. Hurrying and not looking back, they reached the first step.

Scared, she spoke with an intensity in her voice. "Amaury, don't look back, you need to keep moving."

"Why? What's happening?"

Amaury did not fully grasp the urgency of their situation. Although he was trying to listen carefully to his Mother, he missed a step and his foot landed on a broken chunk of cement in front of the stairs. He twisted his foot and fell face-first into the dirt.

Rosa shrieked in fright at the top of her voice. She

stopped short to pick Amaury up off the ground and felt the shadow of the ominous figure close behind her. In her haste, she dropped the shopping bags and the contents spilled out. Her heart skipped a beat as the voice, now right next to her, screamed.

"Lady, don't make me hurt your son, I just want some money. Gimme your money!"

The bum seized Amaury's shirt collar before she was able to protect him.

The community was familiar with outside noises. Screams of joy from passionate lovemaking, domestic squabbling, even cries for help often went unnoticed.

Rosa's terrified screams and the commotion were clearly heard by the residents near the stairwell who ignored her, except for the one neighbor who cared.

Amaury's friend Anton lived in the apartment at the top of the first flight of stairs. Anton's father, Coro, hearing Rosa's screams rushed to the front door to investigate the commotion. He grabbed a large, heavy cast iron pan as he opened the flimsy screen door which closed with a dull slam.

He saw a man standing over Amaury threatening him with the neck of a broken glass beer bottle in his hand, the sharp edge sticking out. Coro was a huge man wearing a yellowed stained tank top t-shirt and undershorts. Amaury saw him fly down the staircase sliding on the handrail and then raise the pan high above his head. Amaury was surprised at how loud Coro's voice burst above the commotion.

"Hey! Let that boy go, you piece of filth!"

Shocked, the attacker looked up at Coro. Surprised at his size, he instantly dropped the sharp bottleneck and stumbled to get away. In his drugged stupor, he lost his balance and fell over. As Coro towered over him, the bum curled up on the dirt, covering his head to ready himself for an assault.

As Amaury looked down at the bum, he noticed a needle with the plunger missing hanging out of his left arm.

Coro approached the man now curled in a fetal ball and said menacingly, "Get the hell out of here and don't ever come back."

The bum crawled away, managed to get up, and then stumbled toward the arch, exiting the Solar as fast as he could.

Coro turned to Rosa, a bit shaken himself, and said, "Sometimes in Cuba, you gotta take matters into your own hands. That guy has been here for quite some time, filthy animal. The police don't do anything, it's pathetic. I'm surprised this didn't happen sooner."

Coro asked Rosa and Amaury if they were okay. Despite her trembling heart and hands, Rosa struggled to gather the groceries. Coro and Amaury both helped to pick up the remaining items. Amaury kept looking at his mom hoping she'd explain this all to him. She thanked Coro for his heroism and then all three slowly walked upstairs together.

Amaury looked at his mom, "Why did that man try to hurt us?"

"No se, dios mijo. Thank goodness Coro helped us. Living in these conditions is so frightening. I wish we could have a better life."

Amaury was forever changed by the events of that day and even though he grew to love Cuba, years later he realized that attack was not unusual.

He never forgot the day that he began questioning their lives in Cuba.

Who are they to decide and dictate how we're supposed to live? Why are we unable to choose for ourselves what our lives should be like? Why must we live like this?

These thoughts gnawed at him for many years. This experience along with his observations of life's realities even as a young boy strongly shaped his thinking as he grew up. For Amaury, no matter how he tried to suppress his feelings of hatred for communism to get along with others, they would surface when he'd least expected it. For Amaury, these moments would come unexpectedly and often got him in trouble.

However, as he grew up no matter how he tried to resolve internal conflicts and put order into his life, communism would always be present.

Chapter 2

A Passion Introduced

By six years old, Amaury was already getting up, dressing, and preparing for school by himself. His mother and grandmother both saw early in his life a behavior, a maturity, to understand and take responsibility for managing tasks normally associated with an older child. His older brother and sister both needed supervision to get their day started and were not as self-sufficient. Amaury was different.

Rosa started her day in the very early morning hours, completed her chores, and was long on her way to work before Amaury awoke. Her three jobs during the week were at a beer manufacturer, a cigar manufacturer, and working as a janitor at the government passport office. His grandmother, Abuelita, visited in the morning regularly to check in on all the children, often arriving as Amaury was already in the midst of his morning activities.

"Hola, Amaury. Buenas días. ¿Como estás?"

He nodded to his grandmother, "Morning, Abuelita." He managed to squeeze the words out while dressing. He watched as his grandmother moved about the apartment.

She went to wake Ernesto and their sister. "Look at that, the two of them, dead to the world like two flounders flat on a grill. ¡Mijos! ¡Rapidamente! It's time to get ready for school, enough already, vamanos!"

Amaury could hear them groaning and complaining about being abruptly ushered out of their deep sleep. He chuckled to himself as he put on the mandatory school uniform.

"Claro, que sí, Amaury. I love watching you make it." She smiled while Amaury began preparing the coffee with a glass press. One pot was enough for two small cups. Within a very short time, the wonderful aroma of espresso filled the small apartment. Amaury loved *Café con Leché*. It was dark and robust, indigenous to Cuba, and made with the steamed milk poured in.

"Abuelita, I just love the sound and smell of the coffee pot steaming. Who invented that?" Amaury asked with a smile.

Amaury was very fond of the old metal coffee pot that was nearly black from years of use. This was a common theme in his household. Many of their kitchen tools had been well-loved, including the clothes washboard which was partly caked with old soap.

The leche was also served with bread, and they called it *Leche con pan* or coffee with bread. For Amaury, *Cafe' con Leche y pan* equaled nothing but pure home and love. It was these early experiences of love associated with his mother and grandmother as they prepared the food for different meals where everyone would be talking, gathered around the kitchen table, enjoying the moment. It was in the kitchen where Amaury developed his fondest memories of home.

When Amaury was three years old, his father moved out. He would show up in Amaury's life from time to time, mostly during times of distress, but for the most part, Amuary's mother was his whole life and meant everything to him.

He knew at a very young age how much she loved and was

dedicated to him and their family. Even at a young age, he wanted to help her as best as he could whenever he could. His brother and sister somehow never felt quite as strongly.

As Amaury picked up his books and pens, he took one last look around his home and thought this was great. The apartment was small, but it was warm and there were symbols of his family's love everywhere. He felt safe there and it made him smile at his Grandmother again, "Going to class Grandma I will see you sooner than later." With a big laugh, he burst out the door and was in his class seat only a few minutes later.

Chapter 3

Los Reyes Magos

"C'mon, Iran, let's get ready to go to the big show today."

All three boys got up and sped out of Johan's house laughing. They jumped down the stairwell several steps at once, slid on the banister the rest of the way down, and hit the ground running. They wanted to get to the courtyard as fast as they could. "Woohoo! C'mon!" they yelled together.

Their shorts were thoroughly worn and stained with rust from constantly sliding on the old banister. Dashing to the arch, they tried to push and trip each other onto the dirt ground along the way. It was a little game they played and from experience, the boys knew they always needed to be alert. No one knew when it was going to be their turn to fly through the air and then crash headfirst.

"Amaury, I know what I want, and I hope I get lucky today!" Iran yelled out.

Johan loudly interrupted, "To be last."

Together they laughed and hollered out loud. They knew last meant first on Government Toy Day, known as *Los Reyes Magos or The Magic King*.

"Let's get to the lottery sheet and see where our names are!"

The three boys pushed and shoved each other to the list at the arch in front of the Solar. Each of them wanted to be the first one to see where the sheet was posted and where their names were listed. The winner could laugh and tease the others if their friend was the loser of the *Reyes Magos*.

Once a year the government would dispense toys to the children in Solars all around Cuba. It was the way the Communists chose to be generous and perhaps garner favor among the less fortunate population. All year long the kids gabbed and longed for the potential gifts they might receive. So excited by the prospect of something new, something different or special, the anticipation of whatever it might be, held a powerful place in every child's mind.

The government was aware young kids needed toys and to fulfill this, they made sure, like everything else, that they controlled the disbursement. When the day finally arrived the distribution of toys was done in a specific fashion in the form of a lottery system.

Each Solar in the country received a numerical list of the families with each child's name. The list was posted for everyone to see before handing out the toys. It was designed to be a *fair* dispersal. But no one knew where they were in the order of disbursement.

The entire toy supply allocated to each Solar was divided into three sections, the first being the best and the last being least desired. The first grouping included items including bicycles, tin Russian soldier figurines, steel tanks with wheels, boats, and the occasional fishing rod kit with a few hooks and floats and several baseballs.

The second level included colored cardboard figurine soldiers, tin navy boat replicas, trucks, and less exciting toys and boxed board games. The third tier, the one Amaury and his closest buddies cherished the most were the drab grey cardboard boxes filled with colorful glass marbles. The beautiful multi-colored marbles coveted by many of the boys were given last as they were not only the least expensive toy distributed but thought to be nothing more than a consolation prize.

If the government knew of the demand for marbles in the Solars, they may not have continued their generosity. Amaury always wanted to be picked in the last group, and it often came true as only a few lucky kids ever received a bicycle.

When the moment finally arrived, the much-anticipated lottery was called out in the courtyard of the Solar by a lowly government official. One by one, each child's name was called out and they would step up to the table to receive their new toy.

At noon, after posting the list, the official began the proceedings. They set up a table in front of the entrance with many boxes and several brand-new shiny bicycles behind them. Quietly, everyone crowded around in front waiting with anticipation as the officials began to call out the names.

Amaury giggled and looked over at Iran.

"Shut up, they're about to start!" he said to Amaury.

Iran elbowed him and Amaury retorted, "Stop poking me!"

With Johan's help, Amaury linked his foot behind Iran's ankle and Johan quickly said to Iran, "Look!" while he pushed Iran back. Iran fell like a bag of potatoes with a heavy thud.

Everyone turned around and stared at them, Amaury's grandma immediately angered and spoke with a harsh whisper and a serious glare. "Boys! Oh, *dios mios*. Stop!"

"But, Grandma, they're always fooling around with me. I swear, it was payback."

"Don't be ridiculous, Amaury, you're such a troublemaker. I know you. Don't you think I saw you push Iran over? Iran, are you all right?'

"Yes. I'm fine, ma'am. Just a little scrape on my hand."

"Now all of you settle down. *Por Favor*!"

Feeling guilty, Amaury apologized to his grandmother and then looked at Johan and Iran. They laughed quietly to themselves momentarily while looking down at the ground kicking dirt.

Amaury said, "C'mon. Shh, it's starting!"

Suddenly, the constable in his most official voice began. "Okay, todos, atención por favor. We will begin this year's *Los Reyes Magos* by calling out your names."

The anticipation was palpable for the children as the proceedings commenced. "Francy Lopez looks like you're the lucky girl; you're starting us off first!"

With a huge smile, Francy ran to the front and jumped with happiness as she got her first bicycle, a cute blue one with a white stripe. As the lottery progressed, the Cuban official continued calling out the remaining children. Little by little, the crowd thinned out. The final ones would be sad because they were at the end. Others happily jaunted away admiring their brand-new toy.

"Look, Amaury," Johan said quietly, "We made it again. We'll be last."

They stared at each other knowing they were getting the marbles again. The kids in the Solar formed a quasi-club for competitive fun. In a sense, it was more than just for entertainment. It created an inner circle of status. Many wanted to compete and become the marble king, *Reyes de Marbol*, at their Solar.

The marbles were delivered in long rectangular cardboard boxes imported from Russia. They had no particular markings other than the Russian word MARBLES in black printed on the top of each box containing fifty marbles. The government would normally give one box, although sometimes two, per child depending on the mood of that official. The boys muted their excitement as best as possible and their happiness for winning that last prize.

Without warning, Amaury realized his name had been called. "Amaury Torres...Amaury Torres?"

He jumped up, stumbling while dashing to the front. As he neared the table, a commanding voice said, "Okay boy. Go ahead and make your choice."

Nervously, Amaury looked at the pile of brownish-grey drab boxes. In his mind, he thought. *Wow! All these boxes look the same.* The word MARBLES printed on top gave no hints of what type might be hidden inside.

He prayed for a box that had the very special shooter marble. It was the one everyone wanted because it was the marble larger than the rest and the one also used to start each game. Since the shooter held special meaning for Amaury, the decision was difficult.

Suddenly he heard the official say, "You know what son, I am feeling nice today. Why don't you take two this time?"

Amaury looked up at the official in shock at his unexpected generosity and wanted to jump for joy, but he contained himself and remained calm. "Oh. Well, thank you, sir."

He had little time to decide, so Amaury quickly made his choices and grabbed two boxes off the top and ran like the wind, with Iran and Johan close behind as their names were called right afterward. They were holding their boxes, as well.

"Figures, you got two boxes this year. You lucky dog."

The very first thing Amaury did was to search for his new shooter—hopefully the one with special markings. The prize within the prize. He loved new shooters, clean, with no scratches, and ready to rumble.

This is going to be a great year.

Chapter 4

Marbles

"Amaury, stop it!" Rosa yelled. "Stop using your brother's socks for your marbles! Do you understand how many pairs of socks you have ruined? I can't keep sewing them. That's enough!"

Mumbling under his breath, he knew his mother was right, but he needed to use something to carry his marbles to the game, and Ernesto's socks were perfect.

"Mama, but please just this last time, okay? It's *the* big match and I need to bring extra."

It was an important competition, and he knew if he lost, he would need extra marbles to make it through all the rounds. The match was the final one for the year, completed in two days. Amaury was fighting to maintain his title of Marble King of his Solar. Normally they played pick-up games, but not today.

Amaury's best skill was shooting the ball forward to spin in any direction with expert wrist control. There were many ways to play marbles, but Amaury's favorite game was called *For Keeps* where the winner kept their opponent's marbles.

Amaury was very skilled, yet there were a few other kids who were just as good. It often came down to an odd spin, a weird rebound, or a chance fractured shooter. The winner would have the whole year to boast his victory. It was a game with risk for many as they often played with the marbles, they coveted the most.

It was obvious which kids played marbles in the Solar because their pants had huge holes at the knees, or their pockets hung low. Socks used as bags were stretched beyond capacity.

The competition took place in the street in front of Amaury's Solar. The double rings were set up in front and a huge crowd gathered around in anticipation. The boys would begin the game by using their main shooter in an attempt to get as close to the center ring as possible. The winner earned the first shot. The goal was to get as many balls as possible into the center ring without hitting their marbles out, but also strategically blocking their opponent's marbles.

This competition was unlike the others. Each player would typically bring fifty marbles to a game. Although there could be as many as eight kids playing in a single game, it only required two players. On this beautiful summer day, it started a game of attrition, and the last man standing to be the eventual winner.

Once the match began, Amaury already planning his path to victory would say sarcastically to his competitors, "Say goodbye to your marbles, my brother," and then laugh out loud to intimidate them.

Winning was important to Amaury because he loved being *Reyes de Marbol.*

Ernesto always came to watch his brother in the matches. It was a popular event for the Solar families too. They all had their favorite players and cheered them on. One by one, the kids who lost then became supporters for the remaining contestants.

When it got down to the final four, things began to heat up. Amaury almost always made it to the finals. This time was no different. He confidently held the victor crown on his head from the previous year and drew the biggest crowds. He loved the attention and wore a huge smile on his face. Inside, his heart was pounding. The crowd never saw it. Amaury was the one to beat.

The larger ring was scattered with marbles, and it came down to Amaury and his biggest nemesis, a young kid named Pablo Ramirez.

Pablo was a short, chubby kid with thick fingers and fat cheeks but an infectious smile. When Amaury looked at him, he couldn't understand why he was so good. His fingers looked like little stumps, although he did have great wrist and finger strength and thus excellent marble spin. This year, Amaury knew Pablo was gunning for him in the finals, but Amaury was up for the challenge. He had to play his best game ever.

"Okay, it's your shot, Pablo."

"Oh, I know it is. I'm setting it up," Pablo said tensely. "You're not going to beat me. I can tell you that. I'm ready, been waiting all year to face you again." Pablo looked angrily into Amaury's eyes but they both started laughing and although he was serious, they enjoyed teasing each other to be intimidating as the game progressed. "You know Amaury, you had a great victory. You took all my marbles last year and it was terrible waiting another six months for *Los Reyes*."

"Let me tell you something, Pablo. This year won't be any different," Amaury shot back. "Six months is hard to wait, but after you count this year's six months, that's going to be a year without marbles. I almost feel sorry for you."

Both boys again started laughing again, but inside Pablo was starting to get nervous. He knew Amaury was going to be tough to beat.

Pablo took his last marble shooter out and although he had quite a few more marbles in his sock, this shot was going to be the one to set up the loss for Amaury.

He had the advantage of positioning the marbles in both rings. Depending on where his shot landed, he anticipated he might end with a two or three marble advantage. He felt this shot would be able to protect his single marble advantage in the small ring.

"You better make this a good one, Pablo. You may have me this time."

"You're funny, Amaury. I know what you're doing."

As they both stalked the ring, Pablo, sizing up his shot, finally crouched down with his knee poking through the pant leg resting on the road. He knew if he could swiftly spin this one to the left, albeit a difficult shot, and knock out several of the marbles in the big ring, he would end up being ahead just enough to finally beat Amaury. Near the end of a match like this, a single marble could very well tip the scale in anyone's favor.

The crowd became silent—this was the moment everyone had been waiting for. They could either cheer for a new winner or look forward to another year of Amaury gloating over his victory. The crowd's energy was clearly behind Pablo. Amaury loved being the underdog. He knew the crowd was rooting against him but didn't care.

Everyone watched intensely as Pablo prepared to take his best shot, and possibly his last shot of the year.

Some people in the crowd started to chuckle, and others were cheering on Pablo, then someone shouted out, "¡Hey, callate! Let Pablo concentrate!"

"Now's the moment, Amaury. I'm going to knock your marbles out."

Pablo knelt so low his face was almost against the street. He reached out with his right hand and gripped the shooter as tightly as he could. With a quick measured thrust, he shot the marble across the ring. It smashed two marbles then one ricocheted off and hit another of Amaury's marbles, which in turn bolted over the ring's edge and out.

He had done it. He had banged Amaury's marble out of bounds and the wicked left spin did the trick. Pablo jumped up, smiling at his achievement. He pumped up his left hand in celebration. The crowd cheered.

Amaury, having been in this position before, fought against his anxiety. Little did he know his next shot would be highly symbolic of his life's destiny. Being pushed out of the ring and presented with serious obstacles never stopped his desire to reach his goals. Deep down, he relished the opportunity to prove his abilities.

"You know Pablo, I'll give you credit," he said. "That was an amazing shot. It really was. But you know when you come to play the best you need to make sure you knock out your opponent without a shadow of a doubt."

Pablo watched tensely as Amaury took a last walk around the ring. He took his time. He looked at the crowd, their eyes glued to him as he circled, analyzing the positioning of the marbles and estimating his options.

There were not many. He knew his string of victories would eventually end, but he was determined that today would not be that day. Amaury wanted to make one last final impression, permanently cementing his legacy.

As he breathed in the humid air, he looked up at the clouds and saw one that looked just like a horse. *Interesting timing*, he smirked to himself and then knelt onto the street. The shot became clear.

Without any fanfare, Amaury flicked his thumb, and in a flash, the shooter jumped up over a marble and landed amid four marbles, each one ricocheting and taking out three of Pablo's positions. Pablo let out a huge sigh of disappointment and the crowd began to groan and speak in hushed tones.

With as quick as a flip of the wrist, the marbles spun out, and the victory was Amaury's. Everyone jumped up, shocked at the ferocity of the shot. The commotion was chaotic, some people yelling or laughing while some were upset.

Amaury hollered, "YES! King again!" He thrust his arm up high in celebration.

It was the tightest match of the year but in the end, Amaury remained victorious and continued his reign at the Solar. He knew this was his last marble ring victory, and he was glad to end it gloriously.

In the glow of victory and celebration, smiling, he suddenly heard in the background a familiar but very loud voice shouting over everyone else's...

Curiously, he looked around.

"Amaury, where are you? Amaury? Did you take Ernesto's sock again?!"

Chapter 5

School Times

The Educational System in Cuba was one of Castro's most highly prized achievements. It was a way to prove to the rest of the world he was unlike prior dictators and prioritized a real education for his citizens.

The typical class in Amaury's school held thirty to forty kids. They sat at old rickety desks that had been handed down for decades from one generation of students to the next. Unless they broke completely, they were never replaced.

Normally Amaury sat near his best friends, and they would play jokes on each other, and steal laughs throughout the day. Occasionally Amaury would get distracted from the lesson and would focus his attention on doodling and scratching words into the wood of his desk with a paperclip or pocketknife. It was clear that many students before him had had the same fascination as there were years and years' worth of scratched words on each desk in the classroom.

As Amaury looked at the random names carved into the wood, one stuck out as it was so much larger than the others. *Palo Diego*. It had a large line scratched deeply under it as though the student who had graffitied surely wanted it to be remembered.

His teacher caught him looking down. "Amaury! Will you please pay attention?"

Embarrassed, he quickly looked up, his face turning red. He could hear his friends snickering, which only made it worse.

Even as a young child in Cuba, Amaury began to evaluate his surroundings in a more adult way. He developed distasteful feelings for the way that the people around him lived. The highly touted advantages of communist life became less apparent and true-life experiences became his reality. The veneer was cracking, and the ugly truth was beginning to be visible to him.

He was young and did not know how to cope with the inner conflicts he felt and subconsciously he developed his ways of managing them. Amaury learned early on that external displays of rebellion were unacceptable. He wanted to stick it to the system in any way he could, and because he was constantly hungry, his mind conjured up a humorous plot to eat more food than was allowed. As he sat there at his desk ignoring the lesson of the day, his mind began to wander to how he would put his plan into action as soon as the lunch bell rang.

"Amaury! Pay attention!" the teacher scolded him. "Lunch will arrive soon enough."

Suddenly the bell rang. Amaury jumped from his desk and hurried to the lunchroom. It was organized chaos, as it was every day. To get their meals, students lined up single file along the counter and took their trays of food before sitting down.

The lunchroom was supervised by two female school monitors, one of whom was stationed at the back of the line while the other observed both the front and students already eating. It was a large task for only two people to manage so many rambunctious children, but they managed.

A stout dark-haired woman in a hair net behind the food counter served the children their small portions. "¡Vamos, niños! Rápido, por favor. ¡Próximo en la fila!"

The large line of kids moved slowly while the monitors watched over them. Luckily for Amaury, the teachers would occasionally get lost in their conversation and their attention would waver. Amaury had already dashed to the lunchroom as fast as he could, and beating the big rush, he had grabbed his tray and had run to his seat as quickly as he could, nearly inhaling his food.

The instant he noticed the two monitors distracted in conversation, he snuck out the back door and sped directly across the small yard to his Solar.

He bolted up the stairs to say a quick hello to his sister and Grandmother. "Hola, Abuelita! How are you?"

"Amaury, what are you doing here? You're supposed to be at school. ¿Que pasa?"

"Nothing happened. I'm just having a little fun with the lunch teachers. Gotta go!"

"What do you mean?" Abuela demanded. "Amaury, what are you talking about?"

"See you after school!" Amaury called to her as he ran out the door.

"Where are you going? Amaury!"

He flew through the lunchroom doors again and got in the back of the food line.

The monitors looked at him, confused. They were unsure if he had already been inline or not. Since these ladies were substitutes, they were not as aware of his tricks. "Amaury, where were you? Weren't you here before?"

He laughed. "What do you mean? I was right here at the end of the line. I don't know what you're talking about."

Occasionally, the monitors caught on and scolded him.

They'd figured out what he was up to. But for the most part, no one ever knew what tricks Amaury conjured.

Amaury wasn't the only trickster within his group of friends. Iran and Johan used class time to entertain themselves by playing jokes on Amaury and each other. On this particular day, Iran and Johan had seen an opportunity to get Amaury into trouble. Before class, they managed to loosen the screws of Amaury's desk. Once he sat down, the desk shook, squeaked, and nearly collapsed. Panicked, Amaury grabbed both sides of the chair to stabilize himself. Glancing back at the two schemers who were grinning ear to ear, he instantly knew they'd done something to his desk.

Señorita Hidalgo Garcia, their teacher, a devoted communist herself, was only too happy to teach the children the required history curriculum and today's lesson was her magnum opus. As she prepared her paperwork, she smiled to herself. This was the lesson she'd been most excited to teach her students.

"Okay, todos! In today's lesson, we will examine the beginning of Cuba's history."

The class groaned. "Do we have to?" a student whined.

"Yes, we have to," Señorita Garcia continued. "These historical moments are very important and required for your tests. And! It's also important to appreciate how our fine leaders have made Cuba the wonderful, powerful country it is today."

Señorita Garcia explained to the class that one of the most important steps Fidel Castro took once he became their leader was distinguishing his style of leadership from previous dictators. His desire to ensure the population understood these differences was symbolized in the improving education and healthcare.

Although it was not explicitly said, it was known among Cubans that Castro wanted his citizens to love and appreciate him as if he were their Big Papa, a father figure on a deeper emotional level. He was not just Él Presidenté of Cuba. He demanded their respect and wanted to appear to be their role model and extolled as such. He installed many important societal norms regarding personal hygiene, such as receiving medicine, through the public education system. The Cuban elementary level students were required to use mouth wash and maintain proper hygiene and teeth cleaning, daily before class. The Cuban authorities made sure young children were being given minimal expectations as some were not receiving care at home.

Amaury raised his hand to ask a question.

Señorita Garcia looked annoyed. She was moving swiftly with the lesson, and she didn't feel like she'd covered enough yet for there to be any questions. "Yes, Amaury, what is it this time?"

"I have some questions about El Presidente."

She sighed. "Amaury, I'd really like to get through the lesson. Let's save our questions until the end."

Frustrated, Amaury rolled his eyes.

Señorita Garcia continued, "Historically former Cuban dictators were terrible leaders who were heavily influenced not only by the United States' physical proximity but its overwhelming influential economic power. From the Middle Ages and for the next several hundred years, Cuba was cultivated and exploited for its resources by many countries. We will cover specific details as the year progresses. The exploitation of these natural resources not only led to slavery and conflict in Cuba but also prevented them from gaining independence for a significantly long time. Castro understood that forced colonization and repression was a serious detriment to Cuba's historic fight for independence."

Once again, Amaury raised his hand, and this time Señorita

Garcia let him ask the question.

"Yes, Amaury?'

"Mrs. Garcia, how did America's influence help or hurt Cuba? I don't understand."

She looked at Amaury incredulously as she'd never known a young child to ask such a question. "Well, Amaury, that's a very interesting question, and it is not easily answered quickly. However, here are a few thoughts to illustrate. Cuba's history was influenced by its northern neighbor. By the mid-century, the United States experiencing a strong industrial revolution created greater consumer demand for sugar and many other products. Havana became the third-largest city in all the Americas. This closeness helped to not only financially elevate Cuba but also exploited it unfairly. Disturbed by this, Castro wanted to cut those ties."

"Now if you turn to page twenty-four in your books, we will begin some reading. Amaury, why don't you go ahead and read for us." Amaury didn't want to be put on the spot, but he didn't dare refuse his teacher.

"The pressures of control from Spain caused other Cuban leaders to rise up in the fight for freedom. One particularly important leader after the 1800s stood out. Jose Marti was known as the apostle of Cuban Independence. Although he unsuccessfully fought for sovereignty, he also hated America's influence over Cuba—"

"Sadly," Señorita Garcia interrupted him, "Marti's life was cut short. He never had the overwhelming success he sought. However, his effort did not go to waste. His achievements and passion profoundly influenced Fidel Castro's rise many decades later. Castro modeled his revolution on Marti's teachings. Continue Amaury."

"Fidel Castro was born in the southeastern area of Cuba in a town called Biran, near Santiago. He attended a private school and was later admitted to the University of Havana Law School where he became intensely driven by the changing political atmosphere. He believed in nationalistic socialism and the removal of imperial America's influence symbolized by Batista's acquiescence to American pressure and money."

"Good," she said. "Early on, Castro's firm conviction in fairness and change for everyone in a society influenced his decision to attempt an overthrow of The Dominican Republic government led by Rafael Trujillo. Castro believed Trujillo was a poor leader and needed to be removed. However, his efforts failed. Iran, continue reading, por favor."

Iran began, "Castro then refocused his attention on his own country and the cruel oppressive rule of Fulgencio Batista. Although his initial pursuits to overthrow Batista failed, he never gave up. He knew he wanted to organize another rebellion effort against Batista and once thrown out of Cuba by Batista, he found his opportunity to begin his plan in Mexico.

While in Mexico he built a small grass roots army of like-minded displaced rebel Cubans. This new group eventually went back to Cuba to begin his new Revolutionary plans. After some time, his efforts finally succeeded and in late 1959 Castro took over the reins of Government. Batista was ousted and fled the country. Castro took on his first role as Prime Minister and then later chose the title of *Él Presidenté*."

"Good," Señorita Garcia said. She continued reading the text. "Batista was a cruel and oppressive leader who, in Castro's eyes, unfairly took advantage of the good nature of the Cuban people and used it against them, including buying weapons from the United States and using them against the population. During this period, Fidel Castro and his loyal brother Raul after they'd been exiled to Mexico, they befriended two very influential men who helped them in their struggle. Camilo Cienfuegos and Ernesto Che Guevara, both men deeply Marxist in their beliefs, helped them to reorganize Cuba into the wonderful country we have today."

Johan raised his hand and asked, "Why are these men so important to the Castro's, Señorita Garcia?"

"Thank you, Johan, for that question. All these men ardently believed it was America and its capitalist ways which created poverty and economic ruin in Cuba and throughout South America." She knew without going much further in her explanation some of these concepts would need much greater detail, but that would come in future lessons.

"Señorita Garcia?" A young girl interrupted,

"Yes, Nathaly?'

"What is economic ruin?"

"Well Nathaly, that's a wonderful question also which requires a much greater analysis, and we'll talk about that later on in the year. However, since time is running out, I'll just give you a brief explanation. Castro, Raul, and Che Guevara, in their travels from Mexico to South America, saw terrible living conditions, social and economic inequality, severe poverty, people starving, and worse. Rightly so, both Raul and Fidel blamed the policies of America for those struggles and wanted to help. Cuba faced a similar fate. *Él Presidenté* Castro made sure life was going to change for the better here at home and made every effort to do so."

Amaury raised his hand again.

"Yes Amaury, I know you have a question, but as you can see, it is almost time to end for today. Hold your question until the next class and take notes for tonight's homework."

The unsuspecting Amaury Torres, who didn't likely know as a young student studying these important historical moments in Cuba's history would one day intimately learn that his very own life had been uniquely profoundly connected and influenced by the very essence, the birth of the revolution itself.

Chapter 6

Water and a New Perspective

In the early years, the most important topic the children learned was Cuba's extensive, complicated history. After his victory, Castro publicly announced he was determined to become a different yet benevolent leader. His commitment to the people was going to save them from the repetition of oppression. Treating the citizenry with respect, equality and fairness were his golden rules of governing. With these tenants in place, he began his reign as the new leader. Castro reinforced his beliefs repeatedly in his annual July anniversary speeches. They were designed to keep the masses in line and give up any thoughts of rebellion.

However, during his years in Cuba, Amaury felt his own experiences were anything but fair. He learned acutely how reality differed from Castro's and his father's words.

Johan left early to head to Amaury's apartment. As he looked at the crowd building from the edge of the staircase banister, he banged on Amaury's front door.

"Amaury, Amaury. C'mon, the spigot's about to blow up."

It was early afternoon in the sunbaked courtyard, a beautiful day. People were busy talking, getting ready for the big moment.

"Quickly, Amaury. Hurry up," Abuelita said, "Johan, how many people are in line now?"

As Johan opened his mouth to speak, some other people ran behind him, nearly shoving him into the front door of the Torres' apartment.

"I can see there are a lot, but the line still isn't too bad yet. But it's building, I'd say," Johan answered.

Abuelita interrupted, "Amaury, hurry! Grab the water containers by the door. We need to get some extra today, enough to make it through the weekend."

"Okay, Abuelita, meet ya down there. C'mon, Johan, let's try to get a good spot in line then we can fool around awhile. Did you see Iran yet?"

"No, I haven't seen him, but I know he had to stay at home today. His mother was mad at him for some reason. I'm not sure why, but I think he left their cat locked in the closet for a joke."

They laughed at the thought.

Amaury grabbed three large cans from the floor; painted on the sides in red was their name TORRES. They looked like old gas cans. Some were plastic gallons, too. Both boys ran down the breezeway headed to the stairs. Each had containers in their grip, purposely banging them on the railings. Not being able to use their hands, there would be no sliding down the railings this time. They hit the ground running and headed straight over to the spigot where the line was assembling. Some containers were already in front near the spigot from people who'd missed getting water the day before.

It was an unwritten *first come first serve* rule to which all the residents adhered. Water was delivered to the Solars through a single spigot in the middle of the courtyards standing straight up waist high with a control valve. Then, unannounced, in the middle of the afternoon, the water would begin flowing. It was a daily ritual for getting potable water for their homes. Unfortunately, the governmental water department did not turn it on at the same time every day.

Abuelita trailing behind finally caught up to the boys who were holding their places in line. There were a lot of people waiting, which was normal right before the weekend. They waited in trepidation, as sometimes the water didn't turn on at all.

There was no rhyme or reason for the inconsistency, but no one asked questions. They knew life in Cuba was a day-to-day experience.

"I hate standing here, Abuelita," Amaury complained. "It's so annoying. It takes up the whole day! Johan, I thought you said the spigot was about to go on. Isn't that what you said?"

"I thought so, That's what my Mother told me. She said to wait in line so we can get enough water. She told me to hurry up and grab a good spot. I stopped by your house first to tell you so we could go together and at least make it fun." He gave Amaury a jostle and they both giggled.

"There's gotta be a better way. Imagine if we have to do this for the rest of our lives?"

"Oh, I know," Johan agreed, "I wonder who figured out this crazy system, to begin with."

Amaury hated to touch the sizzling hot spigot sticking up out of the dusty ground. The courtyard's appearance near the spigot was flat with debris and left behind garbage strewn about randomly. The entire group simply waited. Many stared up at the meandering clouds in the sky. At least it was pleasant to look at.

Solar communities may not have had the best living circumstances, but they all tried their best to maintain a positive attitude. People chatted quietly amongst themselves, waiting for the precious water to begin.

When Amaury was very young he'd never thought about this daily ritual. It was meaningless to him. He was more interested in having fun. He played with his friends and rolled around in the courtyard. His sister or Abuelita would yell at him to stop and stand in line, but he never listened.

"Amaury Torres, will you please get up off the ground!" she'd yell. "It's filthy dirty. What is the matter with you? How many times have I told you to please stop doing that?"

He often ignored Abuelita or his sister Iliana. He was not aware of the seriousness of what the water line meant.

Even as he grew older, Amaury, still hated standing in line waiting every day. He felt hopelessness like he was stuck on a raft in the middle of nowhere with the heat beating down on him, sweat rolling down his temples. He looked around taking in all the anxious faces in the crowd. He understood there was desperation, which made him feel uncomfortable because no one had the power to change anything. He knew the Cuban system was broken and degrading to the citizens and thought to himself this was not the way life should be. Those feelings gnawed at him and despite his young age. Inwardly, Amaury began to seriously question Castro's frequent declarations of what was right and truly fair for the society.

As Amaury stood there with a million contradictory thoughts swirling around his mind, there was a slight rumble beneath his feet and then suddenly water burst forth from the spigot.

The daily ritual of waiting for water sparked a powerful spirit of motivation in Amaury's mind. As he got older, it became more than a passing thought.

At nine years old, he'd discovered that water was available for purchase on a limited basis separate from the Solar water.

There was a water spigot located five miles outside of town controlled separately by the city. Amaury and his friend Johan negotiated and bought a huge twenty-five-gallon plastic container. They built a little wagon from scrap they found then resold the water to their neighbors at the Solar for a small profit. It was quite an effort, but the inhabitants of his Solar always needed additional water and they were grateful for the convenience.

It was Amaury's first attempt at creating a business and he was happy to help his mom with extra money. He also enjoyed the pocket change left over to go to the cinema and enjoy a movie occasionally with his friends, and maybe even some girls from the Solar.

Amaury didn't let the harsh realities of life deter him from turning ideas into action, to make things better for himself and his family. As he got older, he also earned money by selling bodega items and working as a guide for tourists he met at the local church.

He traded for many things—gum, magazines, and anything western which sparked his interest. As an *unofficial* guide, he took foreigners to different parts of the city. Tourists loved the local spots and unknown highlights of Havana. He was engaging and the tourists reacted well to his charm and knowledge of the city. These activities helped him feel productive. More importantly, it fed into his antirevolutionary desires.

Later in life, when he'd finally decided to take life into his own hands and build a small business, he'd develop a sense of greater inner satisfaction. Knowingly, he believed he was able to beat the system directly under their communist noses.

Chapter 7

An Unexpected Brush with Western Culture

While Amaury's resistance to this predetermined Cuban life began in the classroom, his curiosities about the outside world began to gnaw at him even more as he aged. At age eleven, he had a chance experience that would catalyze further exploration.

While at the Church of Santeria near his home, Amaury stepped downstairs to use the bathroom. While washing his hands, he turned and saw something he had never noticed before. Staring at him squarely in his face, firmly fastened to the backside of the bathroom door, was an old enamel-painted sign.

The tin sign was a multicolored advertisement for Coca-Cola, with the contents pouring a bubbling foamy soda into a cold glass. Although rusted and caked with years of dust, the sign was still instantly recognizable by the red, white, brown, and green.

Even after forty years of wear and tear, it still excitedly boasted the virtues of drinking Coke. It mistakenly had been left behind from the Batista era, an oversight in revolutionary societal cleansing. He intently studied every detail and was taken by its compelling visual demand. The sign showed the faded green bottle with the brown soda inside and the famously large white scripted letters across, *Coca-Cola.* As he stared at the ad, he felt as though the bottle was alive and screamed at him, *Please drink me!*

Intrigued by the ad and wondering why he'd never noticed it before, Amaury contemplated its message. The more he stared, the more he wanted to know. The colors and compelling design instantly elicited a strong desire to have a Coke, and he tried to imagine what it might taste like.

He remembered the symbolism of Coca-Cola for Cubans. It was much more than an icon of Western culture. There was a deeper meaning attached with an intensely negative stigma. The fictitious belief was created to influence people against consuming anything Western so they would stay true to their identity. Amaury knew of the old superstition extolling the dangers of having such a drink. If Cubans were to taste Western Culture they would be changed forever, and Coca-Cola was the premier drink to cause this betrayal.

The saying he recalled was choosing *Coca-Cola de la vida falta de perdón.* If you drink Coke, you'll never look back or be forgiven. Affected by these thoughts he tried to push the image out of his mind.

What if it were true?

For another moment, Amaury thought about the revolution's plan and their attempt to create its own style of cola called *Colita.* They believed it was important to counter Western Culture with its own drink for the masses. However, enthusiastically celebrated by the Government, it was highly unpopular and tasted awful.

A couple of years later he was finally able to taste Coca-Cola for the first time. It was an indescribable experience—a revelation even. One summer day his father Nury took him in his Russian Moscobe for a drive. The vehicle was an older model which was difficult to operate and ran terribly. The steering was loose, shifting gears was unpredictable and the brakes required two strong legs to stop. Every drive was an adventure, but amazingly, Nury kept the machine under control.

During the noisy ride, they needed to leave the windows open to provide some draft of air as they sweated profusely. Only speaking briefly during the excursion, his father mentioned a mandatory meeting at a distant government building but wouldn't discuss details.

Once having arrived at the location, they drove up a dusty dirt road. Both Amaury and his father wished at that moment that the Moscobe had air-conditioning. The car's interior became filled with a cloud of sticky white dust, clinging to every surface. While entering the parking lot, Amaury noticed the plain white building which looked foreboding, like most Cuban government buildings.

After Nury parked the car, He turned to Amaury. The Moscobe continued to jerk and belch. It wouldn't shut off.

"Looks like I'll have to have that checked soon," he said. "Amaury, I won't be long. I'm sorry I know it's hot, but you'll have to wait here for a little while. On the way home maybe, we will stop for something refreshing."

"No problem, Dad. I'll just sit here and enjoy the view."

"What a nuisance!" Nury gasped as the car continued to rumble.

The vehicle finally gave one final mechanical pain, chugging, and then with a loud backfire, turned off. Amaury sat silently in the passenger seat and rolled his eyes as the smell of burnt fuel filled the car. He remained unimpressed with Russian auto technology and thought, *American cars were old but at least they ran well, and looked so much better, too.*

Amaury was annoyed that his father wouldn't allow him to

go into the building for some relief from the midday sun. Although he was not permitted to know the purpose of the visit, he was at least grateful his father asked him to spend time with him. It didn't happen often.

Amaury looked around staring through the filthy windshield while waiting. He could see several cows grazing in the distance. The open windows provided scant relief and caused the top of the metal door frame to become hot enough to force him to remove his arm from its resting spot.

From the other side of the parking lot, he noticed an officially dressed man walking to his car. Amaury did not recognize him but saw he was smiling and holding something. Amaury could not initially figure it out. As the man got closer, he realized it was a drink.

"Here you go, my boy. You're very nice father asked me to bring you something cold to drink to cool you off in this terrible heat. So just enjoy it!"

Initially, Amaury didn't realize it was a Coke being handed to him. The official smiled and chuckled, knowing it was a special treat. Amaury with his parched throat replied, "What? Really? For me?" He couldn't believe it. He held in his hand for the very first time, a bottle of ice-cold Coca-Cola. The cool wet drops of water ran down across the painted label and caressed his fingers. "Does my father know?"

"No, no, he doesn't know. Please don't tell him," The man pleaded. "I just knew you were sitting in the car and felt badly for you. It's a tough day here today. Terrible, this heat. I thought you might like to have a nice cool drink. The Coke, it's a small pleasure we have sometimes, just occasionally, I thought you might like to have it. I told your father I was going to bring you a Colita. He probably wouldn't mind, anyway."

Amaury stopped paying attention to what the man was saying. He just continued to stare at the bottle in disbelief.

The deliciously sweet forbidden drink was in his grip and freezing cold. He remembered the old sign and noticed bubbles going upward inside the neck of the glass running to the top. At the opening, they were popping and splashing onto his fingers, never stopping. He thought, *I can't believe it. I'm already in love with Coke!*

He looked at the soda bottle and then slowly lifted it to his mouth. He was amazed at how the bubbles felt ticklish to his lips and palate. He could feel the powerful mini-explosions of the sparkly liquid in a way he'd never felt before. He could never have imagined the wonderful flavor that followed. The sugary sweetness was a life-changing moment for the young Amaury. The revelation and uniqueness were mesmerizing. Once he finally learned what the infamous Coca-Cola tasted like, it was truly love at first gulp. It suddenly made sense to him why Fidel's revolution wanted to keep Coke hidden.

One single taste solidified his disgust of the restrictions that Cubans were forced to live by. It was no surprise that government officials had access to special luxuries, even something as simple as a cold soda. For Amaury, it was another reason to question his father and his intense devotion to the Revolution.

Chapter 8

Boxing

During his formative school years, Amaury preferred physical sports more than competitive ball sports because he enjoyed the ability to test his will against an equal competitor. His half-brother Ernesto had introduced Amaury to Judo in a small class, but when the restrictions of movement of the outfit did not appeal to him, he declined.

Ernesto was not as good a student as Amaury, but he excelled in boxing and sports in general. He was determined to get Amaury involved with exercise and recommended boxing. "You ought to try boxing, Amaury. I think you'd be good at it. You're a strong, tough kid. Come on bro give it a shot?"

"I don't know, Ernesto. I like watching you and know you're fucking great." He paused a moment while he thought. Amaury continued, "I'm not so sure. I'll never be as good as you are. But I'll tell you what, I'll go talk to the coach and see what happens."

Amaury, still a pre-teenager, agreed to meet at the Physical Ed building nearby to observe the class a second time. A few days later he went to see Ernesto practice at the gym. It was near their Solar in an old, repurposed building. The Government knew health and physical exercise was important for children as part of their essential overall development, but despite their educational goals, the Government had little in the budget for building maintenance or the rope, rings, benches, punching bags. All the other necessary equipment for boxing was available but also in extensively used conditions, including the gloves and protective headgear. The building itself showed its age and in general a lack of attention. However, when Amaury saw it for the first time, he was excited and thought it was better than the Solar. At least it had running water for showers, even if they were cold ones.

The large building was a former bank from the 1940s. Under Castro, it had been turned into a community and exercise gym hall because of its large open rooms. The Government minimally retrofitted several spaces with different sports equipment. They tried to accommodate several nearby neighborhood schools and complement their exercise programs.

The building's exterior had two huge white Corinthian columns on the outside front entrance. The interior opened to a large ornate marble hallway that echoed with the sounds of footsteps and voices which bounced off the hard surfaces. However, the location and size lent themselves perfectly to a multipurpose space. The government also provided coaches who were paid separately for teaching and providing physical education. It was strange the ways Castro cared about his people and why it took Amaury so long to figure out that he wanted a life outside of his communist island.

Amaury watched the boys punching, jabbing, moving, and defending themselves practicing the many different moves necessary in boxing. The process was intriguing to Amaury, and as he sat watching his brother and the others, he noticed the instructor kept tight control over the action. He watched his brother intently, as he knew he was up to his tricks and was keen to show off.

Ernesto practiced boxing with several kids. However, one opponent wasn't equally matched for him and got weepy after Ernesto punched his nose. The boy collapsed on the mat immediately. The instructor stepped in right away to prevent further damage. "PARAR IMEDIATAMENTE!! Ernesto. Go to the corner."

Later Amaury asked his brother, "Ernesto, why did you punch that kid in the nose?"

"I know I shouldn't have, but my fist kind of got away from me and it just connected. Oh well. It was kind of funny, though." Ernesto grinned sheepishly.

"I don't think it's a good idea to take advantage of someone just because you can. That may come back to bite you someday." Amaury felt uneasy. Seeing his brother hit someone on purpose hit a nerve. It was the same nerve that pinched whenever he felt the injustices that his people lived with. If this was boxing, it wasn't for him. All the same, he met the coach after the practice at the behest of his brother.

"You know, Amaury you ought to give this a try. When your brother behaves himself, he is one of our best. I'm sure you'd enjoy it! Maybe it runs in the family. It's quite competitive and Ernesto told me you like the battle. We have some pretty serious competition around the area. The other schools are tough, and we mix it up pretty well. What do you think?'

"You know coach, I'm glad to have the opportunity. I know you don't take everyone, but give me a day to think about it. I'll let you know for sure tomorrow." Amaury liked boxing but competing with his brother was not truly what he wanted, it didn't allow for his independence to feel fulfilled.

Ernesto, who was listening to the conversation, was a little disappointed.

"You know Amaury, this is a heck of a great workout, plus

you get to punch people all the time, What could be better?" Ernesto let out a hearty laugh.

"Yeah, yeah, I know how much you like to punch people. That's what worries me. I don't want to be one of them. I already have to fight you at home."

They both laughed but Amaury, slightly serious, knew his brother was a strong kid and thought he liked his nose just the way it was. While leaving the boxing hall, he heard loud cheering and boisterous activity down the hallway from a different room. It caught his attention. He decided to take a look and see what was happening. The commotion grew louder as he got closer to the entrance. Amaury was very intrigued. Boxing wasn't his sport, but what he didn't know was that the sport he'd come to love was practicing right there in the next room.

Chapter 9

Greco Roman

Amaury entered the large room and immediately felt the energy from the activity of all the kids. Once inside, he saw a boy kneeling on a mat wearing headgear and padding on his knees and elbows while another boy was kneeling over him. They seemed to be waiting for a signal. After a sudden quick whistle, there was a flurry of activity from the two combatants. They swiftly started moving against each other and wrestling. After a full minute, the whistle blared again, immediately stopping the boys.

Watching the match, Amaury was riveted by their agility and single-minded pursuit to take control of their partner to pin their opponent to the mat.

Although he knew nothing of this sport, he was instantly taken by the intense action. The two boys would set up in two ways, one up and one down on his knees, or facing off like boxers. Amaury loved the idea they could use their hands while battling. The ability to grab and throw someone down is what he truly revered in the heat of competition, and the idea that he could compete in a type of hand-to-hand combat truly thrilled him. Communism had taught Amaury that fighting was the essence of survival. The communists were always fighting. Amaury knew from school that their revolution would always be a fight. Even if Amaury didn't like communism, its influence was still ingrained in his mind whether he liked it or not.

Each boy learned the wrestling techniques to achieve a dominant position resulting in a true competition of wills. As he continued watching, Amaury instinctively knew he wanted to join.

When the class was over, Amaury walked up to the coach and spoke to him about joining the program. The coach was a huge dark-skinned man with a very kind smile and gigantic hands. His name was El Terry.

El Terry weighed near two hundred and eighty pounds of solid muscle, but surprisingly he was quite athletic and agile for his size.

El Terry looked down at Amaury and saw a young kid who looked very tough but apprehensive. "Hola chico. ¿Qué tal? Can I help you?"?"

Intimidated Amaury squeaked out his response. "Hello, sir, yes. I'm interested in learning about and maybe joining your team here."

"I see," El Terry replied. "Tell me, have you ever wrestled before? Do you know anything about Greco Roman wrestling?"

"No sir, I don't," Amaury admitted. "But I was over at the boxing ring just now and I don't think that's for me. I'm not sure I liked it as much as what I just saw here."

"I understand. This kind of wrestling is a bit new to Cuba, but it's a great man-to-man competition. After some instruction, and of course practice, I think you may find you'll like it and perhaps do quite well. I can teach you all you need to know."

"Really?" Amaury was thrilled.

"But generally, it's a real battle of wills and you'll be challenged every time you go on the mat. Certainly, you'll understand more as you progress. We have school competitions every few weeks, and then at the end of the year, we have a very competitive finals match. It's well-organized and is quite challenging."

"Sign me up!"

"We'd be happy to consider you for the team. What's your name?"

"Amaury Torres." They shook hands.

"Mucho gusto. El Terry."

"How do I start? I think I might like to try."

When Amaury shook El Terry's hand, he couldn't believe the way his hand disappeared into the coach's grip entirely. Amaury looked up at him and thought he was the most imposing man he'd ever seen.

Despite his intimidating size, he was a great coach and a terrific teacher. Amaury eventually learned to greatly respect and admire El Terry. They either called him Coach or El Terry. No one ever gave him a hard time, and the entire team listened carefully to his every word.

El Terry continued, "Do you live nearby?"

"Yes, sir. I live in the Belén Solar #261, close by."

"Amaury. We are glad to have you, why don't you go over to that closet in the corner of the room and pick out a comfortable uniform to wear as part of the team."

The uniform was a one-piece garment that was red and blue, joined in the middle with shorts and a top so it appeared to look like two separate pieces. The tank-style top had open arms with the Cuban flag sewn on the front.

Greco wrestling had been brought to Cuba from Russia as a team sport. However, initially, it wasn't well accepted. They thought it made the participants too physically close together and were uncomfortable with the style. Amaury loved the sport and its pitting men to compete, testing their ability to overtake their opponent through pure strength, skill, and passion. One man against another. It was winner take all, an honest pure simple individual struggle for victory.

One of the first things El Terry taught everyone was about protecting themselves. "Boys, you must be careful of your ears. They could end up looking like cauliflowers from the rough treatment. So, you must cover them and be aware at all times." El Terry gave out a big hearty laugh with that comment. Amaury paid attention and always wore his headgear or waited till one was available.

From the very beginning, everyone noticed that Amaury seemed to have a talent for wrestling. He learned how to use his hands, feet, and weight to overtake his opponents.

Amaury, only twelve years old, was five feet, two inches tall, and weighed one hundred and ten pounds but was formidable and tough to beat compared to the other kids his age.

As the year progressed, he began wining many of his matches and eventually worked his way up into the heavy-weight class. Many of his competitors were a bit smaller and they had difficulty managing his weight and his adept swiftness as they struggled to defeat him. Much like his days playing marbles on the playground, Amaury quickly defeated many of his opponents. He proved over and over that he was talented and fearless.

El Terry, with his athletic contacts, decided they would begin steering Amaury in a new direction. If things went well, he would potentially compete for the National Team and later, if things continued progressing, for the Cuban Olympic wrestling team. To his great enthusiasm and excitement, Amaury knew he was being groomed by his coaches to challenge for the upper ranks of National and International competitions. Amaury was gaining confidence with all his small successes in wrestling.

A series of competitions were scheduled and Amaury needed to prepare. If he were to win them all it would be a big first step to compete for the Cuban National Olympic Team. This was a great honor for Amaury, and he was thrilled about the opportunity. He knew his parents would be very proud of him, and if he did something great and made the team he'd finally get his father's attention.

The competition called the Pan American Games was held internationally as preparation for the Olympics, which were just two years away. It was a warmup, a weeding out process to see who would represent their country on the international stage. If Amaury were to win this match, he would join the national team and possibly get a chance to compete for an Olympic bid later on. He practiced daily and worked out for many hours and months to prepare for the event.

When the big day arrived, Amaury was confident he was going to make his goal a reality. He was scheduled for a total of three matches, three rounds of two minutes each. He would have to win all three rounds to qualify. It was a tall task for the young boy.

Amaury made it through his first two matches without any serious challenge. Once again, just like with the marbles, Amaury proved to be superior.

When the final match was about to begin, El Terry huddled with Amaury to strategize for his next opponent. "Amaury, now you listen carefully. The scouting report I have says Pedro is fast, faster than you've seen before. He's got a significant advantage. You must be very careful and watch his speed. Next thing, like you, he's very strong. Make sure not to let him grab hold of you. His strength combined with his speed could leave you at a quick disadvantage. Be alert and let's go win this. Keep an eye on his midsection—it always tells you where he's going, remember? Buena suerte, Amaury!"

"Okay, Coach. I can do it! Gracias."

Once the official began the bout, Pedro immediately proved he was fast, just as El Terry had warned. He instantly lunged and grappled Amaury's midsection, taking him off balance.

Quickly Amaury found himself down on the mat but partially out of bounds. Pedro jumped, ready for the next setup. The referee awarded Pedro two points for the super quick takedown and one point for Amaury's landing positioning over the boundary line.

Down by three, Amaury, suddenly unusually nervous, was saved from a near-total pinning by being out of bounds and the referee's whistle. He couldn't believe it had happened so quickly.

Realizing he must step up his speed, but careful with Pedro's quickness, Amaury plotted out his next move. If he was able to sidestep at the last second while Pedro tried the lunge again, grab him, and put his weight against him for an advantage and potential takedown, it could work to his advantage.

This time, both started standing up facing each other. The whistle blared out, and Amaury, having correctly analyzed Pedro's thinking, had the speed advantage. Pedro lunged again, but ready for the move, Amaury stepped just slightly to his left and was able to grapple Pedro around his waist and force him down, flipping him over as a major takedown and scoring three of his points.

Tied at three, Amaury discovered he was going to be able to use his weight to his advantage on Pedro from that point on.

Next, from the neutral position on top, he was able to quickly bring Pedro down a second time. Amaury was now a single point ahead. He noticed something about Pedro weakening after the second takedown and thought Pedro seemed to lose some of his energy in that first minute. His eyes showed fear. Amaury believed in himself and felt he could do it. He could finish this here. He could qualify for the Olympic team.

In the middle of the third minute, Amaury took a tactical advantage of Pedro and was able to lift him entirely up, spinning and driving him into the mat in one motion. Pedro landed square on his right shoulder. Pedro thudded hard on the mat and didn't budge. The crowd gasped at Amaury's big move with the added pin. Amaury couldn't believe it.

He'd done it. He'd won! He knew it was over, the move finished the bout, but the referee didn't immediately signal a victory for the match.

Everyone watched in silence while Amaury looked back at Pedro, still not moving, only moaning in pain.

The referee yelled out, "Doctor, please. We need the doctor right now!"

As the medical doctor examined Pedro, Amaury looked over his shoulder at El Terry, stunned, as well. They stared silently at one another. The referee stood over the injured Pedro, watching and waiting for the doctor's report.

After a few more minutes there was an announcement. "Amaury Torres is disqualified from the final round with an injury to his opponent Pedro Hernandez, who has been named the winner of the championship by default. We will begin the awards celebration in ten minutes."

Amaury stood there in disbelief. Everything he'd worked for, struggled, and persevered over was gone in a flash. According to the rules of the Pan Am Games, competitors were not allowed to injure other competitors, or they would be immediately disqualified regardless of how it occurred.

Amaury looked over at his coach, but they didn't say a word to each other. He walked over to his team's bench, plopped down, hung his head, and stared at the floor in severe rejection. His teammates walked by him and, comfortingly, each one put their hands on his shoulder. No one said a word. The entire team was in shock. There was no doubt Amaury would have won the match, but the accidental injury took away any possibility for him to continue forward.

It was over. There would be no National Team, no Olympics bid. Amaury's wrestling career was over.

He never stopped loving wrestling but instead, he went back to being a regular Cuban kid once again. As Amaury, still learning about disappointments and challenges, did not consciously realize, his time on the wrestling mat was a metaphor for his entire life. He believed he'd failed miserably but in reality, he'd grown immensely from the experience. His future, unknown, remained a mystery. Although disappointed with the conclusion of his wrestling, he didn't know he was going to have quite an amazing future.

Chapter 10

Malecón and the Seboney

As he entered his teenage years, Amaury felt it was impossible not to experience or see Fidel everywhere he went. The Revolution was designed to be ongoing and forever. Students learned in school that the life they lived was the best life they could have, but it seldom felt that way.

Having been such good friends since childhood, Iran and Amaury had spent hours outside playing together, discovering the many obscure areas of Havana. Knowing every street, backyard, and hidden farm would prove extremely useful as they aged and felt more and more of a need to rebel.

The restrictions against individual freedom required them to keep their most heartfelt thoughts private, so they made up a word to use when referring to any forbidden topics which could not be spoken of in public without fear of reprisal. The word *LaYuma* was their safe word. It meant anything and everything. When either boy used it, the other one instantly recognized the references without potential fear of listening ears.

"Amaury, you know last night I dreamed about *LaYuma*. It was amazing," Iran said as they were walking down the road. "I was in such a deep sleep when I woke up this morning, I thought I was there."

"What did it feel like?"

"The funny thing is, I have no idea what it's like to be there, but when I got up I felt so lightheaded I had to sit down again."

"Really? What was the dream?"

"I can't remember the details, but it's been on my mind all day. I just know I felt like I was flying, looking down at the world. I knew it was *LaYuma*, though. I'm positive about that." Iran looked so happy as he recalled the dream. It wasn't common for teenage boys to speak so excitedly about anything in life, but at this moment Iran seemed almost childlike in his giddiness.

"What else happened?!"

"I was way up in the clouds. It was weird but it felt nice—floating, kind of. I can't explain it, but it wasn't Cuba." He checked his surroundings before finishing his thought in a whisper. "I think it was America."

The Revolution was heavily reinforced by a bureaucracy of the government called *Comite de Defense*. It was the equivalent of an FBI interior Police Department. Cuban authorities were willing to impugn severe punishments for the slightest infraction, so it was common for the boys to stay guarded when they had these kinds of conversations.

Getting caught with a single American dollar could be the cause of confinement for up to twenty years. Despite obvious dangers, Amaury and Iran often tried to live on the edge and loved to see how far they could push the boundaries before real trouble ensued. Amaury often had more of a lust for trouble than Iran did.

"What should we do today?" Iran asked as the boys walked through the main square in the northern section of Havana.

"Wanna fuck around with the cops and see what happens?"

Iran laughed. He didn't want to get into real trouble, but the thought of messing with a cop was intriguing. "What do you have in mind?"

"I'll tell you in just a moment. I have an idea. Nothing crazy, just a little fun. Follow me."

And off they went. The boy's favorite hangout in the northern shore area of the Havana port was a spot right by the ocean called the Malecón. It was one of the most famous places in Havana, a walking stone esplanade that was originally built by the American Military Corps of Engineers along the coastline to prevent ocean erosion. It was a hugely popular place for tourists and locals alike, especially with fishermen. It was at the Malecón that Amaury loved to use his father's old radio called Seboney, which received a variety of stations.

The portable radio was designed in Russia although manufactured in Cuba had a faded screen, broken edges, and scratched-off numerals. The dial was surrounded by a black plastic frame and a wooden body. The Seboney, although old when Amaury got it, still worked well enough.

Most stations the Siboney received were daily local pro-communist broadcasting in Havana and nearby. However, there were a few other Latin stations that played great jazz or dance music with the deep beat of Cuban Salsa. Amaury loved Latin music, but at the Malecón, he sought out stations that didn't comply with the Communist ideas of what was acceptable for listening.

Inwardly, Amaury enjoyed knowing he could walk the line of rebelling yet seemingly complying. However, on one occasion by pure chance, he discovered a rock-and-roll station emanating from Miami, Florida. One of the first groups he learned of and came to love was Led Zeppelin. Many of the songs he heard sung were about human independence, love, and ultimately freedom of thought, which he later discovered about their lyrics.

The signal from Florida wasn't completely clear nor that strong but still powerful enough to hear.

Once Amaury found the American station, he frequently listened to the forbidden Miami sound. Understanding western music was an impactful revelation for Amaury. He found it louder than Cuban music, stronger, electric, flowing, intense, and with a different rhythm altogether. He always wanted more.

American or British hard rock and roll infiltrated his mind. He listened intently to the names of the groups announced at the end of songs. It was a significant influence for Amaury and a further crack into the hidden world outside. These thoughts were running through his mind when he challenged Iran with his risky plan to chide a policeman on the beat.

"Hey, here's my idea Iran. Let's play WPLJ really loud with the Seboney and walk next to a cop. See what happens. It'll be really funny. Maybe his communist ears will turn red and burn off!",

"That's a really awesome funny idea Amaury. Oh my god! Yes, the cop will be so crazy angry. He's gonna shit. Hey, look, Amaury. There's a cop right over there by the embankment wall. Do you see him?"

"Oh, yeah. There he is! All right Iran. Here's the plan. You'll walk by him, get into a conversation about some bullshit and try to distract him. Then I'll walk up behind both of you not too long afterward with the radio blasting. We'll give him a big ear full of some nice loud *LaYuma*."

With thumbs up, they began their plan. Amaury followed fairly close behind Iran, holding the Seboney on his shoulder with his right hand. Iran walked directly over to the cop and began the nonsense conversation. The policeman, Palo Diego, with his name on his badge, looked directly at him. Not saying a word, he listened and quickly perceived something strange taking place.

"Hi, Officer Diego. How are you today?"

He responded with curiosity but wasn't falling for any falseness in Iran's voice.

"Yeah. What do you want, boy?"

"What do you mean, officer? Nothing. I was merely trying to be friendly."

Diego tried to figure out what Iran was doing. He looked intently into his eyes; his policeman's antenna alerted. Immediately on cue, Amaury shuffled past both of them and dialed up the volume to its highest level. He wanted to make sure PO Diego got a good blast of Led Zeppelin. As Amaury sauntered past both Iran and Diego, music blaring, everyone nearby twisted their heads in disbelief.

Holding the Seboney with both hands, Amaury tried to push the radio toward Diego's face. The two boys broke out in hysterical laughter. Iran followed close behind Amaury as they dashed across the Malecón promenade a short distance along the pier. Diego yelled at the boys as they sped away, turned left, and then headed down a dirt path. They quickly turned at the top of the embankment and disappeared, escaping well ahead of Diego's screaming.

"You sons of bitches, come back here. You're not getting away with this. Believe me, I never forget a face."

While laughing and running as fast as they could, they realized Diego couldn't keep up. Knowing the area well, they continued down the path toward the water and into a small hidden cave they'd visited several times before. This advantage helped them dodge Diego, who was too late to observe where they disappeared. They heard him yelling for quite a while, but he never ventured down the path to continue the chase. Disgusted, eventually he gave up and left.

Not knowing Diego was gone, the boys sat quietly for some time, scared, their hearts beating fiercely. After it quieted down, they began laughing about their crazy fun adventure. They both took deep breaths and agreed perhaps never to try that again, as it had ended more dangerously than they'd anticipated. Happy and relieved, they eventually walked back home.

Chapter 11

An Influential Moment In Time

Around age fifteen, Amaury developed other ways of rebelling, such as letting his hair grow longer. Cuban youngsters displaying this style were considered a rogue type, a hippie, and they were called a *Rockaydo,* a highly anti-revolutionary label most Cubans avoided.

Amaury's choice of friends and his rebellious thoughts weren't appreciated by his father, but he didn't care. He purposely hung out in a district called Copelita on the corner of 23rd Avenue and El Berado in Havana. Copelita was a well-known pro-communist neighborhood. His group of friends went to a small cafe called *The Copolita* where they served delicious ice cream. They purposely chose this area so they could show off their unconventional behavior.

At *The Copolita*, they met Soviets stationed there who enjoyed talking about the world outside of Cuba. Even though Russia was another communist country, any tidbit of new knowledge Amaury heard was exciting.

Equally exciting was a chance meeting with a cute blonde Soviet girl named Svetlana. She was the daughter of a diplomat a few years older than Amaury and lived in Havana because her father was working on a government oil contract. Amaury was taken with her right away.

They became good friends. In some ways, Amaury thought of Svetlana as more than a good friend. Initially, his feelings had to be kept a secret. He would listen to her for hours on end as she described what it was like living all over the world. Svetlana talked about television, movies, music, and interesting books she'd read, but she could have talked about what she ate for breakfast for all Amaury cared. Interestingly, she spoke in a rough Russian-Spanish he didn't always understand, but he didn't care and listened intently to her every word. In his eyes, she seemed very sophisticated. She was attractive, and he was compelled by her physical presence. He noticed other men would look at her while they chatted in that dark corner.

He was hungry for any knowledge of the world outside of his island, and he loved the way she described her stories in detailed verbal pictures. He couldn't take his eyes off her as they spoke. Even later on when he was back home, he'd think about her all night. He closed his eyes and realized he was smitten with her. He secretly hoped she felt the same.

"Amaury, you know it's funny being in Cuba," she said one day in her smooth voice. "It's still communist but so very different from Russia. In Russia, we have a few more privileges. Yes, restrictive, but similarly, I think, being on an island makes it more difficult in some ways. People have fewer things and less money, but they also work harder. More importantly, they are not as worried about the future as compared to what I've learned about Western nations.

"Yes, you're right. I'm sure. I can't even imagine what life is like outside of Cuba. Since we've met, you have given me so much to think about. It gives me hope, considering there's a bigger world out there. I know little about it. I'm so happy you have shared with me your many experiences with me. Svetlana, you know you have the cutest smile!"

She grinned at the compliment and blushed because she knew Amaury liked her as much as she liked him. It wasn't easy for them to share their new young feelings.

"Amaury, you're right." She paused for a moment and chuckled, thinking it might be better to quickly change the subject rather than let these unexpected thoughts linger. "But wait. Don't forget to remind me of the time when we were in New York City, and we had the most delicious pancakes with the cutest little blueberries on top that you could've possibly imagined. Sometimes we don't get any fruit in Russia."

Amaury laughed out loud. "I love pancakes when we can get them, which is rarely. I love them."

Svetlana replied, "I hope to go back to New York someday because they were so amazing."

Lost in a moment of happiness, Amaury looked at Svetlana with incredible joy, but then reality struck again. "I must confess to you, Svetlana. I love Cuba, I do. It's my home. But living here isn't fun. You must always be careful. But I want you to know I love hearing your stories about your life and friends—everything you know. It makes me feel happy to hear about things about which I know nothing. I want to know what the outside world is like. I know it's silly, but you have to tell me about the pancakes again. Please tell me more about your experiences in New York. I can't even imagine what that must be like. Just hearing the name of the city makes me excited."

In her heart, Svetlana knew Amaury was thirsty for knowledge, and she loved how he looked at her. Similarly, to Amaury, she thoroughly loved meeting with him.

On one particular occasion when they sat down to chat, Svetlana felt the urge to reach over and kiss him. Smiling, she cautioned herself and said, "You know, Amaury, perhaps one day you and I will get to go to all those cool places together." She looked at him directly, almost hoping to reveal her hidden thoughts.

He could see her style was quietly seductive. She occupied most of his thoughts in the days since they met. Hidden thoughts and objectives often went unexplained for young people.

Growing was never an easy path. Their relationship only lasted a few months. They often sat in the back of the restaurant by themselves. It seemed the two were quite shy, but their friendship bloomed and was magnetic. Later on, cautiously and happily, they did share one kiss.

One day, however, without warning, Svetlana disappeared, Amaury went to *The Copilita* for their usual meeting and sat at the usual table and waited. As he waited, he read the local paper, *Jeventud Reverde* or the Youth Rebellion. It was a pro-communist local publication often lying on the tables. Amaury would occasionally read them. Looking up at the clock, not realizing hours had passed, he kept glancing around.

Suddenly, the restaurant lights went off. Svetlana never showed up. She'd left for good without saying goodbye. Later, sadly, Amaury learned she'd gone back home with her father. Their departure was unscheduled and heartbreaking. He felt terrible, but when he finally realized it was over, he knew he'd certainly never forget her. He understood the connection they'd established was real and had profoundly affected his life.

Sometime after 1989 when the Berlin wall fell, the Russians officially left Cuba, and everything changed dramatically on the island.

The idea that Amaury might run into Svetlana again someday was most likely never going to happen. In Amaury's mind, the Russians were never coming back again.

Being forced to live a communist life, Amaury always struggled with the obvious deception he clearly understood. He'd learned to love these special dates with Svetlana had taken him away, even if momentarily. His life became significantly less exciting without her. Painfully, emotionally, he missed their special connection immensely. Despite his young age, the loss of Svetlana was difficult to let go of. He would often just go back to Copolita and look around, hoping he was wrong, and she'd be in their dark corner waiting for him. He never imagined experiencing the sense of loss he did. The owner watched Amaury while he cleaned behind the counter and knew he was crestfallen. He could see it on his face—the sadness. He never said anything, but he did offer him an ice cream, hoping he could cheer him up. It took a long time for Amaury to recover. Learning to let go of things and especially people who were important to him, were very tough lessons. It was never easy growing up in Cuba. Life had so many painful experiences to overcome. For Amaury, this was only the beginning.

He eventually stopped visiting *The Copolita* neighborhood and her loss only made his curiosity regarding the outside world stronger. Her insight into Russia further opened his eyes to the realities of life on their island. He'd known in his heart he wanted to be a Westerner, and it was now firmly planted in his soul. But how would that ever be accomplished?

Chapter 12

Genoveva 'Abuelita' Torres

It was a beautiful afternoon in the middle of summer, the blinding sun high in the sky causing sweat to run down her temples.

Back in the old country in southeastern Cuba near the Sierra Maestra, plebeian country farmers scraped out a moderate living from their hard toiling of the land. It was the only life they knew. Farmers grew avocados, mangoes, cocoa, and sugar cane among others produce in the many fields which went on for miles.

The Torres family was small. The mother Genoveva, Francisco, the father, and their son Nury. On that particular day, the two men were working quite a distance from their home tending to their crops getting ready for market.

Just outside the very old one-story farmhouse where they lived was a winding dirt country road. It was bumpy and rock hard from years of use. It resembled the ridges of an old wooden washboard. It was an unforgiving road most people would not drive unless they had specific business being there.

On the farm, there were a few horses, cattle, other livestock, noisy chickens, a few scruffy barking dogs, and many annoying flies. Normally, there were no other souls around unless it was a distant neighbor who ventured by to borrow something or chat. It was known however that the Batista Army patrolled the roads and were an invasive dangerous group of men.

If they came to the door, it typically meant trouble. Rural farmers in Cuba—east, west, north, and south—used extreme caution when observing the Batista Army trucks rolling by. Farmers would keep their heads down and pray the trucks would just pass them by. Batista's soldiers oftentimes ignored these prayers and would invite themselves into many homes.

Genoveva was a middle-aged woman of medium height, and build but looked tired around the eyes from the many years of toiling stress. Her hair was pulled up in a tight bun with a simple pin holding it up to keep cool in the heat. She was always busy in their home, cleaning persistently dusty surfaces. She wore a lightweight house dress with an apron tied around her back and looped around her neck.

Once the dusting was completed, it was on to feeding the chickens then filling the leaky wooden water tubs for the horses, who also needed to stay hydrated. This was the beginning of many chores. The rest of her tasks took her 'til the end of the day when she could finally rest a few minutes before it got dark.

After dinner was finished, she was finally able to get off her feet in anticipation of repeating the same activities the following day and every day after. These farmers took care of themselves, helped others, and did the best they could to get through life, loving God and praying there someday might be a kinder future for them all.

Having been through several generations of dictators, the citizens did not have a lot to look forward to as a country. Most importantly, they tried to make life as livable as possible despite the political atmosphere. It was a habitual process of looking over their shoulders for any potential unknown dangers headed their way. They needed to carry on no matter who was in control of the government.

As the afternoon sun was high in the sky, outside she could hear the sound of crickets only interrupted by the mooing cows or cackling chickens. Mrs. Torres, while busy focusing on her tasks, was surprised when she heard the distant sound of an engine motor. She was not sure she'd heard correctly, but for a moment it distinctly sounded like a vehicle motor. Dismissing the odd occurrence, she went back to work, pushing dust into the dust bin.

The engine became audible, and she froze. Genoveva noticed a vehicle coming up the road by the plume of dirt flying behind the truck and then turning up their driveway heading directly toward the house. She was not only curious but immediately concerned, as this kind of occurrence was hugely rare.

To her horror, it didn't take long before the vehicle revealed itself to be a Batista Army vehicle. It came to an abrupt halt near the unlocked front door.

No one in this part of the country locked their doors. Most doors didn't even have locks on them. Genoveva knew being alone in the farmhouse without her husband and son seeing the Batista troops exiting the truck was a very serious situation. Genoveva heard pebbles hitting the front door and the ominous voices of men as they approached the house. Her stomach tightened with nerves, and her heart pounded in her ears as she attempted to remain calm. She collected herself and took a deep breath, and then a chill ran up her spine as she heard a knock at the door.

Chapter 13

Nury Torres

Nury Torres was a man of average height and weight and later in life was best remembered by his white hair which he'd developed at a young age.

Nury, like many other Cuban farmers, desired a simple life. He didn't seek nor contemplate glory. His singular goal was to make it through each day peacefully. He did the best he could for his family by working on their farm, and in a sense, his life was predictable and predetermined.

Cuban families were generally hard-working members of society and were an amalgamation of many different nations previously brought to the island. They did their best to live decent lives and help each other.

The Torres family lived in the southeastern province of Cuba called *Oriente* in the town known as *Holguin*. It was close to the large city of Santiago and north of the Sierra Maestra Mountain range. As with many others, the Torres' lives were dedicated to farming and getting their products to market as their sole daily effort.

Nury was born in 1929, a unique time in Cuban history. Going through a continually changing political environment affected the quality of their lives. He also experienced changes of a dramatic fashion in a more personal way during the reign of Batista. Even though they were poor country farmers, they worked hard, and while life was a struggle, it somehow seemed worth it. They loved their land and their country.

In 1952 the fascist Fulgencio Batista took power for the second time in Cuba and over time the Army began to prey upon the population. They ran through the countryside harassing people, stealing chickens and food, and pillaging and raping women. It was almost as if the backcountry of Cuba was their own little playground.

On that particular hot afternoon, the Batista Army chose to stop by the Torres' farm. Nury and his father were away farming and unaware of the soldiers' arrival. Once the soldiers stepped through the front door, they quickly discovered there was a woman in the home by herself.

Inside, Genoveva saw the door burst open as she stood there alone in horror, not knowing what was about to happen. All four Batista soldiers grabbed her and took her into the bedroom, doing what power-hungry out-of-control men did when there was no rule of law in the land. Each one took their turn against Genoveva, who was no longer able to fight. Before leaving, they continued to threaten her. If she were to seek retribution of any kind, they would return to do worse to her and her family. The soldiers laughed on the way out as they grabbed chickens and other items while running to their truck. As quickly as they arrived, they were gone.

The next painfully isolated hours seem to take a lifetime to pass as she felt the walls of the room closing in on her. She took time to gather herself and her thoughts, tears streamed down her face. She was terrified for her own life and the safety of her family. Her mind was fogged by the rage, hate, and helplessness she felt. She didn't know how to tell the boys when they returned and knew it was going to tear the family apart. This kind of mental wound would not heal quickly. A dark cloud of hateful contempt for Batista consumed their family bond.

When Nury and his father returned to the house later that evening, they were crushed and shocked to find Genoveva had been raped and left for dead. She was in a terrible condition, and the pain it caused would take a long time for her to resolve. Such a serious event became a beacon that changed the course of their lives forever.

The harm was done and Nury's disgust of Batista evolved into an obsessive rage of despair. He was revolted by the event and couldn't stop thinking about his mom's attack and the deep dark hatred he felt for Batista's out-of-control renegade army.

His rage grew greater with each passing day. He believed to his core Batista was the worst of all the dictators Cuba had ever experienced. The rampant callousness they showed to the Cuban people had gone far enough, and now it was personal. Nury knew he needed to exact revenge for the brutal rape of his mother. The seeds for his retribution were planted and began to grow.

Chapter 14

Nury Plans His Revenge

Some years before the attack on Nury's mother, Fidel Castro attempted a coup against Batista which failed. Several years later after regrouping, Castro plotted a second time. The next attempt was designed to honor the memory of Jose Marti, the historic revolutionary who fought against Spanish repression in the late 1800s, a man whom Castro admired.

While banished in Mexico, Castro developed a plan. It was decided they'd embark their operation in the area of Southeastern Cuba called the *Village Playas Las Coloradas* at *Oriente Pointe.* They deeply believed it was an honor to initiate their fight at the same location in which Marti began his heroic actions against Spain.

The arrangement coordinated Castro's crew of eighty-two men to arrive via the yacht *Granma.* In celebration of their hoisting off from Tuxpan Mexico in late November 1957, they called themselves *Los Expedicionarios del Yate Granma,* The Granma Yacht Expeditioners. They were to converge at the same time with a land-based rebel group known as the *MR-26-7 movement* led by Frank Pais. Their plot was designed to join together to infiltrate Cuba and begin the revolution by cutting off the southeastern third of Cuba known as *Oreinte* from the rest of the country. Pais, who led the largest rebellion group in Cuba known as *The Underground* together, was to meet at the *Oreinte Pointe* beachhead and launch the historic attack from there.

Much to Castro's dismay, the scheme was uncovered by Batista and ended in disaster.

Landing late two days late, Castro was exposed to the remaining rebels. They were attacked as they exited the yacht. In pursuit by Batista's army, Castro's group hastily fled up into the *Sierra Maestra* mountains. Castro, having grown up near the mountain range, knew the natural protection it would provide. Their hideout was coincidentally not far from Holguin where the Torres family farm was located. The only ones to survive were Fidel, Raul, his brother, Che Guevara, Camilo Cienfuegos, and approximately eight more men. Frank Pais was later assassinated, along with the majority of Castro's men.

In the mountains, the remaining survivors reassembled into the core group of a new future rebellion. They eventually evolved into Castro's next steps for his final and successful revolution. Batista's army, not as knowledgeable of the difficult mountain terrain, was never quite able to discover where these rebels were located, and this was a significant advantage for the Castro rebels.

The local population heard of this second attempt and many Cubans thought of it as brave. It was perceived as hope for a real and positive change in Cuba, and it motivated the locals to reach out and assist Castro. It was this emotional movement, the groundswell of support for Castro by the locals that helped to give birth to Nury's planned revenge.

Batista, angry that he was losing his continued control of the locals, encouraged his men to step up their searches and enact greater cruelty to the population. His strategy was to force the people to turn in Castro to him and end Castro's tactical advantage, but the opposite happened. This further motivated the people to rally around and support *Frank Pais's Underground* anti-government movement which later became a major opportunity for Castro.

Nury learned about the rebels and their general location. He realized this was his opportunity to seek revenge. Nury took his time putting together his own plan. After several months, he told his parents he was leaving and would search for and join Castro's rebels. Somehow he believed Castro's group would be a better choice for his plans. Since Pais was dead, *The Underground* no longer had their core emotional leader.

"Mama, the time has come," Nury said to Genoveva. "I have made up my mind, and I must leave now to look for those men. I know they're up in the mountains. I don't know exactly where they are, but I solemnly know I want to do something for Cuba and take revenge for your attack. The time has come for Cubans to fight back for something important and free our nation from the horror we have witnessed for years. I will die trying if necessary. I'm sorry to leave you and Papa, but I have made my decision. I love you very much and will come back as often as I'm able."

At twenty-seven years old, Nury knew the reasons he wanted to go, yet his parents still tried to talk him out of it. His mom pleaded with him. "Let life take its course, Nury. Please stay a few more days and think about your decision."

"No, Mama. This is my future. I know what I must do. I want this more than anything I've ever wanted in my life. I can no longer bear the suffering we incurred, the pain you went through, and the intense disrespect Batista's soldiers have shown Cubans. If I die trying to rid them from Cuba, it will be the last thing I do. Your honor as a mother means too much to me. I finally know my purpose in life now, mother. I love you so very much. But I've made up my mind. It's too late."

Genoveva believed life often worked out for the best, and Cuba would certainly survive Batista. For Nury, however, his hatred was too deep. The rage ate him alive. After packing a few items in his satchel and some bits of food to eat along the way, he got ready to leave with only the clothes on his back. After kissing his mother and father a tearful goodbye, he began his lonesome trek up into the Sierra Maestra in his search for Castro and the rebels. Leaving in the still of the night he was careful to avoid Batista's Army along the way.

As he traveled south with the help of other locals he met en-route, he was given directions to the general area where the rebels were hiding out.

It took Nury several days of searching to find them, and what he discovered upon arrival was a ragtag group of men and boys loosely forming a pseudo army.

Everyone was young and immature. They were undisciplined and undernourished. Though they didn't know Nury, he was welcomed in, even though some of the men seemed reluctant to trust him. They shared what little reserves of food they had with him and began to form a bond.

Eventually the opportunity to discuss with the others his desire to fight arose, and in sharing the story of how Batista's soldiers had raped his mother and threatened to destroy his family, Nury earned their trust and acceptance. They shared the same hatred of Batista. It was the common core of their rage, the glue that kept them together.

Camping outside on a mountain running from a violent army was very different from living in his own house, in his own bed, and working on the farm. As difficult as it was, Nury believed it was the right thing to do and far better than the life he would have otherwise had.

Chapter 15

In The Mountains

Now that Nury was comfortable with his new setting, he began learning more about Cuban history. Fueled by hatred for Batista, Nury had joined Castro's rebel army, but it was learning more about Castro and his ideals that kept him there and turned him into a loyalist.

Castro used four separate encampments in the jungles, which was a safety measure put in place to keep the movement going in-case Batista's soldiers ever caught anyone. Each of the four groups was led by one of Castro's top and closest advisors—Fidel's brother, Raul Castro, Ché Guevara, and Camilo Cienfuegos. Castro kept his own quarters far from everyone else, believing that the safest protection came from anonymity from everyone. Only his most trustworthy people knew of his whereabouts. This frustrated Nury, as he longed to meet their leader, but he knew he had to respect the system that was in place.

Later, Nury learned that the survival plan included emotionally demanding activities such as descending into the nearby towns asking for help, or stealing provisions from the local farmers as necessary. He hated these tasks, as he knew he was taking items from people like his own parents, but he remained convicted in his determination to fight, and so he swallowed the bitter taste left in his mouth. He knew that the rebels needed the townspeople's assistance. Otherwise, they'd starve.

Nury listened carefully to discussions and teachings of communism in meetings with Castro and his three main advisors. They all believed one-hundred percent the doctrines of Marx and Lenin. Nury learned it was in Mexico they'd established their firm beliefs and how positive it would be for all of Cuba if those systems came to their own country.

Nury once overheard Ché and Raul discussing how other rebel groups were forming in Cuba who were competing with Castro's potential revolution, and they plotted to incorporate them into their army. They desperately needed the additional manpower but had to be careful not to fully reveal their true communist intentions.

One of the ways Castro was able to convince them to join was by coaching everyone to read and write. It was a huge inspirational motivation for these recruits, and it worked. By 1957, Castro's rebel soldiers numbered two hundred. The recruits also were eventually taught about communism. If they protested in any way, they received a grave response.

Ultimately everyone had to commit to Castro or face execution. Horrified, Nury saw many men be instantly shot if they didn't comply, but it was for the benefit of the revolution, and he allowed his mind to twist in ways that would keep him focused on the mission.

Despite all he witnessed, Nury's allegiance to Castro was steadfast. He saw Castro as his path to freedom. This passion and devotion to Castro and communism guided his life forward and would take hold of him long into his adult years.

As his time with the rebels passed, Nury's impatience to meet Castro grew, but Castro never individually met with recruits until much later on and sometimes never at all. He felt it important to keep a distance from them as a way to keep his persona a mystery and create the powerful allure he coveted. He believed they would respect and look up to him more if he were unreachable. Castro and his ranking officers, Camilo, Ché, and Raul, planned their actions just as any disciplined army would. They had to account for the survival of their troops, but they also needed to plan their coup against the ruthless Batista and make sure they didn't fail again. Preparing and planning ahead of time was as essential as it was to act at the right moment.

Batista knew he was in the fight of his political life and that he needed to keep favor with the people or risk losing power. He went into the farmlands and towns causing havoc. His army killed citizens then spread rumors that it was Castro who had committed the murders and caused chaos. Later, when Castro's men went down into the towns for supplies, it wasn't surprising the locals no longer happily received them.

Castro learned of this turn of events and developed his own strategy. As many of the small towns were controlled by cruel and illegitimate mayors put in place by Batista, Castro felt he could use the situation to curry favor with the local townsfolk.

Castro's rebels went into the nearby town of *La Plata* where they brutally executed the mayor, Chico Osorio. The townspeople, relieved of this cruel leader's influence, quickly swung their support back to Castro. After that, word spread that Castro truly was fighting back for the people.

Castro was not only able to increase recruiting after that, but also to easily obtain supplies.

It was after these successful raids into other towns that Nury Torres finally met Castro face to face. It was the biggest moment of Nury's life.

"I have heard good things about you, Mr. Torres. I understand that Batista's army directly affected your family." Castro, much taller than Nury, spoke first as he put his hand on his shoulder. "I know that must have been extremely difficult."

Nury was immediately impressed that Castro knew about his family's plight.

"Thank you, Commander," Nury said. He felt intense overwhelming gratitude for the opportunity of the meeting. "I cannot express my gratitude for you accepting me into your group's important efforts. I have learned so much from you and will give you one-hundred percent of my loyalty."

Castro continued, "I know you will. I also want you to know with your help, we will achieve our goal. We face strong enemies not only here but also outside our shores, we will not be defeated. Our power is its own continent!"

Nury felt an unexpected intense rush of strength and warmth from Castro. He perceived it to be an almost religious experience as the feeling washed over him. "Yes, sir, Commander Castro. I cannot thank you enough for this opportunity to fight for Cuba!"

For the rest of his life, Nury never questioned Castro's words or subscribed to any other school of political thought. He believed communism was the answer, the right way of life. He fully complied with and protected it.

It was extremely important for Nury to pass on these beliefs to all his children as his life carried forward.

Nury professed and discussed the value of communism with all of his children and stepchildren as they grew up. He never understood why they questioned and did not fully embrace these beliefs. This conflict became contentious, especially with Amaury and Ernesto.

Ernesto was Nury's stepson, but regardless, he still tried to affect his political thinking. The boys often discussed their dislike of communism and how they hated the repression and the manipulative deception caused by Castro's government. Nury always proclaimed the benefits to them knowing of their contempt. In the end, it was a battle he would never win.

Nury was very protective of his reputation in the government chain of command. He could be severely punished if they discovered his family members didn't fall in line. In 1983, Nury Torres was promoted to the rank of One Star General in charge of the Western Territory. It was a promotion of which he was extremely proud and one he had earned after his years of joining with the original rebel forces. General Nury recalled to himself when it happened—*the old days of living up in the mountains fighting for their freedom, realizing it was worth every minute of his peril and pursuit.* After having made it his life's goal to rid Cuba by destroying the brutal Batista regime, it was finally achieved. The revenge that fed his soul for years was complete. But in an ironic twist, the anti-revolutionary Amaury Torres's life was one single step away from Castro himself.

Chapter 16

A General's Son

From a very young age, Amaury lived without his father, an absence he learned to accept. His father's quick exit at the tender age of four didn't allow for Amaury and Nury to establish strong roots. They didn't have the bond most fathers and sons normally develop and maintain throughout their lives. There was no specific schedule for his father's visits. It was all quite haphazard. Nury's schedule was fluid, and he never made any specific arrangements on how and when he saw his children. All his decisions were based on tasks required by the military's needs. Amaury learned never, ever to depend on spending time with his father.

As a child, Amaury never misbehaved around his dad. As he grew older though and developed a significant distaste for Castro and the communist life, he truly began to rebel. Nury was responsible for three different families with five children of his own and three other step- children. Amaury was clearly the most outwardly rebellious.

As a youngster, Amaury witnessed tourists arriving, visiting Havana on busses from western countries, most often from Europe or other parts of the world. He came to learn that Americans weren't allowed to travel to Cuba but did so illegally on occasion. As a result, by the early age of nine, Amaury was already very politically aware and would often question his father's total allegiance to Castro. Amaury's strongest anti-communist perceptions were his own experiences more so than his natural curiosity of the outside world. He learned to cope with day-to-day issues while the imagination of what the world might be like only provided titillation for his

Eventually, Amaury found the courage to approach the tourists on busses to try and talk with them. He longed to know what they were like. But the first time he approached a bus; a nearby policeman patrolling the streets ran over and reprimanded him.

"¡No hables con ustedes!" the policeman shouted at Amaury.

Amaury despised the local cops but tried hard never to let his true feelings show. He complied with their rules, even when he didn't understand why they were in place.

"Dad, why am I not allowed to speak to people arriving in those busses?" he once asked Nury. "I'm not going to cause them any harm."

Nury didn't take kindly to this kind of question, even if it came from an innocent and curious child. His beliefs were steadfast and strong. "We don't question the authorities, Amaury," he said. "We accept this life. This is the way things are and the way they always will be. Don't cause trouble, and don't ask these nonsense questions. They will not lead to anything worthwhile. Fidel was the savior of Cuba."

"What would happen if I talked to tourists?" Amaury asked again. "Is there something I'm not supposed to know?"

"No. Of course not. They're just different from us. There's nothing to be gained in talking with them."

"You still take their money..."

"Amaury, learn your Cuban history and you will see how Fidel has given us something no other leader in Cuban history has done. We have freedom now. Before, we were a country ruled by a parade of ongoing cruel dictators. This has finally ended. We thank Fidel Castro for his bravery, his leadership, and his foresight in saving Cuba. Look at all the wonderful things we have—health care and education, and we are free from the oppression of capitalist control. We are an independent nation!"

For Nury, committing to communism had been a life-changing experience. The life he'd created would never have happened if he'd stayed on the farm.

Nury was sent to many countries in South America on a variety of assignments, including military commissions to help Manuel Noriega in Panama and other former leaders such as Jaime Luschini and Carlos Andres Perez both of Venezuela. He continued to spearhead influence in other countries including Brazil and Chile. He arranged trading, weaponry, and, in general, anti-American policies which Cuba sought to bring to the southern hemisphere.

As a steward of Cuba's interests, Nury assisted their militaries in securing agreements, purchases of armament, weaponry, and ammunition, including hardware for war. In Cuba, the ends always justify the means. They knew pursuing and promoting their communist progressivism in the South American continent was a necessity even if it potentially caused conflict with America.

To assuage his guilt over his children's curiosities, Nury would buy western-style clothing for them while overseas. His kids began to look forward to these times, knowing he would bring back new jeans, jackets, shirts, and sneakers from foreign countries. Nury knew this was risky but quietly chose to extend these small advantages to his children.

The conflict between Nury and Amaury shaped the kind of man Amaury would ultimately become. He was naturally hungry for his father's approval but his distaste for communism and his curiosities about what lay outside of his home country were more important to him. Amaury became independent and self-sufficient and learned to carve out his path in the world, even if it meant he and his father would never be close. In the end, they both chose their ideals over their relationship with one another.

Despite Nury's internal conflict, he would always appear at critical moments in Amaury's life. Amaury and Nury never saw eye-to-eye, but Amaury knew he had a one-star general in his back pocket if something seriously bad ever happened. Not many Cuban children could boast of the same advantage.

Chapter 17

Camilo

Outside of his relationship with Nury, one of the more complicated relationships in Amaury's life was the one with his stepbrother Camilo. Amaury never spent much time with Camilo, although their paths did cross occasionally. Amaury felt that Camilo received more attention from Nury than he did, and as a result, he grew to resent him.

Amaury and Camilo couldn't have been more different, but the one thing they shared was their mutual distaste for communism. Camilo had his own ways of challenging the system. His choices were significantly more dangerous than Amaury's.

Camilo took a significant risk in selling marijuana to tourists for additional income. He also occasionally used it himself. Amaury never saw the value of using pot as a way of escaping life.

These extracurricular activities in their neighborhood took place at churches, including the illicit sale of drugs.

Camilo, who was three years older than Amaury, also participated in being a tourist guide. The activity of soliciting tourists as a way of making extra money was strictly an illegal side job. They both often tried to meet tourists as they exited the busses and would introduce them to historic parts of town. Taking them to other areas, as well—nearby beaches, small shops for local food vendors, and the retail street experience was part of the service. Most tourists appreciated and loved this personalized attention by the locals when they traveled to the island. They believed Cuba was an undiscovered, unique, and personal country in a busy modernizing world.

When the tourists arrived on the morning busses, they were assigned official government tour guides. It was important for the government tourist department to make sure their experiences were enjoyable, comfortable, and safe and that they didn't get lost. Cuba needed tourism, and it was hugely important for the economy.

European tourists would break off on their own and travel to different parts of Havana. They enjoyed mingling, which became a mutual benefit both for the tourists and the Cubans, who learned about Western Culture.

Amaury, a savvy street kid, finally figured out a way to talk to the tourists. He'd make arrangements to be a personal tour guide and would earn pesos in return for his thoughtful and intelligent guidance and knowledge of the town's historical places.

Despite any potential danger, Camilo sought tourists who might be open to or interested in potentially purchasing drugs. Camilo liked the action and danger he felt from the drug sales and believed his life was elevated and more exciting from this experience.

One afternoon in the early summer of 1989, Camilo was hanging around the inside of a local Church, Iglesia Catolica in Old Havana, and was casually talking to some of his friends. He was, however, more interested in watching the behavior of the visitors. Camilo had become a keen observer of body language. For the locals who went to pray, it was a safe harbor for religious reflections. Camilo saw it as nothing more than an opportunity for the next sale.

Camilo listened to the quiet whispers of visitors as they toured the inside. They huddled in separate spots for chatting and observing details of the interior. As they mingled, they observed the statues of Jesus and the saints. The statues' unblinking eyes followed the visitors as though they were being watched with every step, reminding them of exactly why they were visiting. He could see who the locals were compared to tourists. Tourists carried cameras outside their clothing, hanging by straps from their shoulders. Their clothes were generally nicer and cleaner than the locals. They'd talk in foreign languages, and although some spoke Spanish, their knowledge of the language was not quite as perfect.

Camilo learned how to identify a potential buyer. He listened intently while not getting too close but yet close enough to attempt to make contact. Once Camilo intuitively sized up and discovered a potential buyer, he'd casually walk up to them and start a conversation as best he could. Some tourists were eager to talk to Cubans. Mingling with the population was fun and enhanced the quality of their visit. It created an intimate connection many tourists sought. For others, it was an opportunity to practice their Spanish.

Camilo spoke to the two men first. "Hello, I am Manny. How are you enjoying your trip?" He always used a fake name to protect himself.

"Oh, hello. Yes, it's going quite well. We love visiting the old churches. It's not only exciting but educational. Do you know much about this church?"

Manny would continue courteously. "Yes, of course. I have spent many days here, and there is a lot to see. Its antiquity is amazing. It's one of the better churches in town. So much religious symbolism here, and despite its age, it's still quite impressive. What country are you guys from?"

"We're from Spain. We love Havana. This is our second time here. It's nice to visit a foreign country where we all speak the same language."

Depending on where tourists were from, Camilo would quickly remember a famous person from that country and create an association for their visit to the church. This impressed the tourists. The instant bond would help to get them to become interested and more comfortable in talking to him. Spain was an easy one. "Christopher Columbus came to this part of town, interestingly, being so close to Havana, you know?"

"Yes, we remember. It makes sense he might have been right here. So interesting. Thanks for telling us that. Wonderful!"

Camilo would wink and smile. They'd all laugh. Most people chatted casually or not at all. Others fully engaged in conversations, but it was the occasional person or two who would talk on for a longer time. Camilo was good at reading people and would casually bring up the idea of going somewhere to continue the experience.

"Hey, I have an idea. If you guys are interested in having a beer, maybe get the real flavor of Cuba, I could show you some more places or something?"

The taller of the current two tourists responded, "Sure. What did you have in mind?"

"Come on, let's take a walk. It's not far away."

When the two tourists agreed, guided them to somewhere which was quiet, safe, and most importantly, private. Incredibly, sometimes he brought them back to his own home, the home of his father the general. At least there he was safe and away from the peering eyes of the *El Comite*. On this particular occasion, Camilo brought them back to his father's house. The two men were in their early thirties, friendly, and obviously interested in going off the standard tourist routine.

In Cuba, these types of tourists were known as Guaigos. They were known to have been tourists from Galicia, Spain. Once inside Nury's house, Camilo invited them to sit on the couches.

They began drinking and then eventually Camilo lit and started smoking a marijuana joint. They spent the next several hours laughing, joking, telling stories, and enjoying their time together. As the afternoon progressed to early evening, things quieted down. Everyone fell asleep for a few hours.

Camilo had other hidden plans.

Chapter 18

The Appointment

With Amaury's high school graduation only a year away, he needed to start developing a plan for afterward. Childhood was slowly fading away, and it was time to start thinking about the real world.

In Cuba, boys often never completed school, as families needed to have children bring additional money into a home. Fortunately for Amaury, his mother worked steadily, and he was also earning money in his way. Amaury contributed as best he could to his family unit so they would survive.

In the first part of the month of June 1989, Nury spoke to Amaury and asked him to get together one evening. He wanted to discuss with him some family matters and further, discuss his future.

Amaury was surprised by his father's sudden interest in his life, but he agreed to meet the following night at his father's house across town. Nury was scheduled to leave the following day on business.

Amaury's relationships with his brothers suffered some of the same intimacy issues he had with his father. However, even though they were stepbrothers, Ernesto was more of a real brother than Camilo was.

At nineteen, Ernesto's life also began to change. He was no longer in the house as much because he started working at a mechanical engineering factory on the morning shift.

Ernesto was adept at performing the difficult tasks required of the job. He enjoyed his work, became responsible, and began making a life for himself, meeting new friends, and having a purpose in life. For the first time in his life, he found satisfaction and began to thrive rather than just get by.

Every day after he came home, he'd relax from the hard day's activities and read the local newspaper until Amaury often would prepare dinner. Finally, he'd get ready for the next day's work. It became a daily routine. Much later in the evening, Amaury's mom would get home and the family would regroup again.

Amaury's fifteenth year would become the most auspicious one in his young life, the timing of events would change its entire course. Later that night when everyone was safe at home, Amaury had a difficult time falling asleep. Curiosity over why his father wanted to meet with him was paramount in his mind and he felt unable to rest.

Chapter 19

Being on Time

Amaury left his house early in the afternoon to meet Iran at his apartment. They planned to go together to meet with Amaury's father, with Iran serving as moral support for a nervous Amaury.

On their way there, Iran suggested Amaury blow off a little steam, so they stopped at the park to meet friends and play a quick pick-up baseball game. The sun was shining, the sky was cobalt blue, and there was a delicate breeze in the air. It was a great day for a midday spring game.

Huddled, kidding around with each other about who was the best player, the leaders of each side chose their teams. Amaury was picked on the stronger team. He was well-liked and was a great outfielder. He loved the outfield because had a strong arm from his time in wrestling and he was able to throw opposing players out at any plate. The other kids constantly enjoyed testing his accuracy.

As the game ran into the afternoon and then early evening, Amaury and Iran needed to leave. They said their goodbyes and left the field. While walking, they talked about how sad they were that school was ending, and it seemed clear that what they were both talking about was their childhood ending. Soon there would be no more pick-up games at the field with their friends. They were destined for a life more like the one Ernesto was living. Both boys needed to start thinking about life after school, but neither of them wanted to.

While discussing their options, what kind of jobs they might look for, later on, it became a conversation about everything else, including girls they were thinking about. They laughed about getting chewing gum. "*LaYuma!*" they said in unison and reminisced about teasing the cop. After that escapade, Amaury and Iran also fondly remembered *Chew* and running when they were young looking for a cheap thrill against a tyrannical government. The boys sensed a moment of unabated freedom through those experiences but realized teasing a tiger had consequences.

They needed to walk a large distance to the other side of town to get to Nury's home. The discussion turned to fantasies of what their potential futures might look like. Amaury wished he could leave Cuba and end up in America, while Iran wished he could have a family, a nice job, and hopefully some relief from government interference. His life goals were unlike Amaury's. He didn't have an entrepreneurial spirit or an outstanding rebellious temperament.

Iran could see that Amaury was different from most of their friends. He had an intensity and desire Iran felt was unusual for a boy his age. Iran believed eventually Amaury would have to give in to the system, as overthrowing the government was not an option. It was an overwhelming challenge not worth contemplating. He felt the best way to live was to struggle through managing life as best as possible under the circumstances. Iran may have been a prankster as a child, but he now knew to stay out of trouble and keep hoping a positive change might eventually come to Cuba. Someday.

On the other hand, Amaury felt the need to make his own changes and to live life in the moment as much as possible. He was not the kind of person who wanted to revolt against the system, but he knew conforming and adapting to work within the system and yet still achieving his own goals was impossible.

As they continued walking, they realized they needed to hurry, as it was getting late. The general didn't like lateness.

Across town, unbeknownst to Amaury and Iran, the two Guaigos whom Camilo had lured to Nury's house woke up in a hazy stupor and immediately realized something was wrong. They had been robbed. At first, they didn't know what to do but instead looked around the house, taking a mental assessment of where they were and deciding what to do next.

While feeling panicked, they tried hard to shake off the deep fogging effects of the drugs and alcohol still clouding their minds. Unsteady at first, they saw the house was quiet. The silence caused a strange, disturbing feeling. It contrasted with their terrible fear of having been left alone. Quickly, they tried to assess their whereabouts, yelling out to *Manny* for answers.

There was no response.

Confused and angry, they checked their pockets to see if anything was missing. They discovered, both their wallets and passports were gone. They looked for the door to get out of the house and realized that the man they knew as Manny was gone, too.

As they scurried out of the house, the front door swung closed behind them. Noticing a calmness in the street further disturbed them because it contrasted with their chaotic internal anguish. At the street corner, they saw a policeman and ran directly up to him. Officer Palo Diego turned around when he heard the yelling. In a frantic Spanish, together the Guaigos blurted out the story. "We were in that house over there with a young punk, and now our wallets, money, and passports are gone!"

"Momento, por favor," the policeman said. "Slow down. What's going on?"

Almost out of breath the short Guaigo began again but slower this time. "We are from Spain, and we've been here in your country only a few days. We met this young local man—Manny I think his name was, at the church, and he befriended us. He invited us over to this house, and we went over there. We spent an hour or two just hanging out and chatting. We had a few beers and as the afternoon passed. Somehow, we fell asleep. When we woke up, he was gone and so was our money, wallets IDs, passports, everything!"

Diego replied with a commanding tone, "Okay. Let's go over there and take a look and see what's going on. What was the guy's name?"

"Manny," they said.

As Amaury and Iran approached the house, Amaury took in the sight. His father's home was such a modest house, far simpler than any home of another Cuban general. There was a simple walkway up to the front door surrounded by lots of green plants, foliage, and some colorful flowers. There was an old wooden door with a well-worn handle. The door lacked fresh paint and was stained with yellow oily spots against its white color. Tiny cracks snaked through the surface. Amaury thought about his own future home and the life he wanted to live. In his mind, the image was so different from what he saw before him.

The front path showed signs of wear—small holes, broken tiles, and swarming red ants.

"Amaury, there's a cop in front of the house." Iran pulled Amaury out of his thoughts.

"What?"

Amaury looked up and saw the group of people in front of

them standing at the front door. Not recognizing the two men or the officer, Amaury realized something was wrong.

"Can I help you?" Amaury asked.

The policeman turned around, looked at them, and walked toward them. "Who are you? Do you know whose house this is?" Diego asked.

Amaury paused for a moment. "This is my father's house. We are here to visit him."

Diego then reversed gears. "Do you recognize either of these two young men?" he asked the Guaigos.

The two tourists looked at Amaury and Iran. They seemed to recognize Amaury, which wasn't surprising because he and Camilo were of a similar height and build.

The short Guaigo spoke first. "Well, yes and no. I mean I'm not sure. It was sort of dark before and we were drinking."

"Officer, I have no idea who these men are," Amaury said. "We are just here to see my father."

The policeman, irritated at the mystery of the situation, took a good, strong look at Amaury. "Wait a minute. What's your name? You're that punk kid who played rock and roll music loud with that old radio on the Malecón awhile back. I chased you down the wall. You're a lowlife, a rebel.

"My name is Amaury Torres," he began.

"Yeah, that's his name. That's him! His name is Manny or Maury!" said one of the tourists.

"Same thing!" the other tourist said.

"Why don't we go down to the police station and sort this out?" Officer Diego said, sounding agitated.

"What the hell man?" Amaury cried. "This is bullshit. Who is Manny?" Amaury didn't entirely understand the situation, but he knew he was in trouble. He just had no idea how bad it was actually going to be.

Chapter 20

Police Officer Diego

The scene in front of the house had turned tense quickly and now that there was mention of going to the police station, Amaury felt panicked. He looked at Iran, who appeared terrified, almost as if he was waiting for Officer Diego to recognize him, too.

"You! Go home!" Officer Diego spoke to Iran. "And you two, go back to your hotel, please. Don't leave, as I may need to interview you later."

"Thank you, officer." The two tourists left the area.

"Let's go, boy. You and I are going to have a long conversation." Officer Diego grabbed Amaury's arm and roughly pushed him along.

"Sir, I don't understand why you're arresting me," Amaury said. "I haven't done anything wrong."

The officer continued to question Amaury as they walked to the police car. "Where are the stolen items?"

"I don't know what you're talking about."

"You're under arrest for theft and suspicion of endangering the welfare of tourists and for lying to a Police Officer."

Handcuffed, Amaury was put into the car then driven to the

Central Station, known as the Technical Department and also called *The Departmento Technical Investigationes.* He knew there was no point in arguing with the officer. He'd just have to sort things out when he got to the station.

The Central Station was in Old Havana. Everyone knew it was a terrible place to which no one ever wanted to go unless it was perhaps for a midday school tour to scare children into behaving. It was designed to be intimidating and mean.

Amaury could not have understood the dynamic or the magnitude of the events which transpired before his arrival. The next thing he realized, he was escorted to a chair positioned by the desk of the arresting officer, Diego. "Sit down in this chair. Don't say a word until I tell you and do not attempt to leave."

Amaury responded, "Yes sir."

The police prepared for Amaury's arrest. Diego however, decided to interview Amaury first and try to get more information before the incarceration procedures.

Diego sat at a mahogany desk that looked as if it should've been thrown out along with Batista. However, in communist Cuba, nothing was thrown out until it died on its own or was consumed by the Earth. Diego's workspace was haphazardly covered by uneven piles of papers separated with just enough space to write.

Amaury was seated in an old wooden chair that tilted to one side. It almost made him laugh as he kept having to shift his weight so he wouldn't slide off of it.

The entire office looked like a relic from the 1950s—a Cuban police time capsule.

Amaury was nervous because he knew he was in a tough predicament, a victim of circumstance. But as he sat in the chair he kept thinking he may have an inkling as to what had actually happened.

Police in Cuba always began their investigations and theories of criminality in one way—*guilty*. Everyone was guilty until proven innocent. It was the standard mode of operation. However, that presumption of guilt could extend to an entire family, and that they were all considered in cahoots. Amaury was well aware of this, and that worried him the most.

Diego, determined to question Amaury, seemed disturbed by his very presence. The police disliked tourists being harassed in any way. It was as though Diego was glad to have this case to investigate. His sharp perception and protection of the tourists would make him look like a hero to his superiors.

He had been around the police scene enough to recognize a cover-up, a punk kid hiding the truth.

"What is your name?" Diego asked.

"I told you. It's Amaury Torres."

"Where do you live?"

"I live at the Belén Solar, #261 near the Miguel De Cervantes de Savedra Park."

"Why were you at that house earlier?

"I went to visit my father. I don't understand why you are asking me all these questions. I've already told you all of this. Why don't you believe me?"

"I know what you're all about," Officer Diego said. "All you anti-revolutionaries are the same. You play dumb and act like you have no idea what's going on and pretend you're innocent. But, let me tell you what's going to happen to you if you continue to play dumb with me. It's not going to end well for you. So why don't you just tell me what happened to the passports, the visas, the tourists' money, and everything else missing, and then you will face your punishment like a man."

Amaury bristled. "Listen. I didn't take anything. I was at the park playing baseball. You can ask my friends. We walked to the house after the game. I'm telling you the truth."

Amaury was suddenly pulled from the chair by another cop who had been standing behind them observing. He was abruptly taken to the check-in arresting desk. While being fingerprinted and chastised, he heard muffled screaming and yelling, a frightening commotion taking place in another part of the station. None of the cops reacted or seemed to care about the noise. They ignored it. Once he was finished with processing, he was taken to a holding cell. Diego later returned to have another chat with Amaury.

Aggressive again, Diego said, "I want you to know we will get the information out of you. I don't care how strong or tough you think you are. You will sing. Everyone eventually does, and if you're smart, you'll come to your senses and confess sooner than later. It's for your own good—take my word for it. I know you don't believe me, but I'm trying to help you here. It's easy. Just tell me the truth and we can move on. Be smart. Don't make this worse than it has to be."

Amaury was agitated. "What the hell are you talking about? I don't know how to make this any clearer to you than I've already tried. I was playing baseball, and then I walked to my father's house. I walked into this situation. That's it. Just because those two guys said they recognized me doesn't mean they were telling the truth."

"Let me tell you a little story about how we operate here at the station house. We have a very angry, mean animal we like to call, Buddy. Buddy the Gorilla. He is going to join you in the jail cell. He always gets hungry when he's spending time with people. It's something we can't explain, but for some reason when he sees people, he just gets so hungry and he pretty much eats anything that looks tasty. Now, of course, if you think you can fight Buddy, then sure, no problem. You can try. But I warn you—he is very strong and doesn't like to fight, so he gets things done quickly."

Amaury realized the situation was going from bad to worse. Although he had no way to prove it, he had to assume it was Camilo who'd robbed the tourists. Amaury knew Camilo's schemes, and it made sense why the two tourists would think they had met Amaury before. Amaury and Camilo were, after all, related and looked similar.

He looked at Diego with contempt. "What if I know who did it?"

Chapter 21

Nury Saves The Day!

Iran raced back home, his first stop being Amaury's house. Once inside the Solar, he ran directly to their front door.

Amaury's grandmother, Abuelita, greeted him. In a huge rush, barely able to get his words out, he managed to tell her Amaury was in serious trouble with the police.

"Abuelita, Amaury, and I walked to General Torres's house, and there were people there and an angry cop. He asked all kinds of questions we didn't have answers to."

"Ay! Dios mio!"

"They told me to leave. I came here directly. Amaury is in really bad trouble. Some tourists accused him of stealing. I'm not sure where he is or what's going on, but I think the cop has him. I'm guessing they took him to the station."

"¡Santa Maria! Iran, thank you! I must call Nury right now!" Abuelita responded in shock.

She couldn't believe her ears. Amaury could get into trouble occasionally but nothing so serious. She thanked Iran for helping and for letting her know. As soon as they said goodbye, she immediately got on the phone to speak to her son, General Torres.

"Nury, where are you? Amaury is in terrible trouble."

When she reached out to Nury; she was unaware Amaury had planned to meet him. He was attending a function across the country—a military strategy session of the top military leaders, including Fidel. The general had been called away the day before his planned meeting with Amaury and was unable to change their appointment.

"What? I don't understand. What's happened to Amaury?"

Iran was here just a moment ago. He'd been with Amaury. They were going to your house. A cop was there and Amaury was arrested. I don't know why. Iran's information was confusing. You must return home immediately. Something must be done. You need to help him!"

"Okay, Mama. I made a mistake. I meant to call you and ask you to tell Amaury to cancel our meeting. I see now that was a terrible error. I'll get back home as fast as I can."

"Okay, Nury. I believe he's being detained at *The Departmento Technical Investigationes* in Havana."

General Torres replied, "All right Mama. I need to get off the phone now, but I'll see you soon. As usual, I'll take care of it."

No one mentioned Camilo, as no one knew at that moment that he was the true villain. Camilo had slipped through the cracks and had seemingly got away with selling illegal drugs, and now thievery, in addition to having his stepbrother take the blame for his actions.

He never admitted to his father nor anyone else the real cause of Amaury's arrest. He lied about the tourists visiting and the circumstances of the incident. For Camilo, the entire incident simply vanished.

As Amaury sat in his jail cell, Officer Diego explained to him that there were additional ways they forced detainees to talk. "We will take you to the city morgue cadaver room where the deceased are stored. You'll be tied down in a refrigerated drawer kept at a nice cold fifty-five degrees without your clothes. Small drops of water will fall onto your forehead from a tiny tube placed just above you. These mini drops will eventually cause you to feel as though you're going crazy. After a while, it will have a devastating effect. Crying is the first phase, then begging, then screaming. It's a familiar pattern. But not too long afterward you'll talk just to get it to stop. No matter how strong you think you are, you'll act like a crying baby. Maybe we can see how tough you are then, eh? What do you think?"

In actuality, Diego was trying to get Amaury to tell him what he knew, to get him to crack. However, Diego realized that he'd never really taken the time to completely assess this situation.

An inkling of doubt occurred to him that there might be something more to what Amaury was saying because he was being so stubborn. Diego hoped that Amaury would admit his fault by morning so he wouldn't have to employ these horrific tactics to get a confession out of him.

Nury returned to Old Havana by morning, found out where Amaury was being held, and went there as soon as he could. Together, both Genoveva and General Nury arrived at the Central Station. They immediately confronted the officers on duty.

The police officers became very nervous when they recognized Amaury's father was none other than a general in the Cuban Army. They became panicked with the realization that they should have done a much more thorough job with their investigation before arresting Amaury on circumstantial evidence.

General Torres proceeded with a tongue lashing greater than they ever thought possible. He excoriated them for their particularly unprofessional efforts with the investigation. The general, thoroughly disgusted, yelled, "Who's in charge here?"

Diego spoke up, "Yes, sir, that would be me, sir. I'm the arresting officer, Palo Diego."

"Patrolman Diego, just what is going on here? Where is my son, and why is he being held? You'd better have a damn good reason."

"Well, sir, we had a viable complaint of a crime from two Spanish tourists. It just so happened that your son appeared at the exact moment we began the investigation. It became very clear to me, at least at that time, he may have been the prime suspect and..."

General Torres cut him off sharply. "That's a big pile of bullshit, and you know it. I want him released immediately. Right now. No further delay!"

"Yes, sir," Diego answered. He immediately turned his gaze toward the desk sergeant nearby and signaled to get Amaury out of the cell ASAP.

General Torres yelled, "I don't know who you people are. How do you arrest a boy for all these trumped-up charges with only the story of a few tourists and no evidence?"

Earlier that morning, a Cuban passerby happened to notice the passports and visas in the garbage on the corner where they met. By pure coincidence or luck, the passports and IDs, as well as the wallet minus the money, had been discovered. The police department notified the two tourists, and they had happily retrieved their items.

"General Torres. We are terribly sorry for our error. We only tried to scare him. That's all. We did nothing other than that. Please accept our deepest apologies. It'll never happen again," Diego desperately responded.

After General Torres's arrival, Amaury was released from jail within a few minutes. Nury, very disturbed with Amaury because of this situation, knew his anti-revolutionary way of life, his attitude, and his attire would sooner or later become trouble for them both. The general's reputation was at stake, and he'd no longer tolerate his son to continue being so outwardly rebellious. It was becoming a dangerous situation for everyone.

Nury believed Amaury needed to change his lifestyle. He needed to get in line, get into the fold of communism, adjust his thinking, and finally clean his mind of his rebellious behavior. This adjustment would take some time and would possibly be traumatic, but change needed to come.

The car ride from the station was tense. Nury's mind was busy thinking of ways to try and transform his son. For his part, Amaury was trying to rationalize all that he just experienced. Yet still contemplating why his father wanted to meet in the first place.

"Amaury, I must speak with you later this week. Let's get together on Tuesday at lunchtime and we'll have a chat. This time there won't be any mistakes."

Amaury shot his father a quizzical look. He wondered why he was saying this but knew in his gut it was a troubling request. He felt as though he was being alerted to something. He knew from his father's tone and seriousness it was an ominous warning. Intuitively, he realized something was happening and changes were coming for which he'd better get prepared.

Chapter 22

Time To Grow Up

Tuesday arrived quickly, and after the incident at the police station, Amaury wasn't looking forward to the meeting with his father. He couldn't stop thinking about it. His sixteenth birthday was four months away, and for boys his age, it was the time when young Cuban men faced manhood.

Many boys of Amaury's age often went to work. If they lived on a farm, they'd start working in the fields. Often, attendance at school ended. Cuban life was difficult and helping the economy of the family was an essential requirement. As much as education was emphasized, there were moments in many citizens' lives where it was no longer a priority.

Sitting in a simple chair, Amaury patiently waited for his father. Already, several days had passed, and his anxiety only grew with each passing moment. Staring blankly past his grandmother, Amaury kept trying to conceive of what possible plans his father had in store for him. When he thought about it, he couldn't remember a time when his father made such an official announcement to meet. He knew this time was different and mysteriously uncomfortable. His thoughts consumed him.

"Amaury, what are you thinking about?" Abuelita asked curiously.

"Umm...what, Grandma?" At that moment, Amaury heard the front door open, and like the wind, his father was suddenly standing directly in front of him. Swallowing hard, Amaury stood up. "Oh. Hello, Father."

The general was dressed in a casual yet official uniform with epaulet shoulders and a star on the collar. He was wearing a freshly-pressed shirt tucked in, his tie neatly knotted with the V at the collar and the bottom point of the tie just at the buckle of his belt.

Abuelita prepared coffee in the kitchen while both men sat down opposite each other. Genoveva stood quietly at the entrance of the kitchen listening on her own. She knew this was going to be a pivotal moment in Amaury's life and was not anticipating anything positive coming out of it.

Amaury waited for his father to begin. When he finally spoke, the general's voice was even and measured, but Amaury could feel an edge to it.

"Amaury, this moment has been coming for quite some time," the general began. "Too many problems have transpired since you were a boy, and it's time we sort them out. I've watched you grow up and am not pleased with how you have adopted the mannerisms of the anti-revolutionaries. I can't understand why you've adopted and clung to this lifestyle. Look at the way you dress, your music, your friends, and even your chewing gum. Yes, I've seen you. I've tried my hardest to help you understand the values we have as one of the greatest revolutions in the world's history. We have the honor of living this victory every day of our lives. We bathe in the glory of Fidel's vision and his hard work to save our country. He sacrificed for everyone's benefit and fairness for all."

Amaury's grandmother placed the small cups of strong

Cuban coffee down on the table in front of them. They took sips nervously.

As Amaury drank his coffee, he couldn't believe what his father was saying. He looked down at the cup in front of him and smelled the wonderful dark aroma, but inwardly thought that this could be one of his last cups of coffee in his house ever again. Inside, he already felt the pangs of a loss, the mystery of an unknown was beginning.

His father's words hurt him as he realized the general didn't know who he was at all. He didn't recognize the love Amaury had for his family, nor how much he wanted his father's attention, not his anger. He despised Fidel for infiltrating his father's mind in such a life-altering way. Now he was receiving the consequences of that change. It was anathema to everything in which he believed. As he listened to his father sitting directly in front of him sounding like the Fidel on TV or the Fidel on the radio or Fidel on the 26th of July movement weekend-long lectures, it sickened him.

He respectfully listened, he had no other choice.

"For some unknown reason, you've held the belief all of this is funny, silly, or somehow backward, and at least minimally a joke. The beliefs you hold are painful for me. I have struggled to teach you why we live this life and uphold the values of communism in our hearts. I wouldn't be where I am today if not for the great things Fidel has done for Cuba and me."

"I understand why you feel that way, Papa."

"Castro has made enormous positive changes for our great nation. He successfully ended previous historical dictatorships in Cuba. Earlier generations of Cubans would have been grateful to live in these years, to have today's modern life."

"I know the history, Papa."

"You don't seem to appreciate it!"

Suddenly Amaury wasn't sure why this meeting had been

called at all. He became agitated by his father's words. It was as though his emphasis was meant to specifically goad him. Although he appreciated his father helping him get out of jail, he felt the criticism being hurled at him wasn't entirely justified. After all, the arrest had been a huge mistake and Amaury was still pretty sure it was Camilo who was to blame.

"I'm not sure what you want me to say," Amaury said. "I'm not sure what you want from me."

"Amaury, I have decided it's time for you to grow up and learn to respect and accept Fidel Castro and your government. I want you to learn why we dedicate our lives to Cuba. You're becoming a maggot, and I will not stand for that. Your expressions are too free. A Cuban general's son cannot and will not become that person. You'll be enlisting."

Amaury knew his father was beyond angry, and using the word maggot was extremely derogatory, comparing the behavior of an anti-revolutionary to a dirty bug.

"Papa, I don't want—"

"I have arranged for your entry into the Army this week," Nury continued. "I'll be driving you to the barracks on Friday."

"You're judging my life based on lies and false beliefs. I like my music and my clothes, some of which you actually bought for me, by the way. I like how they make me feel, how they help me to express myself."

His anger now clearly showing in his expression, Nury again interrupted Amaury. "Rock-and-roll music is for people who are in denial of the reality of who they are!"

Amaury felt his anger fill his chest. "No, Papa. You're taking this too far. Let me tell you something. I don't understand why you're so afraid of America. What is it about that country which frightens Cuba so badly? Why do communists cover up everything? Why are we forced to watch the tourists get the best Cuba has to offer, while citizens have to struggle for the little we have? We must work hard our entire lives, and yet we still get practically nothing from the effort. At the same time, Castro tells us this is what fairness is supposed to be. Will you tell me the answer to that? If I don't want to go, you can't force me."

"You don't know what I can do," his father said, gritting his teeth.

"I know Cuba has helped me in many ways. I really appreciate the education I've gotten, and I honestly feel I owe a debt of gratitude to the revolution, without a doubt," Amaury said. "But, how come you are so biased that you can't understand anything else? Did you ever take the time to look at what America has to offer? What it has accomplished as a nation? Look at the freedoms Americans have compared to the repressive life we must live here in Cuba just because Fidel says it's right. Who made Fidel the answer to everything? How is he different from all of the dictators before him? If you can give me one single thing we have here better than America, please let me know, and then we might have something to talk about. Otherwise, we will never understand each other. Violence is the only way communists think. Their methods and goals are used only for control and oppression."

"I've had enough of this nonsense, Amaury," the general barked. "You listen carefully to me. You'll be put through tests to develop you into a better man. It will help to change your mind and ultimately allow you to do something good for your country. We're not America. And you're going to change from being a silly, irresponsible teenager—which is all you currently know about—and you're going to transform into a responsible adult man. This coming Friday, I'm taking you to the Managua Infantry Unit. There you will learn how to shovel, how to shoot a gun, how to clean military trucks, and how to become a great soldier. The army will teach you responsibility and discipline, how to take orders and follow directions. You'll learn how to dress and act like a man, as all soldiers should. You'll learn respect and how to work on a team. You'll find integrity both for yourself and your country. Amaury, you will grow into a man, and most importantly, in the end, you will finally learn how to become a true revolutionary. This will give shape to your life. If you decide against it, you'll be placed in a juvenile detention center. Because of your poor, out-of-control behavior, I've made up my mind. This decision is going to stand. That's it. Finished."

Listening to his father's entire speech, Amaury still couldn't believe his ears. He wasn't surprised, but even so, at that moment, he hated his father. Amaury felt dismissed, his father forcefully changing his life in a way he could neither protest nor prevent.

At that moment, he felt lost, controlled, and helpless, as if he'd been pushed off a cliff. Oddly, at the same time, inwardly he felt a surge of energy. He wasn't sure why, but maybe it was the rage inside of him. Whatever his combination of feelings, it only caused a further conflict. He knew he was going to face this challenge with all the strength he could muster. Amaury's voice carried no weight. He felt defenseless.

General Nury, red-faced, took a moment to settle down and compose himself. He straightened his tie, which had become twisted during the angry outburst. Then he spoke again, calmer this time.

"You must understand, Amaury, that they want to put you in a juvenile detention center because of this incident. It'll be difficult to stop that now. You have been exposed. Your choices are few. Your reputation is now in a grey area of doubt. You did this to yourself. Now you must accept the compromised situation you're in. I've already received the directive regarding this decision. You will now have to choose which direction you want to go. I feel with the army you'll have a better opportunity to repair yourself and have a life. If you go to the juvenile center, you'll continue to be undisciplined and from there I don't know what may happen."

"If you go to the center, it will be on your record all your life. Many of your life choices will be limited. However, in the army, you'll become a respectable, responsible citizen. You'll restart with a clean slate. This formal incident will disappear once you enter the military."

It was evident that Amaury had no choice. He was compromised and caught in a trap. Some of his friends from school were also entering the army. The choice didn't seem so terrible, yet he was scared. The army's unknown mystery swirled around his mind. He sat silently for several minutes. His grandmother and father looked at him mournfully, but both remained quiet.

Both Abuelita and General Nury stared at Amaury, waiting for him to speak. He took a few deep breaths, not completely sure what to say.

Amaury paused for another moment. He already knew what his answer was going to be. He felt numb but knew he was left with a single choice. He spoke softly. "Okay, Papa. I see what's happening here, and I understand what needs to be done. I guess there is only one decision I can make. I'll go into the army."

General Torres responded, "Good! You've made the right decision, Amaury. I will pick you up on Friday. Be careful the rest of this week. Don't get into any trouble. Don't do anything at all. Mama, you keep a close eye on him and make sure he keeps his nose clean. *No mas problemas!*"

It was a difficult few days 'til Friday arrived. Amaury was told not to worry about bringing anything. The army provided everything he would need. His only job was to wait and do nothing.

Meanwhile, he spent most of his time thinking about his life and what the next few years might be like. His thoughts included what he'd potentially like to do if he had the opportunity to do something other than the army. He knew he was astute in math and thought about engineering. He also loved the huge Russian military boats and cargo tankers he saw in the Port of Havana. Amaury had spent many afternoons sitting at the docks staring at them and wondering what life would be like if he could design or work on one of those ships. He enjoyed thoughts about anything mechanical—engine rooms, cargo boats, supertankers, huge tools, and machinery. He believed he could have eventually worked on a ship. It was a career dream to be involved with them. For now, however, those thoughts and desires were on hold. He needed to focus on his new reality.

Chapter 23

The Ride

There was a knock at the door. Amaury looked up, pulled out of his reverie. The moment had arrived. Abuelita welcomed her son General Torres inside. He arrived punctually at noon. Amaury felt numb.

It was happening. He was going into the Army.

With a big smile, General Torres greeted everyone. "*Hola todos. Mamá, ¿Cómo estás?*"

"*Bien, mijo,*" Genoveva said to her son.

"Okay, Amaury. It's time. We need to leave now," Nury said.

Amaury stood up from the comfortable chair, thinking how it might be the last time he'd sit in that chair for quite a while. He glanced at his father, hoping perhaps he might say something comforting like, *Son this will be all right. You can stay here at home, and things will go back to where they were.* But the General said no such thing. He only interrupted Amaury's thoughts again as he walked toward the door. "Amaury! Let's go! Now."

"Okay, Papa. Okay. I'm coming." Amaury turned to his grandmother and noticed she had tears in her eyes. "Abuelita,

I'm going to miss you. I love you very much. Say goodbye to everyone. I'll try to be in touch soon and as often as I can."

With heavy sadness in his heart, Amaury followed his father out of the apartment and down to the military Jeep, where they started the six-hour drive east to the military barracks.

The ride was mostly quiet, as Amaury and his father struggled to carry on a pleasant conversation. Amaury's mind was too full of thoughts and worries. When they did talk, it was about the weather or easygoing topics, purposefully avoiding difficult issues. Finally, several hours into the ride, the general spoke, giving instructions about how things were to unfold, the basics of military philosophy, commanders' directives, and the general chain of command.

"Now I want you to listen to me very carefully, Amaury," he said. "When you enter the Army you'll be completely respectful. Don't talk back. Don't act sarcastically or disobey orders. Do exactly what they tell you and do it quickly. You may very well be given tasks you don't like, but you must keep your mouth shut and obey orders. Understand?"

"Yes Papa, I will. I know this is important to you, and I will do exactly as you expect. I will make the family proud."

Despite Amaury's effort to show his father he would comply, Nury continued to scold Amaury one last time. "Your stubborn antirevolutionary attitude won't be permitted in the Cuban military. You'd better make sure you don't let your normal thoughts slip out at all! Keep them hidden, or better yet just get rid of them altogether. Please!"

Amaury felt tired and anxious, as they drove down a long dirt road, dust flying. His father was used to the annoyance of the dust and how it covered everything as the Jeep pulled up to a Quonset-styled corrugated metal building.

At the top of the building were the words *Managua Infantry Unit* spelled out in large white letters. There was nothing special about the building. It was one story with no personality, simple yet oddly intimidating.

"Welcome to the Army, Amaury," he muttered to himself. "Oh, boy. Here we go."

"What's that?" his father asked loudly.

Amaury didn't answer.

Before their arrival, the general had made sure Amaury would be regarded the same as any other soldier with no special treatment. As Nury turned to Amaury in the Jeep, he said in a shallow, quiet tone, "One last thing, Amaury. They're going to ask about your age and will have you sign papers stating you are eighteen years old. Make sure to tell them you are. Don't worry. They won't question it."

Amaury nodded and got out of the Jeep and then slowly walked up to the entrance. He didn't look back at his father, but he heard the crunching sound of pebbles against the tires and knew that Nury was driving away.

Chapter 24

First Days

There were two men in the office when he walked in. He later learned they were named General Menendez and Captain Sanchez.

"*Hola*. My name is Amaury Torres. My father, General Nury Torres, brought me here to register today. I'm not quite sure where to go. If you would direct me, I'd appreciate it."

"Hola, Amaury Torres. Yes, we were expecting you. Your father informed us in advance. Give us a moment while we get the paperwork ready. Why don't you sit over there in that chair, and we'll be right with you to begin the process?"

When Amaury received the paperwork, he noticed he was required to indicate the subscription of time in the military. He knew two years was the required minimum time to serve, but he believed if he chose one more year, they'd be more favorable to release him when the time came, knowing he'd put in that extra effort. So he agreed to do an additional year.

Amaury was instructed to go down the hall for his full health and physical exam. He was probed, measured, weighed, observed, and questioned. All were requirements to make sure he was fully healthy and fit to join the army.

In Cuba, Bootcamp was called *The Prep,* or the preparation for the next level, which was traditional army service. *The Prep* was extremely disciplined, and they were especially hard on new privates. The army was significantly different from what Amaury had expected and he knew he had to get used to it quickly. *Prep* was mostly developmental and removal of weak recruits' operation. The army used it to evaluate all recruits for later training. If any of the recruits didn't pass *Prep,* they were either assigned other training or released altogether. Staying depended totally on the army's needs.

When the health examination was completed, Amaury was instructed to go to the next stop, where his gear and clothing were provided.

"Soldier, keep walking down through the rows to collect your clothing and gear," he was ordered.

"Yes, sir!" Amaury answered quickly, remembering his father's words in the Jeep.

"It's set up like an assembly line. Take one of everything. Make sure to give your clothing sizes to the lieutenants as you proceed. Please make sure the boots fit correctly. Very important."

The fully-loaded backpack and supplies weighed nearly seventy-five pounds. Amaury was shocked at the number of items he would be required to carry from this point on. It was much heavier than he'd ever imagined, and he suddenly realized that the army might be more intense than he'd anticipated.

It was near evening when he sat down with a large group of other men who had also just joined. Sitting down for a meal, his new clothing felt tight and uncomfortable. As there was no talking, he began eating. Everyone was concerned about what was next on the agenda and Amaury was just as anxious as the others.

Earlier in the day as he rode in the car, he'd tried to confront his own fears. He'd decided he was going to face all the challenges and somehow learn to survive, but while eating and seeing the other anxious faces around him, he noticed how hard it was to stop his nerves from creeping in. Closing his eyes for a few moments, he tried to calm himself down and to focus on making sure he'd have enough energy for what was coming next.

To his happy surprise, he looked across the table and saw a familiar face. It was Umberto from school! Once school buddies and now side-by-side soldiers, he and Umberto Morales were both happily surprised when they arrived at camp and bumped into each other, glad they each had a close buddy with whom to train. They were just about to have a conversation when suddenly there was a loud announcement in the mess hall.

"All recruits please head out to the parking lot for our first meeting and exercise." Both Amaury and Umberto looked at each other, shrugged, and stepped out of the mess hall. The boys quickly returned their food trays.

As Amaury exited the room, he noticed the clock on the wall. It was ten o'clock at night.

Together, all the recruits walked outside in a long, single-file line into the parking lot. It was an hour before a half-a-dozen 1990 BMY Harsco troop carrier trucks rolled up to the standing men. These huge, Russian-made, camouflaged green trucks had thick, heavy canvas tops and carried the men around the base by having them sit on hard wooden benches. Amaury and the other recruits were told to get into the trucks as quickly as they could and take a seat. The truck engines groaned to a rumble and slowly started down the base camp dirt road. The dust began flying, forming rooster tails behind them. Amaury surmised it was about midnight by the time all the trucks began their trek out of base camp and down the driveway. He wondered when he'd ever get to sleep.

The rumbling of the huge Harsco engines and tires

hummed along while the trucks bumped down the highway. There was no talking among the recruits, especially since the roar in the background was overwhelming. The young boys were not only confused and scared but also exhausted. Eventually, Amaury and the other recruits fell asleep.

In the early morning, Amaury woke and saw light sneaking through the canvas top, but the trucks continued to roll one-by-one down the dirt road. As the other recruits slowly awoke, they looked concerned as it dawned on them that they were a significant distance from base camp.

Amaury heard a few nervous whispers around him, and he started looking around trying to decipher if anyone had a clue about what was going on. Then, without warning, the trucks came to a stop. The smell of fuel, road rubber, and early morning dew filled the damp air.

The soldiers hopped out and looked up at the blue sky, then at each other. As they gazed at their surroundings, they realized they were next to an empty field full of high grass. One by one, the sergeants banged on the truck sides to wake up any remaining sleeping recruits.

"Get your asses up! C'mon, you stinking insects. Get your asses up and let's get this going!"

As the men in each truck unloaded, the recruits stood at attention with fully-loaded backpacks, waiting for the next wave of insults and instructions.

They were assembled in rows and told to stand and wait. The purpose of the long drive was the beginning of their training. One row at a time, they were instructed to begin walking in an easterly direction.

"Umberto, you know we're heading east this entire time. I wonder who dreamed up this form of torture?"

"I know. This is a tough one. Man, my feet are killing me.

The boots are great, but they're brutal to break in. Thank god for thick socks."

Both boys laughed but not too loud. They didn't want to stand out with the sergeants monitoring them.

The drill sergeants enjoyed challenging the men with variety and changing the parameters of the march, including sleeping during the day and walking at night. They marched through woods, fields, and streams, over fallen trees, up mountains, and through rough weather. They weren't allowed to stop for severe heat during the day, nor brutal mosquitoes at night. It rained on several of the evenings, but no matter what was in front of them, they walked on over or under it regardless of what the obstacle was. Some of the men fell in their place. Some complained about the duration, the monotony, or the pain. The ones who couldn't make it were taken away. Some were never seen again, while others were encouraged to continue.

They quickly learned stopping was not an option. Learning to walk through the pain was part of the lesson.

The arduous task of breaking in their new Russian boots designed to last forever was a job of its own. They were made of extremely hard, durable leather with a heavy metal embedded front toe box. It took a significant amount of use and pain to achieve basic comfort. Each boot was four pounds, had a massive, curved front and a sole of heavy-duty rubber screwed in from the bottom. The boots, while hated at first, proved over time to be just as important as their rifles.

As the sun rose on the third day, they were given a midday break from the walking. The third day would prove to be an important one for the recruits. Every third day in *Prep* was the first day of rifle training. They were introduced to their most important single piece of equipment which would become their best friend. It would become their nourishment, the most important tool they had to stay alive. It would be with them all the time and help them escape from any tight situations.

They were trained on how to clean it, hold it, maintain it, love it, and most importantly, rebuild it. The entire day was spent in the broiling sun with their new guns. Rifle training went on for weeks from that point on until graduation. The training also included target practice and expertise in guns. Eventually, they were tested and graded for their target-shooting ability.

The third day was also auspicious for an entirely different reason, as they developed a distinct odor due to a lack of personal hygiene. Learning to live with filth and lack of cleaning was also part of the training. Showers were a reward left until the conclusion.

The platoon was followed by medical, water, and food trucks with support and provisions. The trucks followed the marching recruits over the course of the entire exercise.

Amaury realized he was struggling just like his comrades. However, he forced himself to deal with his discomfort as best as he could without complaining or whining. He focused his mind on the single act of putting one foot in front of the other, over and over again. He knew it would eventually end, and he needed to learn to endure, so it may as well be now. It didn't take Amaury long to realize the test of his mental endurance would be a constant part of the training, and he learned to own his pain and accept the challenge to succeed with it.

The moment finally arrived when they saw the familiar dusty road and base camp just ahead. They'd never been happier to be back at the place they'd originally found distasteful. The next day, they were allowed to sleep it off, which most of the men did. Amaury knew better than to relax, though. He was certain that the worst of *Prep* was yet to come.

Chapter 25

Morning Inspections

Recovery time from the first march didn't last long. At 4 a.m. the next morning, they were awoken by screaming and the banging of garbage cans. With hollow pipes clanking, they were being treated like school kids or worse.

The early morning loud verbal assaults weren't easy to get used to. Many of the men couldn't manage. Some quickly lost their mental toughness and literally walked off or broke down altogether.

As Amaury watched the proceedings, he forced himself to bear down, dig in and find it within himself to rationalize what was happening around him. He hated the sergeants. They relentlessly tested and retested just to make the raw recruits struggle. When the recruits were done with one struggle, they'd find new ones. It was an experimental type of physical training structure the Cuban army had created. They wanted to force their recruits to prepare for anything.

Amaury tried talking to some of the other recruits, but often they had little to say. They had to figure out their own path in the face of severe difficulties.

Jorge asked out loud. "How're we going to get through this part of the training? Their expectations seem nearly impossible. They never give up. It's relentless. Sometimes I think it's not worth it. I love Cuba, too, but my life is upside down. It's really starting to get to me. Honestly, I'm not sure I can make it."

"It feels like an impossible mission. We have to help each other, encourage each other to just hang in there. I know I can do it, and I know you can do it. You've already come so far. Look how tough you're getting." Amaury chimed in.

Umberto jumped in, too. "Look, Jorge. We knew this training was going to be part of the battle. So, let's show these SOBs how tough we can be. I've suffered so much myself. It really gets to me, too. But I'm trying to make it. It'll be a great accomplishment for us all when you think about it."

Amaury followed again in. "That's a really good point, Umberto. C'mon, Jorge. You can do this!"

"Okay. Okay, Amaury. I'll push even harder. I've just gotta get my mind into the right place. I'll prove I'm tougher than those bastard sergeants!"

The army experimented with levels of stress and physical endurance their soldiers could manage. Using aggressive exercises, they wanted to explore how far they could push the men. Many recruits suffered broken bones, fingers, knees, or legs. These were the most common injuries, although the men often suffered concussions or complete physical and mental exhaustion, as well.

Another important assignment they were required to perform as part of their training was the repeated cleaning of the Russian Olifant Mk 1 A tanks. The tanks were regularly used to practice general and assault maneuvers in every kind of weather. The bad weather made the tanks dramatically dirtier. Thick, muddy dirt got into every crack and crevice of metal and rubber. Every single surface of the tanks would become covered by either a film of sticky dust or heavy solid mud which emulated dried concrete. It took hours to completely clean a single tank, and it was a job Amaury hated more than anything, especially if he was ordered to clean a tank himself, which happened often. The tanks were required to look nearly brand new when finished. The most frustrating part of this process would be experienced a day later when the tanks were once again used and often became as soiled as though they'd never been cleaned at all.

Amaury had grown into a medium-built man with a muscular frame. He was strong and sturdy. Because of this, he was less likely to experience injuries as compared to other, taller recruits who were smaller in girth. Amaury surprised even himself by proving to be quite durable.

The daily wake-up at 4:30 a.m. was something he never got used to. It felt as if every time he turned around, it was morning, and the screaming began. In very quick order, Amaury learned he needed to get into a successful routine. The entire platoon had exactly twelve minutes to get ready for attention and not a second more. The routine included getting up, showering if they were lucky enough to find a vacant shower stall, washing their faces, shaving, brushing their teeth, getting dressed, combing their hair, and tying their boots.

The next critical step was making their beds wrinkle-free. A single visible wrinkle on the blanket could potentially become a serious infraction. The top had to be tight enough for a coin to bounce off of. Finally, recruits had to straighten up the area around their beds. Amaury's clothing and bedding were always neatly folded or hung up and ready for inspection the night before the sergeants entered the barracks.

Once the difficult routine was completed, the entire platoon needed to stand as still as a statue at attention, waiting for the sergeants to begin the grueling inspection. They examined every inch with extremely critical eyes.

Amaury developed several tricks and blended them into his morning routine. He discontinued using a top bed sheet at night. He left it ironed and folded on the shelf. In the morning, he'd unfold the sheet and make sure it was in place without wrinkles. On some nights, he slept with his boots already on his feet but not tied.

Realizing there was not enough time for the intense rush of morning activities—washing, dressing, straightening, and getting his boots tied and ready for attention—he needed to sacrifice somewhere to shave off seconds of his routine.

Incompletion meant punishment. Occasionally, the platoon sergeant would already be in the barracks as the chaos ensued, berating them the entire frantic time. "Hurry, you insects, you fuckers. Let's go. Hurry. Hurry. Go, go, go! Don't stop! Keep moving. You only have eight minutes left. Keep moving!"

The discipline for the failure of proper execution was doing all the daily military calisthenics exercises at the end of the day. Additionally, they'd be required to clean the entire barracks including the bathroom facilities, toilets, sinks, showers, and the floors of the barracks and the entryway. It was a significant amount of extra work in an already busy and exhausting day.

It was a time-consuming, nasty job. No one wanted to suffer additional tasks as a source of punishment while others watched and commented about the poor job being done, further complicating the work.

The army needed to ferret out the mentally strong, physically reliable, and toughest recruits to move forward. Discipline was the army's true path to being a good, productive, dedicated, and most importantly reliable soldier.

Chapter 26

Decision Time

After inspection, the next activity was breakfast, and then calisthenics for two hours. They were required to do hundreds of pushups, dominoes, sit-ups, and many other kinds of strenuous calisthenics. This section was followed by two hours of class and political studies. Originally, Amaury was surprised by this significant requirement for the Cuban military to reinforce the communist agenda with all the soldiers. The training was more than just physical. They also believed in political education as a way for the army to continue Castro's agenda for communist reinforcement.

Amaury didn't enjoy these classes, just as he hadn't in grade school. His feelings for the government didn't allow his mind to be open to the teachings of the army's communist education program. However, for safety's sake, he needed to learn as much as he could, because he felt his future would be protected by having a wealth of communist knowledge.

Lunch followed politics, and then later early afternoon into the early evening they learned martial arts with three different specific forms of training. The military mixed the styles daily and they never knew until class began which one would be presented that day. This wasn't accidental. They didn't want the recruits to mentally prepare for a specific style, so they constantly changed and alternated between Jiu-Jitsu, Taekwondo, and Judo. Classes were designed to be difficult and aggressive from the very first day of training. It was a brutal assault on their bodies until they learned the fundamentals, learning to block and protect themselves. Fending off incoming blows was their crucial first step.

Many men suffered injuries, and it was normal for recruits to walk around black and blue from constant punches, kicks, and falls. Amaury excelled at all three disciplines, having already shown a natural adeptness in wrestling.

One of the most important techniques Amaury learned early on was how to control his breathing. Over time, he developed the ability to slow it down under severe duress and to regulate his emotions.

The daily routine was demanding and rough on their bodies and the military prepared for this eventuality. Men were sent to a healing facility they'd set up at base camp. It had saunas and healing minerals, an in-ground pool, and separate smaller tubs. The saunas were designed to heat the men's bodies and relax their muscles, while the pools had chunks of ice floating in the water to speed up the healing process.

At the end of a difficult day, Amaury would get into the basin. Military assistants poured hot paraffin wax on the surface, causing the cold water to be contained. The tub temperature intensified, further accelerating healing. Amaury's body was numb after an hour. Years, later despite the extreme difficulties of *Prep*, he nostalgically looked back at his ability to survive an extremely difficult training program.

At the beginning of the third month, the entire platoon was scheduled for a second fifty-mile walk with the full seventy-five-pound pack. They only had four days to complete it. The staff sergeants and other officers walked alongside the platoon, screaming at them the entire time—a final grueling experience. The group walked at a fierce pace. However, this time the slightest hesitation wasn't permitted. As Amaury pushed on, he thought about *Prep* training, his life, and all that had transpired, and he was amazed at his ability to achieve and persevere.

He couldn't have imagined just a short two months before he would be accomplishing a fifty-mile walk with a seventy-five-pound backpack and be doing it with ease.

Three months had passed, and *Prep* was in its final days. Each trainee was required to choose a direction for their next step in the army and had several paths from which to choose. The trainees were given a file of papers including information to help them choose their next career step. From *Prep*, they were able to choose from six areas of specialty, including Special Forces, Armed Services, Coast Guard, Aviation, Mechanics, and Engineering.

Amaury carefully took his time considering this important decision. He'd always loved boats, planes...anything with engines. He felt torn between those areas compared to the elite division of the army called the Rangers, which provided further training that would truly challenge his mental and physical toughness.

He began to realize that he'd developed a true passion for being a soldier. It gripped his heart, the desire to better himself. The idea of being one of the best soldiers in Cuba could mean an opportunity to create a significantly different life for himself. He'd always considered the Solar a tough place to start with little to offer in the way of opportunities, but now he felt he could change his life forever.

Chapter 27

Rangers

Amaury's potential entry into the Rangers was a longshot due to his less-than-desirable height of five feet, ten inches tall. He believed his worst-case scenario was that he'd work in the mechanical area of the military.

Amaury felt confident that he was in great shape. He had a six-pack for the first time in his life. He knew his attitude was excellent, and he felt sure of himself for the first time in a very long while. He may not be tall, but *fuck it,* he thought. *I'm going to apply anyway!*

Amaury knew chances were slim that he'd be accepted, but he still experienced a drive to try to win his father's approval. Joining the Rangers might do just that.

The Rangers were assigned duties separate from the regular military. Their assignments were engineered to protect government officials and the Interior Federation, as well as a variety of specific military initiatives. They were also responsible for protecting and initiating military invasions for Cuba, depending on Cuba's foreign policy decisions. In addition, they were the first line of defense and offense.

Fidel Castro had lofty goals to expand beyond the shores of Cuba with its international military operations. Castro strove to become a significant player on the world stage, a substantial international luminary. With Russia's support, he wanted other nations to be fully aware of his presence and the power of Cuban determination and strength. These goals were driven and displayed through the Rangers' military efforts.

Many years before Amaury applied to become a Ranger, Nury had informed him about the prestige of the Special Forces. The idea of it appealed to him, and he had never forgotten his father's words. On his application, he specifically noted to his superiors that he didn't want anything relayed back to General Torres. Amaury's fate was sealed. The Rangers respected his wishes, and his father was never informed.

When General Torres finally heard through fellow officers that Amaury had successfully graduated from *Prep*, he thought his decision to force Amaury to enlist was working. He believed his son had finally turned the corner to sobriety and had escaped the grasp of lust from Western culture.

Nury was very happy to find out Amaury had not only done well, but he'd excelled. Amaury would follow in his footsteps in the army, and Amaury's decision to join had proved that Nury had been a generous and responsible father after all.

After applying to the Rangers division, Amaury learned it would be another five days before he would be informed of the Army's decision. It was a two-step transition period where they were required to stay on the base and continue their regular training, and then they would receive a three-day pass to go home. Once they returned, they would be sent to their new assignments for the continuation of training.

On the fifth day, the platoon meeting took place, and they were individually briefed in a private room with one of the captains. Amaury held his breath as he patiently waited for the

Captain to enter the office. After some time, the Captain abruptly entered. He spotted Amaury sitting in the far corner of the room.

Captain Sanchez took a seat in front of Amaury. "Private Torres, I have some news for you."

"Yes, sir," Amaury said. His pulse quickened, and he took some deep breaths to regulate his emotions.

"As you know, to make the best decision for each of our recruits, we carefully look at your progress," Captain Sanchez continued. "Our decisions are made with a tremendous amount of consideration and thought based on forty-five days of analysis and data. Each recruit must be placed where they can offer the Revolution the most return on its investment into that soldier. Production, loyalty, and honor for Cuba are utmost. Most importantly, we consider what that specific recruit can offer Cuba going forward as a member of our great military. All these factors are considered."

"Yes, sir," Amaury said. "I understand."

"We put a lot of work, effort, and faith into each recruit to make them the best soldier they can be, helping the revolution continue with its successes and maintaining a military force of which we are all proud. The Cuban Revolution grows stronger with each passing day."

Amaury internally winced with each constant reference to the Revolution. His old anti-revolutionary feelings had never fully left his thoughts. His feelings had changed somewhat, but he wasn't entirely convinced there wasn't more life could offer him. As he listened to the Captain talking about the Revolution, he realized it would be fully integrated into his life in the military, and the realization made him undeniably uncomfortable.

Interrupting Amaury's thoughts, the Captain continued in a proud voice, "Private Torres, we've observed the strong effort you've put into *Prep*. You have excelled in many ways. It hasn't gone unnoticed. We're happy with your progress thus far, and we want to reward you for your outstanding performance. On this basis, Private Torres, we'd like to welcome you to the Cuban Specialized Forces of the Rangers. You made it. I'm sure General Torres will be very proud of you today. Congratulations!"

Amaury could hardly believe his ears. Initially, he was shocked, but the shock quickly gave way to elation. He looked up at the captain, smiling. "Thank you...thank you very much," he stammered. "I'm very grateful you've given me this opportunity."

Amaury stood up and they shook hands. He meandered out of the office, still dazed, and headed back to the barracks. He had two weeks to stay on the base until his weekend pass, and then he would be back to begin Ranger training.

His time at home with his family was his first period of rest in over three months. It was during this time Amaury had a moment to stop and make a thorough assessment of his life.

His thoughts were consumed by his conflicting feelings of enjoying the physical *Prep* training, and yet he'd also joined a communist army.

Unexpectedly, he began to feel an openness to the Cuban system and the hard work of *Prep*. The rough life he'd endured began to make sense for him. He wasn't sure how to manage his feelings, which had developed into an internal conflict he knew he'd have to eventually resolve.

He still occasionally had the same feelings he'd had as a young man. He still questioned the system. But *Prep* had challenged him mentally and physically in a way nothing before ever had, and it had awakened something in him—something he liked.

Amaury couldn't conceive how he could get to a point of accepting the idea of communism, but perhaps there might be a middle ground somewhere. For now, he couldn't trouble himself with trying to figure it all out. He needed to get ready for the new adventure and mysterious future that lay ahead.

Chapter 28

Rangers First Steps

Before Amaury knew it, his time at home ended and he was back on base for the beginning of Ranger training. The entire group sat in silent anticipation. Amaury had a mixture of emotions swirling around inside him. Excitement. Fear. Nervousness. He had no idea what was coming next.

The Rangers officials and the captains started with an initial discussion of the history and the background of the Rangers' purpose. They also covered their intentions and their complex historical missions. The young recruits were told what would be expected of them, the importance of their training, and how they would succeed as the single elite force in the military.

They were commanded to become professional, strong, well-trained, efficient fighting machines. They'd learn the hard cruelties of war and would be tested again and again in this new chapter of their lives. They were expected to succeed no matter what.

As training began, the renewed Amaury Torres, who was highly motivated and ready for anything, couldn't have anticipated how different Ranger training would be as compared to

Prep. He quickly learned they were two completely different worlds.

From the start of Ranger training, *Prep* seemed like child's play compared to the effort exerted and the demanding requirements to succeed in the Ranger class of soldiers. The difference between *Prep* and Rangers training was the same as learning to swim by jumping into a calm pool versus jumping into an ocean during a hurricane.

As Amaury was confronted by the significant constant pressure of hard work and severe challenges, he knew he was in a place where he had to truly allow himself to be wholly drawn into the entire communist specter or be left behind in the heap of miserable failure. He felt he could never again look at his reflection in a mirror if he failed. Emotionally, it was now or never. His life was no longer his, and he needed to give it everything he could. He only worried his body might not be able to endure all that was demanded of him.

From the beginning, training was a strenuous fifteen to seventeen hours per day which occasionally increased to twenty-one hours. They learned quickly that war was not a nine-to-five job. The Rangers' boot camp was a six-month probationary period. Having made the Rangers, Amaury believed he was a pretty tough guy and would get through it with the same confidence with which he'd finished *Prep*. It was more so an affronting brutality rather than strictly endurance with physical conditioning.

The *Prep* trainers had behaved like vultures ravenously picking at carcasses. In reality, they were trying to wake up the killer in each of the trainees, getting them ready for a brutal, unforgiving war. Each trainee was required to learn the knowledge of survival in battle to the point of overqualification. In the eyes of their superiors, success was only achieved if the enemy they faced was annihilated or subdued. Each soldier had the weight of this responsibility on his shoulders—to succeed not only for themselves but more importantly for Cuba.

Ranger recruits were trained in all areas of military, infantry, and survival techniques. The physical and mental toughness, nimbleness, the ability to manage and excel in all kinds of situations and weather conditions were paramount. It included marksmanship, knowledge of diverse weaponry, important AK-47 training, and knife hand-to-hand combat expertise.

They trained in and around jungles in southern Cuba which offered them the unique opportunity to learn to grow into great soldiers. The captains and colonels worked on the recruits' physical and mental toughness as a mainstay of training.

His superiors had thought well enough of Amaury to approve his participation, and it was now his job to prove them right. Each platoon unit had twelve soldiers who lived, worked, and trained together as a single team. Their lives were in each other's hands as they learned to rely on and depend on each other completely.

In their first week, they made clear through their efforts that spontaneity and unpredictability would be the expected norm. This strategy prepared them to develop an innate instinct for split-second decisions under pressure.

Within the first week, the soldiers were directed to go down to the field from the barracks to begin the activities of night drills and preparing sleeping quarters. They dug human-sized foxholes used as homes during their first month of training. Coincidentally, on the very first night of digging there was a driving rainstorm.

As the rain poured down, Amaury looked over at his co-Ranger trainee Marcos. The flooding made digging nearly impossible as the rain filled the hole.

"This is crazy!" Amaury called to Marcos, wiping the rain from his face without success.

"I know," Marcos called back. "Sometimes I wonder why I joined these fuckin' Rangers. I must have been drunk that day!" He rammed his shovel into the mud to take a break.

Amaury also paused to take a break. "You know, Marcos," he said, leaning on his shovel for a moment. "I've lived in Cuba my entire life and I can't ever recall seeing this much rain in one night."

"Yeah, and we get to sleep in it," Marcos said. "That's fucking unreal."

"Hey, you two idiots, who told you to talk?" one of the captains screamed out of nowhere. "Get those damned holes finished. The sooner they're finished, the sooner you get to sleep —and believe me you want to sleep. If you think today is bad, wait until tomorrow!"

Amaury and Marcos looked at each other, then bent over and continued digging while the heavy rain poured down on them.

As the December storm raged on, the temperature dropped significantly. The recruits were wet and cold as they prepared to sleep in a mud hole for the night.

Amaury and Marcos tried to cover their area with a small tarp to limit the water seeping in, but their efforts were in vain. Their training had taught them to cope with suffering and to survive terrible conditions. This would be the rule of thumb for their foreseeable future.

Chapter 29

Digging Holes

On days they were not out in the fields they instead trained at the barracks. At 5 a.m. their morning began with a screaming Colonel or Captain, depending on what was planned for the day, and continued training until 11 p.m. The daily routine allowed for five minutes to get ready, less than half the time allowed at *Prep*. Amaury quickly learned to conform again, sleeping regularly with his boots on as his only option.

Occasionally, they were granted an early return to quarters. One evening at 10 p.m. after another grueling training day, Amaury was able to hit the shower and settle in by 10:30 p.m.. At 11:15 p.m. sharp, the fast-asleep group was shaken awake by the Captain who returned relentlessly screaming at the group.

"Let's go you fuckers, let's get rolling again. We got a lot of hard work ahead of us today and sleeping ain't gonna get it done. Let's go! Get the fuck up NOW!"

At once everyone bolted out of their beds. They were dizzy from the shock of no sleep and the death grip exhaustion had on their overworked brains. Reeling, Amaury couldn't believe that after a brutal day of training, the opportunity of rest was harshly being taken away only to begin another day of agony. No one complained, though. They'd made their choices long before and now had to follow through. Quitting wouldn't be tolerated.

For Amaury, the agony of training was starting to crack his will. There were moments when he cursed and thought he was lost. He never gave up and never broke down completely, and in the end, he survived.

If Amaury had thought the very first night digging holes in the rain was bad, he had no idea what was yet coming. The captains believed digging was their way of teaching self-discipline, strength of character, and toughness to the young recruits. It was hours of backbreaking labor—a true test of a man's appetite and desire for success.

On one particular day, Amaury was told to start digging a hole that was required to be twenty feet long and seven feet deep. His only tool was a Russian-made *Sapler Spade* shovel, which was a compact shovel used for emergencies. The captains made them use the Sapler and nothing else.

They began digging at 7 a.m. and if the hole wasn't completed by 7 p.m. that night or if it was not completed to the captain's liking, they had to dig more. The captains often didn't like the quality of their holes.

On the second night, the rain once again started and continued into the next day. The hole was a slippery, filthy mess, which only made it more difficult to dig. In the middle of the next day, the captain came back to check on their progress. As he looked on during the driving rain, he walked around the hole four times. Each time, his face got redder and redder as the water ran down his cheeks. Amaury looked down at his feet, sensing a problem. He glanced up at the captain from the hole, rain blinding his eyes.

Water running down his face, the Captain began screaming

at the top of his lungs. "What are you fuckers doing? Do you have any idea what it means to dig a proper hole? Is that the hole I need? What kind of soldiers are you becoming when you cannot handle the simplest of directions? If you morons don't have this fucking hole finished by tomorrow morning, I'm going to make you fucking dig two more holes. If I don't like the way those are done, I'm going to think about making you do three more holes. Let's see if you think I'm joking around."

As he yelled, he paced around the hole, kicking wet dirt with his black boots. Mud sprayed everywhere through the entire speech. The captain knew the reason why they were teaching these trainees through toughness and humiliation. The lessons were the discipline of digging until they got the message. Once achieved, they'd rebuild their confidence as a new, stronger soldier.

"Digging their way to knowledge," the captains liked to say. Discipline came with pressure, even if it didn't make sense on the surface for the new Rangers. "The enemy will not care about you. You need to be prepared to mentally defeat them before they meet you," the Captain screamed.

Once again, the captain upped the ante. "I want to see this hole level by morning. If it isn't level, you two fuckers will dig three more holes, and I don't care if it takes three more days. You'll dig until I like the holes. Now you can make these ones twenty-five feet just so you know I'm not joking. Do you get that, maggots?"

The rain fell relentlessly, causing the hole to continually fill up with so much water it was nearly impossible to dig further. A lake of water continued forming at their feet as they futilely persistently bailed it out with their helmets. The hole was easily twenty feet long and seven feet deep. Amaury's hands were burning badly. His back was a painful mass from having to bend with each shovelful. The pain seared each time he bent over to fill his helmet with filthy mud-water. It was a fruitless effort. Marco's and Amaury looked at each other in disbelief. The intensely loud sound of splashing rain hitting the mud was all they knew. But without saying a word, they bent over and bailed.

After another two hours and in complete exhaustion, the boys sat down to eat some food. They'd only taken a few breaks to eat along the way because they needed to make sure the hole was good enough when the captain returned.

Their food was always the same—cans of *Carne Ruso* with Lentil beans eaten cold and never heated. The canned beef was from Russia and the lentils were made in Cuba. The combination of the two didn't taste good, but it was all they had. They hadn't been given a can opener, so they had to improvise with their AK-47 bayonets to puncture and then tear open the metal. It tended to be a messy job, but once completed, they were able to gain sustenance.

After eating, they lay down on the ground and slept until the early morning. The rain continued on and off throughout the night. Finally, in the morning, the rain stopped, and they were able to complete the job of leveling the hole plus adding the additional five feet of extension as per their orders. The torture of digging wasn't over, but at least they made it through this time, however minimally. Upon conclusion, Amaury thought, *What else could they possibly have in store for us?*

Chapter 30

Next Steps

As the training continued, the Ranger captains had further plans to bring training to a higher level and continue to test the trainee's endurance and fortitude. The captains needed them to learn to survive in any kind of theatre of war.

However difficult, the captains believed the true success of survival resided within trainees' own minds. Once the trainees understood and adhered to the disciplines forged by the captains, they learned to adapt to each new level. As each trainee was elevated to the next level, the memory of digging holes seemed gentle compared to the mind-games they faced in later stages. It was a predesigned plan to have recruits cope with stresses on which they knew their own survival depended.

Amaury learned the main tool the captains used to highly motivate their young trainees was anger. Once energized with this intense emotion, they could conceivably accomplish anything. The captains believed it was the only way to get them psychologically primed to correctly attack the challenges of war. The training was working entirely on Amaury. He never realized he was capable of the deep anger instilled within him. He felt an unexpected rage of aggression building. He realized their efforts worked, but he couldn't control it. He liked the ability to be strong and understand how to use that strength. He knew his next personal task would be to properly guide this new knowledge and not let it consume him.

More importantly, they wanted them to recognize and anticipate what their enemies were thinking. Get themselves ready in advance as an emotional edge. They needed the trainees to believe whomever their enemy was, they'd be able to kill them first without hesitation.

With their training, they'd be able to control any lethal environment they encountered. Their critical analysis of a situation was extremely important. If someone was ordered to drop their gun, they had a split second to comply. If the Ranger observed the slightest quiver of an eyebrow, the twitch of a cheek, or a finger movement, they would instantly take a kill shot without hesitation. Amaury and his group learned to live by a motto in war: *Shoot first, ask questions later*. They needed to be prepared to prevent any room for error when confronted by an enemy.

In training sessions, Amaury's group was introduced to two new techniques. The captains brought in trainers from Russia and Vietnam. Captain Vladimir Chooska was Russian, and the other was a Vietnamese Colonel named Cam Truong. Each one brought his own brand of hellish disciplines for the troops.

Captain Chooska was the personal defense survival commander. His goal was to educate each soldier regarding how to kill a person in less than thirty seconds. He taught them how to kill with just a simple needle. Amaury was shocked at how such a little tool could be used to kill someone. Before the army, he'd never thought about killing anyone at all. Now, in the army. he thought about how his father may have reacted to killing. It never occurred to him what that must have been like, and now he was learning the same thing. He knew deep down, though, he must learn and become less emotional about the sensitive effects of what it might be like to kill someone. He kept thinking —*All that needle needed to do was enter a man's temple hard enough, and that enemy's life was over in a split second.*

Colonel Truong was known as the Commander of Survival. He taught the troops how to endure without prepared or canned food in the wild outdoors. They learned how to find whatever was available to consume in any environment. It was his job to teach the knowledge of turning nature into food. In his first meeting, Truong explained to the trainees that nature provided a tremendous opportunity for maintaining life even in the worst conditions.

"As soldiers, survival in any condition depends on your ability to quickly recognize where you are in terms of what's available at any given moment. My job will be to show you how simple that challenge truly is. You may not like the things you learn, but you will eat to survive, though not necessarily to enjoy. You'll get used to eating things you never thought possible."

He showed them how to observe the world differently than anything they'd ever seen before. It was one of the highlights of their training. The skills they acquired enabled them to recognize they could live without becoming desperate for food, which was more than enlightening—it gave them a sense of freedom.

They were taught to find food from hunting, fishing, insects, plants, berries, grains, and catching wild game without tools or weapons. One skill in which Amaury took particular interest was recognizing a poisonous plant used to instantly kill fish in the water. The plant was called *Rarotonga* or *Akai* in Cuba. It could be found in roots, seeds or bark smashed into a paste with a mortar and pestle. Once malleable, they sought out a basin near any water's edge. The paste was dropped and blended into the basin with the natural movement of the water. It created a trap for any fish that happened to enter the basin and ingest the paste.

Once the fish were exposed through their gills, they'd succumb to death or were at least stunned and floated to the surface. The digested plant in the fish didn't harm humans. This method could capture five or six fish with one application, enough for several people to eat. The fish could be eaten raw or cooked depending on what circumstances the soldiers found themselves.

Another technique taught by Truong was the use of freshly-caught animals to trap other animals as bait. Having already become experts in digging holes, this trap required digging a human-sized hole with extremely sharp pointed spikes. These spikes were then affixed pointing up, creating a deathly drop.

They began by using their small entrenching tool to dig holes and then covered them with light branches, twigs, leaves, and other brush. It camouflaged the hole to appear as the rest of the natural environment. The sharp spikes at the bottom were approximately six feet deep from the bottom. They were stabilized in place with several feet of dirt buried deeper. As the animal fell into the trap, the spikes impaled the animal, causing it to die from the force of its own weight.

Peeling the skin of a raccoon or a monkey wasn't an activity Amaury thought he would ever need to learn in his life, but once he realized it might keep him alive someday, he committed it to memory. In time, he also learned to eat insects, bugs, crickets, worms, rats, mice, and snakes—nearly anything that was edible or could be ingested.

He never got over his discomfort of chewing and swallowing live crickets. They were a special treat of a strange nature. Although difficult to catch, they were full of protein and vitamins because they ate grass by living close to the ground. There was no substitute for the nutrients crickets contained and they were a favorite captured out in the wild. All these methods and skills of how to look at the world differently would provide sustenance later on for Amaury and the entire team once they were engaged in war.

Colonel Truong, whose own home country was thick with jungles, taught the unit lifesaving techniques in that environment. He showed the men to look at circumstances in an entirely different way. They learned to consider the world as a source of sustenance rather than simply a place in which to live. They were introduced to important experiences such as getting down on the ground to observe the movement of grasses and to feel and listen to the wind. They learned to watch how insects move. They listened to the birds, viewing various animals' activities, movements, and sounds. They began to recognize whatever environment they were in and use these skills for staying alive.

In later instruction, Chooska taught them how to correctly throw a hand grenade without accidentally killing themselves or others. Throwing a grenade had its own complications. It was not simply pulling the pin and throwing the bomb. They needed to be very aware of their surroundings, their positioning, and how they stood while throwing. Their follow-through as the grenade was thrown was equally important. Additionally, they needed to avoid other objects, branches, a soldier's arm, a foot, or slipping in mud which might interfere with their throw. They practiced the maneuver many times so they wouldn't inadvertently kill a fellow soldier or themselves.

Knowledge and then the skills of these lessons gave Amaury a sense of mental strength. He fully thrust himself into all the lessons. Others around him often grumbled and winced at many of the things they learned. He gave his full concentration to the value he believed elevated his life. He never realized he could experience such a huge change within himself. But it was happening, and he realized for the first time his father's influence may have been right.

The captains continued pushing the recruits' limits to the point of exhaustion, and then they'd push them even harder. If they observed a soldier having a problem with a particular exercise or skill, they'd make them do it dozens of times until they succeeded.

In actuality, Amaury later learned, Ranger training was preparation for life. The training he learned he owned for the rest of his days.

Chapter 31

Rangers - Conclusion

Four and a half months into training, the unit was restationed at a new base camp on an island off the southern coast of Cuba called *Isle de Pino* or *Isle of Pines*. The island was directly south of Havana.

It was established in the early 1980s and was first used by the Rangers for military training. The location was remote enough that the unit felt totally isolated. For the military's goal of toughening up their newest Rangers, this island was the right choice. Once they arrived, it felt as though they had been dropped off and given a prison term on *Devil's Island.*

The mostly jungle location was also known for the citrus that grew there but was used strictly as a military base. Besides being hotter because it was farther south, the island also had a reputation for significant rainstorms which caused large pools of water. These pools became perfect homes for giant mosquitoes who did their best work at night. The mosquitoes were relentless in their choice of food. The men were constantly uncomfortable, and they were nearly eaten alive. Sleeping was almost impossible.

The Rangers' superiors, already prepared for this situation, taught the men early during arrival to use an antidote for the mosquito found in a plant known as *Favela*, a cactus that grew indigenously on the island. Every night before the unit went to sleep and often during the day, they'd break off a leaf of the cactus plant, which oozed a whitish, thick, milk-like viscous liquid which they'd then spread over their bodies as a lotion. Once applied and rubbed in, the cactus juice caused the skin to react strangely. A bright reddish abrasion appeared over applied areas, which seem to rebel from the substance. It lasted throughout the night, helping prevent mosquitoes from attacking while they slept.

In the morning, once the new Ranger trainees woke up, they discovered they'd had a confusing reaction to using the Favela.

"What the hell is in this stuff?" Umberto exclaimed. "Wow, no mosquito bites, but it's burning the hell out of my skin.

"You'll get used to it," Amaury said.

"Shit! Man, I gotta get this crap off of me. I'm going into the ocean!"

"You're right! Let's go." Amaury followed along with the entire group.

The captains didn't care if men were uncomfortable. They were required to train regardless. Irritating mosquito bites were the least of their concerns. There was also the constant threat of contracting malaria.

Days went by while they repeated the same routine. However, the Favela created additional problems over the course of their training. Their clothes—specifically their underwear and t-shirts—began to break down from the plant's sap combined with saltwater. Normally, they spent so much time in the ocean the only showers they had were in the form of rainstorms.

As the six intense months concluded, the Rangers prepared for a barrage of final tests to graduate. They'd always known there would be a variety of *finals* but had never been told when or how they would take place. The entire process was executed and graded in secrecy.

A formal meeting was held before the finals at the main barracks on the Isle for the operations of the remaining weeks of training. It appeared to be a motivational address.

"All Rangers trainees will become the most formidable military in the world, especially in the southern hemisphere. Each of you will become a part of this legacy. To build our nation into a true power the world will never forget, everyone will participate in an assessment of the performance of the knowledge you've obtained in training. We in the Rangers are the most important component of this organized effort. It is your faithful duty to show not only the other branches of the military but the entire world the strength of Cuba and our efforts to build a powerful army."

"We are becoming a well-trained force, Umberto," Amaury whispered to his friend. "Wow. I feel for the first time in my life we are accomplishing something special, something important. You know?" The pride he had felt upon being accepted into the Rangers had now increased tenfold.

"I know, Amaury. I feel the same way. But shit, that element of surprise is still bothersome to me. They have something planned for us. I can feel it. I'm sure it's going to be killer, but then, what isn't?"

"I'm ready for it. We have all the tools, Umberto," Amaury said, grinning with confidence.

The entire group would participate in a variety of physical and mental toughness trials to provide the captains with concluding observations. If the trainees succeeded on the mock battlefield, they would graduate.

They were required to live out in the wild on the island on their own without assistance for over a week. The entire testing program was never discussed in advance with any of the soldiers, making certain that they weren't able to prepare for what awaited them. They needed the soldiers to react spontaneously and watch their natural responses. The last piece of information they were given was the trial could include actual live gunfire and potentially other elements of surprise.

Before leaving on his solo mission, Amaury thought fully about what was ahead. He'd be on his own on this island, and he knew it was going to be rough.

Thank goodness they told us about the favela. Otherwise, I'd be eaten alive.

Amaury was glad they allowed him to use the forty-seven's bayonet, whatever little clothing he had left, and his boots.

Sheesh, these boots are almost more important than my rifle.

The first thing he planned to do was to find a place to sleep. He knew he could maybe use palm fronds and branches for cover. He'd figure it out. Next, he'd look for something to eat for the next few days. He would begin with fishing, for sure.

Each soldier would be judged by how they did.

In the late afternoon, Amaury was taken on a small army skiff to the east coast of the Isle. After a long ride, they finally arrived at the shore. He jumped off with his boots tied together over his shoulder and swam to the beach, his knife in his mouth. His heart was beating fast, but he was determined to succeed.

"Soldier, here you are. You'll need to get back as quickly as you can. You're being timed. Stay alert!"

Amaury swam as quickly as he could to the shoreline. As he walked up the beach, he realized he had no idea where he was. The first thing he did was dump the water out of his boots.

He looked around for food and then went up into the wooded area and looked for a vine to tie his knife to his calf. Next, he looked for favela to cover sparingly, making sure he was protected. As he searched, he heard a noise and squared down in silence. Looking around, he saw nothing. Listening, he heard dropping sounds and realized it was about to rain.

Not good.

It was almost night, and he knew he needed to find some cover. "Gotta watch out for those freaking snakes and those damn bugs," he said aloud to himself.

It was starting to get dark, and he knew he should find a place to camp for the night. As he looked around, he noticed a huge boulder that pointed up out of the ground yet had a wide overhang.

It was a partial cave.

After searching out berries and grapefruit from a tree, he settled in for the evening. Satiated, quietly Amaury leaned his back against the cold rock and planned his next steps. Again, he heard that noise.

Then silence.

Some time passed and he began to get sleepy.

Just as he was about to drift off, Amaury heard movement and a branch crack. Not moving, he opened his eyes and saw two shadows against the moonlit night sky.

Quietly, he scooted over to a different spot, crouching tightly in a ready position, his mind racing. But it was too late. The first figure lunged and without a word, the brawl began. The second figure immediately joined in.

Amaury swung in specific aggressive movements against both assailants. Moonlight was all he had to gauge his thrusts against the mysterious silhouettes.

His karate training kicked in and a brutal fight ensued, with body blows and counter maneuvers. Fists and feet were swinging in every direction. Amaury knew he landed some strong punches but took many himself.

The skirmish didn't last long. Amaury spun around to make a high body roundhouse kick. As he spun, his leg found nothing but air. Both assailants were gone as fast as they'd arrived. It was over. Shaking, he took an assessment of his condition. In the darkness, he felt all over his body. He realized he had significant pain in his right torso. He must have taken a severe blow, but at least nothing felt broken. In the morning when he woke up, he knew he needed to get going early. As he lifted his head, his ear ripped with pain, and when he reached up to investigate the pain and touch his ear, a lightning bolt of pain drove across his torso. He suddenly realized he'd taken more blows than he'd first thought. A significant black and blue sore already began developing on his lower right side. His foot also burned. It was going to be a monumental trek across the island getting back to base camp. His newly-learned skills came with a large cost, but he knew his test was truly underway.

The next day was just as precarious as the first. He discovered two deep raccoon traps along his route and cut his arm from a hard fall. Parts of his body were covered with a severe rash from the Favela with no way to wash it off. The thick blood which had run down his arm and thigh had dried, and combined with dirt resembled mud. He knew he'd finally get the chance to clean the wound only after returning to base camp. After seven days of trekking across the island and nursing his injuries along the way, he finally arrived back at base camp.

Amaury was given congratulations from all his comrades for having successfully achieved passing the challenge. One by one, each of the Ranger trainees arrived back to base camp with many stories to tell. Amaury was finally able to let out a big belly laugh as all his comrades came to congratulate him.

"My God, Amaury. You look like shit. What the hell happened to you? There's blood all over you," Umberto exclaimed.

Amaury laughed, but he was thoroughly exhausted and could still hear the buzzing in his ear from that first night's blow.

He didn't tell anyone about it. It took a few more days to calm down but eventually did go away. His torso, however, took longer to heal. "I swear it was no big deal. It went as smoothly as jumping off a cliff into a pond of sharks." They let out a big laugh.

With the final two weeks underway, their last days came without any special fanfare or celebration the training ended just shortly over seven months.

As in *Prep*, one by one, the men were taken into a large room within the main building back at the original base camp. One by one, their names were called. In a simple procedure, each man was informed of his status by the mere announcement of his name.

Every soldier named was assembled in a short ceremony by the senior officers of the Ranger and some regular Cuban military. It was held in the same large meeting room as the *Prep* ceremony. Each recruit was handed both a medal of *Commando* of Special Forces and a paper *Certificate Of Acceptance.* At the same time, three-day passes were issued to leave the base and take a hard-earned reward of a few days.

Amaury's name was called, and as he walked up to the desk, he was handed his medal and he shook hands with his superiors. They congratulated him, and he proudly walked back to his seat.

That was it. It was done. Amaury's essential training was completed. He was happy to take a few well-deserved days away from the military.

It was his first time off, and once at home, he was glad to sit down and not think about anything other than relaxing. Amaury's body still hurt and pulsed from the final test. His entire family stood around as he sat in the old comfy chair. His legs were stretched out and he closed his eyes, but the questions started flowing.

"*Oh, dios mio,* Amaury. We're so happy to have you home. You look amazing and so fit. But you look so very tired. You must tell us everything. What was it like? Where did you go? How difficult was the training?"

So many questions. It was overwhelming. Amaury answered several and tried to be forthcoming. However, he felt exhausted and fell asleep on the chair. Everyone looked at him with sympathy but let him quietly sleep. He finally was feeling the intense exhaustion of military training. He was home, but his mind was elsewhere.

During the three special days with his family, he enjoyed food, laughter, and contemplating his future. He enjoyed the successes of his military achievements, but at home, although happy, the time quickly passed. He was mostly chatty but reserved. He was unsure of what was coming and didn't feel free enough to be completely open to their many questions.

Nury was nowhere to be found.

It would be a future both certain and uncertain. Commando Amaury Torres knew he was going somewhere, but the somewhere was unknown.

Chapter 32

Cuba & Angola

The fifteenth day of May 1989, was approaching for the new platoon. They'd be shipped across the world some place where Cuba had established alliances and was firmly entrenched. From the early 1960s, Castro's plan was for Cuba to develop a strong international presence in opposition to the United States.

It was important for the Castro regime to show the international community they may be a small country in size but with large political clout. The Castros believed their potential successes and abilities to influence other countries meant more than accumulating like-minded international friends. For them, it meant showing the world Cuba would be a beacon of light in the path of the resistance against communist successes. As such, Castro turned his attention to Angola, which had a significant abundance of natural resources including gas, oil, and important metals used in manufacturing. They also owned some of the world's largest natural diamond mines. The country was so rich in resources that hundreds of years before, Portugal had successfully colonized the various feudal kingdoms to take advantage of its natural wealth. It was known as the Congo and was later organized into Angola. Portugal saw Angola as an opportunity to market their natural resources worldwide, including portions of the population for slavery. Portugal established an export slavery business which finally ended in 1840. Many of these slaves were later exported to what eventually became the country of Cuba.

So many years of subjugation in Angola created a natural resentment within the population. That resentment took many decades to erupt, but it helped to spawn three converging groups who attempted to become liberators inside their own country.

Fidel Castro saw the opportunity to act as a savior rather than an exploiter of resources by helping downtrodden countries. He advertised his motive as a kindred spirit relating to their struggles for independence, thus separating himself from imperialist countries. His true goal, however, was to strategically establish a firm communist foothold in a vulnerable part of the world in need of financial or military support.

These symbolic moments were more important than anything else for the Castro regime. Cuba spent decades fighting in Angola in both an advisory and military role to help stabilize their own embedded communist power structure. Cuba became so deeply entrenched in Angola's affairs that it later conflicted with their benefactor Russia, who eventually withdrew. Russia didn't fundamentally believe a proxy war with America was a worthwhile pursuit in Angola, despite Cuba's lobbying for their continued support.

In the early 1970s, Portugal was experiencing their own severe political strife and economic issues and fell victim to a coup d'état. This resulted in a quick decision to separate themselves from their occupied territories worldwide. Portugal chose to abandon their responsibility from any international and economic obligations, and it was decided all their colonies would be released. Shocked at the quick reversal of fortune, the colonies were forced to negotiate final settlement agreements. Mozambique was first given its independence with an expeditious agreement concluded in June 1975.

Angola, on the other hand, was a much more complicated transition. The transfer of power was contentiously disputed due to significant internal conflicts beneath the surface. The battle for which group would be in control of the new government became combustible. The three parties vied for power divided by a geographical sphere of influence within the country's borders. The three underlying highly-charged political groups were the FNLA, the MPLA, and the UNITA. The Alvor Agreement created in 1975 established the path for Angolan independence. But it was done so poorly that instead only created more severe rifts in the already fragile political structure of the region.

Portugal simply withdrew. Angola instantly fell into a civil war. Three factions were competing for power and looking to foreign nations for financial and military support. It quickly spread into a much larger international conflict.

Conflicting adversaries emerged, immediately supported by Cuba, Russia, South Africa, and the USA. The fight lasted well into the 1990s. Cuba had already fully committed to Angola and had deployed soldiers in the early1970's, but by the early 1980s, it was sending in full divisions to help the MPLA. As Cuba escalated its occupation, other nations followed suit. The number of soldiers from combating nations went into the tens of thousands. Angola faced a full war aggressively played throughout the country.

This background setting predated Amaury's birth and was the path set for any man entering into the Cuban Army afterward. His participation and fate were predetermined once he stepped foot on the very first day of *Prep*. The main military base for all officers, including recently graduated Ranger Commandos, was the Managua Military Base in Managua Cuba. Once Amaury arrived at the new base, he knew his fateful disembarking day somewhere in the world would take place in May.

The time was quickly nearing, and Amaury, along with his compatriots, settled in at the new base. As they went about their daily business, the rumors were flying amongst them about where they might be assigned. The main thought was always Angola, and Amaury felt from his prior knowledge of Angola that once enlisted, he most likely would be sent there. He quietly relished the challenge of the battle ahead and set his mind on how he was going to make sure he'd survive.

While he waited to hear, he thought about his training and the things he'd learned along the way. He knew it quite possibly could be a life and death ordeal. He focused on the positives of training rather than the negatives of what might happen. Mentally, he reviewed many details of training to keep his thoughts fresh and mentally accessible.

The fateful day finally arrived. All assignments designated by mid-May 1989 were established. The troops walked onto the long, sunbaked tarmac. They looked back and took in the full view of what might be the last sight of their home. They could see in the near distance the beige and green palm trees swaying so simply in the mild tropical breeze, so familiar, once taken for granted but no more.

Nostalgically, it reminded Amaury of his youth and how he'd walk to school or hang out with Iran and Johan. It all rushed into his mind's eye. Not long ago, they'd run out to play without a care in the world. None of them thought their lives would ever change. He truly loved his home.

As he contemplated these thoughts, Amaury took a moment to remember how it felt...the sun, the fresh air, that familiar tropical feeling, smooth and warm, embraced him in his fondest memory of home. It was something he'd always experienced but never celebrated. But now it was a pang in his heart as he knew it would soon be in the past.

The simple life he'd once known suddenly got complicated as he boldly stepped over the threshold of the plane. He turned to look back one last time and realized it was not only Cuba he was leaving behind, but it was also his boyhood. It was a feeling he knew would finally happen one day. However, he looked forward and continued into the plane, not knowing what the future held.

Chapter 33

Angola Home Away From Home

The group disembarked on a well-packed propeller airplane to make the long flight across the Atlantic Ocean. The plane was buzzing with loud chatter and commotion as many soldiers put their bags in the overhead bins. Most had never flown before. The energy level was overflowing and distinct. Amaury immediately sought out a window seat, put his seatbelt on, and looked at the runway. It wasn't long before the ocean was far below. Up in the sky, his mind wandered. He reviewed thoughts of his young life, the different events that had led to where he was at that exact moment. Only sixteen-and-a-half years old, a full-fledged soldier, but with some regrets. As much as he hated to acknowledge it, he felt fear.

He thought about what was awaiting him on the other end of this flight, what his new life would be like if there were dangers in store for him, and how difficult his tasks would be. He decided that no matter what lay ahead of him, he must maintain a positive attitude.

The world below looked flat and dark while the sky above quickly faded from blue to black. The fluffy white clouds floating below turned grey. It occurred to him for a second that this was the first time he'd ever flown in an airplane.

Amaury turned to the soldier next to him. "Wow, that's a crazy scary huge ocean. It seems endless and is so much bigger than I imagined."

"It really is," the other soldier replied.

"It looks like a liquid desert. Man, that is huge. Glad I'm on this plane."

The other soldier smiled then closed his eyes, too. It was hours of endless hundreds of miles of forbidding ocean water and nothing else.

In Amaury's mind, the vastness was stunning. He tried not to think about it. It made him feel uncomfortable. As he peered out the window, he could see his reflection and quietly thought, *I'm not going to make it.* Then he quickly shook his head again as if to shake away those negative thoughts, and with great determination, he corrected his thinking. *I am going to make it. I've got to do this.*

Hours passed, and eventually, the din of the propeller's engines cajoled him into sleep.

He awoke abruptly, feeling the plane suddenly descending into the makeshift military airport near Luanda, the capital of Angola. The temporary runway had been built for military planes landing with supplies and recruits. It was essentially a clearing excavated in the middle of the jungle somewhere on the far outskirts of the city. The night sky was as black as coal., and as they approached the landing, Amaury couldn't ascertain whether the plane was still over the ocean or if they were flying near the runway.

Without announcement, the plane finally touched down onto the extremely short, bumpy, and dimly lit runway. As it hit the runway, it lurched and bucked. The squeaking revolt of the seats struggling to stay attached, violently shaking in place, suddenly screeched to a fast and frightening stop. The wings were shaking up and down from the intense braking, skidding, and burning tires. Suddenly the plane stopped, and everything became silent and still. They had arrived.

Amaury could smell the burning rubber fumes slowly infiltrating the cabin. They later learned the runway was very tricky due to its significantly short length and rough surface. The shaken boys looked at each other, blinking and nearly out of breath. The soldier next to Amaury said, "What the fuck just happened there? Real nice welcome. Huh?"

Also shaken, Amaury simply nodded.

Everyone was anxious to deplane as soon as they possibly could. The plane pulled over to the side and stopped where the soldiers disembarked. They gathered their things and assembled inside the tiny airport building for a quick meeting, then they were off to the new Angolan Military base. Amaury took a big breath inside the makeshift terminal. "Well, here we are."

Once aboard the bus, they were given several more instructions as to how their new Angolan base was organized. Amaury gazed out the window and watched the place he knew he would be home for a while.

The first thing he noticed when the bus headlights shined down the road was the trees were completely different from Cuba. They seemed fuller in quantity and taller but were shaped more fully than the palms at home.

He could see brush around on both sides of the dirt road and immediately felt as though Cuba truly was a million miles away. A sudden nostalgic wrenching in his gut told him it was happening—they were in a foreign country and facing many mysteries.

One of the things he noticed right away was the air had a dryness to it and felt different. The familiar salty air of Cuba no longer surrounded him. Instantaneously, his nostrils felt tight and uncomfortable, but he resigned himself to accept it.

While the vehicles bounced along the dirt road in the early morning hours, a dust fog created by the moving busses was flying behind like a crazy horizontal tornado. Amaury intently looked into the distance and thought he saw groups of monkeys dispersing, running, hanging on tree limbs, and playing on the ground. They almost looked as if they were laughing.

Initially, he wasn't quite sure they were monkeys, but then he realized they seemed to be intently looking at the moving caravan. They looked happy. At least those monkeys were free. Next stop, his new home, the Cuban Angola Base Camp, Unit 2675.

Chapter 34

Learning to Kill

Their unit had patrolled for a month. During that first period, Amaury had many new experiences involving some battlefield activity, though his unit never saw an actual head-to-head confrontation. Initially, the unit was lucky without heavy action, but he knew their luck would soon change. His training had prepared him to know exactly what to do when they were confronted with enemy aggression. From this point on it was a matter of mental preparation.

Early in his training, one of the more difficult lessons Amaury learned was consciously forcing himself to separate his emotional reaction when ending someone's life. Learning to kill had to be accomplished. He had no choice. He realized if he didn't vigorously defend himself against a serious threat, his own life would be taken away in an instant. The steps, if correctly completed, surprised him with their simplicity. A life could be easily taken away in a moment, but it was his own life he protected at all costs. His life thoughts changed after the training sessions. The thought of killing a person didn't seem very real until the day it happened. Captain Chooska taught that once a person knew how to kill another, it was a quick process given the correct skills. An enemy would perceive that confidence. Their demeanor in hand-to-hand battle within a fight could potentially end it before it began.

Amaury remembered the first day of hand-to-hand killing maneuvers. The unit had sat on the sand in their green army shorts and shirts and stiff calf-high boots, in a non-defined circle. The intense Cuban sun had caused everyone to burn with sweat. They watched the Captain intently, knowing this day was the most important day of training. On this day they learned to become real soldiers.

Captain Chooska, a crusty old Russian soldier, also had a bit of a sense of humor. He knew the air was thick with anxiety and the hot summer sun. He understood he had to help the troops digest one of their most important days of training in a way that would be very memorable.

Chooska began by barking out instructions. "Okay, listen up, everyone! Today all you young girls will learn to kill in hand-to-hand combat. You will learn what steps you must take both to protect yourself but also and to quickly take out your opponent. Then you can move on uninjured and unharmed. Understood?"

The words went directly into the heart and gut of each soldier. Amaury never liked being called a girl, but he continued to listen.

Captain Chooska intently looked around at every one of the soldiers, then started again in his typical condescending Spanish-Russian accent.

"Killing someone is much easier than you may ever have imagined. I don't know if you girls ever thought about killing someone in your lives, but today you are going to learn how to kill your enemy in less than thirty seconds. Remembering this day of training among the many will be critical."

A small, barely noticeable smile appeared on the captain's

face, much to the curiosity of all those that happened to notice. Captain Chooska asked one of the Ranger trainees, which happened to be Amaury's closest friend in the unit, Umberto Morales, to join him.

"You, there. Yes, you! What's your name?"

"Morales, sir."

"Okay, come on up, Ranger. You're my victim today. Welcome aboard."

Morales walked to the front of all the recruits to help with the demonstration. Uneasy, Umberto looked over at Amaury. He seemed worried about what was about to happen.

Chooska smiled and exclaimed in a loud, transformative, overpowering voice. "Let's see how you do being my subject. Okay, Morales?"

Visibly nervous, Umberto agreed. "Yes, sir!"

Chooska continued, "The first step you need to understand is that when you're close enough to engage your enemy, first strike to the throat with your fist. Aim directly into your subject's windpipe. With a single harsh, massive, quick thrust called a front punch, land directly on his Adam's apple. If done correctly, this single punch will instantly cause the victim to go into shock for the lack of air and the suddenness of the punch. He will panic and grope for air, not thinking about anything other than how he can catch his next breath. It's extremely important to make this blow work the first time. You may only get one opportunity to make that first successful impression," he said sarcastically. Everyone laughed. Though his message was accompanied by the idea of killing, he tried to lighten the information just a little bit to help the recruits absorb the intensity of the subject more easily.

Chooska went on, "As soon as you see your enemy struggling and disabled, gasping for air, you make your second move. Immediately grab the back of his neck. As you bend him over, put your leg in front of his legs, and with a single thrust, you quickly force him to the ground like this!"

With an unexpected swiftness, he grasped the unsuspecting Umberto and completed the move on him. Making it look very official, the captain put his leg in front of Umberto's legs. Without hesitation, he instantly forced him to the ground. With a resounding thud, everyone stopped laughing, shocked as they realized how quickly the move had been executed. The next part of the move caused the class to get very quiet and give the captain their total undivided attention.

Chooska exclaimed, "While your enemy is flailing and struggling on the ground, you have a significantly dominant advantage."

Quietly, Umberto struggled as Chooska continued. "You grab your eight-inch bayonet and thrust it directly into the center-right of the enemy's chest."

The Captain took the knife and thrust it quickly into Umberto's chest, directly into his heart. The class, already shaken, was taken aback. Some of the Ranger trainees gasped at the rapid move. Umberto, also shocked, looked down at his chest to see if he had been stabbed. The class thought for a moment Chooska had actually stabbed Umberto. Umberto, who was on the ground not moving, believed it, as well. His face became red and flushed.

Amaury couldn't believe his eyes. Chooska stared intently back at the class while his knife handle was completely against Umberto's chest. It appeared as though it was embedded into Umberto's body. Then Chooska pulled his hand away, along with the knife blade, which he instantly retracted back into the handle. There was a nervous laugh when they realized Chooska had made a retractable prop designed to create the impression he was thrusting the knife into the volunteer's chest. The effect was stunning and instantly became permanent in each Ranger trainee's mind.

Chooska was extremely serious about survival and his ability to make a first impression count—one they would never forget. He was a no-nonsense army man, and he knew he had to make an impact.

Afterward, Amaury turned to Umberto. "It turns out that Cubans were good at some things—hiring Russians to teach us how to kill!"

It made Amaury feel strong and empowered, and he felt elevated with this new knowledge. Amaury noticed Umberto sweating profusely, not only from the sun, but because he thought his life had ended at that very moment. Umberto looked down at his chest and then at Amaury, disbelieving what had happened.

Amaury said, "Man, you looked like you were about to shit."

They both laughed out loud for a moment. Umberto, however, was not quite so amused. Profusely sweating, he struggled to recover from the shock.

Chapter 35

Learning to Cope

It was not long after Amaury arrived in Angola that the pang of homesickness was upon him. He realized he missed his family. Daily living in a filthy, dirty environment with co-soldiers he didn't know very well made the idea of anything else seem more appealing. As his new life settled in, he would lie on his new makeshift bunk and worriedly look up at the top of the tent. He pondered about the tethered supports joining together at the peak. It occurred to him his own life was similar.

Thinking about his grandmother, mom, and even his brother and sister, he imagined they too were those same supporting joists. He felt that his life was just like the peak only now the supporters were the group of men around him. He worried if they would also support him when the moment came for that dependency. So many threads of life seem tenuously glued together by only their training, no other loyalty necessarily existed. At that moment, the idea alone he now hoped would be his peak coming together.

Their difficult mission was complicated yet simple. They were assigned to help the natives of the country defend themselves against other foreign nationals and domestic aggressive factions. The South Africans and the other home-grown political parties engaged in the civil war were seeking to take over other Angolan territories as well.

South Africans constantly infiltrated Angola through its southern border to disrupt its government and steal natural resources, specifically diamond mines. In general, they wanted to take control of Angola's assets and occupy the country. They stopped at nothing to achieve that end.

All the units were instructed to patrol a 100-200-mile circumference area around the base on a minimum of seven-day patrols. However, those arrangements were subject to momentary changes and often exceeded in their assignments. Always in flux, normal patrol parameters were constantly changing in time durations and directions.

South Africans would often be found surreptitiously mining in remote areas for diamonds and other natural resources. Then they'd smuggle back to South Africa at night. It was an ongoing process as part of their routine, approaching and stopping armed dangerous smugglers.

Cuban intervention was two-fold. They were not only helping the war effort but also spreading the values of communism wherever they could. Amaury, although very dedicated to helping the Angolan people in their fight for independence, never believed nor felt it his duty to spend time indoctrinating the Angolans into Communism. Keeping himself alive he firmly believed was his single most important goal. He never let his superiors know of his motivation.

On the other hand, he was also quite dedicated to helping protect the native Angolans in general and to prevent their country from being torn apart. He passionately used this as his own added motivation to move forward every day. He believed Cuba's presence in Angola was enough of a show of force. The natives could conclude on their own if Communism was a good way of life for them or not.

Once Amaury's unit was assigned their week of patrol, they gathered gear, equipment supplies, anything needed for their assigned period. As the time neared, they would get themselves mentally prepared for the next round.

Out on patrol, they were safeguarding the Angolan countryside in their trucks, on the flat plains or the jungle territories. They frequently faced hidden snipers or other unknown lethal traps. The activity of defending as their main focus also contrasted with days of sheer boredom where nothing happened and then suddenly the air was thick with treacherous confrontations.

Sometimes they'd happen upon another unit wiped out with dead bodies on the side of the road, trucks had been blown up. Amaury learned quickly it was a kill or be killed world he was living in and carried this motto as his daily mantra.

As time progressed the constant pressure of self-survival became debilitating to some of the soldiers. It was mentally challenging and an exhausting experience for Amaury, but some of the other men didn't have the mental fortitude that he had. All units suffered from a lack of sleep. They feared they might be killed while asleep; it was a nightly threat that he struggled with the entire time.

The harsh reality of the dual loyalty of the MPLA did not help with the Cuban endeavor. This complex issue never deterred Castro from his determination to continue in Angola alongside the MPLA but the soldiers in the war theatre had to live with this threat daily.

Angola had many jungles and thousands of miles of land, which went through a significant rainy season each year. The land became a vast wasteland of thick heavy mud nearly impossible to navigate. Conversely, on dry days there were vast open spaces of dusty desert occasionally interrupted with sparse green growth and knee-high bushes. Whatever greenery there tended to clump together, growing wild. As part of their training and current orders, units on patrol needed to be very careful of the numerous native animals... lions, cheetahs, and other wild creatures, all potentially dangerous. Their keen attention was required twenty-four hours a day.

Nighttime guard duties were particularly precarious where the Cuban patrols suffered most of their casualties. The native Angolan fighters only spoke Portuguese and if they did speak Spanish they would hide it, further complicating communication with their Cuban counterparts. Angolan soldiers fighting side by side were excellent with knives but untrustworthy.

Even though the Cubans were assisting the MLPA forces against their two other political foes, they discovered MLPA forces were not one-hundred percent loyal in their war effort. It became apparent in time that some MPLA soldiers were also spies or double agents. Some of these fighters were sent by UNITA (National Union for the Total Independence of Angola which was supported by the USA) or one of the other forces to infiltrate or kill Cuban troops. It was a difficult, strange set of war rules forcing Amaury never to trust anyone other than Cubans in his unit. Watching their backs night and day was required, and as much as their training was required, their real teacher was time on the battlefield.

Several months after arriving in Angola, Amaury's unit 2675, chose a spot to build a camp for the night. They set the barbed wire surrounding the camp, chose the evening guard spots, and set the two-man tents. Once dinner was complete and things settled down the men prepared for sleep. They were fifty miles from the main base. Most of the Rangers, other than the night guards that were active until late into the night had gone to bed and all that was heard was the sound of nature.

Worriedly, Amaury set himself to go to sleep. He shared his tent with Umberto as usual. Neither one had guard duty that night and they discussed the continuing odd feeling they always had about being asleep. The battle to keep one eye open all the time took its toll on them during the day. Sleep was as elusive as coping with the constant danger surrounding the night.

Umberto said quietly, "Let's try to get some sleep tonight, Amaury, we need it"

"Okay, yes tonight. I know you're right. Good night Umberto."

Wild animals and other creatures took over the night's conversation. Unknown to Amaury and Umberto, quietly undercover, several of the Angolan MPLA soldiers traveling with the Rangers had pre-planned a late evening attack. These traitors were a particular group of spies sent by UNITA forces. The Cubans had difficulties distinguishing the native soldiers from enemy to friendly as many grew up in Angola. As they plotted, their contempt thick with revenge, together with the three betrayers stealthily assembled near the edges of the camp and whispered together covered by the darkness of night. Amaury as usual, could not sleep well. He had gotten used to nearly sleeping with one eye open all the time. He rustled around on his makeshift bed while his mind was racing reviewing the next day's activities. In the distance, he could hear some noise that he couldn't quite identify. However not too far away from him the UNITA Captain began giving instructions to the diabolical plotters. Amaury heard whispers and awoke from his sleep. He strained to hear the conversation.

"Go over to that tent away from that guard," the voice whispered. "You'll see two of those Cuban bastards; I'll take care of the two over here." Amaury heard the voice give further instructions. Whomever he was talking to was to jump through a hole in the fence nearby where they had cut the wire. He would meet them here. Amaury felt his heart race as he listened to this conversation. He knew he had to do something but what? He had no idea who these men were and if they were armed or not.

Amaury got up on his hands and knees in the dark and listened. He heard a slight rustling sound of feet moving quickly in the surrounding area, then he heard a loud shriek in the dark.

Amaury jumped up and out of his tent. He looked around surveying the scene. To his right, he saw two men who appeared to be UNITA soldiers. Then there was a loud screaming as other soldiers in the camp began stirring, as well. No one could figure out what was happening. The UNITA soldiers' eyes glazed over in an intense fear in the bright shine of the stars.

Suddenly one UNITA blurted out, "Oh my god. Shit! It's the Macaques Monkeys, they are coming through the wire. We gotta get out of here right now! They'll kill us!"

Amaury started moving in the direction of the two UNITA soldiers, but they were already on the other side of the camp. The UNITA soldiers turned to flee, but one got his foot got caught in the metal tent anchor loop. He tripped, instantly falling onto the tent. His knife blade, already protruding, sliced through the tent surface. The two awoken Rangers also heard the monkeys.

Amaury already running in their direction, heard one Ranger yell out, "What the hell, what's going on?"

The second Ranger spoke, "I don't know but there's something on top of us with a knife that almost fucking cut me."

Umberto also jumped up hearing the commotion, although staggering from being fast asleep. Both Umberto and Amaury ran to assist but the two Rangers had already pushed the UNITA soldiers off. As they shoved their way out from under the collapsed tent, the UNITA soldier whose foot was tangled in the tent wire trapped could not move.

The pack of wild monkeys dashed right past them and ran

through the camp, screaming chaotically looking for food. The entire camp woke up moving around running to get away from the monkeys as well.

Amaury's entire unit discovered their compatriots were dead. Quickly the trapped UNITA soldiers who're now exposed became surrounded. Although the three saboteurs had their knives out to defend themselves, they were subdued in seconds. The UNITA betrayers learned quickly the Cubans were also excellent fighters. All three men were dead moments later.

The other Rangers managed to get the monkeys to leave which was not an easy task. They moved away and let the monkeys take the food they wanted. The canned items were untouched but other food items were devoured. The camp was a mess, torn apart. Satiated, the monkeys simply walked out of the camp as quickly as they came in.

Amaury turned to Umberto, "The entire world has gone insane. Chooska was right when he said war was a twenty-four hour a day job."

Still dark, the unit shocked by the night's occurrences moved away as the monkeys exited. One remained but was severely tangled in the barbed wire and had to be killed. The 2675 unit realized they needed to improve their night routine, which would be discussed the next day with base camp. For now, it was a difficult night for everyone to get through.

Chapter 36

Ambushed!

The Rangers used two kinds of Russian vehicles for transportation in their daily activities, the Kamaz 3 and the Kapé. All Cuban Military supplies were imported from Russia.

Both trucks were mammoth vehicles capable of doing a variety of jobs. The eight-wheeled Kamaz 3s looked like hulking military centipedes covered with dark green canvas interrupted by thick plastic rectangular windows approximately every two feet. The windows didn't provide much ability to see out as they were constantly covered with hazy road dust. The Kamaz 3s were characterized by huge V-8 diesel engines that made a loud chugging sound along with a grinding transmission howl when driven. These vehicles weren't designed for comfort over long trips. The troops often suffered from seat ache and fatigue. The lucky driver, however, had a cushioned seat that was needed for the many hours of driving.

The troops in the back heard mostly the roaring motor and transmission whine, which resulted in little talking. The noise level of the engines normally drowned out any ability for basic chatter. Yelling was the only way to communicate.

Late one afternoon, the three-truck caravan was traveling along a bumpy dirt road with some clearing along both sides. There were scattered trees, clumps of scattered bushes, tall, thick lazy grasses, and soft rolling hills. However sparse, the unit knew with trepidation it provided excellent cover for the hiding enemy SA's. Ditches ran along the edges of the roads on each side. The ditches were important, as they provided some outlet for runoff during torrential rains. The maddeningly rushing water typically flooded the road. To prevent a total washout, the ditches helped allow the trucks to continue moving.

Amaury sat two spots behind the driver in the canvas-covered back holding the twelve men in his group. There were twelve more in the truck behind, with the last truck carrying their supplies. Everyone was sitting quietly while the V-8 diesels roared along causing a virtual sound wall between them and the outside world. Amaury hated the noise of the Kamaz, as it forced the men to become falsely separated from the world with which they needed to be involved.

He looked out of the truck into the distance. The sun that day was very hot. The only breezes he felt were flowing from the movement of the truck. The monotony of the sound and the intolerable heat caused some of the men's minds to wander unfocused. Everyone sweated profusely and couldn't wait until they reached their destination. While the constant noise from the convoy continued to mesmerize, Amaury always tried to keep alert. He concentrated on the tasks ahead for the rest of the day, forcing his mind to stay active and in the present.

Suddenly, he noticed the man sitting in front of him, one of his friends, Jose Juarez, suddenly slump over on the bench. Jose happened to be sitting right behind the driver, who was keeping the truck moving along at a fast clip. The space in-between the Kamaz cab and the men provided an opportunity for a shot to sneak through and hit a target. Amaury stared at Jose, now fully slumped over, and realized he saw blood pouring down his leg onto the wooden floor of the truck. He immediately reached out and put his hand on Jose's shoulder, then yelled, "JOSE! JOSE! JOSE!"

There was no answer. Amaury saw Jose had been shot, the bullet making its way through the one single opening. Jose's body hit the red bloody floor with a very pronounced thud.

With Jose's thick red blood running wildly, Amaury looked to his left and right and saw no one else had noticed. He yelled out as loud as he could that Jose had been hit by gunfire. "Fuck. Jose has been hit! Get alert guys. Guys!"

Amaury immediately got down on his hands and knees on the filthy, muddy floor and quickly crawled back the length of the truck.

Now alerted, everyone instantly moved into defensive positions. The Kamaz had already begun slowing. Amaury was the first out of the back, followed by the others. He jumped over the metal gate chained to the sideboards. With no way to release them at that moment, he hit the ground hard. He landed on his feet and at the same time immediately rolled over into the ditch on the side of the road. Amaury could hear gunshots ringing out and bullets whizzing past, hitting the ground awfully close to him but thankfully none that struck him.

While in his roll, he'd gotten his AK-47 ready to go with his finger on the trigger and instantly realized there was a sniper somewhere in the distance. He leaned his back against the rising wall of the ridge and looked at the positioning of his fellow Commandos. In a flash, he saw the others taking whatever cover they could find.

Because of his advantageous position, Amaury turned and slightly lifted his head to see where the action was coming from. He noticed the roaring of the Kamaz 3s were getting less noticeable as they continued up the road and out of harm's way.

The bullets continued to whizz all around, hitting randomly here and there. Amaury sensed there was more than a single shooter. Just as he looked to make a move, a barrage of bullets came from a distant direction. Hitting in a different pattern, the bullets splattered alarmingly close to his feet. Amaury knew they didn't have a lot of time there before they would either have to move again or do something to quickly change their position. He figured they were being shot at by the SA's, and their unit had happened to roll through an ambush. The terrorists thought they had them cornered and trapped. The SA's loved ambushes. Amaury didn't think—he reacted; his training now deeply seated in his brain. He was ready.

All the training, the preparation, the mental determination in place, his fellow Rangers were also ready. They began shooting their own rebuttals. The bullets flew everywhere, bits of dirt splattering all around and simulating mini earth explosions from the errant shots.

The thought stung Amaury. *We're in a big dirt fishbowl, and I'm about to be picked off any second. Shit!*

Amaury slightly slid up the wall of the ditch, just enough to lift his eyes above the edge of the rim. He quickly looked to where he thought the direction of the gunfire was coming from and saw the sniper was about fifty feet from him. He quickly observed at least one rifle sticking out of the bushes, and it was moving ever so slightly.

"Son of a bitch," he muttered to himself.

For a quick moment, he analyzed the situation and surmised that if he could get a decent shot off on target, he could get this guy. He hunched down again, and just as he got below the ridge, bullets suddenly rang out and hit the top of the edge. A chaotic spray of dirt hit his forehead and helmet with the cracking sound of pebbles breaking on impact and then against his helmet.

One errant pebble fragment flew and cut his face just under his right eye. Although not realizing he had been hit, Amaury felt the intense sting from the wound.

He jumped up and took quick aim, and with one click of the trigger on the AK, he sent a frenzied hail of bullets out of the gun barrel muzzle. In a flash like an intense jolt of lightning, an angry thunderstorm of bullets sprang from his gun. In the distance, the bushes instantly ceased moving. This was followed by another showering hail of gunfire as AK-47s from the rest of the unit followed up aimed at the same location from which the enemy's gunfire was emanating. The firefight went on for some time. They spread the firepower all over the area of the bushes and nearby, directly at the saboteur's nest. The only movement remaining were the branches recoiling from the passing stray bullets.

Amaury rapidly slid down again to take cover as he looked back at his fellow Rangers spread out all over near and behind. They looked at each other, waited a bit, and remained silent for some time. Suddenly, he thought he heard footsteps approaching him, and he quickly crawled away to a spot in the ditch he felt provided more protection. He was able to see the area where the sniper had been silent with no movement. He noticed his knees hurting from the small rocks as they pierced against the fabric of his pants. He also realized he tasted a bit of blood on his lip. He looked over at one of his fellow Commandos and yelled, "Anyone see anything?"

Someone yelled back, "No! Amaury, go up there and see if you can check it out!"

As his fellow Rangers covered him, Amaury slowly crawled up the crumbly ridge, his AK aimed forward. When he got close enough to the bushes, he stood up and saw there was, in fact, a whole group of dead bodies.

In the bloodied mess, he counted ten bodies. However, in

the distance he noticed dirt flying around in the breeze and saw two terrorists chaotically running away as fast as they could. They didn't make very good fighters, but they were sneaky bastards.

He yelled back to his unit. "Motherfuckers are all dead. It's over!"

Amaury suddenly reflected that he'd actually killed someone. Subconsciously, he realized his finger was still pressing on the trigger of his rifle as he lifted it. His finger felt sore from the intense squeezing. He looked at it, then rubbed his hand against his pants. In the haste of the moment, he'd aimed and just pulled the trigger. With his training, plus the threat of death, he'd reacted without thinking, fully immersed in avenging the death of Jose. He'd made sure his unit was protected. The glow of pride swarmed in his mind. Alone, he knew he was finally a successful soldier. A slight smile appeared on his face. The conflict of killing the enemy was not as terrifying as he'd initially thought it would be. At that moment, as he stopped to think about what had happened, it had all taken place so quickly it felt as if it were a dreamlike swiftness—angry, yet flowing. He rubbed the sweat away from his forehead.

The platoon gathered around him, while others walked around the site. They were looking down at the dead bodies, commenting about the suddenness of it all. They realized how lucky they were to be able to have reacted so quickly. As bad as it was, they'd gotten them very fast. Sadly, Jose's dead body was picked up and separately taken back to Unit 2675.

One of the Commandos turned to Amaury and said, "By the way, Tiger, that was a great shot! We'll need to get you fixed up in just a little while. Looks as if you're gonna need a couple of stitches."

Still grinning, blood continued streaking down his cheek.

Chapter 37

Signs of Trouble

Later that night at the new temporary camp, Umberto was quietly talking to Amaury. They were discussing how crazy that entire event had been and how lucky they were not to have lost more men to a stinking bunch of snipers. Umberto spoke softly as he confided in Amaury. The whole process of patrolling and being out all the time on the land exposed to all the dangers they faced daily was getting to him emotionally.

Amaury listened intently as Umberto continued. He explained, "I'm not sure if I can continue over the long term." He quietly revealed, "I feel like I am breaking down, Amaury. It's as if I'm losing my ability to cope. I'm not sure I have the emotional strength necessary to keep up the good fight."

He told Amaury he could no longer handle the continual unknowing, the unending mystery of potential death around every corner. Amaury could tell Umberto was struggling with the mental demands of being at war. It alerted Amaury to the fears he also had, but he was able to process and push aside those feelings rather than allow them to take over.

"Listen, man. Umberto. C'mon. You knew we've all been

trained well for this moment. You and I have made it through the worst training anyone in Cuba could ever have imagined. But here we are. We've made it this far and in good shape, too. You're my best buddy, and you know I'll always be there for you in every way. Umberto, you know you've got this, man. I need to know you're covering my back, and I'll always have your back, too."

Umberto responded, his voice wavering, "I just don't know, Amaury. I am afraid of what's going to happen to me and everyone around me. The constant threat of our friends dying and getting injured is getting to me. What is it for? What about all the people we are killing? There are so many. Why are we doing this?"

Umberto's face turned very red, strained, and sad. He appeared confused. Strangely, after a moment, he told Amaury, "I'm worried I might get badly hurt somehow."

Amaury asked him, "What exactly are you talking about?"

"Well, I don't know. I mean, that's all I think about, Amaury. Ya know, ya just never know when your number is up."

Umberto looked down at his hands and started rubbing them together very tightly, to the point where they started turning red. His face had anxiety written all over it. Amaury saw his friend's hands tightly clasped together uncomfortably.

"Look, take it easy, Umberto. Bro, c'mon. You need to calm down."

Amaury tried to lighten the mood. He figured he would try to change the topic and see if he could get Umberto to think about other things. The first thing that came to mind was food, for some odd reason. They always talked about food, especially out in the field and sometimes before some action took place. They were almost silly as they focused on the danger they were about to face. The topic of food always seemed to lighten the load. Thinking about those moments, Amaury asked, "Umberto, if you could have anything in the world to eat right now, from home, I mean, what would it be?"

Umberto looked quizzically at Amaury for a long moment, his eyes squinting sharply at him. Then he laughed. "I know what you're doin', Amaury! Ha-ha. You're very clever, *muchacho*, aren't you? Okay, fine. I love tamales, and you know that, but yeah, if I could eat anything right now, it would be tamales. And you know, *mi amigo* Amaury, it has to be the old style, too, not that new style crap. The old-style, slow-cook style, ya know, with *mi familia* n' shit. And you knew that, too, you wise guy."

They both looked at each other and bellowed with laughter.

"What about you, Amaury? What would you have right now?"

Amaury thought for a moment and without hesitation said, "Ah, at this very moment, I'd love to have my old favorite *Membrillo's*."

Umberto jumped in. "My goodness, yes! I love those. Oh, and a nice Cuban *pan*, too. Man, I can't believe it's been so long since we've had that."

They both got silent for a moment, and then Amaury thought to himself that he was glad the moment had passed, and that Umberto was able to smile and pass that difficult conversation without any further anguish.

Several weeks passed. Late one evening after a difficult day of ferreting out the SA's hiding places and constantly searching for food or weaponry, they once again retired to the makeshift camp for the evening. They'd eaten, and the few Rangers who were manning the nightshift were posted on the four sides of the camp.

The others were sitting or lying down by their sleeping quarters when Umberto once again brought up his apprehension regarding the patrols. He explained to Amaury that he could no longer take the pressure, and he knew he was finished with the Ranger life. He was ready to leave.

"C'mon, Umberto. We aren't anywhere near leaving yet. You need to cut this shit out, man. You're doing great."

But Umberto persisted, anguished. He told Amaury, "This will be the night I'm leaving for good."

Amaury began thinking about his own time in Angola. Many months had passed, and he'd developed into a well-heeled soldier. He'd seen many battles, killed men, and saw many get killed. The kind of fighting they'd witnessed was ugly and inhumane. It was a wonder if any man, Cuban or otherwise, could walk away from it without some kind of injury—emotionally, physically, or both.

The SA terrorists and the other political groups fighting over land and resources did horrible things to the innocent peoples of Angola. Words couldn't truly describe the human pain the men, women, and children experienced. The children faced the worst treatment of all. Not only were they often left parentless, but then they also faced human trafficking. It was an arduous battle every day.

Amaury always felt the thirst of the SA terrorists, for the killing never seemed to end. He thought it was like trying to stop a waterfall with cups. The Cuban soldiers kept up a good fight and were quite adept and brave fighters. In the end, they won battles, but the conclusion of the fight would take years until all the sides agreed to stop. They fought bravely, but was it a war that could actually be won?

One evening, Amaury said to Umberto, "You know, in war, no one wins. Even if you win, you lose."

Umberto just nodded, understanding Amaury's thoughts. *This entire thing is futile. I just don't know what the hell I'm going to do.*

Chapter 38

A Difficult Way Out

Just a short two months later after a busy day of protecting the Angolan people in the countryside, the unit settled in for the night in hopes they would have a peaceful night to rest their weary bodies.

They had eaten their dinner, and the few Rangers manning the night shifts were posted on the four corners of the camp, while two other guards did foot patrol. The rest of the group were sitting around or lying down in their sleeping quarters. Umberto once again brought up his apprehension of the danger of patrols.

Amaury remembered the last conversation they'd had and thought, *oh, no. Not again. This isn't good.* He felt tremendous compassion for Umberto but wasn't sure what to do for his friend. He continued to listen to him talk about his apprehension and desire to leave.

"I need to find a way out of here," Umberto stated. "I cannot finish my commitment. I've been doin' a lot of thinking about it, Amaury. You're the only one I can talk to."

Amaury didn't notice Umberto concealing his pistol behind

him on the makeshift bed they used each night. Umberto had taken some blankets and pants and rolled them into a pillow he was leaning against with his hand on the gun and his forefinger on the trigger, his helmet at his feet. He spoke to Amaury in a quiet but anxiety-laden voice, and Amaury didn't understand it was an indication of what was about to come.

As Umberto continued talking, Amaury tried hard to hear his whispering. "What if I were to get injured somehow?"

Amaury interrupted him, "What the hell are you talking about, Umberto? Are you crazy, man? Seriously, why don't you just get some sleep, and tomorrow you'll see. Things will be better. Your mind will be clearer. We're going to make it. You know nothing bad is going to happen."

The other members of the unit were sitting around the camp eating and talking. Others were cleaning their guns. Umberto took one last look at Amaury and then looked at his hand and instantaneously took the pistol from around his back. Without any hesitation, he aimed his left hand and pulled the trigger.

The pieces of his bloody hand flew everywhere. Amaury jumped up in total shock and screamed, "Oh my god! Get the medic, quick!" It was a brutal mess. "Call into the base and get the medical team out here immediately!"

Everyone came running over and started helping Umberto, who'd passed out from the shock. They ran to get whatever provisions they could to help him stop the bleeding, but it was done.

One of the Rangers yelled, "Wrap his hand with those towels. Rest his head on these blankets, too. The helicopter has already been called. It won't be here for at least ten more minutes. They happened to be nearby in another situation."

Umberto's skin color became pale, and he looked badly in

shock. What was left of his hand was bleeding profusely but at least it was tightly wrapped. Amaury was sad to realize Umberto had sacrificed part of his left hand, but in his heart and his fading mind, he knew his time in Angola was over.

They rushed to help their injured comrade, and together they brought him to the medics. They said their goodbyes as the helicopter arrived, and Umberto was taken back to base camp.

Amaury took a moment to recover after seeing one of his best friends in the unit sacrifice his own hand. He needed to consider what had happened. Even though they'd been there a substantial amount of time, he realized he didn't know how much longer he was going to be there, and he needed to make sure he was going to survive, as well.

Amaury had doubts about his determination and made sure the rest of his time there was achievable and successful. He rationalized his oath to protect himself and more importantly, his desire to protect his unit.

Being responsible for the lives of his unit meant everything to Amaury, and he knew it was more important than anything else they did.

He took the rest of that evening to calm himself and get mentally prepared to continue the fight for Castro. Many battles lay ahead. He woke up early, everyone piled into the Kamazs, and they left.

A full year later, out of nowhere, orders in the radio blasted the silence. The unit was ordered to return to home base as soon as they could.

Their time in Angola was over. Nearly three years had passed, and it was time to go home. They were told they had to be back in time to catch the scheduled flight back to Cuba in forty-eight hours.

They had approximately one-hundred-fifty miles of rough

terrain to navigate to get back to their home base, which was going to be a challenging task. It was full speed ahead and nonstop, if possible.

They wanted to catch that flight.

Chapter 39

A Happy but Sad Exit

The orders to return to the base for the last time was great news for Amaury, who'd been hoping to hear for a long time that his term in Angola was concluding. Since Umberto had injured himself, he knew the pressures of the constant patrol were getting to everyone.

The South African terrorists were cunning, clever combatants who were cruel and depraved, and every additional day in the field meant another day their lives were at risk. Amaury felt in some ways it was a numbers game, where anyone's name could come up any time—including him.

On his own, he'd also developed into an adept soldier. He owed his successes to his training and experience, as it enabled him to learn the tools and tactics of survival.

The men in the unit were a very close group and decided to make the two-and-a-half-day trip a straight marathon, though they had little choice.

Together, they knew this was going to be another huge challenge among the many challenges they'd faced. They needed to travel quickly through particularly difficult and nasty enemy territories to get back to home base on time. From the moment they reversed course they were counting down the hours and kilometers.

At one point, the driver yelled out loud, "We're almost halfway done, boys!" A cheer could be heard over the chugging roar of the diesels.

Amaury could finally see the light at the end of the tunnel.

They traveled into the vast wilderness of the Angolan desert. They needed to drive through a small village typically characterized by just a few simple structures, each built with long, narrow, thick wooden branches stuck in the ground and held together with a kind of twine. The main street, a dirt road that went directly through the middle of the village, was the hub of activity.

Their Kamaz convoy was six vehicles altogether. As they approached the village, there was another Cuban convoy of Kamazs with a Ranger unit ahead of them. The convoy in front slowed down because of pedestrian traffic. Amaury was seated in the front truck, sitting behind the driver. He watched the activities as they proceeded through the village. He had the one clear spot between himself and the driver. As they drove, everything appeared normal.

Amaury was watching the activity on the street when suddenly a bright flash caught his eye. It seemed to come from several trucks in front of their truck. Out of nowhere, a huge explosion detonated. Everything shook violently. The trucks came to an instant halt. The gigantic blast caused that truck in front to explode into thousands of pieces of hot, angry metal shrapnel which flew in every direction. Shocked at the blast, people began screaming, running haphazardly in utter chaos.

The unit was stunned by the enormous explosion and the amount of debris that flew everywhere. The flying rubble slammed into their truck. Then, only a short moment later, a shower of smoking sharp metal shards started bouncing off the canvas top and all of the Kamazs other surfaces. This was followed by wet thudding sounds; the debris remains of human bodies falling to the ground.

At first, they thought it was an attack and quickly looked to take cover. However, as the pieces were dropping, they noticed there was no further gunfire. No sounds of shooting or any other kind of additional explosions. The only motions were the citizens running, trying to escape and get to safety.

After the initial chaos stopped, the remaining soldiers scrambled out of the Kamaz to assist and help their fallen comrades and the people around them. Amaury saw mayhem and blood everywhere. Disgusted, he surmised there must have been at least twelve to fifteen Rangers in front of them. He conceded a total loss, with body parts everywhere, scattered chaotically about. He realized the explosion had most likely been an IED buried under the dirt road, and the weight of the Kamaz driving over it had triggered the event.

The IED must have been large, as the eruption and damage were massive, obliterating the huge heavy Kamaz. Never had he seen such mayhem in one single explosion. It was a sight he knew he'd never forget. Not only had it annihilated the Kamaz, but it had left an immense hole in the road where the bomb had been hidden.

However, being strong soldiers, his unit helped the living victims to safety. They also swiftly assisted in getting the confusion settled as quickly as possible.

They were on a strict schedule and radioed in the emergency military backup. Emergency medical evacuation immediately assisted. Within a short time, the choppers were heard above, securing the area. Later on, that afternoon, they continued their drive back to the home base.

The drive took an additional twenty hours to complete. It was one of the most difficult drives Amaury had experienced his entire time in Angola as the scene from the IED explosion kept entering his mind. The desire to get back safely in one piece was all he thought about. As he sat in the rumbling Kamaz on the long drive back, he couldn't wipe out the image of the death and destruction he'd seen hours earlier, yet other thoughts took over, as well.

Amaury who was over nineteen years old by this point felt he'd already lived a lifetime of experience. He was very ready to say goodbye to Angola.

The first thing he did when he returned to the base was to get a haircut and shave. He looked like a bear who'd been hibernating in a cave for the past half a dozen months. Normally, he'd cut his hair and beard with his bayonet, as it was quite sharp. However, it never looked neat or trim. He put up with the gruff, unkempt look out of necessity. Getting a shave was a rare luxury he had not experienced for some time. Sitting down and cleaning up for the flight back home signified it was actually happening. On the chair, he concentrated as he watched his hair fall from his face and head. He realized this was only the second haircut he'd had during his entire time in Angola.

He thought about how he had survived the nearly three years there safely and was getting out just in time. He couldn't wait to get on that plane home.

Chapter 40

Home Again

As the Rangers boarded the plane, they each took seats in the rows which were designed back-to-back, while making the other soldiers sit face to face from front to the back of the plane. Amaury was happy he was able to grab a window for his second flight. The opportunity to gaze out the window, see the world below and let his mind wander freely was what he looked forward to the most.

He remembered the previous flight and reminisced fondly about how his thoughts flowed in an unrestricted stream. He liked letting his mind ponder thoughts he ordinarily would not. It seemed to release him from the worldly restraints as he looked at the clouds and stars thirty-five thousand feet above the Earth.

He knew helping the native Angolans was the only activity of valor of duty of which he felt proud and positive during his entire three years. But it barely helped. Witnessing death, or worse, the general fighting, took away from the considerable efforts he'd tried to accomplish in Angola. He was glad to leave it behind. Although he'd made some friends there, he worried about their future.

As the plane flew over the ocean, he looked down, thinking

of how the unit had tried to save people's lives, the necessity of killing some people to save other people's lives, and how nothing seemed to make sense. The fight never stopped. No matter who won or lost, the result was the same. No one won, no one could win, so what was the point of it all?

The strongest test was how each man who was contracted to go to war would survive, both mentally and physically. The question became could they escape with their body and their mental abilities intact?

Amaury had learned to separate himself from the agony and pain of witnessing life in war, to keep push forward, letting go of any emotional connection. He'd chosen to adopt this philosophy in all life's battles. It was an attribute he'd subconsciously developed to survive. It was a way for him to defend his decisions and to rationalize and make himself feel good about what he'd done. Maybe it was a normal response to survival. However, this new quality was something he clung to forever. Running from emotional commitments became part of who he was. The underlying forces of communism had caused Amaury to make many questionable decisions.

As Amaury looked out the window, he saw a brilliant cloud resembling a raccoon. It made him think about how it fought to live every day, even to the point of chewing its own leg off to survive. Umberto had shot his hand to leave the Army. Amaury rubbed his face. The thought of life always being such a demanding challenge was too much to think about right now. He closed his eyes.

The miles ticked by with excruciatingly slowness, yet somehow quickly as the plane flew hundreds of miles per hour over the Atlantic.

Later, the sky was bright and sunny. It seemed as if he could see the beautiful ocean get bluer as they flew closer to Cuba. Maybe it was just his imagination or his impatience playing tricks on him. Whatever it was, the closer they got to Cuba, the more it made him yearn for home. The thought of palm trees, his mom, and being home again was actually going to happen. Some of the fellows sitting opposite him were discussing going back to see their kids, looking forward to finally having a hot shower and washing their clothes to the point that they'd actually be clean. The simple idea of sitting in a beautiful park doing nothing at all other than looking at regular people walking their dogs or enjoying the sun on an uncomplicated calm day was something to which each of them looked forward.

Amaury's feet were in bad condition. He was happy he'd be able to see a real doctor for an examination. He'd suffered from an old soldier malady called trench foot, a toe virus that attacked his toenails and caused them to appear spongy yet brittle. On the battlefield, he was able to use a plant-based powder called *Lisianthus Eustoma*—the Persian violet which caused the feet to stain a purplish-blue on the skin but helped the virus temporarily subside. He'd acquired this condition because he wasn't able to clean and then dry his wet feet frequently enough, causing him to sweat inside the boots. Many of the soldiers had become affected from trench foot, a little gift brought home from Angola.

In the distance, the largest island in the Caribbean appeared through his window. He especially enjoyed the moment when he was finally arriving. A brief announcement was made to the surprise of the passengers that they'd arrive in Nicaragua first for refueling. Cuba was too far for the plane to fly in a single direct flight. A large groan erupted from the soldiers who were awake. When they landed in Nicaragua and were not allowed to exit the plane, it only added to Amaury's impatience to get home. Once again in the air, he finally saw the island of Cuba. He was as happy as he could be as the jet plane hit the runway at half speed and rumbled down the tarmac at Managua International Airport. Unlike his arrival in Angola, the plane landed as soft as a surfer on a beautiful wave.

The two hundred or so Rangers impatiently sat in their seats until they were told to exit the plane. It was a typical glorious sunny morning when they arrived at the Air Force Base. Amaury was so happy to feel the amazing weather in all its beautiful glory. The heat immediately engulfed Amaury as he nearly jumped out of the aircraft. He was so happy to be home.

The men looked up in the gorgeous pastel blue sky and felt thankful that they could finally say, "Wow we made it. We're home. We actually made it." Each of their comrades knew they were the lucky ones to get home alive. For the rest of Cuba, Angola was much like America's Vietnam war. Soldiers were welcomed home, but not as heroes.

One by one, the Rangers exited the plane and walked to the terminal building where the old aromas of beautiful tropical Cuba could be taken in. The sun, breeze, air—everything different from Angola was a stark reminder of their love for home, and it overwhelmed Amaury.

Amaury eagerly looked down the hallway to the terminal exit, and as he walked, he saw a huge crowd waiting, hundreds of eyes searching and straining to see their loved ones first. He kept walking. Suddenly, he saw his mom and his heart almost melted right there and then.

He screamed, "Mom! Mom! Mom!"

He heard her yell back, "Amaury! Amaury!"

He ran over to her. Then he saw Ernesto, his sister, and his grandmother all standing there waiting to give him a huge hug. They all looked so happy, thrilled to see him again after such a long time away. He felt as if he was flying as he ran toward them and enveloped them all in his strong arms. He felt his emotions rising, and he blinked away the beginning of tears. It was so wonderful to be home.

Now back together again, the talking was nonstop, and everyone interrupted each other. They all had millions of questions to ask him about his experiences and what he'd seen, what it was like, how he was treated and all the highs and lows of being in Angola.

He was feeling a bit overwhelmed. Amaury, however, was a very unusual man, and he was somehow able to overcome all the negatives normally a burden to men who'd experienced war. He wasn't depressed and he didn't need significant recuperation time. He was able to mentally let go and leave it behind. Somehow, over the years of his life, the absent father and the rigors of communist life, some people in Cuba had learned to just let go of their feelings. Facing the pain of war and the horrific, mangled life forms, were memories that he mentally chose to forget. For Amaury, he allowed his ego to supersede his emotions. It enabled him to let go when many other soldiers returning needed downtime to get mentally prepared to return to *normal* life. Some never did or had significant problems. Amaury needed no such thing. He immediately returned to being himself back home, a Cuban boy enjoying life again.

Nury made no effort to greet him on arrival, which was a huge blow. Amaury desperately wanted to talk to his father about his experiences. He believed it would have been a great bonding moment, but that would have to wait.

Some things would never change.

Chapter 41

The Cinnamon Girl

At the time of Amaury's return to Cuba, Nury was on official business and on the opposite side of the island. He didn't call, nor was part of the welcoming party for Amaury. He did not attempt to contact him until quite sometime later. While his father's absence was very disappointing, Amaury had already learned to accept his father's distance and lack of closeness and chose to let it go and move on. He was growing up. Despite his young age, Amaury felt he had already lived a lifetime. Once he returned from the agonizing theatre of war, he realized his life was his to guide the way he wanted. No longer just the son of a general, he'd faced tragedy and risk just like his father had. As a result, he knew he had become a man.

The opportunity to be back home with nothing to do, no agenda, no responsibilities of any kind, and only to relax and enjoy himself was the only goal. His only thought was leaving his time in Angola behind him.

Amaury was required to check-in at the Army base at The National Assembly ten blocks from his house once a week to appraise them of his health, status, and location, so he couldn't truly escape. He was still in the Army and had not been released. His participation continued until further notice or until such time that his services were no longer needed, which required an official release notification.

His new schedule included getting up when he wanted to and going to the local corner Bodega where all the bros from the neighborhood hung out. They spent the time talking, kidding around with each other, and bothering familiar customers when they walked in. Everyone knew each other and it was meant to be good fun. At the Bodega were some of his old friends—Coro and his son Anton, another local he knew from the Malecon when he used to fish.

During an afternoon not long after he arrived, Amaury got his usual *Guanabana Batidos*, a popular Cuban milkshake with fruit. The main event for the day was to reminisce with his buddies about their youth. They remembered how they used to sabotage the other kids' kites, and in general about how they caused trouble in the neighborhood. They remembered the fun street parties, and in those moments, he felt free and happy. He teased an old friend, Chepe, about how he never caught any fish.

"You know Chepe, I used to put the worms on your line to give you luck, but even that didn't help." Amaury chuckled.

Chepe retorted, "Ahh, c'mon now, Amaury. You think you're a big shot army guy, but you know what? I always caught more fish than you. Johan will confirm that when he gets here later. You'll see."

Amaury just rolled his eyes and they all laughed.

While sitting in a broken chair and reading the local paper Amaury, watched people walking in the store. He noticed a brown-haired girl enter. She was of medium height and thin with light brown skin. She had a very shapely figure. She was the kind of girl to whom he felt immediately attracted.

I swear she's like a cinnamon-haired girl, he thought to

himself. *A Cinnamon Girl*! He felt compelled to talk to her, but he couldn't find the words, and so instead he continued watching.

She looks like air like she's flowing.

She circled the store, looking at items. Her shorts were provocatively too short, which made her legs appear as though they went on forever. Amaury was completely mesmerized with her as he sipped his *Batidos*.

In the background, his friends kept shouting, "Amaury, Amaury, hola, hola, Amaury?" They started laughing when he finally glanced at them with a blank expression, as though he were somewhere else. "Earth to Amaury!" They continued laughing.

Slightly embarrassed, Amaury suddenly realized he was staring at the *Cinnamon Girl* but didn't want to admit it to his friends. He tried to make it seem as though he was concentrating on his paper.

"What? What's the matter with you, guys? I'm just thinking."

Chepe spoke first, "It's okay, Amaury. We know you're concentrating. The only question is—on what?"

Amaury was in great physical condition, probably the best he had ever been. He'd started to work out daily with weights and it showed. He was proud of his condition, and it made him happy to think he was attractive to women in that way.

Later that afternoon, he was lifting weights at his brother's home when there was a knock at the door. Ernesto answered it. Amaury didn't pay much attention to the conversation between his brother and the guest but continued concentrating on the set he was lifting. He was soaked from the exercise and heat. His brother's apartment didn't have air conditioning, and the sweat ran everywhere. The apartment felt like a sauna set on high.

While he was counting reps, he felt someone's gaze on him

and turned his head to see the Cinnamon Girl standing in front of him, leaning against the door frame.

Amaury was astonished. She was just standing there silently analytically staring at him.

"Who is this?" she asked Ernesto, "Who is this *muy guapo niño* lifting weights in your house, Ernesto?"

"That is my brother Amaury. Amaury, meet Adriana."

"Nice to meet you, Amaury," she said. "How much can you lift?"

Amaury puffed up his chest. "Well, more than a few kilos, I suppose. Nice to meet you, too."

He put the weights down and they started excitedly talking. He then closed the door of his brother's weight room.

"What are you doing here? You know I saw you earlier this afternoon at the corner store," Amaury asked. He was trying hard to hold back his intense feelings of attraction and play it cool.

Cinnamon Girl looked at him. "I have known Ernesto for a while. We're friends. But no, I don't recall seeing you at the store. Where were you when you saw me?"

"You were walking around the store like a floating *Chamaca*, and you knew exactly what you were doing."

"Papi, you don't know what you are talking about. You're just a silly *chico*, you know you really are. I don't float around; I walk like any regular girl—normal. And why didn't you say something to me then?"

"I'm not sure, but you looked as if you were concentrating. And, well, why don't you float over here right now?"

She slid smoothly over to Amaury on the other side of the bench, stopping with one knee resting on the padding, her arms by her sides, and her foot hanging over the edge. They both took a moment, looking deeply into each other's eyes.

In his mind he kept thinking, *The moment is here. This is it. I'm supposed to do something smooth and cool.*

"*Oh my god!*" As he turned, he tried to step over the weights, but his foot caught on the bar, and he fell forward face-first onto the floor.

The Cinnamon Girl burst out in laughter while Ernesto flew into the room. "What the hell happened?"

"El pobre chico is learning to become suave and sophisticated." She giggled as they both helped pick up the embarrassed Mr. Amaury Torres.

Chapter 42

At the Beach

Later that week, Amaury walked to the National Assembly office for his required check-in. He needed to maintain continuity and went directly to the front desk of the small recruiting office on the corner of the block.

The sergeant in front already knew Amaury.

"So, are we ready to go?" Amaury asked.

"Not yet," the sergeant replied. "By the way, you need to finish the paperwork for this next period. Here, fill out those forms, and we will be in good shape with the required documents."

After Amaury handed the papers back to the sergeant, he said, "Two more years and that's it. Then I'm finished with war and the military forever."

"Are you sure, commander? Usually, men sign on for life or at least a ten-year stint. Why don't you try to make it another five?"

"Oh, no way. Are you kidding? Not me. Nope, I am doing two more and that's it. Thank you just the same."

"Oh, by the way—how's your health? Anything to report?"

"Can't ya tell by my tan? Healthy as an ox. See ya next time, Sarge."

"It's sergeant to you!"

Grinning, Amaury turned around and walked right back to the beach.

It was a busy week for Amaury with several events shaping his time at home.

Nury got a break from his official duties out of town and visited Amaury. However, it was a short meeting with an uncomfortably brief conversation.

"How was your time in Angola? Sorry I wasn't able to make it back to see you at the airport. But I was glad to hear you arrived back home in one piece. I understand you've learned to accept your duties as a soldier? Because I was informed you made it into the Rangers division. That's a big step."

"It was fine, Papa, and yes I did, thank you. Yes, I've learned to become a good soldier. I did well. It was a difficult time. However, I got through it in one piece without issues, which is a lot more than I can say about other people. But I'm very happy to be home and healthy."

"I was glad to hear you performed well and made it home safely, without problems. What's your next step?"

"I'm not sure. I have been required to stay close to the local Assembly office. I've heard there may be a new assignment coming." Amaury informed Nury.

"Without saying too much, yes there's quite a bit happening, as I'm sure you can imagine. Learning about it soon is certainly possible," Nury said.

Amaury found it curious his father was as forthcoming as he was, but he didn't ask any more questions. He knew his father would never say anything, anyway.

Amaury was neither happy nor unhappy to see his father. There was so much Amaury wanted to say, but he kept his thoughts repressed. He wouldn't take the risk of revealing his inner thoughts to his father. Outwardly, they didn't have a lot to say to each other. The curt conversation ended quickly. After a few minutes, they shook hands and then left the house.

Later, Amaury started to think it had been a strange meeting. He thought his father would be proud of him and show some greater appreciation for his joining the Army and achieving success as a soldier, but it never came. He didn't see his father again for a long time.

Feeling disappointed as he left the house, he made his way to the beach, coincidentally running into his old friend Umberto, who was working nearby at the tourism board for the government. They were so happy to see each other and hugged.

"Amaury! Amaury! I can't believe it. I knew I'd eventually run into you. How've you been? I've missed you so much. It's been at least a year or more since we last saw each other."

"Umberto! Holy shit, it's great to see you. I haven't stopped thinking about you. My goodness. How've you been? What's happened to you? I felt terrible about not being able to help you more back then. I just didn't know what to do. But I've been so worried about you. You're better now?"

"Of course. I know, Amaury. I'm mortified about what happened. I should never have imposed my feelings on you. But I swear I didn't know what to do. I had such horrible thoughts. I felt hopeless and had such intense anxiety about Angola I didn't know how to cope with it. I was completely lost. Look, I must apologize that I did that in front of you. That was very bad of me. It was my problem, no—"

Amaury interrupted. "It's okay, Umberto. You're my brother. I understand and believe me, I had my doubts there, too. How's your hand?"

"Eh, well, as you can see, my hand is almost no longer, but believe it or not, they did quite a bit of surgery, and it seems I still can use my thumb and the two other fingers, so it could be a lot worse. Thank God I'm alive, and so are you. That's what's important."

They gave each other another hug. As they walked, Amaury and Umberto reminisced about those long ago, far away childhood years and laughed out loud as they continued, ending up in a local hangout, where they got a few mojitos to enjoy.

Amaury offered, "Listen Umberto. Let's get together this weekend and hang out at the beach. We'll bring girls, okay?"

"Yes, that's a great idea."

The afternoon went by quickly, and before closing time, they both went home. However, they agreed to meet the next day to enjoy the beach.

Amaury, who was becoming quite the ladies' man during his time off, got to the beach earlier than Umberto with one of the many girls with whom he was hanging out. About an hour later, Amaury was lying on his stomach when he saw Umberto approach with a female friend. Amaury watched as the two walked toward them and noticed his friend was taller than Umberto, which was intriguing, as he and Umberto were about the same height. Amaury couldn't believe how beautiful she was. Her name was Lonna. He liked that she was taller. As a natural gut reaction, he felt challenged and was excited.

She was very thin and darker-skinned than he was, although her hair was lighter with blonde streaks mixed with beautiful light brown highlights. Amaury was taken by her smooth gait, which was undulating fluidly as though she was water flowing on her own. She had a beautiful smile framed by her bright white teeth. She smiled at Amaury. He knew he wanted to kiss her. The entire period after having left Angola had been punctuated by his overwhelmingly strong desire to live life to its fullest, with no responsibilities, no attachments, or encumbrances by responsibility to protect people from anything. He was allowed to feel free for the first time in a long time.

For a few moments, he was able to forget about the former enormous stresses of life and death on the war stage, now only being entirely interrupted by the smooth skin of a woman who singularly captured his imagination. He watched Lonna glide over to the blanket where they were lying and take a spot near Amaury. He couldn't help but notice how amazing she looked in her bikini. Quietly, he admired her and realized he was immediately profoundly attracted to her. Remembering how silly he felt tripping and falling just a few days before, Amaury realized he had to stay calm and collected before he started trying to make moves on Lonna.

Amaury tried to make conversation with Lonna as she relaxed next to him. He chatted about life in general and how much he was enjoying being back home, as well as his time in Angola and the potential of going to Nicaragua. Most of the conversation was about what else they would do for entertainment in the afternoon. His mind wandered again.

He nearly ignored the girl who accompanied him to the beach, but she didn't seem to mind his momentary preoccupation with Lonna. Although she was friends with Amaury, she knew his time home from Angola was about letting go and freedom away from what was. She also liked to carry her own style and independence. She knew it would be difficult to expect him to feel obligated to anyone at this time.

Amaury felt as though the air of opportunity was thick with excitement, and it showed. Lonna listened to Amaury, and Umberto talk to the girls about fishing, and then it was decided a little later on they'd go over to the Malecon to fish rather than stay at the beach all afternoon.

Umberto and Amaury got up together, put on their well-worn Cuban leather slider sandals, and walked to the Malecon with fishing rods and a small bucket of bait in hand.

Amaury's feet were covered in sand, and he said to Umberto, "Listen, my brother. You know your friend Lonna is really nice. I like her a lot, and you know we have known each other for a long time. I want to be honest with you I'd like to hang out with your friend for a night, like for a date. Maybe tomorrow night."

Umberto wasn't shocked about Amaury's request at all. In fact, he expected it.

"I had a feeling you were going to ask me about her. You know, what the funny thing is, I think she already likes you, too. I could tell by how she was very quiet and was sneaking glances at you. You've become quite the ladies' man, haven't you? Well, I guess it's not a big deal. She's a friend, but not my actual girlfriend. I'll talk to her for you, but I'm sure it's pretty much gonna be okay with her. It's not like I have any say in it, but I'll see what I can do. I kind of owe you, anyway."

"No, man. You don't owe me anything, but if you'd put in a good word, that would be great."

Umberto smiled, and they both chuckled.

In some strange, unexpected way, Amaury felt at that very moment he was changing, maybe becoming more western. The odd move of asking another man to meet his woman and being completely open-minded regarding this unusual potential request from his best friend was an expression of a shift to a new life, a new philosophical vault across the mystical ocean to a place where he'd never before been but where his heart seemed to reside. He wasn't sure, but it seemed an odd moment of self-realization for Amaury. He even surprised himself.

"Amaury? Amaury? Hello?" Umberto said.

Amaury looked at Umberto and said, "Huh? Did you say something?"

"Yes, I was talking to you. You looked like you were dreaming. What gives with you?"

Amaury just looked at Umberto. "Yes, yes. I'm sorry. I just was thinking about something."

"Anything you want to share?"

"No. It was just a strange thought I had. Hey, you know what? Let's go back to the beach. Screw this fishing. Let's go talk to the girls. They're a lot more fun, anyway."

"Oh my god, you are so right. What were we thinking? By the way, I'll get that done for you."

Amaury smiled, knowing his friend was the kind of brother he had always hoped for.

"This is why I love you because we can talk about everything and just be who we want to be with each other without prejudice or criticism. We're like real brothers."

Chapter 43

Time For Another Change

Both couples spent the next day together at a local bungalow near the beach, where they also spent the evening, Umberto with Amaury's friend and Lonna with Amaury. It was a humid evening, with rain falling on the bungalow roof all night.

The couples were up long into the night enjoying each other's company. The next morning after they woke up, they laughed together, wearing only their sweaters and smiles. Amaury thought to himself that it was one of the best nights of his life he'd ever had in Cuba.

The weekly requirement had once again arrived, and Amaury made his way over to the National Assembly to do his weekly check-in. The sergeant at the desk spoke first as he immediately recognized Amaury.

"Buenos días, Ranger Torres. ¿Cómo estás?"

"Great!"

"How have you been this week? You didn't get into any trouble, did you?" he asked with a wink.

"No sir, but you know, maybe just a little bit."

"You know, Commando Torres, things are changing again

around here, and you'll need to stay close by at least for the next week or two."

As Amaury listened, he looked around the recruiting office walls. He couldn't help but notice the huge cartoon-styled picture of President Fidel Castro in an old-fashioned dark brown broken wooden frame. It was splintered on the corner—perhaps it had fallen on the floor.

The profile showed Castro with a full brown beard wearing a green army jacket and a green military hat with the Cuban flag behind him. Amaury hated seeing Castro on posters. It reminded him of his youth and the entire communist style of government. He felt it to be a fraud. People's lives were under the control of an entity that didn't allow for anything other than what was declared by the leaders. It disgusted him.

He looked over at the sergeant. "Yes, of course, sir. I'm not going anywhere, and I'll check in next week as usual."

"No, commander. You'll need to check in a few days. Make it two days. Oh, and by the way, how's your health?"

Amaury shrugged, turned, and left the recruiting office, wondering what that was all about. H*e sure was acting strange.* For a fleeting moment, he realized all the fun in the sun very well might be over, and his life would quickly turn real once again. He knew that Cuban forces had been in Nicaragua for many years providing similar support to the people and government as they did in Angola. He guessed his participation would most likely be required soon.

Chapter 44

Nicaragua

In Nicaragua, the Castro family saw another opportunity to spread communism regionally. Being a protector and enabler for foreign nations was too compelling to refuse. Cuba had positioned itself in Nicaragua years before by training and giving support to the Democratic Socialist Sandinista who believed in a Marxist-based government. They were countered by the USA/CIA-backed Somoza's dictatorship, pitting Cuba itself squarely against America a second time but more importantly in the same hemisphere.

The Sandinistas governed from 1979 to 1990 and inherited a country severely in debt and near-total ruin from the battle against the former Samosa government. The Cubans were involved with the Sandinistas early in 1967, where they trained and helped rebel revolutionary groups through their intelligence division, the *GID,* or the *General Intelligence Directorate*. Once the Sandinistas took over in 1979, the Cuban government quickly involved itself with the new Sandinista government.

This was a double-edged sword, as any country helping another country against the approval of America found itself at odds with the USA and CIA. On the other side of the argument, the USA's policy saw the influence of communism on the small nations in South America to potentially become mini-Cubas. Eventually, America tried to invoke policies to help countries in South America to steer clear of potentially negative influences. The USA was most strategically concerned with Nicaragua because of its location near Panama and the canal and would never allow Cuba to gain control.

Cuban soldiers who traveled to Nicaragua stepped into a theatre of war where the only value they reconciled in fighting was preventing the country's population from annihilation and slavery inside their own country by actively producing drug cartels. The drug cartels' usurping of the native farms were converted to poppy growing fields for the illegal production and sale of narcotics. The Cuban soldiers desired to return the country to its people and to restore its original rich history and heritage.

The Cuban Military assisted in the fight against the USA and Contras (the remaining anti-government forces), which played out in the countryside from 1981 on. This rebel militia got their name for contra-revolutionaries or *contrarevolutuinarios*. The Contras attacked schools, health centers, and the rural population anywhere they could damage the Sandinista government's standing. Once again, the battle for control played out on the population and was used as a tool of terror.

The Contras terrorized the country in any violent way achievable by raping women, destroying property, torture—anything to destabilize the government. The Contras, however, were a divided militant group, each with their own independent goals preventing them from becoming a more cohesive unit strong enough to defeat the Sandinistas.

With all the effort and energy put into the fight for power, in the end, the Sandinista didn't lose their power to the Contras. In an odd twist of fate, the Sandinistas stunningly lost their control a few years later in an internationally forced and monitored election completed in 1990, when they were voted out.

In the end, Cuba, after decades of covert and communist influences, did not turn Nicaragua into another friend of communism. This part of history was yet to unfold as Amaury with his Ranger Comrades were about to be a part of the fight yet to come.

Amaury was officially ordered to be in uniform and deployed to Nicaragua seventy-two hours after receiving his orders. As a child, Amaury knew Cuba had been involved in the Nicaraguans' fight for many years, and going to Nicaragua was a very real possibility for his continued military activities.

Upon his weekly check-in, the sergeant looked at Amaury and delivered the news.

"Nice to see you, Commander Torres," he said. "I'm happy you've arrived right on schedule. The time has come, and you have been reassigned to continue your budding career overseas again. You're headed to Nicaragua. I'm sure you are surprised."

"Of course, I'm not surprised. I think someone would have had to live in a closet for the past ten years if that were the case."

"Always with humor, Commander. Well, you have about seventy-two hours before you must meet at *de Missiones Internationalists*. The International Mission will be presented to the Commandos. The mission briefing detailing our involvement will be explained to you then. Just be ready, and we will see you soon."

"Okay. Thank you, sergeant. I guess I won't be seeing you anytime soon, so you take care."

Amaury appeared three days later at the *Unidad Militar Es de Tropas Terestre*, the military base of the Army at the Havana International Airport where the Army had its own facility adjacent to the main runway. At the base, men were given equipment, boots, armament, helmets, and any items needed for their participation overseas, including the very important newly-developed and required anti-snake venom kit.

The entire group of men, dozens of them, jumped into the many Kamaz 3s waiting for the trip to the airport taking them to their destination. Once at Havana International, it didn't take long before the men were in the air and well on their way to Nicaragua.

The flight arrived later the same day in the afternoon at the Nicaragua Managua International Airport. In one single day, Commander Amaury Torres found himself in the middle of another war. On the relatively short plane ride to Nicaragua, once again, Amaury had time to reflect on life. The old feelings of a war quickly conflict returned. He knew he was being thrown into a second battle where he had no loyalty other than to the orders given to him. It was a strange life to live. Thinking back on his Angola days, he reviewed his experiences once again. He knew Nicaragua was an entirely different scenario, but war is the same no matter where it was.

Those familiar fears crept into his mind again. He hated how that felt but knew it was normal, yet tried hard and forced himself to push it all away. It didn't work. He continued to stare out the plane window, truly appreciating the window seat.

While concentrating what was going to happen, he knew he would be required to follow through and perform all given orders. *This time it just feels so mechanical.* He had no desire to accomplish anything other than what he was told to do. This new battle was going to be different from the last, as these combatants were killers who only cared about money. Castro was once again sending troops into the theatre to force his brand of communism on another continent.

At the initial strategy meeting, they were given orders to patrol specified areas near the airport, how to patrol, and ultimately more details of their purpose there and the military's expectations for their mission. At the briefing, Amaury learned Cuba's goals in Nicaragua. As a professional military organization, it had an obligation to assist and serve other counties in need of their help.

After they took their seats in the newly created troop assembly room,

Sergeant Major Nestor Martez addressed the troops. "In today's meeting, you'll fully understand why we are here, what our jobs are, and our goals regarding helping Nicaragua overcome the challenges they currently face. We will be divided into groups. Once you get your assignments, you'll get further instruction on your specific duties. On this whiteboard here, you'll see how all of you will be disbursed in the field zones. Please make note of the jungle areas, which will be part of all investigations. Everyone will spend equal time in the jungle, no exceptions."

Everyone looked at each other, knowing they were going into dangerous territory shortly.

"Further, essentially the official proclamation of our military is cooperating and assisting with the construction of hospitals, clinics, schools and seeking and stopping international drug dealers. We will assist the population to feed and protect itself, to survive and generally help the country to defend itself and reestablish its former self-rule."

The Sergeant Major continued. "Lastly, you will be briefed on the snake venom kit shortly. This is one you will want to pay attention to, as there are many dangerous snakes in the jungles. Please make sure to carry the kit with you at all times. Be aware when moving around. This is for real, Commanders. Make no mistakes about it, please."

Nicaragua was a country deep with thick jungles, and the kit was necessary, as many dangers lurked and presented significant varieties of problems.

Castro's true motivation for Cuba in Central America was to establish an influential foothold in the Southern hemisphere. This goal was purposely hidden from the soldiers sent in to fight. The Commandos were informed only of the players involved, aspirations of their presence in Nicaragua, the goals of achievement, and intentions of how they were going to proceed. These limited organizational goals were all they were given. Additionally, the cartels' drug trafficking activities were used to create governmental instability the Cubans intended to end.

Nestor made sure all the Commanders were fully aware of what was expected of them.

"All Commanders will be assigned to look for specific individuals for arrest and or killing depending on the circumstances. Once these orders are given, it will be up to you to discover ways of finding these people or groups. If anyone is apprehended, your only duty is to return them to the Nicaraguan police. We will be working with them daily on most situations. More on that later. The several Generals who are stationed in Nicaragua to guide our effort are General Ignacio Gutierrez, General Estavio Vizcaya, and General Alfredo Mora. General Nury Torres will unfortunately not be assigned on this mission. His participation is required elsewhere in this time of need for Cuba's international relations. We will miss him, however. Further, these great men will be leading you on the Nicaraguan front. You will be taking orders from the command, but know they are the ones designing our overall effort here."

As he continued, another Ranger turned around to whisper to Amaury, "Amaury, isn't that your father?"

"Yes, it is, I'm as surprised as you are. I had no idea."

"I had no idea your father was a general."

"Well, that's a story for another day."

Some of his fellow soldiers turned around to look at Amaury, who couldn't believe they'd just learned his father was a general. He was as surprised as the others, but it went no further, and he continued to listen to the rest of the meeting.

Amaury believed their presence in Nicaragua was a guard policing action and a reconstruction project with the emphasis on helping rather than an all-out war. No matter how it was perceived, though, their presence in Nicaragua was fraught with danger and death always around the corner. The drug cartels were brutal and didn't care about how they were seen worldwide despite their illegal activities.

Chapter 45

Stake Out

The Nicaraguan people, especially the farmers, were useful tools in an operation to serve drug cartels' needs to do drug manufacturing, sales, and their distribution business. It didn't matter to the cartels' native Nicaraguan families who had lived and worked their land for hundreds of years prior. The natives, who were barely scraping out a living, had to face farming slavery or death in their own homes, which in the drug manufacturing process had stolen from them.

They became the drug lord's slaves in their own country. Either cooperating or dying were their only options. The cartels were ruthless in their pursuit and had only one goal—money.

Amaury, who was only nineteen-years-old, resigned himself again to be disciplined, sharp, and alert in order to survive another dangerous mission. He dug deep into his mind to maintain his same philosophy in survival as he had employed before. The unit was to be prioritized over anyone else if his or their lives were endangered. He never forgot this principle, knowing this would only be two more years, which was his agreed time on his final mission.

Nicaragua posed a different kind of threat than Angola. The patrols were largely out in the open with an enemy who was sneaky, determined, and cunning, however sloppy. The ruthless enemy used the jungles for cover, and night patrols were precarious. The thick forestation provided unusual visual protection and often became impossible to negotiate. The jungles also contained many other dangers. Animals, snakes, strange jungle creatures, bizarre insects, and other unforeseen hidden vulnerabilities all had to be factored into the equation. New unexposed, unknown illnesses were often more difficult to manage than bullets and were quite dangerous and prevalent.

Initially, the soldier's tasks were guarding new infrastructure construction of schools, hospitals, and roads. Their most challenging times on duty were at night when the anti-government forces and drug cartels would carry out their many illicit activities. It became an extremely frustrating regular cycle of building and rebuilding.

To halt the interference, the Cuban Command Military sent troops on police action to take down or arrest pockets of drug cartels or rebels hidden in the jungles. As part of an offensive unit of five hundred soldiers, Amaury was sent in a single sweep operation and attempted to locate the suspected enemies.

First, they searched for mines and booby traps and then camouflaged IEDs. If the assignment was scheduled for an open poppy or marijuana field, it would be immediately chopped down with machetes or burnt with gasoline until it was a leveled black field. Often the military was called in to simply blow up the drug plant fields.

Amaury's main function given the assignment was to perform radio communications, where he was responsible for the thirty people in the unit. In a patrol of one hundred soldiers, there were four communications commandos, and often

Amaury was required to make his own decisions for air, ground, or sniper support and report back to the Cuban rear official command.

When a command base was set up for a patrol, he'd send in snipers to begin the process of clearing for patrolling. They were called the *eyes* of the unit. The *eyes* would go in to begin the process of establishing the rules for the engagement of the target.

The *eyes* would be set up on a rooftop of a building, near the top of a canyon or at the tops of tall trees, if necessary. They could set up a defense with an anti-grenade unit. Amaury could coordinate ground forces or air forces to establish safety for his troops. He enjoyed having this authority, and in a sense, it was an honor bestowed upon him. He felt a sense of accomplishment with these new responsibilities.

Several months into the tour, they were given instructions to patrol and do a secret reconnaissance mission in a very thick part of the jungle a significant distance from the Managua main base. Amaury's unit was required to observe a drug cartel group's activity deep in the jungle. Often the jungle foliage was so thick they never saw the sunset as the trees obstructed their view of the horizon. This made their maneuvers difficult.

The sun's light caused huge dark shadows in some places, contrasting with severely bright blinding shafts of light in other spots. It was extremely challenging for their eyes to constantly adjust and then readjust to the differences. Amaury's unit felt the shadows toyed with their minds as sometimes things weren't as they seemed, while at other times they were exactly as they looked. Moving in late afternoons was a slow process with each step taken with care. The ones in front signaled instructions to the rear of the group as the machetes continued chopping.

On patrol one afternoon, they discovered the whereabouts

of a hidden jungle runway that the drug cartel used to fly drugs out of Nicaragua for their distribution. This was an important find by Amaury's unit, as the Cartels maintained it as one of their main distribution points.

"This is *Operación Uno*. Main base check, come in."

"Go ahead, *Uno*,"

"We have uncovered a private runway, not on the map. Will send coordinates momentarily via the closed radio. Please confirm after. Will await further instructions, over."

"Okay, *Uno*. Will confirm shortly."

A moment later a voice came back over the radio. "Uno? Come in, Uno?"

"Yes, this is *Uno*, go ahead."

"*Please* do a further investigation and report back with details ASAP."

The Cartels used small airplanes which could fly low, appearing invisible to radar, light on sound, and easy to land on short runways with moveable temporary lights. The military knew of a runway but not its location. They also discovered there were several flights daily from the airport, and it was decided the Rangers were going to infiltrate and then destroy the runway and put an end to the flights once they established a foothold near it and could coordinate the attack. This would be a huge coup if they were able to accomplish shutting down this part of their operation.

"Hello, *Uno*. Based on the investigation of this site, we are setting up the observation plans. Will be sent to you via closed radio. Name changed to Cartel flight V*uelo del Cartel* from this point on. Over."

"You've got it. Main base, out."

The military wanted to send a message to the drug lords that they knew where they were and that they were ready to take them down. Amaury's unit, which had been downsized for this part of the initial surveillance, was required to establish a remote temporary camp to do nothing more than observe and note the activities surrounding the runway and the activities taking place at the location, including the airfield rebel barracks. It was going to be nothing more than a surveillance and reconnaissance observation camp but was an important first step in their planning of the mission's final goal.

The initial mission was seven days of continuous communication back to the rear Military High Command detailing their observations. On the fifth evening, the interior command instructed Amaury to move the unit to a new location to get closer but to make sure not to be seen.

"Come in, *Vuelo*?"

"*Vuelo* here. Go ahead."

"Listen, we want you to be very careful. Don't be seen. Make sure to stay hidden. Keep moving if you have to. Go further back. Just make sure you can observe but remain invisible. That's the priority. Over."

"Okay. Confirmed, sir. Will do. Ten-four."

They were taught not to stay in one spot for any length of time. Moving provided safety and the ability to be fully aware of their surroundings.

It had been a full day of communicating with the rear command and watching the drug cartels' activities when they pulled up camp to move again. They saw loading and unloading of planes taking off, landing, and setting up.

Shortly afterward, they received instructions to immediately move again to that new location, where a new unit would relieve them several days later.

Chopping through the thickness with their machetes, the jungle foliage roots, branches, small trees, vines, and horribly ugly flying insects slowed their process. They trudged and slogged through the dark, unforgiving mud, and Amaury felt as though they were wearing cement shoes. The mud was so dense that it caused their thighs to feel as if they were on fire, aching from the constant lifting. The mud seemed to grow thicker and heavier with every step.

The unit finally found a location perfectly situated near the middle of the runway. Smaller, heavily armed militias were set up in small low-lying bunkers along either side of the runway, yet were far enough away from their location. The smaller unit chose the new temporary camp at a new spot as it gave them a great vantage point but with cover.

Amaury, who was very tired from the day's activities, knew he was running low on reserve energy as they began to set up. It occurred to Amaury they needed to move back only about thirty feet from a nearby shallow creek. He felt being near the water could be a disadvantage, and to move only a few feet up the ridge to higher ground would make a lot more sense.

As they picked up their packs, gear, and equipment, Amaury reached down to his right near the ground to grab his pack when he saw something. It was fast and direct. Confused, he thought it seemed like an arrow moving in his direction.

In a split second of confusion, he watched as it headed directly toward him. The thrust happened so spontaneously he did not understand what it was as his body motion continued downward to reach for the bag. Suddenly, he felt a tremendous pain on his left side by his hip. Shocked and panicked, he instantly looked over to his right, yelling to his co-commandos as he realized he'd just been attacked and bitten by a snake.

He simply couldn't believe it. Amaury screamed in pain as the unit came running to his aid. He fell to the ground, grasping his side. The pain was excruciating and quickly moved up his body. He immediately realized it was very bad. He tried to stay strong and lucid and not lose his composure or consciousness and to help instruct his buddies, but it was a fierce struggle.

"Get the kit," he screamed. "FUCK, FUCK, FUCK! I've been bitten by a snake! Shit. Hurry! Quickly! Holy Fuck!"

His words in his mind became confused, and he felt his body go slack.

Chapter 46

Snake Bites

One of Amaury's comrades, Javier Silva was immediately at his side and quickly began giving Amaury firm instructions.

"Okay, Amaury, take it easy. We've got this. You're gonna be okay. Hang on. Keep looking in my eyes. I'm with you. You'll be okay. Amaury? Do you hear me? Blink if you can. Stay with me. Look at me, Amaury. LOOK AT ME, AMAURY!"

Amaury mumbled, almost unconscious.

Silva spoke louder. "Amaury, stay with me. Look at me. You must stay awake!"

Amaury's mind was racing, and he struggled to formulate thoughts and find words. His mouth wasn't working. His breath was panicked, and his eyes were wide open in fear, staring up. Javier already knew what to do. Everyone was trained in snake antidotes and carried their supplies with them. They were well within reach.

"Don't close your eyes. Blink! Blink!" Javier yelled.

"Oh my god, this hurts!" Amaury kept thinking about what Silva had said to him. He was desperately trying to resolve his commands and follow what he was told to do. He realized it was nearly impossible to control what was happening. He struggled with breathing while his thoughts became intermittently mixed with anger and shock. As he looked up, he saw shadows of light and dark intermingling in a strange menage of confusion. The only sound he heard crept up on him from inside his head. It was a high-pitched whistling tone of frozen panic.

The others managed to quickly corral the snake, which seemed confused itself and tried to slither quickly away. There were enough commandos to keenly observe its direction and hurriedly shoot it. They were completely taken aback when they realized this was not just an ordinary venomous snake but was, in fact, a cobra. The cobra was one of the most dangerous snakes in the entire world, especially in the Nicaraguan jungle.

Amaury had been bitten by this cobra, which was easily eight feet long and angrier than a raging bull in the run of Pamplona. The commandos, all expert shots, quickly neutralized the snake whose body continued to fight to escape, wriggling with remaining life until they were able to cut off its head. The Rangers knew if they didn't cut off the head of the snake it still could bite for as long an hour after dying by simple reflective impulse, the venom still present. The head was easily eight inches wide with eyes that looked as angry dead as when it was alive.

"Amaury, I can see your eyes open, but I'm not sure if you can hear me or not. I'm going to inject you now with the anti-venom, and it ought to go to work quickly. We've already radioed headquarters, and we need to move you immediately. Hang in there, Amaury. Stay with me."

Amaury could only stare at the soldier's mouth, not moving. As much as they'd prepared for this situation, it was still an intense moment of stress. Amaury fully felt the venom coursing through his body, slowly moving into his lower torso. He knew this was bad. The venom had a strange sensation as it flowed through him. At first, its effects were a numbing sensation, but he knew eventually he'd feel paralysis. Luckily, he'd been attacked on a fleshy spot on his hip. It would take longer for the venom to move up to his diaphragm and affect his breathing.

The boys in the unit moved quickly to his aid, and more importantly, their swiftness and skill managed to help Amaury immensely. He was able to fight the effects of the fierce bite. They all moved back with him to a safe location where he was able to begin the process of recovery in peace and with minimal discomfort. Calling to the rear command they explained they needed to abandon their surveillance due to Amaury's injury. Calling in to get assistance and an exit out of that area was their priority. Although it happened so fast the Ranger Commando's swift action saved Amaury's life

He was ill for over a week but managed to recover from the attack. The venom of a cobra bite causes the victim to stop breathing and die of eventual lung paralysis. Amaury developed fever and shakes at night which lasted for three straight days. Later, he was moved to a nearby village to have a doctor tend to him, and then finally to the makeshift military hospital for the duration of his recuperation.

His recovery was slow, and it took a couple of weeks for him to feel well enough to get back on his feet and back to his job on the patrol. The Cuban Command made sure he wasn't in the main area of fighting and had him supervise the building of a nearby hospital.

Later, the reconnaissance mission for the hidden runway paid dividends as the Cuban military sent in several hundred soldiers and overran the drug dealers using the airport. They took it over completely and shut down their activities there. Amaury had to observe the remainder of the operation Cartel Flight from the sidelines and was not a part of the final steps in the attack and the dismantling of the airfield.

Time was winding down in Nicaragua for Amaury. His military career—at least in his mind—was nearing an end. He longed for the time when he could return to be a regular Cuban citizen without the military telling him how to live. He was as proud of his service, but the time had come to leave it behind.

He knew in Nicaragua, they tried to teach many of the natives to read, how to build buildings, medical clinics, schools and to learn at least in some ways how to improve their ability to defend themselves going forward. Those thoughts also made him think about his own country. Although it was great to help these other countries, Cuba needed the same kind of help.

Amaury believed that in many ways, Cuba wasn't much better than Nicaragua or Angola, and yet Castro sent men to help foreign nations to get better and their own country was neglected. Amaury found himself once again on the final plane ride home thinking about these conflicting ideologies. Knowing his service was coming to an end, he felt himself starting to slide back into his old ways of thinking, which in many ways were his truest, most honest feelings about his home country.

He had joined the military to attempt to make his father proud, to stay out of trouble, and just to be a good Cuban, but his father was no different, and Amaury's relationship with him had not improved. And now that he'd seen some of the world, and had some life experience, he realized his line of thinking had been right all along. He wasn't a communist. He'd never be a communist, and he needed a life that was bigger than the Cuban government would allow.

Chapter 47

A Fine Welcome Home

It was summer, and Amaury arrived home to the overwhelming congratulations from his family and friends a second time, his father being the only exception. Many Cuban soldiers returning from Nicaragua experienced splendid reunions with their families, as Cuban people are family-oriented and love to be together. Amaury loved the attention and the chance to be back in the family fold. Finally, he felt he was home for good after five-plus years of battle.

It was comfortable in his mom's house, familiar. There was nothing like mom's cooking with all his favorite foods and drinks. With any good fortune, he'd leave the soldier's life behind.

The military, however, was never too far away, and even as an inactive soldier, Amaury was required to check in weekly. Once settled in, they were debriefed about their past mission, and they gave reports about their experiences and passed on information so the units coming in behind them would be brought up-to-speed. Subtly, he could tell from the way they addressed him that his time in the military was not necessarily over. In his mind, although he didn't discuss his displeasure with their insistence, he continued in the army. He was sure he wouldn't acquiesce to their desires.

Amaury was anxious to get out, but as prior, he was required to turn in his Military ID. Everyone in Cuba was required to carry an ID with them wherever they went, and without his, he was at a distinct disadvantage. Originally, he'd signed on for three years and then agreed to two more and served an additional half year more. He'd originally thought the five years would satisfy the army and they would positively discharge him once his subscription period had been completed.

After the debriefing, he returned home and saw his mom struggling to maintain enough food for the family. Additionally, her refrigerator was broken. The simple convenience of a cold glass of water wasn't even available. Amaury was angered that he had given a third of his life to the military but minimally in return, the government wouldn't even make sure his mother had a decent refrigerator. Although he knew it wasn't required, the indignity of her having to do without one he felt was insulting beyond imagination. Whether this conclusion was right or wrong on its own, it hurt him fundamentally to his core.

This single small issue concretized in his mind how much he hated the Castros and the Cuban government's revolution. He'd had enough and decided he was not going to continue with the Army. It was time to leave and resign when the timing appeared right. He wanted his life back, and he wanted to move on with living his way and not the way the Army decreed. Amaury was determined to live a life where he could get a job and help his mother live better. He'd observed his father's military-driven, pro-communism life over the years and knew he didn't want to duplicate it.

The Army saw in him someone who'd inherit and continue in his father's footsteps, a continuation in the Torres' military legacy. The desire to leave the Army became his first firm decision once back home. Amaury decided he would discontinue checking in, instead of disappearing into the shadows of daily Cuban life. He began staying at different locations with friends or family and not frequently in the same place. It wasn't long before the Army realized Amaury was no longer following his orders. They didn't wait long before staking out his mother's and father's homes.

Several weeks went by, and although things appeared calm on the surface, it was not over and became an uncomfortable situation Amaury had created for all those protecting him.

Despite the inconvenience, however, his network of family and friends continued to help him hide, slipping through the cracks and remaining invisible. Amaury knew deep down he'd never be able to continue on this insane path long term. One evening in the darkness of night while he was quietly sneaking back to his mother's house, the Army caught him. They didn't initially realize who he was, as he'd tried to change his looks with a beard and hat. The soldiers were thorough in their questioning but discovered he was without his ID, and so they quickly realized they'd caught Commander Torres.

"We've been looking for you, Torres. You think you are so smart, huh?"

"I don't know what you're—"

"We knew you'd eventually come back here. Did you think you could play these silly games and get away with them?"

The communists spoke in a condescending tone which made Amaury feel even more disgusted.

"We've been waiting to speak with you, and tonight we will. You're under arrest."

Amaury responded, "Yeah, sure. Lucky for you, I guess."

Once they arrived back at the military station, the commanding officer saw a handcuffed Amaury coming down the hallway with the two army patrol officers by his side. Having radioed ahead, they were waiting for his arrival.

"Hello, Mr. Torres. Where have you been? Care to explain?"

Amaury glared at the commander. "I've been a little busy," he said.

His wrists hurt from the tightness of the handcuffs, which they'd neglected to remove once inside the office. It was a dreary room with numerous file cabinets along the far wall in the typical boring Army grey. Amaury noticed two very bright naked light bulbs hanging from the ceiling, causing a glaring intensity that hurt his eyes. He stared squinting at the sharpness of the unforgiving lights. Sitting on his hands against the hard wooden brown chair with the uneven leg, he knew it was going to be a long evening.

"So where have you been hiding, Mr. Torres?"

"Here and there. You know how it goes."

"It's always a busy time when you're running, cheating, and hiding from the Army."

"Well, I wasn't hiding. I was just busy. I didn't realize the time had gone by so quickly. Funny thing about life. Some things go by quickly, like time."

"Why haven't you checked in? You know you're required to. Plus we have your ID. You must have known you wouldn't get too far without that..."

He realized this was the moment. It had finally arrived. No matter what he said, it wouldn't matter. From the time was a young boy growing up in the Solar until today, all the years of internal conflict, the mental battle he'd faced along the way—his hatred for communism had finally come down to this moment in his life.

He needed to take a second to collect his thoughts. He was having to finally stand up for himself and tell them it was over.

His time in the Army was over. He contemplated how he was going to make his explanation work.

"You know, Mr. Torres," the commander said with an edge to his voice. "We believe you are looking to get away from your responsibilities in the Army. You knew you were supposed to be checking in every two weeks here. We haven't seen you in at least three weeks. Now I realize you may have enjoyed your time at home, but until you are officially released from the Army, you're required to follow the orders given to you. Do you understand that correctly? It's nothing new, is it?"

Thoughtful for a moment, Amaury look directly at the commander. "Yes, I do recall that requirement, but my time is just as valuable as yours and—"

"Listen, Mr. Torres. We realize you may need some time off, but three weeks and the failure to check-in is neither allowed nor tolerated," the commander angrily interrupted.

Amaury now gathered up the strength and confidence and all his resolve and began to speak. "Commander, my time in the Army, as you say it, the Cuban Army, is over. I'm not going to continue my service in the Army. I've given you over five years of my life. I have already decided that I'm resigning here and now and that's that."

"Let me inform you, Mr. Torres—your time is not only not over, but in fact, you will spend your *life* in the Cuban Army. That decision has been made for you!"

"The Cuban Army no longer represents the life I want to live," Amaury said firmly.

"Mr. Torres, you will do as you are told. This is not a discussion. We feel you may be the victim of war-weariness. This is a normal result of war for the length of time you have been involved thus far. We want you to take some time to think it over and consider this important decision. We don't want you to feel any undue pressure. With that in mind, we're going to send you to the *Hospital Disciplinario Mental* to speak to the doctors there and let them spend time with you, allowing you to get these anti-revolutionary thoughts cleared out of your mind. It's something that we feel will be very good for you to help you make a positive change," the commander continued. Amaury couldn't tell if he was being sincere or sarcastic. "We want you to feel refreshed and start anew. Since that is settled, we will be seeing you soon enough."

Staring down at the floor, Amaury thought to himself, *this is taking a turn for the worse.*

Chapter 48

The Hospital

Amaury looked at the Commander with anger in his eyes, knowing these words were all bullshit. They had no meaning. He knew damned well that the Army didn't care about his mental health. The hospital was just an excuse to keep Amaury under their thumb...under lock and key until he acquiesced to their will. Plus it gave them time to create their own plan of how to deal with him.

"Mr. Torres, you will be sent to the Cuban Havana division of the Army's Psychiatric Center, which is just a few towns over, and there you'll have an opportunity to calm down and reset your mind. You have been labeled with exhaustion. Some call it PTSD. We just think you were in the field for a long period, and it's a difficult issue to resolve. This will help you."

Amaury knew this was a manipulative game they were playing, and the requirement for his mental toughness would be paramount. It's what had kept him alive for the last five years, and he would have to dig down deep once again.

"Look, Mr. Torres, you will think carefully about your choices, and the next decision you make will be especially important. We want to prove you aren't truly suffering from

PTSD because you've taken a position that is, shall we say, very disturbing."

The commander interrupted himself to look around at the military policemen who were also standing watching the proceedings. He laughed out loud at his comment, then continued.

"We believe the hospital will help straighten out your way of thinking. You'll be taken there tonight, where you can begin processing your trauma and recovering."

Amaury knew they were going to coerce him into staying by laying a trap for him. He'd have to play this out until the end no matter what the result.

Sometime later that evening as the handcuffs continued to cut at his wrists, he arrived at the Army mental hospital. It appeared to be a starkly austere place. There were several typical institutional-styled taller buildings with a simple metal staircase on the exterior.

As they walked toward the main door in the darkness, it was hard to discern the color of the buildings. But what did it matter? They appeared to be in disrepair. All government buildings were similar. Entering through a small door, Amaury could hear the sounds of screaming in the distance, the only sound without clarity. Amaury wasn't sure if someone was being tortured or was simply protesting their situation.

The very first thing they did upon his arrival was to strip him and hose him down as though he were a dirty plant. They sprayed him harshly from head to toe with a terrible smelling disinfectant liquid delivered through a hose. As he drip-dried walking to the next stop, he saw uniformed workers talking, but he was quickly taken to another room with a single striped white and blue cot with no sheet. Amaury counted fifteen other inmates in the room of various sizes and shapes and levels of mental health.

He had one towel, a small bar of soap and a few minimal pieces of folded clothing, a blanket, and a strangely odd pair of sandals which appeared to have two left feet. He was told to change and then was left alone.

As he lay down on the bed and looked up at the ceiling, he noticed a single dim bulb screwed into the ceiling socket. He covered his eyes with his arm. Even though he was feeling depressed, he was worried about what might happen next. He tried to focus on how he was going to manage and get out of this predicament unscathed. It was one of the few times in his life where he felt trapped without any possible escape.

Early in the morning after he awoke, he got up and looked out the meager window near his bed, which was corrugated glass crisscrossed with thin metal wires embedded interfering with any view. The window was so filthy it barely allowed daylight to shine through.

The nurse entered the room and abruptly told him to get dressed and follow her as the day began. After dressing, he tried to place his feet into the odd-shaped sandals which didn't fit correctly, being tight in all the wrong spots and forcing him to shuffle along with the others. The sandals made rough scraping sounds on the tile floor as he took each step.

I think they want us to shuffle while walking.

As he trudged along with the nurse, he noticed the flooring was grey tile with an occasional unorganized red stripe blended into the shiny surface. The next things he noticed were the other residents and the surreal constant flow of their walking habits. They tended to aimlessly head in all directions and appeared to be doing nothing other than walking without talking. Amaury observed that some of them must have been there for a very long time, as from the knee down, their long cotton pants looked like jagged triangle stalactites ending near their ankles which flipped around as they muddled along the hallways.

Some of the less lucky ones had thin underwear, which was dark and dirty in obviously wrong spots, showing a severe lack of care from the staff.

The staff had no intention of changing, which made it an awful, hateful place. People were thrown in to be ignored or to get rid of rather than help to improve in any significant way. Amaury instantly felt it was the true way of communism to generally treat the population with contempt in a condemning, dictatorial authority. The government became a substitute parent who knew all that was good for society yet truly did not care.

He observed the healthcare workers to be very busy with their activities, but Amaury never understood what they were doing. Using his keen observation skills, he spent his first week watching their movements but not interacting with anyone. The nurses were neither aggressive nor neutral with him. However, it was the ranking medical doctors who behaved roughly, inquisitively and at times cruelly, manipulating him to try to get him to rescind his anti-government stance. The doctors were more spies than medical investigators for the government.

Amaury believed they were building a case against him, and he felt this through their questioning. He knew he needed to be careful with his answers. In his mind, it was as if Castro himself might be listening. This most likely was a fantasy, as his situation would never get high enough in the military chain, but he felt it was possible because of his father's connection to Castro. Nury had always tried to keep Amaury's rebellious attitude hidden from higher authorities.

Despite all his efforts to stay strong, his duration in the hospital suddenly seemed to stand still.

Chapter 49

A Shake Down

He spent several hours each day talking in a type of therapy, which was more of a grilling than a conversation with the military doctors.

For the remainder of the day, he sat on the floor of the main hall or alone in his room with only his thoughts for company. It stayed this way for several weeks. He felt truly alone, as he had neither seen nor heard from his family. He didn't know if they even knew where he was. He dared not ask the doctors about them in case they might consider retribution.

One of the disciplines of his training taught him to stay resolved within himself and be patient, to keep his mind and emotions private.

As the days passed, the doctors became impatient, irritable, and increasingly aggressive in their questioning. He withstood the verbal assaults as they continued trying to force him to change his way of thinking and commit to remaining in the Army.

Every day was the same routine—morning breakfast that was a bowl of some strange mush he swore looked as though it had worms squirming through it and a brown powdery topping he was disgusted to look at. However, he was still alive and felt he must provide himself with some nutrition. Otherwise, he *would've already died.* The duration was taking its toll and wearing him out.

One day, the head nurse informed him he was leaving. Happily, he knew it was over, but what lay next was a mystery.

He was handcuffed again and brought back to headquarters where he'd originally left six weeks prior. Once he arrived, he was approached by the commander and was verbally drilled about his visit.

"How was your time off, Commander? Did you take the time to think about your future? Have you learned anything in your short stay at the hospital, Mr. Torres? Do things make more sense now?"

"You already know my answer. Why bother with your questions?"

Amaury fully knew this wasn't the answer they wanted to hear and dispensed with any respect to their authority. The commander, who also realized he wasn't going to pull rank, had other things to settle on his mind.

"Okay, Mr. Torres. We're going to change our philosophy. Let's try a different method. You'll spend some time in solitary confinement to do some personal introspection and see if you can come up with some better answers. You know your remaining time is limited, and things will get worse from here. Why don't you smarten up and realize you are in no position to negotiate? Why don't you simply comply and renounce your former statement? If you continue to choose not to, you'll be taken in front of the military tribunal judge for unpatriotic anti-Cuban actions. We know what you are all about, Mr. Torres. We will not tolerate any kind of maggot behavior. We've looked into your past. We know about you. Let's hope you can find the right path in the time you have left. Why don't you save your own life? Don't you want to?"

Amaury realized this was the moment where he was no longer going to hold back. His feelings about the war, the inequities in Cuban life, and communism's hypocritical rules of living had come to an end for him. He believed no matter what happened, he wanted to make clear his thoughts about his life.

"I have given nearly a third of my twenty-one years serving my country. I have done my time honorably, and that is enough. No more! I have fought in wars that made no sense. I've helped you to bring communism to the world and kill people who didn't deserve to die just so you could wear a badge on your chest and those stripes on your shoulders. Let me live my life as an ordinary Cuban. This is all I want. It's a simple request. I will not join your revolution. Ever. I'll go my way and you go yours. I renounce the revolution completely and fully!"

"Mr. Torres, you cannot and will not continue to walk around society harboring anti-communist thoughts. We cannot have that, nor can it be allowed. You are an infection to society and the Army, and infections must be treated as such."

The commander continued. "Sergeant, take this maggot to the brig. Let's help him make the correct decision. And throw away the key! He may be with us for a while. This maggot!"

Several days went by, and suddenly he was dragged out of the solitary confinement cell. The next thing he knew, his grandmother was sitting directly in front of him in the holding room. He couldn't believe it.

"Grandmama, what are you doing here?"

She looked at him startled and started to cry. Tears ran down her cheeks. "Amaury, what are they doing to you? What's going on? Why is this happening?"

After seeing his grandmother crying, he also began to get a

bit teary himself. She'd found him unshaven and weary, having lost a ton of weight and generally looking unhealthy.

Amaury knew the game. This was part of the Army's strategy to break him down and use his emotions against him, get him to regret his words, succumb to throwing in the towel, give up on his life and adopt communism.

It wasn't going to work. He knew what they wanted, and letting them win wasn't part of his plan. He didn't care how difficult it was going to get. They didn't talk much, but she was able to ascertain he'd had several difficult weeks, which was why he looked drawn and exhausted. She knew based on her knowledge of the military in general they would not tolerate any openly anti-Cuba, anti-Castro behavior and going against their will. She sensed he was facing serious times ahead. They only spoke for a few minutes and needed to be careful.

"They want me to stay in the military like dad and give up my life to communism. I'm not going to do it. I've refused to let them break me down, and I will never let them take my life from me."

She understood. "Don't worry, Amaury, I understand, and you know I want you to stay strong. Yes, I will be back to visit again very soon, okay, so don't worry."

She wanted to hug him, but she understood they weren't alone, and she did not want the commanders to recognize their sadness. They played it safe, a quick kiss on the cheek, and said their goodbyes. She turned and walked out, and Amaury was taken back to solitary.

Chapter 50

A Crescendo Moment

His grandmother immediately went home and contacted General Nury in Panama, who was away on military business. She exclaimed over the phone in a panicked, rushed voice what terrible things had been happening to Amaury and that he needed to come back to Cuba as soon as possible. No matter how Nury felt about Amaury, his mother loved him unconditionally and wouldn't stand by while her grandson was mistreated.

"Get him out of there!" she screamed at her son over the phone. She explained his condition and how he was being treated. She knew he was in confinement and in poor condition.

"All right, Mother, I'll come home." Nury hung up the phone and quickly made his plans to return to Havana.

Two days later, Nury drove up to the detention center where Amaury was being detained and walked directly up the stairs into the military jail and right into the main office. "Who's in charge here?" he shouted. "I want to know who is in charge?"

Commander Rodriguez walked in and immediately saw it was a general. Confused and shaken from the intensity of the yelling, he stepped forward and looked the general right in his eyes. Commander Rodriguez knew deep down that this confrontation was going to be an issue but didn't quite understand why. His hands started shaking terribly, sweat began beading on his forehead and upper lip. He could instinctively feel its ticklish wetness, and it was disturbingly distracting from the berating he knew he was about to receive.

General Nury gave him a direct, intense look for what seemed like an eternity. Then he spoke. "Where is my son?"

Commander Rodriguez responded weakly. He couldn't get his voice to work well. "Er, umm. Your son? Sir?"

"My son. Yes, my son! Ranger Captain Amaury Torres. I was told he was being held here against his will. Where is he, Commander?"

"Yes. He's right here. Sir in a holding... we're—"

Livid, General Nury cut him off, not caring for an explanation. "Listen, you stinking maggot, bring my son to me immediately." The General was so angered and enraged that he turned red as a beet from head to toe. With a single breath and motion, he drew his hand across the shirt of the Commander, grabbing the Commander's stripes by the edge and pulling as hard as he could across his chest, ripping the stripes completely off his arm and taking part of the sleeve with it. The Commander's shirt was torn, and his arms were scratched and red. A little trickle of blood appeared on the surface from where the general's nails had scratched his skin.

The general, having the remainder of the stripes in his hand, threw the cloth at the commander's face.

The utterly flustered Commander Rodriguez immediately turned and said in a clear voice to the private standing at attention to go and retrieve Captain Torres. Rodriguez knew he'd just been taken down several ranks.

"Rodriguez, you are done. Collect your belongings and get the hell out. This man is my son. He served this country, and he served it well. You have no respect for human life. Get your things and get out. You're finished!"

A few moments later Amaury appeared in the room, looking disheveled but surprised to see his father. General Torres looked at Amaury and signaled him with his gaze to follow him out the door. They both walked quickly out and down the steps and around to the side of the building.

It was early evening, and they took a brief moment to hug each other. For one of the few times in their lives, they had a momentary emotional connection.

The general was genuinely happy to see his son, and Amaury was also truly glad to see his father. Nury, never one to show affection of any kind, knew this moment was a watershed event. He realized Amaury's future was badly damaged forever by these latest developments. However, their closeness only lasted until they finished embracing.

"Amaury, we need to talk," Nury said. "You're in serious trouble. I was afraid you'd face this sort of scrutiny from the Revolution. I've tried my hardest to prevent this from happening to you, but in the back of my mind, it was always a concern. I'd hoped being in the Army with the training you've received, you'd begin to see things differently and discover the true beauty of the Cuban way. But it's too late for that now. It's out of my hands. Whatever happens now, you're on your own. If you stay in Cuba, you'll either end up in jail for the rest of your life or worse. They may even consider execution after a trial if it were to get that far. I'd hoped we'd never see this day, but I believe you must leave Cuba."

"I know we've had our differences. I can only express to you my appreciation that you have taken this moment to save my life. Thank you very much for your help today, Father," Amaury quietly responded.

Nury nodded as they made bonding eye contact.

The crescendo moment fell upon Amaury in a split second as he realized his life in Cuba was finished. In that exact minute, he shivered from the intensity of his father's words, and it was horribly scary and overwhelming.

Amaury didn't know what to think and stayed quiet. He instantly knew few choices were remaining. The life he wanted in Cuba was not going to evolve. It had been taken away from him in a snap of the fingers. The carefree fishing on the Malecon, the familiar warm breezes, the always present ocean aromas, all his fond memories of normal life, his family, everything in his past, and his potential future, too. So many thoughts crossed his mind. The idea it was all going to stop was impossibly hard to grasp. He shook his head to wake up from the suddenness of reality.

Was this really happening?

Although only twenty-one years old, he felt it all had gone by as though it were a dream. As he looked out of the window of the car, he imagined a dark, heavy blanket had been suddenly dropped over him. He felt smothered. He was alone in the darkness. A foreboding, unfair feeling surrounded him as he considered his limited solutions.

I'm not ready to give up, Amaury kept thinking.

Always the optimist, he knew there was a gun at his head and a knife at his back, and as desperate as he felt, his decision was clear. It was time to go. Trying to work something out with the military definitely could not happen. He'd have to become a lifelong communist or face jail or possible death if he wasn't careful. As he stared into the depth of desolation, a strange occurrence happened. He could not explain it, but he saw a tiny pinhole of light shining through and realized at that moment there actually might be a chance at something else.

A possible solution. A way out, he thought.

Giving into communism was a life he simply could not live.

Confronting his fears and left with limited choices, he realized he needed to choose a path that provided him with the best chance for staying alive. Then he thought about how his life had unfolded and the realization of his predicament seemed predetermined in a strange way. He'd always wondered about the outside world. He'd always had it in the back of his mind, but he'd been too afraid to seriously consider it was the only choice possible.

He didn't belong in Cuba anymore. He *couldn't* belong in Cuba anymore. His plan to escape had to start immediately, and it would begin tonight.

Chapter 51

Brothers

Amaury started right away. He didn't waste a single minute as he developed an exit strategy. He knew he needed money to accumulate the provisions he needed to get off the island.

The first step was selling or trading all his belongings of any value. He sold an old bicycle, some clothes, shoes, and sadly even his marbles—anything with value that could be used.

A day later, Ernesto heard the news and went straight away to see Amaury. He couldn't believe it was true.

Was Amaury going to escape Cuba?

He was stunned and intrigued at the same time.

"Amaury, I heard the news. Is it true? Are you seriously leaving? What the hell happened to you? You were in some kind of jail and some kind of hospital, too? Tell me!"

"Yes, Ernesto, it's all true, but I don't have time to go through it now. Believe me, we'll have time to talk."

"Amaury, I want to go with you," Ernesto blurted out. "I've thought about it, and I want to go along. I don't want to stay here." Ernesto sounded nervously excited, as though an escape from Cuba might be a fun experience, a great adventure, something brothers would do together.

Shocked and in disbelief, Amaury stared at Ernesto. "Seriously? You want to go, too? Together?"

"Yes, yes. I do. Look, I love Cuba as much as you do, and you're my brother, but still, what an adventure it's gonna be, right? C'mon, Amaury. You can't go alone. That's just way too dangerous, anyway."

"Ernesto, are you kidding, would you really go? I mean, this is no joke, you know. We'll be going across the fucking Atlantic Ocean!"

"I'm serious, brother."

"I can't believe I'm even saying this. But yes, let's do it!" Amaury smiled and grabbed Ernesto in a big, happy hug.

Ernesto balked. He'd reacted impulsively to the idea of leaving. Although he'd said it, he truly hadn't given it enough consideration. He wanted to be with Amaury, and the idea that they could start a new life together had an incredibly strong allure, but Ernesto hadn't completely thought out the reality of such a trip and what it might be like. However, dismissing those thoughts, they agreed to start immediately with a plan to leave together.

"Maybe this will be a brother's adventure of a lifetime," Amaury exclaimed. Amaury was feeling a strong sense of relief in not having to take on the trip alone. Inwardly, already in survival mode, he'd also removed the idea of any danger from his mind, except the knowledge that his life was being threatened while he stayed in Cuba. His motivation was clear—leave and hopefully live, or stay and most likely die. Either choice was not optimal, but in leaving there was at least a chance of survival.

For Ernesto, it was the idea of being with his brother and the adventure that lay ahead. The emotional tug from the other side of the ocean created an overwhelmingly strong allure for him.

Ernesto's choice was far less urgent than Amaury's, but he trusted his brother, and going to America was in a sense a victory he wanted for his own life. Amaury thought it could be great having Ernesto there, with both working together, helping each other face the ocean rather than him doing it alone. He happily welcomed the opportunity to have Ernesto with him.

As they began to plan, they chose to collectively ignore the harsh realities that were facing them and just stay positive—or maybe it was naive. At the same moment, they both said together. "It's going to work out fine," and then laughed at the spontaneity of their combined thoughts.

Ernesto and Amaury, although close, had not spent a lot of time together as brothers other than when they were young. In their youth, they'd forged a close brotherly relationship that had never waned. However, as close as they were, there were many years they'd not spent together, especially when Amaury was in the military. The few times Amaury did return home, they'd gotten together and reestablished their old bonds. The idea of leaving and being together in the United States only heightened the dream of a successful new life and presented the opportunity for a more meaningful bond as they crossed the ocean.

The next step in their planning was determining what they needed to bring and dividing up the tasks as to who would do what and what they would do together. They didn't apply a lot of emotion to the chores and went about their activities in a very methodical, almost businesslike fashion.

From the moment the general had told Amaury he'd need to leave Cuba to save his life to the moment Amaury and Ernesto planned to leave was exactly ten days.

The escape plan was utmost in their minds, and they didn't allow for any kind of distraction. Their behavior and activities were deliberate and determined.

One night as they sat planning, Amaury had a funny realization that he shared with his brother. All of his life, he'd felt as if the outside world was so far away, but as he sat there looking at a map of the Atlantic ocean, it finally dawned on him. He looked at his brother and said, "Ernesto...when you think about it, it's only ninety miles to freedom."

They smiled at each other.

Chapter 52

The Planning

As the plan unfolded, the boys wrote a list of items they needed to obtain by importance from first to last. The first and most important piece of equipment they needed was the rubber raft. The trip could not happen—no escape, no liberation, and no freedom without it.

Both boys knew the consequences of getting caught escaping would be dire. It had to be planned right the first time. They didn't want to get caught.

Amaury learned from friends there was a very large tractor truck tire inner tube available, intact and good quality. These tractor tubes were the holy grail of any escape plan from Cuba for any individual, but they were dangerous to possess. The military knew their worth and made sure these tubes were confiscated when discovered.

The next day, they borrowed bicycles and traveled an hour to a nearby town to get the tube. Their endeavor to get the tube was serpentine, slipping through the countryside on dirt roads and through back yards reminiscent of scenes from a spy movie. Most of the plan was accomplished at night under the cover of darkness, as many Cuban roads didn't have a single streetlight. Generally, the only lights were the headlights of other vehicles or the occasional house door lights close to the road.

The Cuban countryside was beautifully tropical, with lots of high grasses that undulated from the breezes seemingly with a life of their own. Amaury fondly memorized the scene even as he was focused on the job ahead. Wistfully, he dearly wanted to remember that moment as he peddled. The night's full moon also helped them with lighting their path to the house where the inner tube was located. Once they got to the farm, they both took a moment to laugh out loud at the crazy circuitous route they'd taken.

Amaury whispered to Ernesto, "That was crazy, right?"

"Yes totally. But let's go."

Along the way, their knowledge of the area and the moon made the trip work. Once they arrived at the farmer's home, they quickly negotiated a price that was too much for what it was, but they didn't have the luxury nor the time to be picky.

They completed the deal and quickly went back to their mom's house to hide the large tube. It was thick, heavy, and unwieldy, but they found a location and buried it underground, covered by a mound of dirt smoothed over to look natural.

The next day, the most difficult task was to gather the parts to build wooden and leather bellows so they could blow up the tube and make sure it was viable. Building the bellows took a full day itself. However, once completed, it became quickly apparent the tube they'd bought was leaking and deflated in such a terrible way it was not usable. Even if they could fix it, it worried them to consider whether or not it would be safe enough to use across the ocean. Their lives depended on it.

Stoically, they stared at each other, knowing the search was on again, and set out to find another tube. Not long afterward,

Ernesto learned of another farmer whose house was further than the first one who had an even larger tube to sell.

The next step was selling anything they could get their hands on to get enough to buy it—old clothes and a few old military items, and a few friends gave them random items to sell.

Ernesto sold all his weightlifting equipment, bench, clamps weights, and gloves—every single item. He raised enough money on his own to buy the tube. Out of goodwill, many of the neighbors bought the equipment to help the boys out.

A day later, they took a three-hour bus ride to the second farmer's home. These tubes were highly sought-after items on the local black market. Word of one would get around from one friend to another and then finally that information was passed on. Eventually, it found an interested party.

Openly discussing the purchase with the wrong person was also another dangerous proposition which they had to navigate correctly. Back at home, they once again hid the inner tube underground.

Later that night in the house, Rosa asked Amaury when they were embarking. The only thing he quietly said was, "Soon, Mama. It will be soon."

Amaury wasn't able to hide the truth from his mother. She knew leaving was terrifying, and the prospect of both her sons leaving at the same time on a dangerous adventure didn't make it easier. By herself, alone and overwhelmed with sadness, she cried in her small solar apartment.

The next job on the list was gathering the other provisions, including five plastic gallon bottles for water, extra t-shirts, shorts, several hats, and an easy to assemble fishing rod with fishing wire, hooks, and bait. They made a few sandwiches just before leaving and carried rope to tie themselves to the raft. They also bought two towels to lie on, sunglasses, and a needle and thread.

Ernesto made sure to bring five packs of cigarettes and several lighters. They were also able to obtain and trade a box of *Cohiba cigars* for two swimming flippers for paddling off the shore with an old Russian neighbor they knew.

The flippers were critical in their escape. As was typical with Cuban possessions, everything worked but was often not in the greatest condition. Hopefully, the flippers would last long enough to get them out into the deep ocean, but beyond that was anybody's guess.

They'd have to share the one pair so each of them could help kick the raft out to sea. They kept looking, but unfortunately, they never found another pair. One fin was going to have to suffice for both on their swim into the depths of the Atlantic.

There were several more important items remaining. After they successfully tested the inner tube, they needed to get something to sit on, as the rubber sides alone would be disastrous. They both knew that not too far from their mom's house was a soccer field. Later that night, they took two knives and quietly walked over to the field. While looking left and right and running from bush to bush and behind each tree making sure they weren't being followed or seen in the open field, they made their way to a goalie net.

As dangerous as it was, they both began laughing, trying to lessen the anxiety of their adventure, but it was an extremely important piece of their escape puzzle. Once at the soccer goal, they quickly cut off the net and its post moorings and rolled it up.

The next day, the kids playing soccer were going to be upset that the net was missing. It took a while for things to get fixed by the government in Cuba, and they knew they had maybe five to seven days before government officials would discover the missing net, which would be a signal something unusual was happening. They needed to leave as soon as possible once the net was gone.

The netting would enable them to lie down or sit but at the same time, it would also prevent sharks from potentially jumping up at them through the hole. Amaury and Ernesto knew their time in Cuba was concluding fast.

Chapter 53

The Escape

Their departure was imminent, and their final planning stages required crucial decisions.

Where were they going to push off from the coast? When would they leave?

This task was as equally complicated as many of the others. Several issues needed to be resolved. The preferred location had to provide the ability to hide their entire collection of traveling gear. Everything had to be well buried in advance of their departure.

They also needed the ability to push off from where they had the most time before the Cuban Coast Guard might spot them, a secure vantage point where they had enough time to observe the shoreline in both directions before pushing off. Leaving successfully depended on when the Cuban Coast Guard boats passed their location. They needed to know the Coast Guard's schedule on the morning of departure so when the brothers pushed off and were still close to the shore, they wouldn't be seen. Otherwise, their trip would be over before it began.

All these questions needed to be figured out in advance, and they had very little time remaining to fully complete the analysis.

Amaury discovered the final spot in a little town called *Guanabo.* He chose the location because it was further west and afforded them natural ocean currents and the ability to watch for patrolling Coast Guards' boats. The local 400 bus ride that night was anxiety-filled.

On the last two nights before their departure, they went to the launch site for a practice run. They had to take the bus late each night so they wouldn't be seen taking all the provisions at once with them on the bus. They couldn't risk arousing any suspicion.

Once they arrived near the launch site, they walked quite a distance to the push-off spot on the beach. It was near trees, sand, and tall grasses, all of which enabled them to find camouflage enough to dig holes for all their provisions. Then they covered the ground with grasses and other brush lying on the ground nearby.

The launching site enabled Amaury to verify the Coast Guard's shore pattern schedule, which he noted and then calculated the time between their passes and their patterns in the very early morning hours. With his military experience, Amaury knew how the Cuban military thought and what to expect of them, and this was no exception. The timing would present itself as he watched.

The final calculations showed they needed to be far enough offshore so once they were in the ocean, they would safely float away unnoticed. Amaury knew that an object six feet tall can be seen with the naked eye at sea level to a distance of about three miles. The curve of the earth allowed for them to see far into the distance; however, the Cuban Coast Guard patrolled off the coast as much as fifteen to twenty miles into the ocean. If the Navy saw them, everything would be lost. They needed to be close to twenty miles off the coast before they'd be free. This single step was the most critical to accomplishing their escape.

Amaury estimated they needed to paddle with their feet nonstop for fourteen to fifteen straight hours. Starting out, this would be a very difficult job to achieve while constantly looking around checking for the Coast Guard.

On their last night in Cuba, they took the final scheduled bus ride, which left at midnight. Amaury and Ernesto told their mom they were leaving. Rosa knew of the circumstances of the predicament and of course, had no choice but to accept Amaury's departure, but she never expected to lose Ernesto, too. Both boys walked into the apartment to see Abuelita and Rosa one last time.

With tears welling in his eyes, Ernesto looked at both his stepmother and grandmother. "Well, this is it. We're about to jump on the 400 bus. I think this is the hardest thing I've ever had to do. I'm sorry. I love you both so very much. I don't want to say goodbye."

"I know, Ernesto. I understand. It's the first time our family has had to face separation like this. It feels completely different when it's your own family."

Abuelita nodded her head in agreement as tears streamed down her cheeks. "Come here, you two. I want to give you both a big hug. I know we'll see each other again someday. It will probably be a while, but I feel certain about that."

Amaury quietly sobbed while hugging his mother. "I am truly sorry, Mama, I never, ever figured it would feel as bad as it does. I don't know what to say. I will love you forever."

Inwardly, Rosa never thought she'd see either one of them again. They gathered all their fishing gear with them, including the fishing line, rod, reel, and bait. Their premade sandwiches were packed into a fishing box along with Ernesto's cigarettes.

They made sure they looked like two typical locals going out for the catch of the day.

The bus ride to their final destination was fraught with fear, anxiety, and apprehension. They couldn't look at each other on the bus and had to act as though nothing unusual was going on, just two fellows going fishing.

The bus arrived, and they made the long walk to the departure spot. The stars were very bright above, sparkling and enveloping them in the universe of opportunity. Next, they had to dig out their stored gear and clean off the wet sand as best that they could while making sure they weren't being seen. They constantly looked around. Concentrating without interruption, they worked on each task in order. Both boys watched moment to moment over their shoulders to see if the Coast Guard was lurking about. Highly focused on getting everything set up and prepared, the boys worked together nonstop. The sun was not up yet, and the sky was a dark blackish blue. On the horizon, the ever-so-slight ribbons of dull sunlight beaming completely across the ocean focused like lasers and landed haphazardly. The final moments of the mysterious night quietly slipped away to the west. Second by second, nearing the final moment, they looked at each other.

Inside, they felt fear and intense apprehension. However, they said a last-minute prayer for their safety and survival along the way. They also thanked God for the chance to one day live in a free America as an American.

There was little room for error on the precarious trip on which they were embarking. It was an adventure based on faith, hope, and destiny. Amaury truly felt his entire life had come to this moment, although he didn't think his life would go on the path in which it appeared to be headed. He wasn't quite sure what way it would arrive, but leaving on a makeshift tractor tire inner tube seemed like a far cry from an airplane ride or simply walking out of the Nicaraguan jungle up to America. In retrospect, that certainly would have been an easier way to have left Cuba.

Although he felt it was not the right thing to do, abandoning his family or putting them at risk would be the result of his actions. He realized he might be second-guessing himself and rolled his eyes, laughing for just a second.

"No going back now," he said.

Five years of facing death every day didn't seem as bad as this moment.

Now the future truly feels unknown. I have no idea what to expect, nor what life is going to be like or choices I'm going to have.

He always felt he would survive the war theatre, but here facing the unknowingness of the huge ocean seemed unimaginable. He took a moment, and although still fairly dark, he looked out at the huge, dark water.

The ocean is a vast surface and can swallow you up in a split second, especially being on the surface the entire time.

It seemed all of a sudden quite daunting and terrifying.

For a quick moment, he remembered flying thousands of feet above the ocean on his way to Angola and recalled watching it go by for hours. He swallowed deeply at the thought of its immensity. He had to let that thought go. It was too overwhelming.

"Make sure to tie your tether rope around the tube, not the netting. It's safer that way," Amaury told Ernesto.

"Si, I understand," Ernesto said. He looked at his brother, who was checking the knots of the netting on the inner tube and didn't let his brother know he was having his own compelling thoughts.

"Ernesto, how are you doing?"

"Good, Amaury. Good." Amaury knew it was a lie.

"Okay, Ernesto. That's it. We're ready now." They soaked their feet in the wet sand at the water's edge, the little waves splashing against their calves. "The sun is going to be breaking fully in the sky soon. We need to push off."

This could be suicide.

"Okay, Ernesto. Let's go!"

Both Amaury and Ernesto took a last look across at the shore to their country. It was a beautiful morning. Cuba looked amazing, so much better than they remembered. If Amaury could have turned his mind into a camera and taken a snapshot of that single moment, it's what he would have forever remembered.

There was such clarity in the early morning hours. It looked surreal with its beautiful blue sky, not a cloud around, its deep green grasses, beige sand, and the striking sound of the ocean lapping against the shore. Amaury knew they had about two hours to get just far enough out at least in the very early stages to get away. Their escape moment had arrived.

They dragged the tube to the water's edge. The cool, friendly water was blueish-green and had a nice, silky feeling to it. It was coming into the shore in a rhythmic small-sized wave pattern. The familiar lapping sound of the waves breaking rushed against the light beige sand. Little crabs, tiny ones almost invisible due to their sandy color, ran like chickens without their heads, although they knew what they were doing. Going sideways was the easiest way for them to move forward, an interesting comparison, Amaury thought to himself.

Going sideways to go forward seemed like the path his own life had taken.

They were about calf-deep when they both looked out on the horizon and saw the sky starting to truly break out of the dawn, a good part of the sunlight shining through. With a very deep breath, they pushed off. They took a quick look at each other and then both grabbed the tube and started paddling. In the back of their minds, they knew the fins had cracks, but at least they were holding up. They were also praying that the fins would withstand the rough treatment through which they were about to put them.

Just before they pushed off, they tied their midsections to the inner tube with a prickly thick beige marine rope they'd brought to be their tethers for safety. Amaury glanced over at Ernesto, who seemed to be doing okay.

"Ernesto, this is the hardest part. Once we get out there, we'll be able to rest, so just remember to keep going."

Ernesto said nothing. He just nodded at Amaury and continued paddling.

"And don't stop 'til I tell you."

Chapter 54

The Atlantic Ocean

The initial period of paddling was extremely important as well as backbreakingly difficult. They both vigorously pushed on, holding and paddling, holding and paddling, pushing and kicking, the water splashing everywhere. Saltwater scratched at their eyes and throats as they furiously worked their escape.

Pain first developed in their legs, then their arms. With effort, they achieved a rhythm that guided them to continue straight and not make the fatal mistake of circling around, a potential common error.

Once the water got deep enough, they pulled themselves up onto the tube and while lying on their stomachs with their legs over the sides, both paddled equally, relentlessly kicking over and over, pushing their legs to their limits and beyond.

Both boys constantly strained, continuing to see if they could catch a glimpse of the Navy anywhere. Within the first two hours, Amaury had calculated that there would be no Cuban Coast Guard interaction with their raft, but they knew their chances of being spotted increased as time went on.

Both their legs and feet were in extreme pain. Amaury glanced back at his legs and noticed at one point he'd begun to lose the hair on his inner thighs. Paddling on the heavy rubber tube had caused friction so severe the chafing had worn away the hair. The chaffing then became a strawberry rash and bleeding on his inner thighs. It already burned like hell, especially because of the constant saltwater and friction.

Turns out that was our first mistake. We should have gotten longer shorts.

Ernesto never said a word, but Amaury knew he was in just as much pain, maybe more so, as he hadn't been prepared for the severity of the escape. He'd never done any military training of any kind. Amaury realized upon looking at the sun that they were still only several hours in the ocean. As they glanced back at the island horizon, it had already shrunk and looked to move level on the ocean's surface as they continued to paddle and push on, never stopping.

It was hard to believe it was really happening. The outline of Cuba was disappearing into the ocean surface. It was only another hour or so before they both realized they were completely alone in the middle of nowhere. It was an odd feeling. Maybe had they been in a boat they may not have felt so singularly alone, but out there on a makeshift raft, exposed to the elements, they felt the weight of the risk they were taking.

"Being on the ocean is very different than I ever imagined," Ernesto said. "It's so fluid and yet so flat. A liquid desert."

"That's exactly it," Amaury marveled. "We're in the middle of nowhere."

The feeling of aloneness crept in, but the fear of being seen was still prevalent and they continued to paddle and push against the will of their bodies, their numb legs begging them to stop.

"Amaury, can you believe we're so far out that the island is already gone?"

"I know, Ernesto. It's pretty amazing and scary and sad at the same time."

It was noon when the hot, lazy sun was the highest in the sky. They had been nonstop paddling for many grueling hours and they both wanted nothing more than rest.

"How much longer do we need to paddle?" Ernesto asked.

"We've probably been paddling for six hours or so, but we must keep going," Amaury replied, based on where the sun now was. "We need to be at least eight to ten hours out before we can truly relax. We'll stop around dinner time. Like when the sun gets really low. Okay?"

Both boys' legs were so fatigued they couldn't feel them at all. Their feet felt like wet, sloppy appendages dangling from but unconnected to their bodies.

Cuba was long gone in the rearview now, and they were alone in the calm, glasslike ocean. There wasn't a single wave in sight. All they saw and felt was just a slight heaving and rolling motion. There wasn't a cloud in the sky. It was truly a beautiful day. The sun was hot, though. They could both feel its intensity on their skin, and it caused sweat to run down their faces. Occasionally, they would reach out to the ocean and pull the water up and splash the sweat off, but they continued to paddle, push and kick, the taste of freedom their singular focus.

The two said very little, but continued moving, pushing more and more, unsure of where their strength came from. Neither one could understand the intense determination that was their only motivation. A lifetime of oppression can do that to a man. They didn't want to think about the pain, nor how far they had gone, but they just continued focusing on the future and the promises of the new life they hoped was straight ahead.

The sun drifted toward the horizon, and as the day passed, they realized they were nearly safe. It was possibly two or three in the afternoon before Amaury felt it was finally okay to take a break, yet they continued for probably a final hour more.

For many hours, their legs were just numb. Occasionally, they would punch their legs just to make them feel something.

Amaury believed they still needed to be farther out beyond the shore. He wanted to be certain they were clearly past the imaginary line. There was no way to judge how far they'd gone or needed to go other than his gut feeling, but his survival instinct correctly guided him.

Amaury, the survivor, was facing the most difficult test of his life and was taking Ernesto with him. He could see Ernesto struggling badly. It was clear he didn't have the mental ability to continue the way Amaury did.

Amaury constantly gave him words of encouragement. "Keep going, buddy. Keep going. We're almost there. You're doing it. You're doing great!" Ernesto looked at him in disbelief. This was certainly more than he'd bargained for.

"I don't think I can take much more of this."

"You just keep moving. We're gonna make it, you'll see. I'm telling you; we're making it. See? Look how far we've already gone. Once we stop, you'll be able to rest the entire trip. Think about that."

Promising him they were going to be okay did have a positive effect on his brother. Amaury always thought positively and truly believed they were eventually going to get to America and then would be able to live life on their terms. That was America's promise. and was what drove him.

However, internally, Ernesto was fighting his demons. The struggle was much more than he'd bargained for. Over the years of his life, Ernesto had developed some bad habits, including smoking and drinking. In fact, he'd become an alcoholic. He hid this from everyone including Amaury and maybe even himself. Before the trip, he'd badly miscalculated and hadn't planned to bring alcohol with him or to accommodate to this sudden change of life. Without alcohol and only limited cigarettes, he'd underestimated his body's ability to manage such a trip.

As they progressed over the course of that first day, he started to think this had been a huge mistake. He didn't realize how bad he was going to need to drink and how incredibly difficult traveling across the ocean was going to be.

His body was already reeling from the sheer physical effort the trip had demanded. His mind was a frightened squirming raccoon caught in a corner. There was no escape from this predicament. Ernesto would look over at his brother and see he was a never-stopping machine. While it motivated him, even that motivation ebbed as time went on. He couldn't understand how he was able to just constantly keep moving seemingly without pain or stress.

Of course, it wasn't true, but Ernesto's mind was not only clouded by the physical requirements of paddling but also the constant mental demand for a break, a drink, a smoke... some kind of relief.

Ernesto's romantic notion of leaving Cuba and starting a new life had been so alluring and seductive that he'd failed to consider his own physical frailties. He'd misjudged his demanding daily needs and how seriously his addictions were going to impinge on his performance during the escape. His internal mental fight was as intense as the pain in his legs and arms, his mind yelling at him to stop and rest but also to keep going, keep moving.

Where Amaury had been training from a young boy how to survive, the true battle of survival, the mental tug of war, was only just beginning for Ernesto.

Amaury continued to gaze out at the horizon to see if the Cuban Coast Guard was anywhere nearby. So far so good. However, the Cuban Coast Guard was the least of what they needed to worry about.

Chapter 55

June 1994 Rebellion

There's a funny thing about living on an island—private conversations circulate. Bubbling just below the surface was a grassroots conversation, an effort the population in Havana knew was happening. Amaury was knowledgeable about the stirring anticommunist fervor developing on the streets. In the background, he'd heard a rumor there would be changes taking place against the government, and soon. He did not know the specifics but learned the people were planning a significant antigovernment event. The anger was a palpable boiling rage of tension that had been provoked by a recent tragic incident.

Amaury considered this might impinge his plans, but he never allowed it to interfere with his escape efforts. He made sure to stay knowledgeable of what was being said amongst the people, but his own intentions remained quiet. His life depended on a successful escape regardless of what was happening locally with the civilians.

Three weeks into June, the population witnessed a rare display of Cuban unrest. Anger had developed earlier in March when a group of seventy-two people tried to leave Cuba only to be caught mid-escape. During the attempted liberation, half the group was purposely and savagely killed by the Cuban Coastguard, who discovered the tugboat carrying dozens of desperate people. The Coastguard rammed the tugboat from behind, splitting the stern and causing the boat to begin sinking. At the same time, other government boats speedily circled the badly-damaged tug, causing a massive whirlpool. They sprayed high-pressure jet water from cannons into the sinking boat, forcing some passengers to jump off or be pummeled. It was a cruel act by the Coast Guard, who laughed as they continued to flood the listing tug.

In later reports, the Cuban government excused their actions, falsely explaining they'd attempted to put out the fire on the damaged tugboat, while children had been ripped from the clutches of their parents and had been eventually swept out to sea where they'd drowned. The fierce jet cannon water pressure forced other passengers down into the engine room for shelter, but those passengers perished, as they'd also drowned when the tug finally succumbed to the ocean's unforgiving grip.

Altogether, the passengers—men, women, and children on the boat—could do nothing to stop the onslaught and screamed in vain as the ship went down. This callous and heavy-handed show of force by the Coast Guard conveyed an intense disrespect for the population, causing an open public wound. Nationally it became known as the *Marzo de 13* event. Only thirty-one people survived on that horrific day, and the resulting anger rallied an open public revolt.

The blatant deadly action taken by the government made an example of what citizens could expect if they tried to illegally leave the country. The populist rage of thousands of Cubans evolved into a full-fledged rebellion the government was seemingly unable to quell. Afterward, several more copycat escapes took place. Another three more ferries were stolen, and the death of a Cuban police officer caused further retribution by the government against its people.

Later, to further punish the population, the government imposed a punitive food tax. As a result, thousands of pro-revolutionary workers entered the streets and began to fight the anti-revolutionary protesters. It became a show of force for their continued support of Castro's Revolution. It was a chaotic time. The government seemed incapable of stopping the new potent anti-revolutionary fervor.

Amaury knew of the incident, but he had to prioritize his escape from Cuba for his safety. It was difficult traveling around the island trying to make deals, accumulate provisions, and remain safe and invisible. Amaury the smart survivor worked quietly, continuing his activities unabated. He moved forward, staying in the shadows and never letting his guard down.

By the time he and Ernesto had pushed off, the anti-government revolt had not subsided and there were many small, oddly-timed outbursts of anger. Amaury and Ernesto had already been in the ocean several days when suddenly, in a strange turn of events, Castro, as if by a miracle, decided to change tactics. Without fanfare, he announced anyone who wanted to leave Cuba would be allowed to do so immediately for a limited time. A large exodus began to take place and lasted for a month.

Thousands of people risked their lives to leave in makeshift rafts or boats of any kind, giving them a chance of survival across the ocean. The Cuban Army was instructed to passively stand by while they watched crafts leave their shores. Castro thought allowing whoever wanted to leave would mitigate the intense anger he'd seen undermining his revolution, which by that time was many decades old. It was a gesture he felt would end the rebellious thirst. They'd realize they had gone too far. At that time, many Cubans chose to legally leave the island behind.

Amaury and Ernesto were already well on their way, never having known about the mass exodus soon after their exit.

Chapter 56

Realization

The moment of relief finally arrived. Amaury and Ernesto were able to stop kicking and paddling. They could finally rest. The feeling of simply floating was wonderful. Seeing the ocean from their vantage point the calm solitary confinement of the water contrasted with the knowledge they might be free for the first time in their lives was exhilarating. They were exhausted but also conflicted. This juxtaposition of the unknown versus the pain of leaving their old lives behind wasn't easy to digest as they felt the continued throbbing of pain in their legs.

Now, they were completely alone, probably for hundreds of miles, and they could hear the silence of the ocean. Their view was only the rolling movement of the ominous vast water as far as their eyes could see. It was a powerful reminder their trip was still in its infancy. The entire moment was surreal.

Later that afternoon, as they watched the sun overhead slowly fading into the distant horizon, the last few rays of light meant the change they sought was real. Time was definitely passing. Both boys rested, enjoying for a brief moment their feelings of elation and the total exhaustion of the day's adventurous escape.

Mutually, they thought the worst of it was over. They'd succeeded in getting away from the sphere of communist control over their lives, and a momentary elation set in. The idea of finally being away from Cuba was not only an emotional hurdle, but the prospect of a brighter future tugged just as hard. It was amazingly silent other than the occasional lapping of water against the curve of the rubber raft. Their muscles still ached. Amaury noticed how badly chafed his legs were. There was even some bleeding.

Ernesto's voice was dry and scrabbly. "Wow, we did it. And now we're out here all alone...It's strange. I feel trapped but free. Odd, isn't it?" He looked over at Amaury, who didn't respond but agreed in silence, too exhausted to say anything.

Who knew what could have been done?

Amaury looked across his feet and as far as he could see, surveying the ocean. It was amazing, huge and vacant with nothing but blue sea. He breathed in the ocean air and let it settle inside his lungs. Occasionally, he saw seagulls flying overhead, squawking as though they were saying hello to their new neighbors.

Amaury and Ernesto felt the rumbling of hunger in their stomachs, so they sat up and took a few of the sandwiches from the fishing box. Every bite was an effort. The fight to get away from Havana had left them without energy. They had just enough to chew and swallow. Hopefully, the night would bring rest and relief. As they reached for the food, Ernesto noticed the sky getting cloudy. Oddly, it wasn't quite as clear as it had been.

Amaury knew that they had no control over where they were going and that they could just as easily float right back to where they came from, but they wouldn't know until it was too late. While he wanted nothing more than to sleep, he was afraid to relax too much for fear that their efforts would be in vain. They ate slowly. The small sandwiches were the only food they had, another reminder of what little they had in their lives. It seemed strange to both of them that the life they loved was gone —it was almost as if it had never happened.

For the remainder of the early evening, things were still and quiet. No Coast Guard, no sharks... nothing. Just ocean water and the breeze.

Back home and with no sight of Amaury for days, the Cuban government wasn't satisfied nor finished with him. They knew he had gone rogue. He was a pariah to the community despite his father being a general. It was finally time to bring him to trial.

They sought him out everywhere. On every corner and street, his friends, family and anyone who might have had contact with him was subject to questioning.

General Nury had tried his best over the years to reign in Amaury to make him heel to the communist way, but it was not going to happen.

The government positioned policemen on each corner outside of his solar. They were stationed day and night with shift changes. They were out in the open while other operatives hid in dark corners. They thought he was around and needed to watch every possible location he might frequent. They planned to bring him in as soon as they saw him. His national ID and Army card were confiscated, and they knew he'd have limited access to free movement on the island. The government didn't like the sudden mysterious disappearance of Amaury Torres, and so they decided a full-scale search for him was necessary.

Chapter 57

Life is Always a Challenge

At the time of Amaury and Ernesto's departure, the rebellion was still in full force, although the release of the people had not yet taken place. Meanwhile, as the brothers looked up at the sky, it was completely dark until finally interrupted by the brilliance of the moon which eventually rose in the east. "Ernesto, can you believe how beautiful the moon is?"

"It's unbelievable, Amaury. As I reach up, it almost feels as if I can touch it."

Witnessing the billions of stars as far as the eyes could see made them suddenly feel very small in the universe. The sight of the heavens looked so vast without any lights to block its view. They were surrounded not only by an ocean of water but an ocean of stars to entertain their eyes.

Together, they talked about the constellations and tried to test themselves and see if they could figure out where they were. The solitary floating was beautiful and made them a little bit sleepy, while the sound of silence was alive in their ears.

"I will tell you one thing, Ernesto. The ocean has a natural current that will guide us to America. I learned about this in training. They tried hard to keep it a secret, but I figured it out. Some of the Rangers were headed to the Coast Guard, but to us other guys, I'm pretty sure they wanted to make sure we never understood. It had to do with Cubans escaping. I later discovered it's the natural movement of the Caribbean Sea. That's why I wanted to push off in *Guanabo*. I figured it gave us the ability to catch the current and move us toward America."

"Ah okay, now I get it. You're not that crazy after all." They both laughed heartily.

Not long after that, they began noticing it was becoming darker. Clouds covered the moon and visibility in the water disappeared. Soon the moon disappeared altogether. It was total darkness. They couldn't see each other nor their own hands in front of their faces on their little raft.

"What's going on?" Ernesto asked, his voice full of fear.

"I'm not sure," Amaury said. "The sky looked clear at sunset..."

The wind began picking up and the temperature dropped significantly. Quickly, they became uncomfortable when the calm water started rolling and splashing across their raft. It was nothing too alarming but was not the peaceful ocean they'd experienced over the last few hours.

In the distance, they could hear thunder, and then suddenly small drops of rain began to trickle down onto their skin. Realizing the Atlantic Ocean could very well experience hurricanes and tropical storms, Amaury felt they could be in for a troubling evening.

"I hope we aren't going to see a hurricane," Ernesto said.

"I was thinking the same thing, Ernesto."

Even though it was hurricane season, they didn't know what possibly could be happening. It was, however, a severe tropical storm descending upon them. The ocean heaved as the winds picked up and the water started to splash onto their raft. The waves grew bigger, and the little raft started to rise and fall with the growing waves.

They held on tightly as they could.

"Ernesto!" Amaury shouted. "Tie the end of your rope around your ankle very tightly! We cannot afford to drown after all this! We're hitting a storm!"

"This looks pretty serious. The waves are getting really big!"

"Yes! Stay alert. Hang on, here comes another one."

Thunder boomed right above them, while huge branches and bright bolts of lightning crackled around them. The sudden white light enabled them to clearly see the water for quick moments. The sudden view of giant waves was frightening. They both looked at each other in horror. The storm sounded as if it was right above their heads. The rain was coming down in sheets directly into their faces and often at odd angles. The rain and salty ocean water blew in every direction, and they had to cover their eyes.

The ocean current became severe. The rubber raft followed up an ocean mountain only to slam down again landing at odd angles. The boys grabbed the netting under them as tightly as they could muster. Amaury looked at Ernesto to see how he was holding up.

"Ernesto, I think we're going to end up in the water, so hold onto the rope as tightly as you can."

"Okay, Amaury. I've got it. Oh my god, this is bad, brother!"

Then without warning, the lightning flashed, the thunderclap crashed, and the raft flipped completely over as a wave slammed directly into it. Amaury and Ernesto were knocked out of the raft and into the water, and Ernesto felt one of the bottles of water hit him square on the side of his head. They could still hear the muffled booming of the thunder as they struggled under the surface.

Submerged under the raft and trying not to drown took

nearly all the strength they had to give. Everything they'd brought with them was gone in that instant. Still stunned from the blow to his head, Ernesto made his way to the surface and tried with all his might to grab the rope but missed it twice, although his ankle was still tied to it. Panicked and gasping for breath, he reached several more times to grab the rope, but his fingers grasped nothing but water and air.

Amaury had also breached the surface, and in the flashes of lightning, he could surmise that the waves were easily fifteen to twenty feet in height. He hadn't expected this kind of weather event and was intensely afraid that Ernesto wouldn't be able to survive.

"Ernesto!" he called to his brother.

"Amaury! Over here!"

Amaury looked around but couldn't see his brother through the angry churning of the water.

"Ernesto! Where are you?!"

"HERE!" he heard Ernesto call again. The lightning flashed again, and Amaury caught sight of him. He started to swim to him and then helped him swim back to the raft. Somehow, they were both able to climb back on, but the raft was of little refuge as the waves were way above their heads. They continued to crash down around them. The severity of the storm's anger only seemed to increase as time went on, while the wind threw them about as they struggled to hang onto the rope and the raft. Paddling during the day now seemed like a slight effort compared to the punishment they were receiving from the storm. It was an altogether different kind of battle, a life, and death, moment-to-moment struggle. The only thing they had left in life was the rope, the raft, and exhaustion. All they could do was to try and make sure they were able to catch their next breath between mouthfuls of saltwater.

Several more times, waves knocked them into the water, and

each time they would hang onto the rope until they could try to climb back onto the raft. Amaury watched Ernesto struggle and did everything he could to help him get back onto the raft. Getting himself above the surface to breathe and occasionally up onto the raft was a herculean task all on its own. The only moments Amaury could see Ernesto was when the lightning cracks illuminated the sky. He'd look to make sure Ernesto was attached and above water every time he caught a glimpse of his brother.

Amaury surmised if they could manage to get onto the raft together lying down at the same time, they might be able to aim the raft up and then down depending on the waves' motions. With one huge breath, Amaury screamed out, "Ernesto! follow me onto the raft right now!"

Chapter 58

Momentary Relief

It took every ounce of strength they both had left but somehow they managed to get on top of the raft one last time together and hold on as tightly as they could. It worked well as long as they lay flat, but it was a few more hours of struggling to stay alive in the ferocious, unforgiving liquid monster of the storm.

Ernesto had never imagined that his flight to America would result in such devastating circumstances. Shocked at the severity of the storm and how hard he had to struggle to stay alive, his resolve began to slip. His thoughts became compromised and disoriented, and he believed he might not make it through the night.

During the course of his struggle, he realized his years of drinking were a terrible mistake and that they'd stolen from him his confidence and his determination to succeed. He hated himself for his failings. He could hear his brother calling to him in muffled bursts.

"Ernesto! Ernesto! Are you all right?"

Ernesto could barely respond as he tried to keep his strength within himself to maintain any equilibrium. Barely able to get the words out so Amaury could hear, he called out, "*Bueno, bueno*!!" He knew, though, he was not doing well. He was slipping very badly. Mentally, the sheer exhaustion weakened him alarmingly. He prayed it would end soon. Unconsciously, he was consumed with terrible thoughts, and his muscles hurt so badly. His mind played tricks on him, the kind he didn't want to mess with. His thoughts kept whispering.

Let go. It's easier, Ernesto. Let go. You'll finally be free.

More than anything, he didn't want to disappoint his brother, and that one single thought helped him to stay with Amaury and make sure he'd be all right.

Ernesto knew that in America they'd be a better team than Amaury being on his own, so Ernesto held that thought in his mind as he cried alone in the ocean as the storm tossed him and his beloved brother about.

I have not lived my life correctly. I've let myself down badly.

Gripped by an immense sadness, he was afraid Amaury would see him sobbing.

As time went on, all they could think about was surviving the next wave, the next gust of wind, and the next breath. Everything was so punishing.

Amaury figured they must be dealing with forty to fifty mph wind gusts. He was furious with himself for not paying better attention to the skyline earlier in the day. But then again, what could be done? There was no turning back. All they could do was hold on for dear life and hope they made it to the other side of the storm.

They desperately continued to position themselves so they could direct the raft to get it to the top of waves and use it for safety, but it was close to impossible to consistently make it work.

Amaury quickly thought that the raft traveled better sideways, much like the sand crabs they'd left earlier in the morning at the beach. They were doing the same thing. Perhaps that was the answer.

Either way, it was a test of their will against nature's will. The only things keeping them alive were the ropes tied around their ankles. Amaury focused on the one thought which kept him going under all the pressure, and that was the thought of not seeing the American Flag one day. He pictured the flag in his mind, praying to see it, and repeated the image over and over as a goal to distract his doubtful thoughts in a positive way to keep himself strong. He'd always wanted to see the flag and be part of something so beautiful, and it helped him make it through the stormy night.

Their ankles became severely raw from the friction of the tied rope. Amaury had been through many hardships in his life but at this moment, it seemed like the hardest challenge he'd ever faced.

Finally, the storm began to subside. Thunder and lightning dissipated, and the gale became a steady light rain. Eventually, the ocean surface calmed and became friendlier once again. Exhausted, the boys had nothing left. Lying on their back, they faced up and contemplated their fate. Amaury realized the trip had been much more than they both could have possibly imagined it would be. The fight to get to America was a road paved with many unknown debts.

The storm finally petered out in the early morning. Amaury estimated it was around maybe 5 a.m. based on the light in the eastern part of the sky. As they tried to regroup their strength, Amaury knew from experience that they were very possibly in the early stages of hypothermia. The physical tasking and exhaustion with no food to replace the energy expended and without any physical protection meant they both might very well become ill.

The morning came and mercifully with it came the sun's

heat. Both brothers were starving and were without food. The only thing they both had were the shirts and shorts they were wearing.

Early in the morning, a delirious Ernesto began to complain. "I don't know where those damn cigarettes are. I know they were here. I'm sure I brought them. Damn it. I need those cigarettes!"

Not knowing what to say or do, Amaury just remained silent.

Chapter 59

Ernesto

On their second day, without much to do, Amaury quietly began reviewing his entire life. He thought about his childhood and what had brought him to this day. How did he get to where he was? Had it been a mistake? And what would his life be like in the USA if he made it there? What happens when dreams do come true? He was happy to have his brother with him and face their new life together. It was much better than facing one alone. Quietly, on his own, he kept praying to God to steer them to safety, hear his prayers and keep them both alive.

Both Amaury and Ernesto didn't talk much on their second day. The exhaustion and the physical fight they individually faced were so overwhelming they needed to find strength within themselves to recover and to be thankful they were still alive. Their bodies were equally beaten up, and they needed to find the energy to continue for the remainder of the trip, however long it would take.

Their only desire was a peaceful day to recover. However, they also needed to manage the intensity of the sun, as well. Amaury realized he needed to teach Ernesto how to endure the sun's heat for the balance of their trip. Their next goal was trying to stay cool.

His Ranger training had taught Amaury to use his sweat to keep the heat off his body. He explained to Ernesto to use their shirts as a towel to capture the sweat, as it was much less salty than ocean water. When it was soaked with sweat, they could squeeze the shirt to pour it over their bodies to cool their skin. Similarly, in the jungle, they'd use their pants as a towel to catch the morning dew and then squeeze the water from their pants for water to drink.

Amaury knew survival.

Ernesto struggled with the cooling-off procedure. He seemed confused and not disciplined enough to follow through, but mostly lamented not having a drink and a cigarette. His need for nicotine was relentless and he continued loudly struggling all day.

His body begged for just one smoke, and his mind continued playing tricks on him. There were moments when he thought the cigarettes were right near him as he reached out to grab one, even though he remembered they had disappeared in that very first crushing wave. His struggle was not only in meeting the demands of the trip, but his body and mind became twisted in angry confusion. He couldn't control his feelings. They were becoming irrational. Now and then he'd suddenly blurt out loud, pleading, "I need just one. Just one, please. Only one!"

Amaury ignored these calls for the cigarettes. He knew there was nothing to do. Ernesto quietly worsened, although he never admitted it to Amaury. Ernesto's mind became a rat on a wheel, a rage of internal uncontrollable emotion.

Amaury could see his brother was having a difficult time but also didn't understand how severe it was. He kept his eyes shut and tried to retain his strength, knowing he needed to be calm for his brother's sake.

Ernesto was so focused on cigarettes and alcohol, he lost track of where he was, what he was doing there, and why he could not have that cigarette. Conflict and confusion were his only thoughts as little by little he broke down throughout the entire day.

The hours went by slowly, especially as they did not have a clock to check. They never knew what time it was, other than looking at the sun's positioning overhead or east then west. When it was directly above, they knew it was around noon, and as the sun headed west they could see it was later in the afternoon. Both boys continued to feel the intense pangs of hunger. Amaury knew this was going to be a bigger problem if they weren't able to get water and/or food soon.

Slowly, the afternoon became early evening, and strong sunburns appeared on their exposed skin.

The hours passed with darkness fully enveloping the now calm sea. They didn't see a boat or a ship the entire day. Amaury knew there might be a shark around eventually, but other than the occasional bird, it was a quiet, solitary day.

Amaury always looked straight up to the heavens contemplating the stars, allowing his mind to wander in a meditative stream of thought with no barriers. He was relaxed and mentally floating when he heard his brother once again mumble something.

"I'm going to the corner to get some cigs," Ernesto said.

Amaury didn't so much as look at Ernesto, as he'd been repeating those same words all day.

He continued to doze slightly, occasionally gazing up and concentrating on the stars. He felt as though he were watching a movie of the wondrous universe. The gift was the enormity of the heavens and how it made him feel momentarily happy.

As Amaury lay on the other side of the raft, Ernesto spoke again. "Amaury, I'm going to the corner to get a pack of smokes. Be right back."

Ernesto, then quickly and quietly slipped off the raft and into the ocean. For a moment, Amaury didn't realize Ernesto had left the raft. It was only a moment or so later when he rolled over and realized the raft was leaning down slightly toward his side that he bolted up to his knees.

"Ernesto? Ernesto?! Ernesto! Ernesto!!!" He screamed it over and over. His eyes darted in every direction in the darkness of night.

He searched the dark water, looking for any sign of his brother. All he had was the moon's light causing shadows and a few reflections in the blackness.

Amaury tied the rope to his other ankle and jumped in the water, screaming Ernesto's name at the top of his lungs. He desperately felt around in the water in a circular swimming motion around the raft, then dove under it as deeply as he could, trying in vain to see if he could feel him anywhere at all. He bumped into Ernesto's rope underwater and vigorously yanked it up until the end was in his hands.

Ernesto was gone—completely gone, as though he vanished into thin air. Amaury climbed back onto the raft and sobbed. His body convulsed in agony as his tears streamed down his face. He realized he must have underestimated the pain Ernesto had been in and the severe confusion that must have shrouded him. For a while, Amaury thought maybe he was trapped inside some unimaginable nightmare and prayed to wake up beside his brother. But when the sky started to turn pink and morning's light began to break, Amaury knew he hadn't slept and there was no denying the truth.

Ernesto was really gone. He was gone forever.

Chapter 60

New Friends

Amaury felt destroyed. As the sky grew brighter, he slowly sat up and tried to evaluate his remaining choices. Over his life, he'd faced many adversaries, the death of friends and his own potential death, but this was different. He was truly and totally alone for the first time in his life.

He'd known from the beginning that Ernesto couldn't handle the trip, but he'd been afraid to admit the truth to himself and should never have allowed his brother to go. For the first time since he'd entered the ocean, he felt scared that he might not make it to America. The intensity and weight of being alone were overwhelming, more than he ever could have imagined.

No matter how tough you are, nothing prepares you for this.

Without his brother, he felt fragile and vulnerable. That morning, he allowed himself to grieve, but as the sun rose high, he knew he needed to move forward. His survival was his only motivation. He had no choice. He was determined to be a free man, and he knew he'd have to make a difference in his own life.

Using these thoughts and his brother's memory, he forced himself to keep going. Amaury's instinctual survival abilities helped him move forward. He kept considering how to save his own life. He constantly thought about Ernesto, never forgetting the huge effort he'd contributed and the debt he owed his brother for his dedication, sacrifice, and love.

Later that day, Amaury fell asleep thinking about the night he'd spent looking for Ernesto. He thought about the day before and how his brother had had a difficult time staying strong in the fight and had suffered because of it. The lack of alcohol and those damned cigarettes had been too much for him. He must have finally given in to its demand. He'd underestimated the intensity of Ernesto's struggle because he'd been thinking about his own instead. They'd been in the part of the ocean where the currents were strongest and must have quickly taken him away, as he'd swiftly disappeared.

Amaury had been fast asleep for hours when he felt a strong tugging, a brushing, and bumping of his raft. His eyes were closed, and he was half asleep, and he thought it must be his imagination. He continued to keep his eyes closed, but the raft was being touched by something. After all, he was alone. For a moment, he thought it was a shark and his heart started racing. Suddenly concerned and feeling uneasy, he lifted his head to see what was there. If it was a shark, he could get knocked off.

The way this trip has been going, nothing would surprise me now.

Slowly, he took the shirt off his forehead and looked around. Again, he felt a strong bump on the other side of the raft. As Amaury sat up, still feeling the constant rubbing sensation, he looked down through the covered hole and saw a very large fish. He peered over the raft's curved edges and thought he saw a shark, yet although the fish was quite large, it wasn't the least bit aggressive. It appeared to be pushing his raft, almost guiding it. There was no dorsal fin sticking up, and Amaury heaved a sigh of relief. He looked out at the ocean surface and, upon seeing a lot of these fish, suddenly realized it wasn't a shark but a family of dolphins. Rubbing his eyes, he couldn't believe what he was seeing.

There was a family of dolphins swimming alongside him. As he watched in amazement, he saw they were playing with each other and him. It seemed as though each one took turns bumping against his raft in a game-like fashion.

As the afternoon progressed, he watched them push him and stay with him, swimming as escorts. They jumped out of the water near him, splashing him with a cool refreshing mist. there were other moments when they were so close that he could look directly into their generous eyes and easily could have reached out and touched them.

He was amazed. A gift from God, perhaps!

As night fell, they seemed to disappear and reappear over and over. Each one took turns bumping him and swimming and increasing the speed of his raft. He could hear them squeaking almost as though they wanted him to know they weren't leaving. They stayed with him for the next three days and nights, never straying from his raft.

Oddly, Amaury felt they were trying to help him keep him going in the right direction, but the truth was he had no idea. As the days progressed, he found although he loved being with the dolphins and knowing they were there, he felt he rapidly was losing his strength. Each day he knew his physical condition was worsening. The heat of the sun and the lack of food and water were all taking their tolls on him.

Amaury thought if he was progressing toward Florida, it was quite slow and had no idea where he was. Amaury knew his time to live was limited. He calculated if he didn't get help soon, he'd die within a day or two at the most. The moon's blinding light high in the night sky appeared again.

Alone.

Chapter 61

Dehydration

Amaury had been drinking his urine for hydration for days and calculated his production was less than a third of a cup every eight hours. It was important to gauge the amount as a way to actively monitor his physical health. Amaury realized it was only a matter of time before he was no longer able to produce enough to maintain his life, and the toxicity levels of drinking his urine over and over could easily become life-threatening in its own right.

In his Army training, Amaury had learned the body didn't digest all the nutrients and vitamins ingested each day. As he drank, he was essentially recycling whatever value he was producing. Amaury hated urine. It tasted horrible, like an old nasty warm beer, only to be consumed in emergencies. He would drink it as quickly as he could because his life depended on it.

As he looked down at his body, he noticed the welts growing in size, the boils covering most of his body. Struggling to reach up and touch his face, which was the worst of all, round painful balls enclosed liquid welts and his skin was extremely sensitive inside his elbows. Dehydration was taking its toll, as well. He realized his mind was cloudy, and he often saw himself from above lying on his raft. It made him feel uneasy and out of balance.

The sun's rays against the ocean were particularly painful. He left his shirt over his eyes most of the entire day. Lifting his head was a task of its own. Lying on the netting, he felt the ropes piercing into his back, which had already been hurting for days.

His body was shutting down little by little. Inside, his kidneys felt sore, his stomach was cramping from lack of food and his entire physical state was in significant decline. He knew death was closing in. At night, it was physically more challenging, as the setting of the sun left him cold and shivering. He rolled into the fetal position to create and maintain some heat. Nothing worked, other than praying he would make it. He kept trying to stay positive by imagining what it would feel like lying on American soil, kissing America's ground, and knowing his predicament had finally ended.

He realized though his body was giving up, for better or worse, he knew he had done his best. He gave it his best shot with everything he had. He'd made the tough struggle and had done what he could to fight communism and be his own individual against the tyrannical system. He'd taken the world on his terms and would not cave into the pressure to lose his own. A funny thought popped into his head.

Who was the bastard who'd started communism to begin with? He was an evil asshole.

That was the last funny thought he'd had for a while. Amaury looked at his body again and noticed his blistered hands, his dehydration so severe that surprisingly his vision had become compromised, as well. He was only able to see a little beyond his raft and, shocked by this new realization, he tried to reconcile again that he might not make it. He tried to find a peaceful spot for his soul to feel a sense of satisfaction and serenity. It was all he concentrated on, and as time continued, he tried to calm his mind and get ready to accept his fate.

Amaury had already been in the ocean for seven days and until now had been lucky, as the weather had been calm since the first evening.

As the sun rose with the dawn, he dreaded the morning brightness most. It was arduous, punishing, inescapable trap when the sun rose and the rays forced him to keep his eyes shut. As each minute passed, he believed it was possible he would die that day and felt himself slipping in and out of consciousness. While floating, he started hearing unusual sounds, faint but not from the ocean. Amaury found them baffling, and he wasn't sure if they were real or a figment of his frail imagination.

However, although the sounds were confusing, they seemed familiar but distant. He focused as hard as he could and tried to separate reality from illusion. His mind scrambled hard to mentally untangle his thoughts. Already so dizzy from days of drifting, the sounds became audible voices. He was able to establish it was the sound of a man and a woman conversing in both English and Spanish. Struggling to lift his head to see, Amaury turned to look backward, and stunned, he saw a large boat's bow directly above his head.

It was huge and white with a big blue stripe down the side. He tried to make a sound, but he couldn't get his voice to work. He kept blinking and trying to get his eyes to refocus.

He took his sweat-soiled T-shirt and wiped his eyes but was unsure what to do or say. He saw two people staring back and understood were discussing him. As he stared at them while trying to avoid the intense sun in his eyes, he saw to his immense surprise an American flag flapping in the ocean breeze, flying high atop the main mast of the yacht.

In total disbelief, tears immediately welled up and he couldn't stop himself from crying. They called out to him in both Spanish and English. "Hello? Hello? Are you all right? Who are you? We want to help you."

They pulled aside his raft with a long-hooked pole and tried to grab ahold of his raft. The woman appeared anxious as she quickly spoke to the man in Spanish. It appeared they were arguing, but regardless, they pulled Amaury around. She kept pointing at him and talking to the man. They were out in a fishing yacht when they'd come upon Amaury.

Both were just as stunned as he was, Amaury noticed. Their demeanor wasn't hostile, and he realized they were going to help him, hooking the long aluminum pole onto the netting and proceeding to pull him around to the stern. While the crew pulled, they followed and continued talking, but he couldn't understand what they were saying.

At the stern, he saw a square opening entry to the boat. It was used to pull fish onto the boat. They reached for him, pulling him through to the other side and onboard.

Immediately, they started to dab cool, fresh water on him gently with clean white towels, slowly washing his body and taking care not to disturb his many welts. The man seemed to know exactly what to do. After a few minutes of washing, they carried him to a lounge chair, where they sat him down and carefully gave him water to drink. Amaury had never tasted anything sweeter than those first few drops of fresh, clean water. He tried to sip it carefully, but still sputtered and coughed a bit, as it was hard for him to keep himself from guzzling it down.

"Cuidado, bebe despacio," the woman said as she held the water bottle to his lips. "Drink slowly."

As he drank and soothed his parched mouth, Amaury was able to find his voice again. "Gracias," he said.

Over the next few minutes, they asked him questions about who he was and how he'd ended up in the ocean. They asked about his life. They understood he was a refugee but wanted to know as much about him as they could. As they were talking, the man put a cream on Amaury's body and told him that he was a doctor, a pediatrician who knew what to do to help him.

Amaury realized this was another strange twist of fate, a gift perhaps, to have a doctor as the first person he met in America. As the doctor placed the cream on him, he was careful to first wash the salt out of the wounds. Once cleaned, they completely wrapped him in a blanket for extra warmth due to his severe exposure. It was still difficult for Amaury to talk, and the next thing he remembered, he passed out.

Chapter 62

First Taste of America

"How are you feeling Mr. Torres?" A voice stirred Amaury from his sleep. He awoke in a hospital bed. Staring up, he realized it was a nurse who was talking to him.

Answering in Spanish, he tried to communicate his needs. "I'm doing okay, but I could use some water, please. Where am I?"

She didn't know Spanish. However, she understood the words *agua* and *por favor*. She went to get him some water. He drank the water and then looked down at himself, remembering the last time he'd seen his body he'd been covered in painful blisters. He saw bandages everywhere. The wounds were still painful and burning, yet some were less so now.

There were many machines and wires around him, as well as people wearing white uniforms. He realized they were nurses who were speaking English, but most weren't paying much attention to him as he dozed on and off for the next several hours.

Occasionally, a nurse walked over to him to check the machines and not say a word and then would walk away. In the evening, he was left on his own to rest. He discovered he was healing fairly quickly after receiving lots of medical attention and care from the nurses. Six days later, he was well enough to be released.

The Immigration and Naturalization Service came to visit within the first few days and in Spanish, they told Amaury he would be taken to their offices and remain under their control. They asked Amaury many questions. "Who are you, Mr. Torres? Why did you come to Miami? What happened to you and why were you alone?"

Under questioning with an interpreter, he answered as many of the questions about his life as he could.

"I'm a political refugee and had to leave my country to stay alive. I was in severe danger and was forced to flee. I was in the Cuban Army and refused to continue. They were going to put me on trial for antirevolutionary behavior if I refused to join the communist party. I would probably have been executed. Therefore, I am seeking political asylum."

The U.S. government officials described to Amaury how his case would be handled and what to expect under U.S. custody.

Once he was approved to leave the hospital, he was taken by the immigration department directly to a U.S. Coast Guard ship where he was transferred to Guantanamo Bay to await his immigration status review. He was worried about the process and how it would unfold on his behalf, but as an illegal immigrant, he accepted what he was told and did not ask many questions, and only contemplated what his future would be.

Initially, the Mother Ship, as it was called, sailed a perimeter around Cuba for a twenty-four-hour period. He spent time looking at his homeland from the ship's deck and could not believe he was back home looking from the outside in.

While he looked at his home country leaning on the deck railing, he thought about how crazy life was. He had almost lost his life to get away, and barely three weeks later, he was right back where he'd started. The irony of what had taken place was not lost on him.

The entire trip back to Guantanamo took four days. Before leaving, they were given instructions on their assigned sleeping quarters. They'd be separated into three groups and then further divided into smaller groups in the camp, which housed thousands of people.

In his tent, Amaury learned of a surprise. His departure from Cuba coincided with the *Marzo de 13* exodus. Once again life moved in Amaury's favor. When he'd fled Cuba, it had coincided with the Castro temporary exit sanctioning, resulting in his ability to keep his Cuban citizenship.

He was amazed at his good fortune. He'd thought he would never be able to return to Cuba or see his family again. The irony didn't seem to end. They were going to put him in jail minimally for refusing to become a communist, and with this change, he'd be able to return legally someday in the future without fear of retribution.

Chapter 63

Guantanamo

The U.S. Marines were in charge of refugees at Guantanamo Bay, and they required separate assigned quarters for men and women. All in all, the total number of detainees was over thirty-thousand people. Each tent housed approximately thirty residents. The accommodations were basic and relatively clean, but no one cared to complain. Everyone lived peacefully. The tent walls were made of wood fastened to dirt floors with spikes, cots for sleeping, and two small shelves for personal items.

When Amaury found his assigned location, he met his new tentmates and quickly became friends. He spent much of his time playing card games with the others but always tried to inquire from the Marines how the process was moving along. Each night, the tentmates talked about their prior experiences. In the bed next to Amaury, a new friend Chago Valdez's family had originally been from Africa, although they'd emigrated to Cuba decades before. Chago had also tried to immigrate to the U.S. and told Amaury a story about his cousin.

"My cousin wasn't a good boy and found much trouble in Cuba. That's why he tried to escape. He got pretty far, though.

Initially, he'd left with a bunch of people, but somehow the had Marines found out about his history. Once the Cubans somehow discovered he was here in Guantanamo, they'd managed to get the Marines to return him to them. He'd been here for a month before it happened."

Thinking quietly to himself, Amaury was shocked to discover the Marines were working with the Cubans.

Helping them get wanted criminals out of Guantanamo.

"That's interesting to hear about, Chago. Are you sure that's what happened?"

"I'm as surprised as you are. He wasn't a bad guy, although honestly, he'd done some pretty bad things. In a way, it wasn't unforeseeable. I'm not sure what'll happen to him, although, I've heard those Cuban prisons are really bad places to be."

"Yes. I'm sure you are right. They never sounded like a lot of fun." Amaury hid his background. He was very nervous that he might get turned over, as well.

Slipping out of Cuba quietly and having never found out exactly what had happened after he left, Amaury was more than a little worried. He thought the Marines might return him, as well, if they learned about him. He was extremely uncomfortable once he realized he was going back to Cuba via Guantanamo. It was his first thought when he'd been informed—he was going to be brought to Guantanamo by the U.S. immigration authorities. He didn't want to advertise his history to any of his tentmates by revealing intimate parts of his past. He believed sometimes people talked.

Amaury took a big gulp. "Chago? Tell me how it happened with your cousin."

"He was here like you are and I am. However, one day out of nowhere, a group of Marines came over and talked to him. They asked him to follow them to their office. He looked nervous. And then, I never saw him again. It was mysterious. It's as if he just disappeared into thin air."

"Man, that's scary."

"Yes, it certainly was, especially since he'd been here for a month or so. I remember talking to him. He thought he'd made it."

Amaury rolled over in his bed, closed his eyes, and tried to calm himself. He didn't want to let his tent-mates know how terrified he truly was. The night passed quietly.

While at Guantanamo, they were given three cold meals a day. Within six months, Amaury became excited when he learned he would be given the option to move to Panama at the second military facility, thinking it would speed up the immigration process and give him some additional much-needed separation from Guantanamo.

Amaury was always looking over his shoulder to see if the Marines were approaching him. He never felt comfortable.

Being in Panama might allow me to get away from Cuba and will give me some relief from my fears. It's eating me up inside. I'm going to take them up on their offer. I'm out of here!

Chapter 64

Homestead

Upon arrival in Panama, Amaury found a camp prepared in much better condition with many surprising new amenities—running hot water, showers, hot meals, plus his old favorite, Coca-Cola in the tents. The Panama location provided other surprises, as well—weird creatures and another old favorite—dangerous snakes. Luckily the tents were predesigned to protect the inhabitants from the slithering creatures.

Despite his uplifted spirits in moving, daily life remained the same, with not many options for activities. Similarly, they ate, played cards, and reminisced about home. Most of his time there was quite boring; however, this stay ended quickly. Amaury learned the journey to America was a test of patience. After six months, there was an announcement.

"The Panama camp will be closed in a week. Please prepare yourself to return to Guantanamo for the remainder of your processing period. More announcements will follow over the next several days. Thank you."

The detainees were surprised by the suddenness of the changes. Unfortunately, during his stay in Panama, out of anxiety, Amaury began smoking cigarettes. Cigarettes also became a base of currency in card games and other transactions inside the camps. Amaury was torn. He was both happy yet nervous to go back. His fears of being returned to Cuban authorities never subsided despite being in Panama.

Once back in Guantanamo, Amaury continued to look over his shoulder, yet still, nothing untoward took place. One day the local priest who visited the camp to help the spirits of the inhabitants became friends with Amaury. To his surprise, the priest brought Amaury a full assortment of fishing gear, a rod, a fishing line, and lures. This made his second stint in Guantanamo quite enjoyable because he loved fishing. He was delighted, and it didn't take long before his tent became the most popular in their area. Everyone came to eat and spend time with Amaury because his fishing and cooking skills were the highlight of their neighborhood. He became an expert in fish preparation despite the minimal tools and seasonings available. More importantly, he perfected his fish-filleting abilities.

One evening while Amaury was cooking on his makeshift rock-built barbecue, he was tapped on his shoulder. He looked back and his face went white as a cloud. Standing next to him were two Marines, Sergeant Paul Madison and his assistant Joe Halliday.

"Mr. Torres, we'd like to speak with you in our office in fifteen minutes, please. It's important. We'll see you momentarily. Okay? Thank you"

Amaury was shocked and didn't know what to think. He quickly became very nervous. Remembering Chago's cousin, he now believed his time was over. It was happening to him, as well. His past may have finally caught up with him.

Shaking, Amaury responded. "Yes sir, I'll just clean up here and be right there."

Amaury took the long, intense walk near the center of the

camp to the Marines' main tent offices. In the darkness, he heard laughing and talking as he approached. There was a screened metal-framed door that he knocked on to announce his arrival. A single dimly-lit lightbulb highlighted the middle of the tent.

"Hello, Sirs? You wanted to speak with me?"

"Oh, yes, Amaury. Please come in. Why don't you take a seat for a moment? We called you into the office tonight because we've heard about you."

"Heard about me?" he asked. "I don't understand. What do you mean?"

Sergeant Paul Madison spoke first. "You know, the fishing and grilling."

Shocked, Amaury hesitated for a moment. "Oh, yes. I guess that's true."

"I am not sure if you're aware, Amaury, but it's against the rules here. We know it's been good for morale in your area, and more importantly, we've heard you're an amazing cook. Frankly, the thing is, we cannot talk to you in front of all the inhabitants. We were wondering if you wouldn't mind making us some. We'd love to taste your Cuban fish. Truthfully, we're all a little hungry. We'll keep it on the hush-hush."

The other Marines chuckled as he concluded their request.

Amaury couldn't believe his ears. He knew the word had got out about his cooking, but he had no idea it had gotten back to the Marines. He almost fainted from his nervousness but then agreed.

"Of course, you can. It would be my honor to prepare fish for you. I have a few *Sabalo* and *Mojará* left that haven't yet been claimed. Both are very *rico*. I'll bring you the assortment right over. You'll really enjoy it!"

Smiling, Madison responded, "That would be great!"

Amaury walked out feeling one hundred pounds lighter and

felt his life begin anew. It was another eight months before Amaury, and the rest of the group learned they were finally going to be brought to America and be permitted into the country. Amaury couldn't believe it.

The exit process took an additional two months based on a lottery system. However, once his name was announced, he had to be prepared to leave in two days. It was a long, arduous wait fraught with anticipation, anxiety and jealousy as he watched many friends leave first. As the Marines dismantled each tent, the immigration paperwork had to be finalized. As family names were announced each night, approximately three hundred people would be flown to the Florida area with two to three flights a week.

The tents quickly emptied. They were not allowed to take much of what they had accumulated, leaving an enormous mountain of items behind. The remaining clothing, food, and cigarettes were burned in huge piles.

Amaury saw hundreds if not thousands of boxes of cigarettes and hundreds of shirts, shoes, shorts, and sandals that remained to be disposed of. His group patiently continued to play cards as their names were called one by one.

"We have several final groups to leave over the next few weeks. However, here are tonight's names. They are as follows: Alejandro, Alicia, Alejandro and Ricardo Balmana. Next is Torres—Amaury Torres."

The announcement of names went on for a few more minutes, and Amaury jumped up in elation once he'd heard his name. Everyone cheered for him, and some of the others in his group were also called.

"That's it for me. I can't believe it. Finally, the time has arrived. Wow!"

The few guys whose names had been t called danced in a circle, thrilled with the great news. That night, Amaury couldn't stop thinking about his new life's potential. He remembered conversations with Ernesto discussing this very moment. In their conversations, he recalled thinking how great it would have been if they were together with new horizons and a fresh start in Miami.

Ernesto was now forever in Amaury's heart, and Amaury knew he owed it to Ernesto to honor his memory throughout his new life in America in the best way he possibly could.

The move back to Miami meant his life was changing. While looking out the plane window leaving Cuba for the last time, Amaury realized he had done it.

He would be an American.

He smiled the entire flight until the plane touched down at the military base in Homestead, Florida.

Chapter 65

Through the Threshold!

Everyone walked single file into the military terminal, and once inside, a surprised Amaury was approached by an immigration officer in the hallway.

"Mr. Torres, we'd like to speak to you for a moment. Please follow me."

"What's going on? I don't understand."

The man didn't respond. They took him aside to ask him more questions about his military background and experiences. Amaury looked around realized he was the only one who'd been taken aside. They both slowly walked to an austere office separated from where the other immigrants were taken.

"Continue to follow me, please. It's right this way, just a little farther."

"Okay. Yes, officer."

The empty office contained a green metal military desk, where he was asked to sit while they waited until two additional men walked in together. An FBI agent and a second immigration officer quickly took their seats across from Amaury. They started by asking him more detailed questions about his military experience in Cuba.

Here we go again.

He tried his best to explain a third time about his full military experience from when he was a soldier. He went into further detail about his time in Angola and Nicaragua, but they appeared much more interested in learning all he knew about Russian involvement with the Upper Cuban military. They also wanted to learn as much as they could about his Ranger training and experience during those periods. They were specifically interested in the criteria they'd used for training. Initially, he was disturbed at being taken aside. However, as they spoke, it dawned on him it was not an investigation, but more of an exploratory conversation, which surprised him.

Although he was tired from providing the amount of information they wanted, he continued to comply.

He told them all he knew, which took a significant part of the midday. He went into detail about Chooska and Truong, his experiences in Angola, and the police action in Nicaragua. Additionally, he explained as much as he knew about the Cuban military's plans in those countries and why in the end he was forced to leave Cuba altogether.

They understood his knowledge was limited, but there was a moment of tension when they purposely asked if he was in the U.S. to spy on behalf of Castro.

He was shocked by the question. It had never occurred to him they might consider he was still working for the military, especially after what he'd gone through to get to the United States.

He explained he wasn't a spy at all. He loved America and had specifically come here because he hated communism. He emphasized his near-suicidal attempt to escape Cuba. It meant everything to him to finally live a free life with a government that would let you live a life you chose. "Freedom," Amaury said. "That was the only reason I risked my life."

While sitting and talking to the FBI in the office, he began to think about things for which he felt passion. "I have lived in a communist country my entire life. I vowed to myself if I ever had the chance to see America or perhaps live there, it would have made my life and all I'd fought for worthwhile. The military wanted me to become a communist, and unless I went along with it, they threatened to either put me in jail forever and throw away the key or kill me. The Cuban government doesn't like people like me to get away with escaping or resisting. I gave up everything I had, including my brother, to leave. I would have killed myself rather than stay there in prison, and I nearly did!"

He continued to tell them how he'd wanted to be an American from the age of nine years old, and how he wanted to prove he could be a good, productive, hardworking American citizen. He'd waited his entire life for this moment.

They seemed to like his answer.

Looking back on that day, he was never sure if it was this answer which helped him or not, but they had finally told him he was going to be allowed permanent entry.

"Well, Amaury, we have a bit of a surprise for you. Your Aunt Adana is outside waiting for you."

His heart jumped and skipped a beat. He'd made it. He was going to live in America and his Tia was here?

They continued, "When you leave the building, you'll be given a temporary green card. Then you'll need to report to the government office in downtown Miami to finalize your papers. But essentially, you're now an American citizen."

The officers shook his hand and then gave him some information about what he was supposed to do to get his green card. He was also handed an envelope with one hundred dollars in it. They wished him the very best and told him to go through the door at the other end of the hallway, where his aunt would be waiting.

As they walked him to the door, he glanced up at the sky. It looked so blue. He consciously took one deliberate single step over the threshold, and that was it.

He was in! He was finally legitimately in America.

The sun beat down on his skin, and this time the heat felt great. His mind instantly went to Ernesto, and as he proceeded, he quietly thanked Ernesto. Without his brother's help, he never would have made it alive. "Wow, that is the American sky. Thank you, Ernesto."

He smiled and took a deep breath of fresh new American air. Right in front of him was Aunt Adana.

"Amaury? Amaury? Oh, my goodness, it's you. I cannot believe my eyes!"

"Aunt Adana. This is fantastic. It's amazing to see you, too! Thank you for picking me up. I wasn't sure what I was going to do, and can't be happier to see you. I'm finally here!"

"I briefly talked to your mom, and she said maybe I might see you someday. It took such a long time."

Amaury responded, "It's a very long story. I'll tell you all later. I'm so happy to see you."

They gave each other a huge hug, and both smiled. Together, they walked to her car and talked a hundred miles an hour as they drove.

Amaury was in America. It was overwhelming and exhilarating all at once.

Aunt Adana mentioned they would go home first, get something to eat, relax a bit and then go shopping at the mall to buy him some clothes.

She was so excited that she hardly let Amaury talk. He didn't mind, though. Everything seemed okay now. Exhilarated, his new life was just beginning.

Chapter 66

The United Way

In the early evening, Aunt Adana drove Amaury to his first mall visit in his whole life. The building was huge and beautiful on the inside. People walked around as though it meant nothing. They were used to shopping. But as Amaury walked along the hallway and marveled at all the stores, his heart swelled with amazement.

Amaury was shocked at the overwhelming grandeur of the mall. "I can hardly believe my eyes, Aunt Adana. This is what people have in America? It's no wonder they suppress information in Cuba. The entire country would swim in here."

With every store imaginable, he looked around like a child seeing his first birthday present. The tile floors and fountains and the sound of the splashing water were so simple and delightful to his ears. Everything felt fresh and clean. He was truly amazed.

They walked slowly from store to store. With his one hundred dollars, he bought a few necessities including pants, sneakers, t-shirts, and one regular short-sleeved shirt. The simple concept of shopping was so new he could easily understand why people nearly kill themselves getting to America.

Life seemed so easily pleasant, and he would remember this day forever.

By 10:30 p.m. they arrived home. He was happy and ready to sleep on a real bed on his first night in his new country.

The next day began early. They went to the social security administration, where he was registered, and then he began the required paperwork for the green card and registration for residence. Aunt Adana took Amaury to different sights around Miami. They also met her friends and other family members while visiting. He learned about an available job at a Dunkin Donuts in downtown Miami, which he happily took. The delivery job required him to ride a bicycle round trip from the store at 27th Street and then north to 140th Street and back. It was a strenuous seven-mile daily ride, but he was happy to learn his Ranger army legs were still up to the task.

The job started at 4 a.m and ended at 8 p.m. every day. He happily earned over one hundred dollars a day. In Cuba, it took five months to earn that amount of money.

Later on, he was required to dress the donuts and prepare them for patrons. It was an extremely fast-paced, detailed job. Initially, he enjoyed it. However, it only ended up lasting four months. The time soon arrived when Amaury realized he'd seen enough of Miami, and it was time to move on to another experience.

He decided to visit another half-brother Rudy in Jacksonville, Florida. While there, he lived with Louis, a good friend of Rudy's. He wasn't terribly tall but was a full-sized man with a crazy large thick mustache and intense green eyes.

Louis had come to the U.S. during the Carter administration Mariel Boatlift from Cuba. Over seven hundred boats left Cuba at the Mariel harbor at the western port of Havana and had emigrated to America in a single day. Castro coyly wanted to clean out his jails by releasing criminals while also taking unfair advantage of American generosity. Despite early warnings, the Carter Administration was unaware these immigrants were mostly criminals.

In Jacksonville, Amaury met many people through Louis, who eventually got him a job working at a Publix supermarket. This job also lasted only a few months. On one particular afternoon, Amaury went to the local deli to buy cigarettes and a lottery ticket. Once at home, he discovered the numbers on the ticket were winners and he'd won $275. He was thrilled at his sudden windfall and thought America really was such a fantastic place to live.

Soon the year passed, and the ever-ambitious Amaury still felt he hadn't accomplished enough. The itch to excel returned, and he continued to move forward again. This time, however, he made the big decision to leave Florida altogether. He wanted to experience American life on his terms. He felt his life wouldn't take shape unless he could grow as a person. The big question was—where would he go?

He'd learned about the charitable organization called The United Way, whose mission was to relocate immigrants in new cities around the country through their nationwide network. Amaury visited their local office and discovered options available to him.

At the downtown Miami United Way office, he met Sally Yearwood.

In her best broken English and Spanish, she said, "Hello, Mr. Torres. It's a pleasure to meet you. I understand you want to leave Florida. Is that right? Where would you like to go?"

Amaury responded as best as he could. "I want to go somewhere where there are no *Cubanos*! No Latinos at all, *por favor*! Somewhere very new."

Sally's gaze widened in surprise, but then she said, "I understand. Let's see what I can do for you. She explained to Amaury that he was entitled to receive Social Security every month for a specific period in the amount of $210. She explained they would also help him move to a new location somewhere of his choice within the country.

"Gracias," he said.

"Do you mind if I ask—what is the reason you don't want to live near Spanish-speaking people?"

"I grew up in a Latin country, and although I love being Latin, I'll finally have a chance to learn more about my new adopted culture and maybe finally learn English, too. I'm so happy I'm finally going to have this opportunity. I want to learn what it's like to get to know America like an American."

"I understand completely," she said. "Let's see if we can help you make your dream come true. After all, America is all about dreams and opportunities. If we make the effort to work hard, we can achieve them. Let's get to work!"

Sally sat quietly and looked at the computer screen in front of her. There were many travel books at her desk, as well as registration sheets. Pausing now and then, she leaned back in her squeaking chair to think for a moment. Amaury looked on quietly. He watched her as she sifted through many pages while referring back to the screen. Suddenly, she perked up her head and looked directly at Amaury.

"This is interesting. Have you ever heard of a place called Kentucky? It's in the middle of the country and there are most likely not many Spanish-speaking people there. We have a connection to recommend you for a job at the Perdue Chicken facility there. I am fairly certain we could set that up quickly."

"Oh, no. Sorry. I won't work with chickens. I did that back in Cuba. I cannot do that again. I swore I would never do that again. No chickens," he said definitively.

Sally chuckled and continued. "Okay, then, I'll keep looking."

A few minutes later, although struggling to make herself understood, Sally tried again. "I have an idea. Tell me, what do you know about Oregon? Have you heard of Oregon?"

"No, I haven't. What is Oregon?"

"Well, it's on the complete other side of the country on the West Coast. It is between Washington State and California. It's quite a nice place to live, and we have some contacts there, too. We can arrange a place for you to stay and perhaps you can start out working for the city of Portland. It's a good-sized city and the best part where you are specifically concerned, is there aren't a lot of Spanish speakers there. It may be a perfect place for you to start according to your desires."

For a moment, Amaury was surprised.

How interesting this sounds. Just by coming to the United Way office and asking a simple question, my life is about to change yet again.

Initially, the cocoon of Florida and being among Latinos had made his adjustment much easier. It seemed as though many Cubans were living in America waiting to go back home one day to a new and different Cuba when communism would finally be over. Conversely, Amaury genuinely wanted to start a new life in America.

"You know what? I'll do it," Amaury declared, "What's next?"

A huge smile appeared on her face. She was quite proud to be able to find a satisfactory solution for Amaury and began instructions for her new client.

"Amaury, give me the rest of today to make the arrangements. It will be done by tomorrow. You must go home and pack whatever you have and get ready to change your life. I'll expect you to be here early tomorrow morning at 9 a.m. and I'll give you all the final details."

"I'll be here."

"Thank you, Mr. Torres, for allowing me to help guide you on the next step in your journey of life. I think you'll be quite happy."

With the money the United Way gave him plus the few extra dollars he had to his name, Amaury had $200.

In the morning, Sally gave him his plane ticket and he boarded the plane. Six and a half hours later, he prepared to walk off the plane in Portland, Oregon.

This is incredible. In just a few hours, not only am I thousands of miles away from Cuba, but this is also the first time in my life I've been somewhere so completely different than anything I've ever seen before.

From the airplane, he'd seen mountains, valleys, lush green trees, thick clouds, flowing rivers, and the Pacific Ocean not far away. He was proud to call himself an American. *America is beautiful! Life is great, and America is definitely the land of opportunity.*

He smiled widely.

Chapter 67

The Grind of Life

Amaury's new home was a hotel converted into a halfway house for United Way immigrants. He was assigned to a room upstairs in a makeshift apartment with a Russian roommate who was not often around. The roommate worked many hours at a commercial laundry company in Portland. He was a direct and abrupt man, talked very little, and was uninvolved. He did, however, recommend Amaury to work at the same company called Aramark Laundry.

In the beginning, with the UW's help, Amaury started working for the city of Portland driving garbage trucks. After difficult work hours, he decided to try the laundry company and was immediately hired.

Amaury quickly discovered the work was laborious and difficult. The company cleaned commercial-grade carpets. They were extremely heavy and difficult to move to the various machines. They had to be dragged into giant washing machines and then loaded into massive rotating dryers. The operation was a long process that ended with the workers manually refolding the carpets and then putting them back on racks. Later, they were redistributed to their customers. Aramark paid Amaury six dollars and twenty-five cents per hour for a nine-hour day. One cleaning cycle took three hours, and he worked daily, from 7 a.m. to 4 p.m.

While at Aramark, Amaury began attending the local community college to take English lessons. Although his English improved, he continued to speak a combination of broken English and Spanish. His ability to speak English more clearly helped with future job opportunities.

He eventually discovered another job at a large pipe manufacturing company called the Siedel Marine Company, which made industrial, commercial piping for manufacturing plants, shipping companies, and oil rigs. The new job was just as demanding as Aramark with even worse working hours. Amaury's new schedule was a graveyard shift, 4:30 p.m. to 5 a.m. Amaury discovered that working life in America came with its own sets of problems, too, but despite that, he was glad he had freedom of choice.

He felt the hardships were worth it, and he was determined to forge ahead. Inside, Amaury felt struggling was very American, as well. At the end of the day, working hard and feeling the benefit of his effort was the reward.

Another six months passed, and despite all his life changes, Amaury's efforts to move forward and create a better future for himself were still falling short. He concluded he needed to transition to a more substantial career path, as he knew continued physical labor would eventually be too demanding on his body as he got older. He wanted to build a future with a solid foundation that would be a career rather than just a job.

He began to take a true assessment of his life and thoughtfully considered what he wanted to do. He fully began to assess his skills and his passions and turn them into goals. Most importantly, he wanted to prove the sacrifices he'd made coming to America were meaningful.

As he took stock of himself, he thought about the fishing skills he'd learned in Guantanamo and how much he loved those days despite his circumstances. Even working at the donut shop in Miami had had its pleasantries. He loved working with food, and he loved feeding people. He started to realize his true passion was cooking.

To start a professional career, his plan included graduating from high school, continuing to learn English, and eventually applying to a culinary school.

Getting a GED was the first step, which he completed within the year. The GED given in Spanish enabled him to obtain the certificate for completing a basic high school education. He then continued his studies at the Portland Community College to take English classes.

Amaury noticed his bills piling up and knew he was falling behind financially. It wasn't going to be easy, but he felt the struggle of life would be worth it.

While living in Gretchen, Oregon, he was unable to afford to leave and live closer to work and school. He didn't have enough money for a deposit on a rental in downtown Portland. Gretchen's living expenses were becoming a burden for Amaury, including his commute on the local MATT train.

He fell into a terrible rut. He didn't want to jeopardize his jobs, but it was just as important for him to continue his education. He realized the only way to do both was to make a sacrifice. He weighed his options and decided the idea of living on the street for some time would allow him to get ahead. As crazy as it sounded in his thoughts, he realized the benefits of savings and believed it was something he could accomplish.

He created a step-by-step plan he knew would help get him through it. After surviving life-threatening conditions in Angola, Nicaragua, and crossing the Atlantic Ocean, he thought he could survive on the streets of Portland for a few weeks. The plan merely needed to be executed in a very logical way.

He knew his choice was fraught with trepidation, but if calculated well and organized, he could accomplish the plan. He proceeded with specific plans for clothes, cleaning, showering, and eating. Once he figured out his strategy, he set it in motion. Amaury became homeless on the streets of Portland. Thankfully, the weather cooperated, as well. He knew the adventure was part of his life. This was going to be another chapter.

Homelessness was his path to freedom.

Chapter 68

One More Hurdle

Homeless life for Amaury wasn't fun, but he had a method that worked. He had two full sets of clothing he used and cleaned several times a week at a public laundry. He alternated bathing days using wipes on some days and public showers on others due to convenience. His possessions were stored in a public storage locker. Once he chose to move forward with his plan, he found the perfect spot under the Burnside Bridge spanning the Willamette River in Portland. He figured it gave him protection from the elements and allowed him to be close to the MATT, as well. Amaury found the plan to be an energizing challenge.

The place he chose was at the point where the bridge created a triangle and joined the road as it tilted upwards. It allowed him invisibility, dryness, and safety, but more importantly, he was alone at night and not bothered by the police or anyone else who might try to harm him.

The first few nights were very strange. He realized it was one thing to think about living on the street, but it was entirely another to live it.

Amaury bought a tent and set up an outside home that

could easily be folded and stored in his backpack daily. Initially, he didn't sleep well. Although he had significant experience living outside in dangerous situations, he felt he needed to keep an eye open all night. He heard and felt strange things crawling around, as well as the distorted sounds of car tires rolling by at 40-50 miles per hour.

Unexpectedly, his mind began playing strange tricks on him when he was on the verge of sleep. Bright lights immediately woke him, and he thought it might be the police. In reality, they were reflections from boats on the water, streetlights, or the headlights of a distant car. He felt as if he was both protected and naked at the same time.

Over the following few nights, he became more comfortable and familiar with the environment. The regularity of nightlife under the bridge became ordinary, his fear subsided, and he started sleeping better.

Several weeks passed, and he realized living on the streets was not so terrible. He began to enjoy his new circumstances. He found a strange sense of freedom living purposefully yet hidden. His body got used to the ground's hard surface. His survival training had again prepared him in life to manage and deal with nearly every situation and turn it into a positive.

Always an open-minded optimist, Amaury saw the positive in whatever circumstances he was in and made it work in his favor.

His street life lasted for six weeks, and he was able to save enough money for the deposit. Although he wasn't unhappy living homeless, he was happier to have a place to call home.

While living under the bridge and continuing to work at Seidel, Amaury was already planning his next steps. He knew his passion and happiness were in cuisine and food service.

When he was young, he'd loved learning to cook with his

mother and grandmother and even his father, who also happened to be a wonderful chef.

In his research, Amaury had discovered that the world-famous Le Cordon Bleu French Culinary School, had a division in Portland and was accepting applications.

He applied and was thrilled when he found out they'd also provide him with a loan for the $77,000 tuition. He was accepted to begin in the fall of 1998. For the first time in his life, Amaury began on a path of his true life's calling. He was on his way to becoming a classically-trained chef.

Chapter 69

Le Cordon Bleu

The demanding daily schedule didn't change. Amaury slept from 5:30 a.m. to 9 a.m. so he could be ready for school in half an hour. This new and exciting period in his life created other issues, though. He started falling asleep on the production line at Seidel. Keeping the tight schedule was difficult and caused tremendous pressure on his mental state. Although he'd always been a stocky man, his weight dropped to 170 pounds. For Amaury, it was a significant weight loss.

When school began, he discovered he was one of the only three Latin male students attending. The entire program was taught in English, including textbook materials, classes, and tests. He realized it was a significantly more difficult program than he'd expected. Amaury needed to buckle down, not only to concentrate but to understand the English as presented.

He felt this was a once-in-a-lifetime opportunity that he took very seriously. Although his English was still rudimentary, he managed to succeed with significant concentration and constant review. They didn't cater to his deficits, but he was always ready for pop quizzes and regular lectures regardless.

Amaury saw school as a battlefield. Acquire the knowledge,

be prepared, stay ready, minimize surprises and figure out a way to make it work.

In the first month, students at Le Cordon Bleu studied the different processes used in cooking, temperatures, ingredients, and an immense variety of kitchen tools. The curriculum was designed to teach the culinary skills a chef needed to know and how a professional kitchen operated. The kitchen was called the laboratory, and Amaury had a lab every day which required hands-on cooking and notetaking as part of his daily routine.

Tests were given every Friday. His cooking classes did not begin until the second month when they started with healthy foods, international foods, proteins, wine, French, English style, French pastry, and then finally baking near the end of that period.

The next section they learned was Administrative Management and food cost analysis, and then lastly the business of running a professional kitchen, commercial food ordering, reorganizing food, recognizing food quality, and menu design. They also learned about shopping for menu creation, refrigeration, food rotation, and safety and health in food processing. Working and food handling in a professional kitchen and butchering came afterward.

As in most classic culinary schools and especially Le Cordon Bleu, cooking was taught with an emphasis on French Cuisine and preparation. Amaury's favorite areas were sautéing, stocks, and pastry; however, he excelled with protein carving and he adored making bread.

As he progressed, he discovered many things that fascinated him. For example, there was a big difference between the American way of preparing stock and the French. In American style, for example, vegetables were thrown into the pot, boiled and strained, whereas in the French all the vegetables were precleaned, then boiled and removed. Amaury loved that there was so much to learn. The possibilities seemed endless, and it excited him.

He also discovered through learning, he had a special passion for preparing foods he had never before experienced—the five basic sauces, pastries, and how to make the correct cuts of high-quality meats. He discovered so many areas of new cuisines and grew a strong appreciation for Japanese sushi preparation and variation of rice styles including Mexican. Amaury also learned about Kosher food being blessed before preparation by a Rabbi, which gave food an entirely new meaning. For Amaury, culinary school was exactly where he wanted to be.

Life took on a new meaning in general, and seeing it in a promising new light enabled him to accept his past and look forward to a future he could embrace.

As the school continued, he realized for the first time in his life he'd made the right life choice—he truly loved the creation and preparation of food for others.

He thought about the amazing difference between life in Cuba and life in America. In America, he was allowed to create greatness in his own life for himself and not for the benefit of tyrannical government. His effort and ambition as an individual were applauded in America. He discovered this was the real reason America was so special.

In Cuba, life was severely controlled to the point that individual choice was not an option. The ability to think positively was the meaning of freedom, and his desire to break out from under oppression had been valid.

As Amaury continued his studies, his knowledge of the culinary world seemed to explode exponentially. As they moved forward in the curriculum, there was particular emphasis on red meats and learning how to butcher proteins correctly. It was an extensive part of the semester, and was very intense, as they used actual animal products in class. Amaury could see how important it was to listen and watch very carefully, as wrong or wasteful cuts became expensive mistakes.

They had pigs, cows, chickens, and ducks in the class, and they were taught the exact way to butcher so they would make perfect cuts every time.

They were taught a two-pronged strategy in managing proteins—the first was understanding an animal as a plated product and then correctly butchering. Individual cuts of meat had to be planned, portioned, and plated for the correct profit. Protein preparation was the lesson of these classes. A professional chef must consider the entire animal as a source of income for any menu where the end usage is considered first. Once decided, there was no going back to change the plan. It had to be correct every time, and for any chef, this part of the preparation was quite stressful.

Considerable thought was put forth to be sure every animal was used to produce the most product for a restaurant's purchase. Wasted protein meant lost revenue for the restaurant and an angry restaurant owner. These classes were the most demanding in his training, and it took considerable concentration to succeed in them.

While Amaury had very little experience with baking, he grew to love it. In class, he learned dessert occupied a large part of the menu, which was creative, used less complicated ingredients, and still provided a great profit source for any restaurant. These techniques he was learning opened up a new world of ideas and he developed a sense of accomplishment.

While in school, he started to think about his future. In the back of his mind, he'd considered the idea of opening his own restaurant, but he never gave it much thought. As he learned and grew as a chef, the idea began to feel more and more possible.

He knew this could only take place far into the future if at all, but the idea became a powerful motivator in his mind once the seed had been planted. This was a personal goal that he never discussed with anyone.

In the back of his mind, though, memories of growing up in a Solar made him doubt that he could achieve his goal. The idea of attempting to open a restaurant and failing would be an embarrassment too much to bear.

How could a kid from the worst Solar of them all end up in America and dare to think he could become a successful restaurateur?

But in America, he realized, he was allowed to have those thoughts. He was allowed to have a dream and commit to himself. If he truly wanted this career, it could be achievable, although for now, it had to be correctly planned. Thankfully, time was on his side.

Chapter 70

A Night to Remember

Almost as soon as Amaury started school, he knew he'd have to start paying back the tuition loan, so he quickly found several jobs, since he was not working at Seidel anymore. Never one to sit idly by, he started working at a restaurant called the Josh Café, a local well-known pastry café on 26th Avenue in downtown Portland. Amaury worked from 9 a.m. to noon, preparing traditional French pastries which the customers adored. He was already putting his school knowledge to work!

Soon afterward, he began a job at another local restaurant, Wildwood Pizzeria. Wildwood's owner was very innovative and offered custom-made pizza rather than strictly traditional-style. Wildwood introduced many ingredients not normally associated with pizza, especially in Northwest America, and they became famous for it.

Corey Schreiber, the originator of Wildwood Pizzeria, used unconventional foods such as artichokes and pineapple as toppings. He was the first in the Northwest to put Gorgonzola cheese crumbles and pears on the same pizza, combined with roasted garlic and Spanish anchovies.

These odd combinations worked well together and became extremely popular, and as such, his restaurant became famous in Portland. With many obligations, Amaury knew he needed to continue earning more and always be seeking new work opportunities. Before long, Amaury also started working part-time at Higgins, known for their huge tap beer inventory. Higgins had one hundred choices of draught beers, and the place was one of the busiest beer joints in the city.

Amaury had been in America for over two years by his time, and for the first time, he was finally enjoying his life. Culinary school and learning to cook around adults his age with similar passions released his creativity. He finally felt as though he'd left his past behind. He knew he was on the right track.

In the middle of his last semester, his buddy Juan asked Amaury to take the night off and join him at a cool nightclub to explore the perks of nightlife in Portland. Amaury felt fatigued from his demanding schedule, and he was reluctant to go out. He wanted to stay in and relax, but Juan insisted.

"For once, Amaury, c'mon!" Juan begged. "Let's go out and have some fun. Take a one-night break from school and enjoy ourselves!"

Amaury paused for a moment to think about Juan's offer. "Okay, let's go. What the hell, you only live once."

They decided to get very dressed up and make it a real night of partying.

Amaury figured if he was going to do this right, it may as well be fun and exciting. What he didn't know was that Juan was actually setting him up on a date with his girlfriend's friend Ruby.

Ruby was forty years old and thirteen years older than Amaury. She had recently retired from twenty years in the interior design industry and was moving on to other ventures. She was medium height with a shapely figure, brunette hair, and a wide smile. Her eyes sparkled when she smiled, and she enjoyed a freedom-loving lifestyle.

Having grown up in the early 1970s, she took life at face value, yet at the same time, she always made things work in her favor. Just like Amaury, Ruby approached every opportunity as moving forward in her life path.

On that very special night, both Amaury and Ruby were getting ready to go out but had no idea it was to meet each other. Ruby wasn't actively seeking anything romantic but had reluctantly agreed to go to the club with her best friend Amy. She had another busy day scheduled the next day in her new business, a retail lingerie shop for women.

Her clientele was mostly loyal locals who saw her sense of humor as endearing and knew her to be a trusted friend in the neighborhood.

Amy helped them feel confident and uninhibited, so they'd spend time and money in her shop, and they often returned.

One of Ruby's best friends and former employees Amy was dating Juan. Amy worked at the community college in Portland, where she taught English to many new refugees, including Juan, and after several classes, they began dating.

Sometime later, Juan and Amy decided to introduce Amaury and Ruby because they thought they'd be a great match. Ruby was laid back, and Amaury could use a new friend, not to mention he was a cute catch. Initially, Ruby didn't want to go, but eventually, she gave in to Amy's pleas and figured it would be a fun night out. Ruby had no intention of meeting anyone, let alone an immigrant who had difficulty speaking English.

Ruby dressed to the nines. "What the hell," she said, "If I'm going to do this thing, then I'm going to do it right."

While they walked out of the house to the car, Amy hesitated. "I just wanted you to know that we sort of set you up on a date..."

"What? What the hell are you talking about?" Ruby protested. "Oh, Amy, you know I don't like blind dates. I've told you that a million times! And who is *we*?"

"Juan and me. It's his roommate!" Amy defended herself with a laugh. "Juan says he's really nice and super cute! A hot Cuban. You'll love him!"

"Fine." Ruby laughed a little. "But it's only because I'm already dressed."

They arrived at the club and met up with Juan, who animatedly told the girls Amaury would be along shortly.

"He went to the little boy's room. He had to make sure he was perfect," Juan said, rolling his eyes and chuckling.

The club walls reverberated with the rhythm of salsa. Ruby returned from her tour of the dance floor, and she saw her friends at the bar. She immediately noticed a young man dressed in a loud purple paisley three-piece suit, a white shirt, and wire-rimmed glasses already seated.

Intrigued, Ruby was taken with his fit and healthy style. He had a Latin Marlboro man look and a cigarette hanging out of his mouth. They were introduced. Ruby knew there was a large difference in their ages, but as they talked, she started getting more comfortable. She found him refreshingly funny and attractive. He ordered them Mojitos.

As they talked, Ruby realized quickly his English was poor. Despite his continued efforts to learn, he still lagged in his control of the language. She had to focus carefully when he spoke.

As the evening went on, both Ruby and Amaury began to think favorably about each other. Amaury felt she was a challenge and she found it hard to look away from his eyes. Sometimes life forever changes on a dime, and for Amaury and Ruby, this moment had subtly arrived. As soon as Ruby watched him dance, she realized she was smitten. He was a great dancer, and she loved how he smiled at her while he moved. He looked deeply into her eyes, and she felt a gripping in her stomach. Ruby imagined this might be her final blind date.

Ruby stayed over at Amy's house at the end of the night, and they gabbed about the boys all night long. However, once at home and after several days since their fateful night together, thoughts of doubt crept into Ruby's mind. She began to weigh her options and feelings. She knew she was very attracted to Amaury but was he right for her? She had a million questions about being ready or not to be in a new relationship. The nagging thoughts wouldn't leave her mind.

Amaury persisted and called Ruby daily, but she stridently avoided his calls and didn't dare to listen to his messages. He was undeterred and continued for several more weeks. Juan and Amy questioned her and tried to persuade her to change her mind.

Ruby knew Amaury wanted to see her again, and she needed to make a decision. She thought about what was in her heart and finally concluded that she did want to see him again.

Amaury called several days later, and this time she picked up. Once she heard his voice, there was no turning back. They agreed to meet at the beach a few days later with their friends. Quickly after the beach day, they jumped directly into a serious relationship. They were both delighted and looked forward to enjoying their time together. After several weeks, Amaury resigned from his job and moved into her home.

Ruby firmly felt Amaury was an old soul and wise beyond his years. Despite his inability to speak English well, he was able to communicate his thoughts profoundly. They fell madly in love and just six months after they met, they were married.

Their ceremony took place at Ruby's home. A pastor

performed the ceremony, with friends and some family in attendance.

Ruby insisted Amaury finally learn English correctly and hired his own tutor. He learned to speak well enough to discuss his lifelong goal of opening his restaurant, but now his plans included Ruby. He was thrilled to have her be a part of his dream, and he expressed that to her.

"Together, we might be able to make this happen one day," he told her, but this vision for the moment remained just that in their imaginations.

Chapter 71

Final Achievements

Amaury's career in the restaurant industry had several benchmarks of achievement. He wanted to build a resume highlighting his time at top-quality, high-end restaurants in Oregon. After graduating from Le Cordon Bleu, he was highly driven to apply his new skills.

His new chef's aspiration was to become the Captain in the kitchen of a tablecloth sauté restaurant. He loved tablecloth service establishments and knew people enjoyed a gourmet meal with a beautifully-paired bottle of wine curated by an experienced professional.

His satisfaction came from being part of a team responsible for the diner's experience.

As a highly trained chef, sauté custom cooking was also his path to obtaining a higher salary. Working in reputable kitchens and establishing a name for himself was the first step. He envisioned his daily life as managing legitimate dinner preparation pressure, high customer expectations, and designing proper wine pairings with exquisite platings. The restaurant owner and patrons would be the final judge of his abilities.

Nearby and among the best restaurants in Lincoln City was

a well-known first-class establishment called The Bay House. This beautiful historic restaurant had an incredible view of the water, and their unique location and their superior menu made The Bay House Amaury's top choice of places to work.

The menu included many different cuts of high-quality beef, pork, fish, and gourmet salads along with an excellent selection of wines. Although he was interviewed to be the Sous-chef, which would be the second in command under the Head Chef, he was offered work on the grill. Amaury initially took the position and worked it for three years. Eventually, he was promoted to Sous-chef for the next four years. He learned to love the grill, and it helped him enormously in later years. Amaury's first stint at The Bay House was for a year-and-a-half. However, he returned to work there on and off several times over the course of the next seven years. While at The Bay House, he worked under Jesse Otero, who was famous on the West Coast, and Jesse and Amaury grew to become great friends.

Normally each evening, the Bay House had nearly three hundred covers. It was a significant number of people to come for dinner in just six hours. At the grill, Amaury moved swiftly and carefully each night because mistakes were costly. Every incredibly busy evening consisted of grilling fifty or more protein entrée servings per serving hour.

He was under severe stress, and intense concentration was required to perfect the correct temperatures of a significantly large variety of proteins.

"What's my time look like on that five-top, the three T-bones, the lamb, and that pork chop? Plus, we have those other orders waiting. I know we have two more salmon coming soon, as well. What's my timing? Where are we on those, Chef Otero?" Chef Otero barked at Amaury.

With sweat rolling down his forehead, he rapidly reported

back, "I have three in one minute, the well-done in four more. I have the other two scallops ready momentarily, and the other order two beef tenderloins, that'll be ready in two. Also, a medium duck and salmon rare in five more, Chef. Two veal chops will be plated in forty-five seconds!"

Chef retorted, "Also just in, drop three more New York cuts, two mediums and a rare. Then, a pork chop medium well, and now those salmon medium up on another five-top with those next, ASAP! And more tickets are coming in right now. I need it all quickly! Plates are waiting! Thank you, Chef!"

"Yes, sir, Chef. You got it!" Amaury replied.

On any typical day, Amaury would arrive at the Bay House at 7 a.m. and Chef Jesse would already have completed the list of items Amaury needed to prepare. He pulled all the meat including lamb, duck, and pork and he'd ice the fish of the day, cut them, and get them ready for preparation. His next steps included getting the daily house stocks and sauces started. All these tasks took four hours to accomplish.

While working at The Bay House, Amaury added another important name to his resume and took a part-time job with Cathy Block at The Flying Dutchman in Otter Creek. Like The Bay House, it was also on the southern part of the Siletz Bay but even closer to the ocean. The prices were lower than The Bay House, but people still loved and flocked to the restaurant.

The Dutchman also had an amazing view of the Pacific Ocean and boasted fifty-four gigantic panoramic windows of the sea. People would not only come for the amazing food but also enjoy a meal with the glorious scenic backdrop. Chef always paired wine with dinner, and he'd specifically design the dinner menu to compliment the incredible sunset and sea. For example, a bowl of chowder to start, then a fabulously tossed salad with herb-grilled, wild-caught salmon.

Once Amaury began at The Dutchman, his day started

quite early, first stopping at The Bay House to get Chef Jesse's morning list prepared, and then at 11:30 a.m. sharp he'd go to The Dutchman until closing time at 8:30 p.m., ending a twelve-to-thirteen-hour day. He knew from the start kitchen work would never be a regular job. It was his passion that made it possible to maintain these stressful work requirements.

Restaurant life, especially the rigorous demanding work a professional kitchen requires, depended on each person's love of their craft. It was what drove Amaury to succeed in a professional kitchen. His sweat-effort and hard work created the result —a well-made meal. Food as art from the heart of the creator was how Amaury saw his life.

After he left The Bay House the first time, he ended up at the Side Door Café on the Oregon Coast, another esteemed restaurant. The Side Door Café was located in the coastal area known as Gleneden Beach. After several years working the high-end restaurant market, Amaury succeeded in working at many of the places he deemed necessary for the experience he desired. He was pleased with his efforts to create the life he wanted in America, but there was more to come.

During this time and while being married, Ruby wasn't working. She shut down her retail store and never went back to work. Amaury was now the sole breadwinner of the family. Despite his perseverance as their future took shape, the itch to move once again came back. Both Ruby and Amaury needed more challenges to accomplish.

Chapter 72

The Mineshaft Tavern

By the time Amaury had been in the United States for twelve years, he was considering where he had started and where he was headed. He'd made incredible strides. He had a career, a marriage, he'd learned English, and he'd accomplished a predominantly satisfying life.

Amaury earned approximately $50,000 a year, and the last year of Ruby's retail business had been quite lucrative, so collectively they were able to buy a home in Lincoln City, centrally located near the three restaurants where Amaury worked.

Not long afterward, however, Ruby and Amaury felt the urge to move again but to a completely new area. Many ideas came to them. However, the one they clung to was to be somewhere away from the ocean—somewhere warm. The location had to have work options for them, but more than anything, they were interested in a completely different environment.

One location that immediately came to mind was New Mexico. Amaury liked the concept of a new experience living in the desert. As they began their search, they discovered online an intriguing, yet oddly located Cuban restaurant called Tocororo situated in a small town called Madrid in New Mexico. The quaint little spot was located on the main drag called Highway 14. As they discussed the opportunity, the temptation to be in a place where they could live close to work in a more intimate setting was extremely attractive.

They liked the idea of a desert climate with the surrounding mountains, fresh clean air, bright clouds, and high above sea level. They could live amongst the cactus and the dry climate but not far from the main city of Santa Fe, where Amaury could find a chef position, if necessary.

Amaury found the contact information for Tocororo and gave them a call. An older woman named Olga, who happened to be the owner, answered his call. During the conversation, Amaury learned she was closing up for the entire winter. This was her normal schedule because she was a snowbird in Florida for the winter and would reopen in the springtime.

As their conversation progressed, Olga told Amaury, "I must tell you there is a rumor in town that the restaurant across the street called The Mineshaft Tavern is changing hands, and I know the young lady who is buying it. She's a friend of mine. I think you ought to call her and find out. From what I know, they're looking for a new chef."

Amaury immediately became curious. "Wow, Olga. That sounds very interesting. Can you please give me her number? I'd love to talk to her, since I'll be moving there, and I would definitely like to have a job secured before arriving."

"Absolutely, Amaury. Her name is Lori Lindsey." Olga then provided Amaury with Lori's number.

Amaury thanked Olga, slammed down the phone with excitement, and ran to Ruby with the new information. "Ruby, you're not going to believe what just happened. Olga, the woman who owns Tocororo, told me about a potential job at the restaurant across the street called The Mineshaft Tavern."

"Oh my goodness, that's amazing, Amaury. You need to call immediately."

Olga had told Amaury that Madrid was an old coal-mining town that had started many decades before but had now turned into a skilled crafts business town where about 450 people lived.

It was twenty-five miles south of Santa Fe but still part of Santa Fe County. The Mineshaft was directly across the street and had been there since 1947. Amaury was hooked. He loved the feel, and he loved the back story. He found the antique ambiance of the town extremely compelling. He called Lori right away.

Lori was from a city called Beaumont, Texas. She was tall and blonde with a strong personality. She was a true Texan, of course with an accent. Lori had previously traveled to Seattle, where she'd spent a decade working in the restaurant industry. She had a widespread and thorough knowledge of every aspect of foodservice. Furthermore, she also owned a very successful vintage boutique in Madrid, New Mexico, called Cowgirl Red. Her personal lifetime goal was to eventually own her own restaurant.

Amaury's impatience was palpable, and his calls to Lori were repeatedly met by her voicemail. After a few days of anxious telephone tag, they managed to speak at length. During the conversation, he discovered that Lori lived in Madrid, and she was, in fact, buying the restaurant with a business partner from New York. As their discussion progressed, Lori learned Amaury was an experienced working chef in the Pacific Northwest.

His heart was beating out of his chest as he finally heard her answer his phone call.

"Hello Lori, this is Amaury Torres. I got your name from Olga at Tocororo. I recently called her for a job. I'm a chef and I'm considering moving to Madrid. She mentioned that you're opening a restaurant there and you might be looking for a new chef?"

"That's right. She told you correctly," Lori said. "Nice to talk with you, Amaury. I have a partner and we're in the process of buying the tavern here in town. It's right across the street from Olga's place. Perhaps you could tell me more about yourself."

"That's great!" Amaury cried. He took a deep breath. "Well, first, I'm from Cuba, but I've lived in this country for twelve years now. I graduated from Le Cordon Bleu here in Oregon, but my wife Ruby and I are thinking of moving to Madrid. I'd like to secure a job before we leave. I'm a highly-trained chef and would like to see if there is a potential fit. I've worked at quite a few wonderful places in our area including The Bay House, Flying Dutchman, Side Door Café, and Higgins. I mean, there've been quite a few restaurants..."

Lori laughed. "Wow. I know several of those spots. I've been there. We should talk more, but listen, I have a meeting and I need to hop off this call. I have your number, and I'll call you back later tonight. I'm interested in speaking with you further."

"Absolutely! We'll talk soon." He turned right around and looked at Ruby in shock. "Ruby, you're not going to believe who I just spoke to!"

For Lori, Amaury's experience strongly resonated with her love of Pacific Northwestern cuisine. Lori was a real foodie herself. She had a highly developed palate and loved food prep, service, and cooking, of course, but also had a passion for the business side. Her energy for the foodservice industry equaled Amaury's in many ways.

By the end of the second phone interview, Amaury was really excited, and Lori clearly seemed ready to hire him. They also discussed potential salaries and plans for the type of cuisine she was interested in serving at The Mineshaft as the new owner. Menu preparation was extremely important for Lori from the onset, and their decisions about the food offerings were paramount to anything else. She liked Amaury's ideas.

She did say, however, that there was one final hurdle for Amaury to overcome. She had a partner in the purchase who was a full owner, and before any decisions, Amaury would need to interview with him, too. It just so happened her business partner lived in New York. Jeffrey Kutcher's background was as far from the restaurant business as you could possibly get. He had a background in financial services as an advisor who had no prior restaurant experience other than a summer stint as a busboy at an Italian restaurant when he was seventeen. He was planning a career change to something completely different. An antique American biker bar roadhouse in the Southwest was about as far from Wall Street as he could have possibly imagined.

Amaury had no reservations when he learned about Jeffrey's lack of experience in the foodservice industry. On their call, they discussed menu ideas and what a work schedule might look like. They discussed how Amaury planned to operate the kitchen, his general philosophy of cooking and food preparation, and how it would apply to their Southwestern roadhouse. They shared information about their backgrounds to become more familiar with each other.

Amaury told Jeffrey his idea was to continue the traditional burger joint style, but he would look to make some fresh changes to the Mineshaft Burger which was currently on the menu. Jeffrey found Amaury's background fascinating. He liked the idea of a Cuban chef in a Southwestern biker bar.

As the conversation progressed and was going well, it became apparent to Amaury that both partners were pleased with the idea of him as their first chef. Lori and Jeffrey mutually agreed privately that they were interested in hiring Amaury.

Lori began the process of getting the menu started, along with other operational activities in preparation for opening day early in January.

In one of their meetings, Jeffrey turned to Lori. "Amaury sounds great to me, other than the fact that he speaks too quickly and he's not easy to understand all the time. But I like the idea of a Cuban Chef at an old American roadhouse in the middle of nowhere. It's a unique twist!"

Lori chuckled. "I know we'll have to work on that. So, let's hire him. That's one less issue we'll have to deal with. He certainly has a lot of skills, and his experience working on the grill makes him a super great fit. I'm very happy about that. By the way, we'll deal with the closing next week when you arrive. Also, the *Santa Fe New Mexican* wants us to do an interview. How about that?"

"No kidding? We're big shots now!" Kutcher exclaimed.

Not long afterward, Ruby and Amaury found a cute little house not far from the restaurant on an old dirt road in Madrid called Back Road. It was a small two-bedroom house with all the necessary amenities needed for living, although it was quite outdated. Madrid wasn't particularly modern in general. The house was small, but it had a nice kitchen and bathroom. The Mineshaft was located within short walking distance for a very easy commute.

The Mineshaft Tavern had been built just a few years after WWII on the property of the original coal company and housed their main offices. The restaurant, though originally only a stand-up bar built by the ACC Mining Company, was constructed to allow the miners to unwind after a hard day of mining in the cramped coal shafts. It stayed this way until approximately 1955 when the United States coal demand slowed enough to put a quick end to the town's coal production.

They closed up shop, shut their doors, and everyone vanished. Almost overnight, Madrid became a ghost town.

By the early 1970s, a population of hippies had settled in. They inhabited the abandoned coal miner cabins dotting Highway 14, which was also known as the Turquoise Trail. As time went by, the hippies began creating quality fine arts, glass blown pieces, leather items, and crafts. It reestablished itself as an art destination by the late 1970s, which is how it remained when the new Mineshaft gang rolled into town.

The Tavern was the focal point of entertainment and was an important hub for town events. It was an eclectic and unique setting for any newcomer, but Amaury was not ready for this new experience. As the new head Chef of the tavern, he became a town celebrity and a topic of discussion and attention. Initially, he enjoyed the notoriety, but over time, his passion became tested. He loved working at The Mineshaft, but it was in other areas of work where he found unexpected surprises.

Once new ownership took over, the rehabbing took more than a week of hard elbow-grease cleaning and scrubbing and stocking food. Organizing and preparing to get the restaurant ready for the reopening was the single most important goal.

A new kitchen was designed with updated equipment to help develop a more appealing menu and hopefully bigger crowds. Initially, the local townspeople were resistant to the new ownership and a new Cuban chef, but as time progressed, the locals and the tourists who stopped in grew to love the new Mineshaft Tavern and Amaury's food. New changes in life are never easy to digest, and Madrid's locals' eventual acquiescence was no exception.

Lori, Jeffrey, and Amaury worked on an entirely new menu together, providing much more exciting entrées than had previously been used in years. The updated menu featured a very popular chicken and turkey combo burger named after the owner—the Jeffrey Burger. There was lots of delicious Southwestern fare, including the star of the show—the Mineshaft Green Chili Burger. Soon after the first big staff meeting, the doors were opened, and the reopening day arrived. They were quickly a huge success!

The Mineshaft would be forever known for professionally homestyle-cooked meals by Amaury. This was a big change for the town, as the Mineshaft was in definite need of an image makeover.

In addition to Amaury's creations, they made real corn chips with hot salsa, roadhouse style fresh guacamole, real potato fries, and superior cheeses with lettuce and tomatoes on a grilled bun. The local townspeople were very happy to see the transformation.

In the first few months, the employees who stayed on were stuck in the former owners' culture, which often included a few illegal activities.

Amaury tried his best to have Lori and Jeffrey release everyone and rehire an entirely new staff to establish a new culture, which would be standard procedure with any new ownership of a previously established restaurant. However, the owners believed they needed to keep old staff symbolically to show their support of the local community, as they also lived in the town. As much as he argued to make important changes, he lost some battles, which was an important test of his passion and his required dedication.

On most days, Amaury arrived at work around 8 a.m. and often worked until closing at 1 a.m. or later on weekends. A tough schedule was normal for all management working at The Mineshaft. The staff pushed against what Amaury wanted, which caused additional stress in the kitchen, and he struggled to initiate things the way he'd learned from his training and experience.

It was during this period of instability that Jeffrey and Amaury cemented their friendship, which lasted much longer than their time together at the Mineshaft.

A short eight months later, Amaury decided he wanted to continue to chase his goals, and a new horizon once again formed in the Torres' family future. More changes were developing.

Chapter 73

Amaury's Mineshaft Final Days

As time progressed, Amaury realized Lori and Jeffrey had profoundly different personalities, and he learned to communicate with them individually. He respected both owners. However, on one side he had a strong Texan woman who had substantial beliefs about restaurant operation and kitchen preparation. She knew exactly what she wanted and gave the restaurant firm direction, but her style was not often negotiable.

Amaury struggled with her stubbornness. He understood her and knew her desires were important, but if he held a different viewpoint, he had to fight to get his needs met. Unknown to Jeffrey and Lori, he eventually became resentful of something he loved so much. Ruby understood the way this conflict suffocated his passion and motivation. It was more than friction—he was a highly-trained professional chef used to fully built-out, functional high-end kitchens with a well-trained and motivated staff.

The Mineshaft quickly proved to be the opposite of what he'd anticipated, and although he initially accepted it, over time it began to wear on him.

Jeffrey, although open-minded, often sided with Lori, as they were business partners and had a common focus on the betterment of the restaurant and its future. Amaury felt stuck in the middle without a voice.

He confided in Ruby. "I can't understand how these two people can be in business together. I love them both, but it's getting too difficult to manage and succeed in the kitchen. I'm not happy about continuing. I'm not sure what to do."

Ruby responded quietly. "Perhaps you already have your answer, Amaury."

As the kitchen manager, he was expected to join in and take part in the management roles in some areas of the business, which was more than he'd originally thought. He'd believed his job was only in the kitchen, but it soon became apparent he'd be helping in every other area of The Mineshaft's business.

The Mineshaft was more than simply a restaurant—it was a tourist center with several different businesses on the five-acre property. There was a vintage photography studio which they turned into a back bar and a coal miners' antique museum.

The partners also got involved with using their portable liquor license in other areas of Santa Fe to sponsor and cater events and work music festivals. Amaury was there to prepare the food but also help oversee those events. It was an all-encompassing job which Amaury tolerated, but they did take their toll on his true passion.

The Mineshaft was an extremely fast-paced and challenging environment. There was never a dull moment or an easy task to complete. It required hard work and strong mental fortitude. The New Mexico heat beat him down after eleven-to-fifteen-hour days. Sometimes the only thing they could do at the end of each day was to grab a beer and sit at the sixty-foot stand-up bar and just stare at each other quietly, beers in hand.

Amaury spoke up. "How the hell did we make it through that day?"

Laughing, both Jeffrey and Amaury nodded at the profound common experience and agreement of the sheer physical demands of working at The Mineshaft, while sweat trickled down their temples. Together, they both called it a *meatgrinder*.

In the end, Amaury didn't want to lose his friendship with Lori and Jeffrey and thought it was better not to clash, as it seemed that's where he felt it was heading. At the same time, his friendship with Jeffrey seemed to go in a different direction. Over the many months of their friendship, Amaury grew to deeply trust Jeffrey and revealed to him his full life story.

Amaury went through many changes and experienced busy days that never seemed to end. There were days where he sweated completely through his clothes (and while living 6,000 feet above sea level). After a few months of contemplation and discussions with Ruby, he finally made his decision.

With a very heavy heart, he gave notice of his resignation. He wanted to make sure the owners were going to be able to find a new chef and gave ample time for their search, helping with the interviewing.

Over the months of his employment, their relationship was more than just that of a boss and employee. It had become an emotionally-charged familial bond that would last a long time.

Chapter 74

The Decision

Upon leaving Madrid, Ruby and Amaury moved back to Oregon to get their house sold. Before they had a chance to get settled, Ruby's mother passed away, and because of the suddenness, they had to switch plans, leaving for Arizona to finalize her estate. The passing of Ruby's mom became an emotional watershed moment for them. It helped stir their spirits and not allow more time to pass without creating a path to a new future. They looked at each other and knew their moment arrived. It was time to make Amaury's American dream a reality.

Although it was not Ruby's dream, she was happy to go along for the ride. Amaury was a great chef, and in his heart, he knew whatever menu he designed would resonate significantly with his clientele and become successful.

New Mexico had always been a place they loved, so it was decided they would continue to make their future there. With the money Ruby inherited, they bought a home further south in Cedar Crest, NM, and began the process of their next endeavor. Having been away, Amaury joined a few local clubs to meet people and used his former chef fame to mingle with the locals again. He found a breakfast club in the town of Cerrillos. One of the members told him about an interesting restaurant space vacancy available in Lone Butte just a short drive away.

He met the Realtor, who also owned the property. Her name was Nai. Oddly enough, a former chef from The Mineshaft Tavern had opened a lunch place there; however, it had lasted only a single year. While considering this location closer to the city of Santa Fe but not as far south as The Mineshaft, it needed a lot of work to get ready for usable working conditions. Generally, it appeared to be quite attractive and had potential, and there were a lot of positives. It had a nearly complete working kitchen great for sautéing and grilling. Although it needed a serious deep cleaning, it had the right qualities desired for his tablecloth service dining room.

Excited, Amaury went home that afternoon and started preparing his calculations on its viability. He spent hours working the numbers over and over with Ruby. They became quite enthusiastic as they both mutually visualized the opportunity.

Nai gave Amaury a great deal—he'd only be required to pay $1,000 a month in rent for the first year and a free month upfront. It was a huge bonus he didn't expect. His next step was purchasing chairs, tables, flatware, additional kitchen equipment, and decor for the space. He started creating a menu and establishing relationships with food and beverage supply vendors.

Amaury took another few days to let the idea settle in his mind, but he knew this was his golden ring moment. He realized for the first time in his life, he could obtain a lifelong achievement. He thought about where he'd come from and all the experiences he had been through along the way. He decided to drive to the downtown Albuquerque Burger Boy, one of his favorite spots, to be alone with his thoughts.

He needed to sit outdoors, feel the breeze and imagine his life as a restaurant owner. He called Ruby, who was in Santa Fe. "Ruby, I've made a decision. I'm at Burger Boy's in Albuquerque, and I want to talk to you. When will you be home?"

"I'll be back later, so hold your horses until I return. I think I'll open a bottle of bubbly when we get back. I already know what you're going to say."

Amaury laughed to himself, but later that night when Ruby got home, they sat down together at the table, and he took her hand.

"Ruby, this time has long been coming. You know where I came from and know about my life, and this is an opportunity of a lifetime. I've wanted to do something on my own for a very long time. You know how I have given my passion to others. Well, now I'm finally going to do it for myself."

"I know, baby." She squeezed his hand.

"We're going to open that place, and it's going to be called *Babaluu's Cocina Cubana*. I've been giving it a lot of thought, and I know exactly what we're going to do!"

Ruby's face broke into an ecstatic smile, and she jumped up and hugged Amaury tight. "Hold that thought!" She ran into the kitchen and popped open the bottle of champagne she'd set out on the counter just in case. She poured them two glasses and returned to the table, where a beaming Amaury sat there waiting for her. She handed him a glass and they toasted. "Okay, tell me everything!"

"I've come up with a clever new concept. We'll have a rotating menu that I'll change every few weeks of operation. No matter what week it is, we'll always have the appearance of a fresh new menu for repeat customers."

"I've never heard of that! How does that work?"

"Okay, here's what I am thinking. We'll create twenty-two separate menus which we'll rotate every two weeks. Since the